**FALLOUT**

Colin T. ock

Also by Colin Nelson:

Reprisal

FALLOUT

Colin T. Nelson

North Star Press of St. Cloud, Inc.
St. Cloud, Minnesota

Writing a novel is never done alone. In my case, the following people helped me immensely.

My wife, Pam, is my muse, my support, my best editor, and comes up with the best ideas. My group of readers who spent their time and generously made critical suggestions to the manuscript include: Mary Stanton, Carol Epstein, Jessica Austin, and David Epstein. Officer Dale Hansen from the Minneapolis Police Department educated me about data retrieval from cell phones as did expert John Carney. Jennifer Adkins contributed vital editorial help and corrections. And, of course, the team at North Star Press who do such a good job and are so supportive: Corinne, Seal, and Brandon.

First Edition: June 2012

Printed in the United States of America

Published by
North Star Press of St. Cloud, Inc.
P.O. Box 451
St. Cloud, Minnesota 56302

www.northstarpress.com

DEDICATION

To my parents

Sherry and Vern Nelson

Who always encouraged me to "just try it . . ."

"Godly violence. Violence prescribed by divine law and Holy Word. Violence pleasing in the sight of the Lord."

John Brown, Abolitionist and American terrorist

"An old monk once advised a traveler: in the desert, the voices of God and the devil are scarcely distinguishable."

Loren Eisley

 # PROLOGUE

Early September

MARKO KNEW IF THEY CAUGHT HIM, they'd kill him.

He had been hidden behind locked doors in the basement of a church, the nerve center of the operation geared up for the End. The preparations had taken years of networking across the country. Infiltration of the plants to discover the security codes and learn the layouts, and the secret consultations with engineers to decide where to place the charges—it had been a struggle for all of them.

Marko had hoped to slip out the side door of the church undetected. Before he could reach his car and escape, someone burst through the door and came after him. He panicked and ran. It was probably Menendez, the most violent member of the security detail hired by the church.

Marko slowed as he reached his car. Did he have time to unlock the door, get inside, and escape before he was caught? No. He veered off toward the long street that ran into the small town of Hamel, Minnesota. It was a quiet area, except for the closed bars and a strip joint. Maybe he could outrun Menendez.

This late at night, the town sank into quiet sleep. Marko knew there was a Super America station still open at the far end. If he could make it there, he'd be safe.

He ran harder, hearing his leather shoes slap on the damp pavement. Earlier, a soft fall rain had drizzled over the streets. He felt the burn in his lungs, clawing for more air as he lunged ahead. Somewhere to Marko's left a dog barked twice. When he dared to glance back, he saw Menendez gaining on him. The yellow light from a street lamp glinted off the silver gun in Menendez's hand at the end of his pumping arm.

Marko dodged around a parked car and up across a lawn that smelled of wet grass. He slipped but gained traction as he ducked behind the only house on the street, hoping to lose Menendez.

His mind darted back to better times, when he and Menendez and the others from the church had come down from Canada for the first "test run" to see if they could make it. Marko remembered the dangerous journey across the border at night and how they had traveled down through the lake region of Minnesota. In the morning he'd seen men out in fishing boats, pulling golden walleyes out of the clear water. The fish had flopped and jerked in an effort to get free of the hook—just as Marko did now.

He curved around the back end of the small house, saw an open alley and ran for it.

Between the house and alley, Marko hit a low chain-link fence. It was too tall to jump over, so he stopped to climb up the edge and fell over the far side. He gasped for breath, certain his chest would explode. He had to get up and run. Feeling in his pocket to make sure he still had the flash drive, he scrambled to his feet. Menendez grunted as he rounded the corner of the house close behind, and Marko spurted toward the alley.

Two years earlier, it had all seemed so right to him. A friend had introduced Marko to the church that seemed to offer answers for all the things he knew were wrong in the world. It was a small congregation and their secretiveness had startled Marko at first, until he realized that their message caused people outside the church to become upset. But without a family, he had found warmth and friendship there, so when they'd asked him to use his software skills for their plan, he'd readily agreed.

And he agreed with their message that the End Times were upon them. Americans were too consumed by material matters and hedonism to recognize the signs, but the church saw them all. Marko felt reassured to be one of the "chosen" who would survive.

But when the plans had mushroomed across the country, he became worried. Security increased and they forced people like Marko to finish their work. Marko discovered the plans were more destructive than he had ever imagined. The leaders blackmailed him with threats of going to law enforcement if Marko didn't cooperate. He was scared for several months until something inside him snapped, and he knew he must act first to protect himself. He stole the flash drive with all the details of the network's plan.

It was the only thing he could use to try and cut a deal with law enforcement.

Marko gained speed down the alley. Without street lights, he could fade into the shadows. After years behind desks, he knew his body was out of shape and couldn't run this hard for very long. If he could elude Menendez for two more blocks, he'd reach the gas station.

He tried to push himself faster, hearing the gasps from his lungs pumping harder. His head hurt. Behind him, Marko heard the splash of Menendez's boots through the puddles in the alley.

Coming out of the alley, Marko leaped toward the street again. He had to run between two deserted buildings, turn hard to the right around a bar called "Inn Kahoots," and sprint one more block to safety. Sweat dripped into his eyes, making it hard to see. Long before, his glasses had fallen off his slippery face. That also made it difficult for him to see well.

His legs screamed in pain and his chest heaved up and down. In the darkness next to the last building, he tripped over something on the ground. His face scraped across the pavement, shredding his skin. He knew Menendez was close behind. Marko struggled up, found his footing, and lunged toward the open street in front of the building.

He heard the slap of Menendez's arms along his chest. Marko saw the Super America ahead. Maybe he'd make it.

He dodged to the right. He saw a man accompanied by a woman in a short pink dress stagger out the front door of the strip joint. He meant to avoid them, but in his exhausted state he smacked into her. People screamed and Marko fell, rolling across the pavement to stop on his side. He saw a crushed Budweiser can at the curb. Marko struggled to his feet and heard a flat pop that echoed off the building behind him. He could see the golden yellow lights reaching out to him from the windows of the Super America. He would make it.

That's when something slammed into the back of his head and threw him forward. Marko had just a moment to look across the street again and see a golden fish getting free from the hook before he died.

 # CHAPTER 1

October

T HE NINE MILLIMETER SEMI-AUTOMATIC Glock 26 jumped in Zehra Hassan's hand as she fired it for the third time. It felt warm to her touch, and she thought of the Beatles song, "Happiness Is a Warm Gun."

"Another kill. Great," the other woman said.

The gun itself didn't make Zehra happy, of course, but the thought of protecting herself sure made her feel secure . . . which for now, was happiness.

Her instructor, Mavis Bloomberg, a former law enforcement officer, coached her. "Remember the support from your left hand on your forearm," she shouted to be heard through the ear protectors.

When Zehra had first come to the gun range an hour south of Minneapolis, she couldn't believe what she was doing. Driving down the Minnesota River Valley to turn off at Le Sueur and continuing on through the small town to the east, driving into a narrow valley across a rusty bridge over Sunderman's Creek, where the Raccoon Hollow Gun and Rod Club was located—these seemed like the actions of a person alien to her.

But that was before the man she loved had revealed himself as a terrorist and tried to kill her.

Since then, her life had submerged through fear and panic, guilt, and finally anger to surface in a debilitating Post Traumatic Stress Disorder. As she worked her way through the trauma, her therapist had recommended the gun course. To her surprise, Zehra discovered that shooting a gun felt pretty damn good.

She just wanted to figure out a way to get back to "normal."

On the range, Zehra rotated her shoulders a little more and cupped her right forearm in her left hand and arm, which in turn braced against her chest. She let out her breath slowly and pulled evenly on the trigger. The gun exploded. The flat *crack* rolled across the range and echoed back from the narrow valley walls. She could smell the sweet odor of gunpowder float toward her.

Mavis ran a course called Defensive Shooting 101 for Women. There had been a morning of classroom work that included fundamentals of firearms, ammunition, cleaning, and the paperwork to obtain her permit to carry a concealed weapon. The afternoon class moved out to the range, where Zehra learned how to draw and holster the weapon. She was taught correct grip, stance, sight alignment, trigger control, and rapid accurate firing. Finally, she started to move, shoot, and hit a target. Zehra fired over one hundred rounds of ammunition. The advanced session taught her how to reload under stress. Mavis used timed shooting drills to teach Zehra how to stay calm enough to move, shoot, and hit her targets under pressure.

When the work on the range was finished, she and Mavis walked back to the red frame ranch house with white trim. A wrap-around porch held rocking chairs and refreshments. A sign near the front door read: "The Second Amendment Applies to Women Too!"

One of the best parts of the course for Zehra had been the support of the other women in the class. She had felt awkward coming here in the first place until she met Mavis and the others. Mavis had stood before the class and said, "From now on, your motto is: 'Not Me. Not Anymore.' Girls, you need the tools to make this motto effective." Mavis showed a sly grin. "You'll be able to finally kick some ass."

An appreciative murmur circled the room, and one woman in front of Zehra even held up a small gun with pink hand grips. A gift from her daughter.

On the porch, Mavis sat next to Zehra. Zehra pulled out an iced tea drink from a cooler Mavis offered. "How'd you like the course?" Warm air smothered them until a puff of wind blew up from the creek.

"It was . . . different. I've never had much to do with guns before. This made me more comfortable and gives me confidence for . . ." She felt hot from the work out on the range.

Mavis waited for a moment. She'd worked with a lot of traumatized women. "You told me you had to kill someone. In self-defense?"

Zehra looked up across the twisting creek that wrapped around the south end of the house. "At least I survived—physically. I'm not so sure about psychologically." She didn't want to bring back the memory, so she simply said, "He tried to start a pandemic and kill me." Zehra switched the subject. "If I'm carrying a weapon, should I put it in the small of my back like I see on TV?"

Mavis laughed. "Worst place."

"Why?"

"What if the attacker pushed you backward and you ended up on the ground on your butt? How would you reach the weapon?"

Zehra nodded.

"Thanks for the tips." Zehra didn't want to bore Mavis, but the effects of the trauma trailed her like the humid air did now. She said, "How do you deal with taking another life? I'm just a normal person, raised in a middle-class family, working as a government lawyer and . . . how does a person deal with the guilt? The 'what if' I'd done something different to protect myself?"

"I've heard that many times. What are you doing about it?"

"This course, for one thing. Also, I went back to work. I switched from working as a public defender to being a prosecutor for Hennepin County in Minneapolis."

"Sounds interesting. Does it take your mind off the memories?"

"It's helping." She sipped more tea. "Besides, I'm just plain mad."

"Good."

"I'm sick of extremists, crazy people holding innocent people hostage and as victims. I want to do something about it. My own experience changed me, and I'm mad."

Mavis smiled and rocked.

Back in Minneapolis the next day, Zehra walked into work. Nothing in her thirty-four years had prepared her for the trauma she'd experienced. She hurried across the circular plaza on the north side of the towering Hennepin County Government Center where she worked. An Indian summer day bathed her in soft and peaceful warmth. Humid air pressed around her, making it feel like she was swimming through a pool of water. Behind her, across the street, the hulking pile of stone called City Hall looked like it held all the heat of the day. From its own tower, sonorous bells clanged at noon to the melody of "Amazing Grace."

Amazing was how Zehra thought of her life right now.

Her plan for recovery seemed to be working. For now. She pushed through the revolving doors on the ground floor of the Government Center to enter into the coolness inside. In spite of budget cuts, at least they still provided air conditioning as a public service.

An old friend, Elizabeth Alvarez, had suggested that Zehra become a prosecutor. She had hesitated, wondering if she'd be able to get back to the rough work of a trial lawyer. But then, as Zehra put her life and career back together, she'd realized her future opportunities for a judgeship or promotion would be enhanced if she got some prosecuting experience.

Liz was a senior attorney who headed a trial team in the Adult Criminal Prosecution Division. Zehra remembered her conversation.

"Someone with your cred is always welcome here, girl," Liz said.

"Sounds good. I'm not sure I can handle it yet, but is anything open?"

"Let's see . . . there's a position on the Gang Unit."

"Umm . . . don't know about that."

"Yeah. Might get tired of prosecuting Tre Tres, Vacos Locos, Surrenos, and Murder Boyz all day long."

Zehra laughed. "I still get panic attacks. It's getting better, but I'm still not fully healed." She trusted Liz to keep this confidential. In the professional world of trial lawyers, weaknesses often hurt far beyond their seriousness.

"Hey, I remember what you were like in a courtroom. Don't worry. What about joining my trial team? We lost Ben Johnson to childbirth. He's on paternity leave for four months. Give it a shot?"

"Well . . . I don't know."

Seven months later, Zehra had been hired and was still working with Liz, handling major felony cases. Ben had returned, but the elected county attorney, Ulysses S. Grant, wanted Zehra to stay. Part of him respected her immensely, but he was still a politician, and the fact that she was a progressive Muslim-American wasn't lost on the boss and his next election campaign where he could boast of diversity in his office.

Zehra walked up a flight of stairs in the Government Center to the second floor. In the open indoor plaza, above the square fountain, rose two identical office towers on either side. In the middle, to the north and south, glass walls enclosed twenty-four floors and opened the entire interior to sunlight.

After gathering her files for the day from her office, Zehra rode the elevator back down to handle new cases that had been scheduled for that day. The pre-trial calendar contained the cases of accused felons.

Although it resembled a factory assembly line, all the participants tried to give each case and each defendant adequate time. The public defenders who represented most of the accused juggled dozens of clients each morning and gave everyone attention and respect, whether it was returned or not.

Zehra handled this calendar one day a week as part of her assignments when she wasn't in trial. By ten o'clock, she'd met with seven defense lawyers, settled six of those cases, and appeared before the judge on each one. She glanced at the gold watch that contrasted with her dark skin on her wrist.

She felt calm. Things finally seemed to be getting better. At noon, she'd go back to her office and perform one of her prayers for the day.

When she looked up, an older public defender she'd known for years approached her. "Todd, how are you?" Zehra smiled at him and straightened her legs.

"Busy. The defense never rests." He laughed at his own joke. Except it wasn't much of a joke, since the PDs had so many cases they never rested at all. "I got Andre Evans. Jacked the pickup in Loring Park."

Zehra shuffled through the pile of folders until she found it. "Yeah. Read it this morning. He's so small, when he stole the truck it looked like no one was driving."

Todd laughed. "Can you imagine? The truck moving without anyone in it."

"Uh, this is his fourteenth stolen vehicle."

"Well, as his mama says, 'Dre, he sure do like his cars.' I got a reason to deal on this one." Todd leaned over the table toward her. His voice quieted. Instinctively, she rose up a little to hear him. That's when she caught the whiff of onions on his breath.

A gush of heat tore through her torso from a burst of adrenaline that shot into her stomach. She lurched back from the table. Even though her hands and feet felt frozen, her body started to sweat. A thought stabbed through her mind again and again. *What if I can't get away?*

Zehra fought to gain control. She tried the yoga breathing she'd been taught. She raised her arms from her sides to reassure herself that she wasn't trapped anywhere. Nothing worked. The panic flooded her, and she struggled to push it back down.

What if I can't get away?

Her heart raced faster than she thought possible and burned in her chest. The panic gripped her to the point she thought she might lose her mind. Claustrophobia closed in on her, black circles at the edges of her vision. She pushed people away to give herself enough space to remember the imaging exercises the counselor had taught her.

Zehra took as deep a breath as she could. Out went air with the fear and tension. Zehra closed her eyes and wiggled her feet to catch the sense of sand underneath them. She listened for the hiss of waves and soon the image of her favorite beach came into her mind while she smelled the salt in the hot air and started to feel sand against her bare skin.

Zehra sat down in the chair and felt completely wrung out.

"Are you okay?" Todd asked as he hovered over Zehra.

Zehra nodded slowly. "I'll be fine. This still happens. I'm sorry." She felt like an infant, embarrassed and unable to have any control over her body.

She saw her files scattered all over the table. She gathered them and stood on shaky legs. "I'll get a drink outside. I'll be okay." Zehra walked slowly to the courtroom's big wooden doors, turned left, and found the fountain. After a long, cold drink, she retreated to the bathroom and found shelter in a stall.

It was finally over. Zehra hung her head. Why did she still get the panic attacks? Of course, the smell of onions had triggered it, since she remembered the faint smell of onions on Mustafa's breath as he leaned in to choke the life out of her on the muddy ground with the cold rain splattering around them and his black wet hair brushing against her face as he grunted with the effort of killing her. Would she ever get back to normal again?

It was so damn scary. In spite of the passage of time, the sensations were so vivid and palpable . . .

Her hair, normally shiny and black, hung limply on either side of her face. She could even detect silver strands deep in the part. Where once it had sparkled, now it looked flat, like dull coal.

It was the randomness of the event that scared Zehra most. She'd learned from her therapy that people take their daily lives for granted. The mindless routines. The place where the toothbrush sits each morning, the same faces at work, the same corner stop with the overhanging tree that scrapes the roof of the bus where they meet their children, and the automatic payroll deductions every two weeks to deposit their salaries.

When the routine was shattered in such a violent manner, lives got broken apart—if they even survived.

During her time off work on paid medical leave, the psychologist Zehra worked with had told her, "Post Traumatic Stress Disorder is like there's a dividing line between the person you were before and who you are now." Her doctor offered imaging therapy.

"I'll think of a beach. I've also bought a cat, an Angora. My parents have been great and have tried to support me, but even with them, I don't feel the old trust I had."

"Start with the cat. Maybe go back to work to keep your mind challenged," the doctor said. "What's the cat's name?"

"Larceny, because he's so sneaky."

Zehra turned to the mirror in the bathroom over the sink, looked at brown eyes that had sunk so deep she could barely tell the color. She washed her face twice. Her long nose she'd inherited from the relatives on her father's side. The dark skin from her mother. She twitched her hands through her hair to try and give it some semblance of life.

Back at her office, she shut the door, sat in the leather chair, rocked back, and put her feet up on the desk before her. Zehra worried the job might not work out. Could she really handle it? She was going to kneel on the rug and start her noon prayer but decided instead to turn on Minnesota Public Radio.

She heard familiar news: "Here at Fukushima's Unit 4 nuclear reactor in Japan, Dr. Karen Jones from the U.S. Nuclear Regulatory Commission said that radiation leaks will continue, and it could take fifty to 100 years before the nuclear fuel rods have cooled enough to be removed. Many of the workers who battled the leaks are expected to die from radiation sickness within weeks and . . ."

At a soft knock on the door, Zehra lowered her feet and said, "Come in." She turned off the radio.

Liz Alvarez walked to the low couch in the corner and sat at one end. She carried a cup of coffee in a pink mug. "Tough morning?" she asked carefully.

Zehra nodded. She stood and moved around her desk and collapsed on the other end of the couch. "I had a bad one." She shook her head, picked up a lint brush and scraped it down across her suit pants. "My darn cat. Sheds all over the place."

"I've got something to tell you." Liz cleared her throat. She was middle-aged and had made a career of being a prosecutor. A little overweight, she had a pretty face, a small nose, and blonde hair pulled back in a curl behind her head. She joked that people were often surprised that a Latin woman could have naturally blonde hair.

"Yeah?"

"Drake Chesney, the sheriff's detective, finally found the shooter in the Hamel killing." She paused. "I just charged Roberto Menendez with murder."

"Really?"

"It's a God damn thin case, but I think there's just enough to convict this guy. We're gonna have to work fast. The defendant will probably demand his speedy trial rights."

"What do you want?"

"I need a good second chair I can depend on and trust."

"That was a horrible murder. Something to do with that church, wasn't it?"

"Zehra, the pressure on us to win will be unbelievable. You sure you want . . . ?"

"Uh . . ." Her mind swirled. Did she really want it? "Yeah. Yeah, I'd love to help you convict the killer."

 # CHAPTER 2

Francisco Estevez sat next to the tomato plants staked on wooden bars in the sunny calm of his enclosed patio, reading the Spanish language version of *The Godfather* for the ninth time.

He loved the book, and the more often he read it, the easier he could understand the words since he couldn't read very well. Here in the Campestre section of Ciudad Juarez across the Rio Grande from El Paso, he was *El Padron*, the Godfather. Like the Godfather in the book, Estevez controlled the operation and money for *Los Lenones*, the pimps, and the sex industry that supplied big parts of the United States. He also sold drugs, of course, as well as babies, weapons, and explosives, and ran a profitable illegal immigration service to get people into the country to the north. In fact, he would sell anything illegal if he could make money.

It wasn't his fault. He was a simple, uneducated businessman offering all the illegal things the *Nortes* wanted. That demand was what drove the business, thank the saints, or Estevez would be delivering barrels of beer to the cantinas for a living.

Today, he was apprehensive. The North American buyer, who called himself the "Horseman," was going to be at the plaza again. He'd been meeting with Francisco about a huge shipment of explosives that had to be delivered in less than three weeks to reach Minnesota on Sunday, November 30th. The date was absolutely firm.

Getting the explosives wasn't a problem. The buyer was. Although Francisco was tougher than most other men, he was scared of El Norte. The man was smart and violent. Unpredictable.

Francisco's mind swam with the details he had to get ready for the shipment. The buyer wanted an unusually large amount. It would take time to assemble. Francisco was worried that if he didn't perform, the Horseman would certainly kill him and his sons.

Pushing the thoughts away, Francisco thought about Ciudad Juarez. Although the drug wars in the last few years had led to many murders, it was still one of the fastest growing cities in the world. North American companies had been building assembly factories for years and were actually increasing their purchases. The real estate was cheap and the workers, *maquiladoras*, were also cheap.

Twenty-three million people crossed the border every year—most for legitimate business. The lawlessness and corruption didn't seem to slow down the industrial growth or the flow of legal and illegal items either way across the border. Cash and guns came from the north, while almost any illegal product moved in the opposite direction.

That lawlessness attracted men like Francisco. He could run his businesses without interference. He lived in the old country club area, which had been deserted, for the most part, since the drug wars began. People had even left huge boulders in the streets to deter the movement of drug cartels. It was a perfect spot for Francisco, and he had plenty of his own protection.

The large house they'd taken over after the rich family who built it had fled to Guadalajara had excessive security systems, high walls, dogs, and cameras everywhere. When he and his boys left the compound, they rode in Hyundai SUVs that Francisco had taken to chop shops, where the mechanics had layered bullet-proof steel into the doors and replaced the windows with inch-thick glass.

He'd been blessed with a large family, a wife who'd grown ever larger, and a group of mistresses who had also grown larger over the years. He had three loyal sons who all worked in the family business along with four of their male cousins.

At one o'clock his maid came out to the patio. "*Padron,*" she called, "*esta caliente,*" as she fanned herself from the midday heat. "Do you want a beer before lunch?"

Estevez nodded, and the maid returned with a Pacifica from Mazatlan, where he'd grown up working with his father unloading the fishing ships early every morning. He'd promised himself that if he could ever escape the hard work, he would, although sometimes at daybreak he could still remember the fresh, salty smell of the silvery fish as they flopped out of the plastic crates, trying to get free. He lifted the expensive glassware and drank deeply. For lunch, he'd have the same thing he'd eaten for most of his life. Two bean-and-rice tacos with tomato sauce.

He carefully returned his bookmark between the pages he had read and set it on the stone table next to him. He reflected on how well his life had gone since he had gotten the family involved in crime and the sex industry.

When each of his boys and the cousins had turned twelve, Francisco had removed them from school to start their training in the business. They were each given one or two girls to rape and pimp out to learn the trade and, more importantly, how to control the girls. He emphasized the arts of kidnapping and seduction, as both methods worked equally well, depending on the prey.

While his maid served the small blue plate with two tacos, Francisco made a phone call to one of his nephews. "Carlos, you have the explosives?"

"*Si, Padron*. But such a *grande* shipment? What is the buyer going to do? Blow up Las Vegas?" The young man laughed.

"I don't know or care. Just make sure it all gets here on time. We don't have any room for mistakes." He hung up and sipped his beer again. "*Otra vez.*" He ordered another.

He had also trained the boys and their cousins in firearms, knife fighting, kidnapping, drug sales, and security. Someday they'd take over the family business, so they needed to know how to move drugs, launder money, trade in stolen guns from the U.S., and to deal with the bankers in El Paso who were happy to accept the cash deposits without asking where the money had come from. Francisco didn't trust any of the Mexican banks and only worked with those across the river.

He'd handled explosives before. China was the best source. Now he worried the timing of the delivery had to be perfect in order to get the shipment to the Horseman.

Francisco looked up at the sun. Clear blue skies stretched across the horizon to disappear behind the mountains to the west. Apprehension grumbled in his stomach that no amount of beer could eliminate.

Tonight, he and the boys would take a sample of the explosives to Anapra, one of the poorest areas of the city next to the Rio Grande. The police were afraid to go into the area. The North American would meet them there.

Francisco disliked the filthy streets. It usually smelled of cooking grease and gasoline and the exhaust from dozens of motorcycles.

But that was the traditional area for the "coming out" parties of prostitutes. It had been so since the turn of the century. He remembered the family had started displaying their products there in the early 1990s when the sex trade bloomed like the desert cactus after a spring rainstorm around Juarez. Also, any other business deals could be transacted there without interference from the police or *federales* poured into the city to try and stop the drug wars and killings.

Five hours later, Francisco walked down the narrow Calle Santa Maria with two of his sons. They towered above him, both heavy across the chest. The sun, setting to the west, cast the street in deep shadows except for the end, where it opened onto a small plaza. A sand-colored church steeple rose to three stories and caught the evening sun, making the tired, dirty brass of the dome shine like gold. They all carried heavy pistols that sagged the fronts of their jeans. He carried a large old briefcase packed with the plastic explosive samples. Without detonators, they weren't too dangerous.

Above them, small balconies hung out, separated by lamp fixtures that were starting to glow in anticipation of night. When they reached the open plaza, Francisco motioned toward the sidewalk café they always used. They settled into the chairs, and all of them ordered twenty-year-old tequila. Even after all the years and the business he'd done here, Francisco was still nervous.

Francisco had met the Horseman right here in this plaza many times. The man had come down looking for guns at first. Once he'd bought what he needed, he asked for explosives. Lots of them. He paid top dollar for the guns and always smiled. That bothered Estevez, made him uneasy in the presence of the man.

He saw a dead dog flopped over the curb. The air smelled stale, stagnant, of death and spilled beer across the stones in the street. The roar of motor bikes echoed down the narrow street they'd just walked along.

The square filled quickly with dozens of men. Some were buying, some trading, and some drinking. Almost anything illegal was for sale. Some men were there to buy the young girls who would soon parade in the street or be rented by the quarter hour. Many were there just to leer at the flesh on parade.

As darkness fell, the streetlights and café lights gave a golden patina to the open space. More laugher rose and more liquor drained into dozens of mouths.

"*Chicas, chicas,*" the men shouted for the girls to begin the show.

Soon, an endless parade of young girls came out from the side streets that flowed into the square. Over fifty would gather eventually to make a slow *paseo,* or walk around the square in front of the men, dressed in halter tops, tight t-shirts, and even tighter pants.

They walked in a pattern that rounded the area in front of all the cafes and men. No one spoke, but Francisco always swore that he could hear a collective panting, as if the men were all lost in their private fantasies. The important men sat toward the back. These were the buyers and money men. They'd come to sample and buy whatever they needed for their own operations.

The man from Minnesota walked up to Francisco and his sons. He was tall, handsome, well-built like an American football player and walked with confidence. He smiled at the group and sat in the chair next to Francisco. Without saying hello he asked, "Do you have my order, *amigo*?" He carried a well-worn brown leather Bible with him that he set on the table off to the side.

"Of course. We can fill it completely."

"You'd better. If the product doesn't work . . ." He smiled directly into Francisco's eyes. "Or if it doesn't come exactly on time, I'll be back for you and your family." He lifted his head. "I can get all the money I need from the church and my investors. Because I'm doing the Lord's work, I won't fail."

Estevez let out a breath quietly. That was the other thing that scared him about the North American—he was *loco.* His eyes had opened wide to stare right through Francisco, and he talked all the time about the "holy war" that the Horseman would start.

When a girl in a green t-shirt came forward, his son nudged his father. "Esperanza. She's ours." He turned toward the Horseman.

"I'm not interested in that sin."

"*Si, senor.* Of course not."

Her larger-than-normal breasts jiggled under the shirt, and a man from behind Francisco whistled softly and nodded at the girl. She stopped and walked among the plastic chairs to reach the man. He stood and led her further back in the café to a wooden door that had an iron handle in the middle of it, black with age and use. They hurried through to the rooms with dirty cots in the back at the end of the hallway.

Next to Francisco, two men argued about drugs. Meth sold better than ever in the States now, and the seller complained he couldn't get as much product as the buyer wanted.

"I'm squeezing my factories out in the brush to add more workers, but it takes time."

Nodding in agreement, the buyer said, "I can take all you've got and more. These gringos can't get enough." He laughed and slopped a shot of tequila down his throat.

And Francisco also remembered the time the North American had become angry at another man and a whore. The man had beaten the girl in front of everyone. Coming at the man in a holy fury, the Horseman had shot him in the head, the sound echoing out around the plaza until everyone stopped talking. Standing up, the North American threw $3,000 on the table to pay the owner of the bar for the trouble of cleaning up and walked away. The seller's *compadres* had planned to kill the Horseman later that night but instead settled for some of the money he'd left on the table.

After several tequilas, Estevez started to feel light-headed. He wanted to pick a girl himself before he left for home, but he was much too nervous. Reaching for the leather satchel he'd set on the pavement beneath the table, he pulled it over to the North American. Francisco peeled back the top flap to reveal the explosives inside. The Horseman studied them carefully.

Francisco retrieved his phone and clicked open the calculator. He poked at the keys. For the amount of explosives the North American wanted . . . Francisco tapped away. When he finished, he leaned back in amazement. The amount was astounding. His sons would help him pack the shipment and send it north. It could keep the family business running for months.

Francisco smiled. Not that he cared, but what the hell was the *Norte* planning to do?

 # CHAPTER 3

Monday, October 17

ORDER YOU TO DISMISS THE CASE! No deals. Just dump it." Ulysses "Bud" Grant shouted. He was the elected Hennepin County attorney, with absolute and final authority over all prosecutions. He yelled at Liz and Zehra, who sat in the leather chairs before his desk.

A few weeks after charging Roberto Menendez with murder, the thought of dismissing it churned Zehra's stomach. Liz turned slowly to their boss and said, "No. Can't you see there's something bigger here? Something's going on at that church. This is the only chance we've got to stop it."

Zehra looked at the man she respected and now worked for. Grant rubbed his hand over his bulging stomach. Gray hair curled around his black skin like smoke hugging a log.

"It's too bad. But even after all the work on it, we still don't have a solid case. A prosecutor has an ethical duty to dismiss if he doesn't think he can prove the case. You're gonna lose the trial and your reputation and maybe your jobs, too," he warned them. Grant turned his back on them and faced the window in his office at the Government Center.

"We've got a young man who's been murdered, that's what we have! We can't give up," Liz said.

Grant spun around and scowled. "What'd the judge do today?"

"Screwed us."

"Huh?"

"Denied our motion for a continuance. Trial starts in seven days on Monday the 24th. But we're appearing in front of the chief judge. We'll renew our motion."

"Ah . . . shit! Liz, what do you think the voters will do to me when you lose? And the press is on my ass, too."

"We're not going to lose," Zehra added.

She knew that Grant, nicknamed "Bud" after the famous Vikings football coach, had legendary political abilities. But recent polls had put him in a precarious position. Crease lines furrowed across his face.

Zehra had mixed feelings toward him. Grant could be charming and anyone's best friend, but when his own interests were on the line, Grant always voted for himself. He was a clever man. If they won, Grant would take credit for solving the case. If they lost, Grant would distance himself, saying that Liz and Zehra had lost it. Obviously, he didn't even want to take that chance now.

"Here's the deal, guys. As the elected county attorney, I'm ordering you to dismiss it. If you go ahead and lose, I'm not going down. I'll fire you two and tell the public it was your fault. Got it?"

Zehra's breath caught in her throat. He would do it, no doubt. She thought of the repercussions for her career as a lawyer. Would she ever get a job again in the county? Her dreams of being the first Muslim judge in Minnesota would go out the window. Zehra hesitated.

"Defense lawyer's good. He knows we're in trouble, so he's pushing for the trial to start immediately and he's got the judge siding with him," Liz said.

Outside the window, wind-blown leaves pirouetted from one rooftop to another. People had finished raking their leaves, cleaned out gutters, tuned up snow blowers, and covered rose bushes, preparing their homes against the coming storms of winter.

"You know I got confidence in you guys personally," said Grant, turning toward Zehra.

"I know," she snapped. Blood rushed through her cheeks and up across her face. Her family had come from Iran to America decades ago, when the shah fell, but the dark skin and long nose heralded her as different. Her parents must've felt like Martians amongst the hordes of Nordic blondes. A deep breath calmed her.

Zehra could smell the faint odor of old cigar smoke. Even though the entire Government Center was non-smoking, Grant occasionally broke the rule and smoked in his office. She dropped her eyes to notice white hairs from Larceny sticking to her pants.

On Grant's desk beside his computer rested a pair of designer glasses with bright-blue frames as well as two books, one about the inner game of golf and the other, one of the Easy Rawlins mystery series. He trudged over and sat down, then flicked at the cover of the case file on his desk but didn't open it. "Well, let's go over it again."

Liz cleared her throat. "Young guy, Marko Sundberg. Software engineer. Seems he was working at the church most nights. Found across the street from a Super America gas station. Shot once in the back of the head."

"Which church?"

"Church of the Rapture."

Grant squinted. "The what?"

"One of those 'end times' churches. Think the world's about to come to an end." Liz glanced at Zehra, then looked back to Grant. "Chesney, the main detective, is sure the church is tied to an armed militia group, but he can't prove it. Bud, that's another reason the case is so important."

Grant sighed and, for a moment, looked like he'd seen too much of human cruelty in his prosecutor's career. He swiveled in his chair, leaned back, and rubbed his chin. "Just focus on the murder. When did it happen?"

Liz nodded. "The 911 call came in about twelve fifteen in the morning."

"Signs of a struggle?"

"No, but it looked like the victim had been trying to run away."

"Find anything on him?"

"No. Except for his wallet with cards and driver's license."

Grant took a deep breath. "Murder weapon?"

"A .22 was found near the body, dropped in the street. A Ruger, Win Magnum. Dusted, no prints. Forensic can't ID the bullet positively because after going through the guy's skull, it had mushroomed beyond recognition. They can't give us any more to hang onto."

"Traced it?"

"Can't. Serial's filed off, and even the sheriff's lab couldn't lift it." Liz sighed. "Wish I had a cigarette. By the time the cops got there, the occupants of the church had fled."

"Check out the staff?"

"Only one minister. Reverend Josiah St. Peter."

"Really?"

Zehra said, "You think we could make up a name like that?" They all chuckled.

"He had a part-time secretary, but everyone else was volunteer like Sundberg," Liz continued.

Grant shrugged. "What'd you find out?" Grant's eyes grew in size as if he were pleading with Liz to reassure him.

"The reverend confirmed that Sundberg worked there, one of their best employees, can't believe anything like this would happen, yada, yada, yada."

"What about the defendant?"

"Menendez's prints did show up all over the church, but we can't prove *when* he left them there. St. Peter told the cops he was hired to mow the lawn and do janitor work. Shocked that he would be accused of murder. Must be a mistake. With a search warrant, cops seized three cell phones. One belonged to the minister, one to a girl there, and the last one was our boy's."

"How do you know?"

"Hennepin County Sheriff's crime lab did a quick check of the data stored on it. They ID'd it as Menendez's."

"So, how'd they grab him?"

"Cops canvassed the area. At first, nothing. Then a few weeks later, they find a bartender at Murphy's Tap. Really a bowling alley. He tells them that the night of the murder a guy he'd never seen before showed up right before closing time. Described the guy. Anyway, not only was the guy new to the bar, he acted nervous, was sweating. Had a couple shots and took off."

"And?"

Zehra laughed out loud. "You won't believe it. Sometimes, these perps are so dumb. He used plastic."

"You're shittin' me."

"Yeah. Cops did an NCIC data base check with the name, and he comes up as Roberto Menendez, with a record in Texas. Got his address here from the plastic and popped him. Says he was at the bar for hours, drinking."

"But the bartender . . ."

". . . says he only had two shots. The tab was for two shots and a beer. Menendez lied."

"Confession?"

"Said he left before the shooting," Zehra added. "Then he got lawyered up and stopped talking."

Grant grunted. From a drawer in the credenza behind him, Grant pulled out a Punch cigar. He unwrapped it and stuck one end in his mouth. This time, he chewed silently. "Okay. Where's the smoking gun?"

The door to the office popped open. "It's a circumstantial case, Bud." Jeremy Brown rushed into the office. Their best investigator had volunteered from the start to work on the case. "And we've all been working hard."

"'Bout time you got here, Hollywood," Liz joked with him.

Brown smiled broadly. He was tall, dressed in a blue sport coat that hung over tan slacks. No tie. He was a former highly decorated Minneapolis detective whose intense eyes always moved and never missed anything.

"You give me a little bit of hope," Grant said to Brown. "You sneaky son of a gun." Grant closed his eyes. "How you gonna prove the defendant pulled the trigger?"

Liz paused as a smile creased his face. "Thought I'd save the best for last. Tell him, Zehra."

"Cops found a witness out in the street who puts Menendez there at the time of the murder. Says she saw Menendez chase Sundberg outside with a gun, then heard the shot."

Breath wooshed out of Grant. "Why the hell didn't you say so in the first place?" His soft brown eyes searched Zehra's face as he stood then he walked toward the window.

"Well . . . 'cause the witness is dirty."

"Huh?"

"Yelena Mostropov, a prostitute with a long record of everything you can imagine someone like that gets into. . . . History of drug addiction, can't remember the details real well. She'd just gotten off her shift as a pole dancer at a club near the murder scene. Says she was with some guy, but after the shooting he disappeared. Local police are looking . . ."

"Oh, damn." He stabbed the air toward them with his cigar and rushed toward his desk. "You're telling me our main witness is a goddamn hooker?" He slumped into his chair and threw the soggy cigar in the trash. In five minutes, Grant calmed down.

"Bud, I've tried the tougher cases over the years to big wins," Liz said.

Grant cleared his throat. Something was coming. "I'm ordering you all to dismiss it. End of discussion." He waved the hand across the desk.

Liz exploded out of her chair. She let everything from the past few months, the pressure, her reputation, and her future pour into her voice. "Investigative reporters are hounding us, the advocacy group NorthStar is attacking us. . . . We're keeping it, Goddammit." She stared into the eyes of their boss.

Grant blinked first. "This will ruin both of your careers forever in this town."

Zehra smiled to herself. The only reason she hung on was her trust in Liz and the fact that Zehra had been in a similar place once. Unlike the victim Sundberg, Zehra had survived. Deep down, they both felt the suspect was guilty. They had a duty to go after him.

Grant looked at Brown. "You're one of the best cops I ever knew. Twenty years on the force until I snagged him out of retirement," Grant said to Zehra. He turned to Brown. "Tell me, can we convict this sucker, Hollywood?"

Brown shrugged. "It'll be tough to get a conviction, but we have to try." His voice lowered. "I didn't win all those awards by giving up." He was a rugged man, powerfully built across the shoulders. Still deeply tan from the summer, he had intelligent eyes. He cut his shiny black hair short. Severe. Zehra had always thought that made him look like a gangster, except that he was too put-together, handsome and erudite.

Zehra had first met him when he'd joined the trial team with her and Liz. Up to now, he'd communicated mostly with Liz, who adored him. Of course, Liz had always had a thing for cops anyway. Zehra sensed he was a man who usually got his way.

Brown's face flattened into seriousness. He lifted his arm and a pink plastic band dropped down. He toyed with it in his left hand. His little finger bulged purple and distended.

"What happened to you?" Zehra asked, pointing at it.

"Huh? Oh, hit myself with a hammer. Nothing I didn't deserve." He changed the subject. "I'm talking to the witness, the stripper, Bud. Sparkle's her name." He grinned. "All those hookers lie. That's the second best skill they've got." A dark expression crossed his face. "I'll make that sinner talk."

"I don't want to know," Grant said.

Brown circled the chairs where the women sat. His eyes focused on something behind Grant. "Bud, this was as cold-blooded as it gets. We should get this perp off the streets. I've seen too much of it as a street cop and detective, and it sickens me. The whole country's dropped into a cesspool of depravity and moral collapse. We have to fight back," he urged.

Zehra could hear the bitterness in his words as he spoke. Clipped and short. She felt pride and renewed enthusiasm. He felt the same way that she did: mad at the crazies and criminals who preyed on innocent people. This case gave them all a chance to try and stop some of it.

No one spoke. Finally, Brown said, "And I've warned you about Mezerretti, the defense lawyer. Don't trust him." He spoke fast and with authority.

"I never tried a case with him before," Liz said.

"When I was a copper, we had a case that involved a pistol. Six chambers in the cylinder. That was critical because the victim said six bullets were fired. Mezerretti took the gun to his expert and it came back with a five-chamber cylinder. We raised a stink about it, but no one had guts enough to take on a big shot like Mezerretti. He got an acquittal and got away with it. See what I mean?"

Grant blew out a burst of air. "Liz, you know the detectives always promise more than they can deliver. Why'd you bite so hard on this one?"

"Like Hollywood said, this is so cold-blooded. Besides, if there's some connection to an armed militia, we've got a duty to run it down." She looked at Zehra, who nodded in agreement.

"Sure . . ." Grant still wasn't convinced. He lumbered back to his desk. "And if you're forced out to trial on Monday?"

"As things stand now, we lose."

"Guys . . ."

Brown glanced at a gold watch on his wrist. "Hey, gotta run. Governor's Citizen Council is meeting in an hour, and I'm supposed to be on it."

Grant followed him toward his door, which he never locked, threw a blue suit coat over his shoulders, and shot his arms down the sleeves. They all followed him out into the lobby.

Brown walked closely behind Zehra. When the others moved away, he said, "You look lovely, Zehra."

"Uh, thanks. It's been difficult. I'm glad I'm not in Liz's place, the lead attorney."

"You got a lot of cred around here. I'm sure you could do it."

"What's the pink bracelet for? Breast cancer?"

"Yeah. My mother died of it."

"Must've been hard on your family."

Jeremy shrugged. "Yeah. My wife and I are on the board of the Susan G. Komen 5K run. You know the one that raises money for breast cancer?" When Zehra nodded, he said, "I'm doing what I can to fight the disease." His eyes expanded and seemed to look right through her. "I've got two daughters of my own."

The power of his presence caused Zehra to step back. Chilly, controlled. "That's wonderful."

He broke his expression with a generous laugh. "Hey, we've been pushing hard on the case. Let's have some coffee."

"Uh . . . maybe later, Jeremy."

Brown's face creased in apparent pain. "Okay . . . later." He leaned closer to her. "I know you're Muslim. I'm a Pentacostal Christian. There are many things I must tell you."

Zehra found him attractive, but his proselyting made her uneasy. She listened to her inner voice. *Take it easy*, it told her. On the surface, he smiled and joked and charmed. Zehra could sense something deeper, inflexible, and sharp. "This is business. I don't think we should."

"What's more important than your soul?"

"Besides, you're all flash." Zehra laughed and pushed him aside. An angry look brushed across his eyes, which hardened, and unmoving, he stared at her. A jolt of uneasiness pulsed through Zehra again. She thought momentarily of apologizing, but then the expression disappeared.

Grant had stopped outside his door. Looking at his watch, he said, "I gotta meet the county commissioner at Peter's Grill." He turned to the team and said, "Okay. I've got years of ulcers invested in my career, and I'm not gonna let this case pull me down. You lose and I gotta throw you to the wolves. Not only will the killer walk but your careers as lawyers will be over."

Zehra knew he meant it. Cradling the file under her arm, she locked eyes with Liz for a moment and followed them out of the lobby.

CHAPTER 4

Wednesday, October 19

At the Minneapolis/St. Paul International Airport, Jeremy Brown made a quick call on his cell, talked fast, and lied. "Liz? Yeah, I just got a call from my sister in Boston. She's worse, and I gotta run out to see her. Be back tomorrow. I know . . . now's not the time. Promise I'll be back."

He flipped the cell shut and waited for the Delta clerk to give him a seat assignment.

"There you go, Mr. Brown. You're booked for the non-stop to Santa Fe." She flashed a perfunctory smile and waved the next person forward.

The phone call to Alvarez reminded him of the problem he faced. Since Brown still needed more time to bring about the End and usher in the Kingdom of God, he had to stop the investigation and trial of Roberto Menendez as soon as possible. Luckily, Menendez had managed to retrieve the flash drive that Marko Sundberg had carried when he tried to escape. If Menendez collapsed and took a deal to tell all that he knew, the plans would be stopped and the powers of evil would prevail.

That could not happen.

When he arrived in Albuquerque a few hours later, Brown walked through the new airport. It was immaculately clean, and he loved the colors on the walls that echoed the desert colors: mauve, tan, orange, purple, and turquoise for the jewelry the Indians worked to perfection.

He stepped outside in the shade of an overhang and looked out across a wide shallow valley with Albuquerque spread out at the bottom. He breathed deeply and felt the dry air. God's country.

He remembered the need for more cash to finance the final purchases, as always. The supplies they would need for the plant were expensive, particularly since they were illegal and difficult to bring into the country. He smiled at the clever plan he had for that.

Using an encrypted cell phone, Brown texted someone in the network identified as "Mr. Han" for more cash. Brown didn't understand why the cash source had come forward, but he didn't care. Mr. Han must be a guardian angel, sent by God.

A new Lincoln Navigator pulled up before him. Brown threw his carry-on over his shoulder and moved out of the shade toward the car. Heat from the sun wrapped around him like a wool serape.

"Hey, Jose." Brown grabbed the dusty door handle, tossed his bag in the back, and climbed into the Jeep.

"Ah . . . it's the Horseman. How are you?"

"Tired. But the Lord provides." He laughed as Jose pulled around onto the tan road that led to Interstate 25, heading north toward Santa Fe. They crossed under freeway overpasses also painted in the desert colors with fading turquoise stripes along the top edges.

"What's the problem?"

"As you know, I'm planning to move my family down here to be safe from the storm that will grow out of Minnesota."

Jose frowned at him.

"Don't worry, my friend. You will be safe with us." He turned to the man he'd hired three years ago to be the part-time manager of his horse ranch.

Jose grinned under a black, drooping moustache. He wore a white cowboy hat pushed back on his head, both sides of the brim rolled tight to the crown. "I know you'll take care of me and my family."

This old guy would probably work for one third the amount he was paid. But Brown liked him and knew he supported a family of five kids. He made a note to raise Jose's salary. Besides, when the End came, they should all be safe from the holy war out here in the fortress he'd constructed.

"How are your children?" Jose asked.

"The two girls are in school. My wife and I home school them. The public schools are worthless and full of people with no morals."

Skirting around Santa Fe, they rose into the mountains covered with thick pine forests that looked, from a distance, like moss growing over large humps. To the northeast, standing flat and dark and stretching as far as Brown could see, was the Black Mesa. Wispy clouds clung to the front edge of the cliffs.

The Lincoln climbed higher and both men could feel the difference in altitude. The air smelled clean and carried the dry odor of pine resin. Brown had never believed that air itself could possess color until he saw it in New Mexico. Land of enchantment . . . indeed.

The sun passing through it seemed to shimmer and change colors as it moved across the huge sky. Near the horizon, it wavered in blue tones that matched the turquoise stone until it rose and, as if the full sun bleached out the color, the sky faded to pale blue so thin there was hardly any color left when one looked straight up. No wonder the painter Georgia O'Keefe had skipped out of New York City to her studio at Ghost Ranch, obsessed with the stark simplicity of landscape and the bleached animal skulls she found.

Forty miles north of Santa Fe, Jose crossed the Pecos River that ran to the southwest. One could hardly call it a river, smaller than Minnehaha Creek in Minneapolis. Just past the river, Jose turned off the freeway onto a tar road that wound around jumbled piles of red and tan rock. When they reached a railway line, they turned right and paralleled it for about a mile. Then the tracks curved south toward Santa Fe and the road dipped deeper into the river valley.

"Still pretty lush?" Brown asked.

"River's up this year. Yeah, you'll like the ride today."

At the end of the gravel road they bumped over, Jose slowed to make a sharp turn directly down toward the river. Years ago, the owners of the ranch had piled the local red rock into two pillars to mark the entrance to the property. Cradled between the towers was a worn wooden sign that announced the name: Four Horsemen Ranch.

With his wife's inheritance, Brown bought the place and he'd asked Jose about the name. "Sad story. The ranch was owned by four brothers from California. One day, the youngest was getting married, so they all piled into the car to go to the wedding. When they got to the railroad crossing—the one from Santa Fe where we turn—a train bound for West Texas hit 'em broadside, killing all of 'em."

Every time they turned under the sign, Brown thought of the Four Horsemen of the Apocalypse. Now he was one of them. Considering his family tree, it was destined. He was in direct lineage of the fiery abolitionist John Brown, who had raided the federal arsenal at Harper's Ferry prior to the Civil

War in a plot to steal weapons, head into the South, and help the slaves rise up and kill their masters in order to end slavery.

Beyond the entrance stood three adobe buildings. The largest two-story was the main house, and it sprawled in several directions. Updated with the most expensive and modern facilities, he'd made it into an impregnable fort. The ranch was completely self-sufficient in food, water, and energy. There were three wells, fruit trees, a large vegetable garden, cattle for beef, and plenty of fuel to run the four generators.

Hidden out of sight were all the security precautions and protections that he'd built into the property. He didn't expect the storm to come this far, but just in case, his family would be protected and secure until the Rapture. After that, of course, none of them would need any protection, because they would have won and the Second Coming would be upon them.

Brown used another building for storage, and the third was the granary for the horses. Next to that structure, a large corral circled out across the field that sloped down to the Pecos River. An old cottonwood fence surrounded the corral. A Morgan and an Arabian stood inside the corral, both their necks bent down as they chomped on feed. The Morgan jerked its head up as the Lincoln lifted dust in the driveway before the main house.

"Jose, get them saddled. I'll change and be right back. I want to check the perimeter and our security systems."

Brown hurried to the main house. The front door was a weathered wooden one with Indian motifs carved deep into its surface. Inside, the adobe did its work. The house remained cool and quiet. He climbed the stone steps to the upstairs bedroom, dumped his bag, and changed into riding clothes. On the way out, Brown lifted a hat with an extra wide brim off the peg by the door and placed it firmly on his head.

He stood a moment outside the front door, studying his property. This was his secret fortress. Fully protected with security and armament, he could withstand the chaos and fighting that would result from the plan to blow up the nuclear power plant at Monticello, Minnesota. In staged succession, seventeen other plants across the country would be blown. The resulting mass death and panic would cause people to turn on each other with murderous fury. That would bring on Armageddon, the end of the corrupt human existence, and the return of the Lord.

Through blogs and chat rooms, Brown had found the Church of the Rapture easily. They agreed with his view of the End Times and, like many others, were simply waiting. But it was too late to wait any longer. Brown had been called to fulfill God's plan and to make the Rapture occur. Over the years, he'd persuaded the church members to take more proactive steps, which had led to establishing a network of believers across the country, prepared to act at their locations. Because the actions would be necessarily violent, the church and other groups had to remain secret.

Brown would bring in the explosives and distribute them to all the sites for the final acts. The other explosions would be staged to occur right after his attack. The timing was critical because the relentless disasters would overwhelm the first responders, the local law enforcement, and finally even the Army—leading to chaos and a breakdown of all aspects of civil society, making the country ripe for the Apocalypse.

He smiled to himself when he thought of how important the work would be in service to his Lord. He would hasten the Second Coming of Christ and save the Believers all over the world. Just as his distant relative, John Brown, had been selected to fight the evils of slavery, Jeremy Brown had been divinely chosen to do the Lord's work and save the country. Most other Christians thought he was an extremist. Maybe he was, but he had the truth.

The trees along the river had turned to their fall colors. Grasshoppers clicked in the bushes, and when he walked to the corral, they popped out and struck him in the legs. Wind from the west blew into his face, sounding like someone trying to blow across the top of a bottle.

When he got to the corral, Jose had prepared the horses. Brown liked the dark Morgan. He walked up to it slowly and ran his hand along the horse's neck, calling it by name, Apple Jack. It smelled faintly of old sweat and heat from the sun. Not unpleasant. Brown grabbed the dangling rein, lifted his foot up into the stirrup, hoisted himself upward, and heard the leather stretch when his weight filled it.

"Let's go down by the river," Jose called to him. Brown liked Jose's company. He was a simple man with a plump wife who adored him. Jose saw life in black and white, and Brown agreed. There were the people of God and all those who weren't. Simple. Didn't the Holy Scripture say so? As a cop, he'd seen how depraved and hopeless the human race had become. It was time for the Second Coming and he, Jeremy Brown, would be the ultimate instrument of God to make it happen.

They worked their way down the field that sloped toward the river. Birds swarmed them as they got closer. Doves in the trees. A greater roadrunner darted into the cover. Above, a Cooper's hawk circled. They called in chirps and long whistles, warning the other animals of the riders' presence.

Brown thought of the men who were working for him now in Mexico with the explosives. They had to be assembled, packed, and ready for transport within a few days, or his entire plan would collapse. Every twenty-two months, the power plant was shut down for its regular replacement procedure and he would strike at that precise moment.

The timing was so critical. The explosives, weapons, and his hand-picked team of operatives all had to come together for transport at the same time, when Brown would meet them in Minnesota the next Sunday. From the northern border, where he'd smuggle the explosives into the state, they'd be distributed around the country, some moved down to the small city of Monticello, located on the Mississippi River. Before it froze, the plant had to be blown so that the radioactive material would not only spread in the air, but also be carried down the river to sicken thousands and millions of people.

He tasted dust in the wind, blown from far away and bitter. Across the expansive valley, he looked up at the high mountains, purple and dark blue. Further down, the forest thinned and the colors changed to lavender, saffron, rose, and mint. The Pecos whirled in bottle green eddies that looked like smooth, soft glass as it rounded over submerged rocks. Near the bottom, along the edges of the river, cottonwoods and quaking aspen shadowed the water. They were covered with clattering yellow leaves that clapped in applause for the gift of sunlight.

He thought of the Robert Menendez murder trial in Minneapolis. He'd stop that dead in its tracks before they could figure out what was really going on. Menendez would keep quiet—but only for a while. And the prosecution team? If necessary, he'd do whatever it took to stop them. None of them would stand in the way of God's plan.

"Mr. Brown," Jose shouted.

When Brown looked up, he saw Jose waving wildly at him to come over. Brown spurred Apple Jack and reached Jose in a few minutes.

"Down there. Get your glasses out. It's a coyote on the hunt."

Brown reached into the left saddlebag and pulled out some Steiner binoculars. He tilted his hat back, adjusted the glasses and scanned the low country ahead of them. There! He'd spotted the slinking coyote. Unusual that he'd be out in the heat of the day and that he'd hunt alone. Must have been really hungry.

Brown moved the binoculars up the incline to see the prey. He circled the field, but couldn't see anything obvious until at the last moment before he shifted back to the coyote. A small deer, probably this year's fawn, dark-brown against the sun-washed soil, feeding peacefully, unaware of the predator stalking her.

Suddenly, the coyote leaped.

In a flash of light, the doe cut to the left and started across the field, hoping its superior speed could save it.

The coyote dodged right, left and kept closing. Brown watched it run flat-out across the short grass, both of them in the open now and crossing in front of him. The coyote bounded in a rhythm that to Brown seemed like someone hitting a drum in triplets. The muscles in its shoulders bulged with the effort.

The doe skipped and jerked to avoid death. Its neck stretched out far and Brown could see the nostrils in the unusually long nose flared wide. Her eyes, dark-brown and almost human. Fully open.

Suddenly, the coyote burst to the right, leaping at the tender neck. Mouth wide open, it clamped down and jerked the neck to the side which caused the doe's body to flip over upside down. As the coyote squatted over the ground, its legs spread wide to brace itself for the killing work, Brown could see the jaws moving. Digging down through windpipe, gristle, and spinal cord.

It was over in a minute.

The young doe's body twitched a few times, the graceful neck hung at an unusual angle, broken now, and the coyote lifted its face, red around the snout, and looked to the left and right for his competitors. Life was truly "eat or be eaten."

He marveled at the cunning and strength of the animal. Brown tried to hold on to the feeling, but it passed through him like the wind through his hair. He lowered the glasses and pulled his hat down to protect himself from the bright, hot, uncaring sun above.

CHAPTER 5

C AN'T YOU JUST GET OVER IT?" Martha Hassan told her daughter, Zehra. "It's been over a year."

Zehra held her anger in check. She'd heard this so often that if her mother said it one more time, Zehra might become a murderer. "You can't 'just get over' PTSD."

"But I heard this doctor on *Oprah* say that most people don't have any symptoms."

Zehra had driven west on Highway 62 and exited at Boulder Creek Drive to her parents' home in the western suburb of Minnetonka to meet for dinner. The road curved up and around spacious but not expensive homes in a leafy tunnel of green. When she pulled into the drive, Zehra saw her father's ancient Toyota, held together in many places with duct tape—his favorite reconstruction material.

Her mother's call had hinted at some other reason for wanting Zehra to come over. As usual, her mother would approach it Iranian style—from some indirect angle. "I'm working on it. People react differently." Zehra tried to end this part quickly as it always led to an impasse, and she wanted to have a peaceful dinner with them.

Martha frowned as she thought over what Zehra had said. "You've been so sad. I'm worried."

"I'm worried too. Sometimes, it's like I'm bobbing in the ocean with all my senses cut off from everything and everyone. Occasionally, I climb onto an island where I can hear again, feel good, and feel like I have a purpose. Then I drop off into the water again."

Even though her parents had immigrated to the United States years ago and had become citizens and embraced everything American, they still retained some of the old culture they had fled after the Shah of Iran fell. After

34

all, they'd had plenty of traumatic stress in their history. If it ever bothered either of her parents, they never admitted to it and simply shouldered on with their lives.

"Lots of people have trauma."

"I know, Mom. But how many people do you know who were forced to kill someone?"

"Well . . ."

"The guilt gnaws at me. I can't sleep. But I'm working at it, and things are getting much better. I don't feel so depressed and lonely anymore. I know you disagree, but the firearm training has made me feel safer. My job in the prosecutor's office has really helped, too. The trial I'm working on is important, but luckily I'm only the second chair. I really want to convict the defendant, but since I took off the time from the courtroom, I'm not sure I'm up to handling it by myself."

Martha called out to Joseph, Zehra's father, who stood on the deck off the kitchen. "Don't burn the vegetables." Joseph moved from the edge of the deck to a large grill wreathed in smoke. He disappeared into the cloud as he attended to the dinner of lamb shish-ka-bobs.

Her mother said, "There's another problem I need to talk to you about. But I still think you should get out of law. Go into medicine or engineering. I know I promised to keep my mouth shut, but you aren't going to meet any nice Muslim men in law. Lots of Christians and Jews, but no Muslims. Go into medicine. Do something good and save some lives."

"What about the last man you two introduced me to . . . Mustafa? Turned out to be a terrorist who almost killed me."

Her mother blushed. "We've apologized a thousand times. If anything had happened to you . . ."

Zehra forced herself to remain calm. She changed the subject. "If we can convict this defendant, Menendez, we'll keep a bad actor off the streets for a long time. That could save the lives of future victims. Did you ever think of that?" Zehra stood in front of her mother with a finger pointed into her face.

Martha paused and looked up. Dark eyes sat deeply in her head, surrounded by dark smudges. Her black hair, streaked with silver, was pulled back into a loose bun that fell down around her shoulders. Outside the house,

Martha wore *hijab*, the head covering favored by many Muslim women the world over. Although the Qur'an didn't mandate the wearing, Martha chose to do so. "My 'Benazir Bhutto look,'" she'd say, hoping to resemble the stunning former prime minister of Pakistan.

"Sorry," she said to Zehra, "but look where it got you a year ago."

Zehra could see the genuine strain and worry in her mother's eyes as they pulled downward around the edges. "What's the 'other' problem, Mom?"

"I just know you'd be happier if you had a man in your life to help you."

"I'm fine on my own." She had to force the words out in a cheerful tone, since underneath Zehra felt the loneliness that had surrounded her even before the trauma had made things worse. Cut off from most people as she recovered, only her old friend Paul Schmitt had been a comfort because he'd been there.

They'd met and dated in law school. Now, after both had been through so much together, Zehra had a different picture of him. Of course, he was German in his discipline and orderly life, which at one time had seemed boring to her. Now those same habits were comforting. He was handsome and rugged, and she had started to see him in a new light. She liked what she saw. "Besides, Paul's been there for me."

Martha shook her head, her lips thinned, and she turned back to the stove with the simmering rice. From over her shoulder, she finally said, "He's wonderful, but he's a Christian."

Zehra threw her hands up in the air and yelled, "It's tough to find eligible Muslims in Minnesota. Most of them are African or Asian, not American." She paused, unsure if she should tell her mother. "Besides, Paul's a Christian, but he's leaning toward being more of a Universalist."

"I don't care. People who are married need to be on one page with religion and . . ."

"Hey," Zehra shouted. "Who's talking marriage? And I'm not so sure about the whole idea of Islam anyway."

Martha spun to face her daughter. "I noticed you broke the fast this past Ramadan. Allah does not require much to be faithful."

"I can interpret the Qur'an any way I want, so don't lecture me. Maybe I have a different viewpoint on Islam. Maybe mine isn't as strict as yours." Zehra felt moisture brimming in her eyes. "Besides, how could Allah allow what happened to me? I doubt . . ."

"Don't say any more. Your father may hear. It would hurt him."

"What about me?"

"We haven't said anything over the years as you dressed in American clothing all the time, didn't cover, and even drank wine. But when it comes to men and your marriage . . ." Martha checked herself and stopped talking. Instead, she changed the subject. "You need to eat more. You're too skinny."

"That's one good thing to come out of the PTSD, although I wouldn't recommend it for everyday weight loss." Zehra laughed in spite of the tension that bubbled around them like the water over the rice. "What's the problem you wanted to tell me?"

"It's your cousin, Shereen."

"I hardly know her."

"Of course you don't. My youngest sister, that my parents always said 'was a mistake,' and her husband have been working in Saudi Arabia. He's an electrical engineer, remember? Updating their electrical grid. Probably made a fortune. Anyway, when the government started restricting foreigners, they came here. He's got a wonderful job with St. Jude Medical. Your cousin came too, and that's the problem."

"What?"

"Well, she's taken on all of the worst traits of American teenagers. She's fifteen and after the repressive life in Saudi Arabia, she's gone wild. She no longer covers, wears revealing clothing, and talks foul words."

"What happened?"

Martha paused as the breeze blew in from the deck. "Ah, can you smell that? We've got lots of fresh lamb on the grill."

"I'm vegetarian."

"Since when?"

"Oh, I don't know. It's part of what I've changed."

Martha shook her head. "Anyway, Shereen has been arrested and charged with shoplifting at the Mall of America. My sister's beside herself with shame and anger."

"I'm sure it's a misdemeanor. She's a juvenile, so it won't be a permanent record."

"Zehra, you've forgotten. My sister's family is very conservative Muslim and proud to be American citizens now. To break the law is the worst thing their daughter could do. Can you help her? She's appearing in court in the next couple days."

"Ah, Mom. I'm really busy right now with the trial."

"It's family."

Zehra sighed, knowing because of that she couldn't refuse. "Look, I can't get her off. Professionally, I can't ask for any favors for her, and I wouldn't do it anyway because I don't think that's right."

"Of course not. But could you go with her to court and at least help her? Make sure she doesn't do something else stupid?"

"I don't want to. I don't have the time. I don't even know her." Zehra threw up her hands. "But I will."

Her father came in from the deck. He brought in the greasy, tantalizing smell of grilled meat with him. "My Zehra." He wrapped his arms around her, careful to keep the long steel tongs away from her. "You feel thin. Don't worry. We've got lots to eat."

"Don't burn those vegetables, Joseph. You always do," Martha warned.

"I'm on top of it. How are you?" Joseph asked Zehra.

"I'm fine."

"Panic attacks?"

"Not many. It's getting better."

His eyes grew larger in their dark recesses and circled around her face as if to assess her condition. Zehra felt the warmth of his love and concern. Through her worst times, they had always been with her. For that rock and support, she was always thankful.

"The vegetables, Joseph," Martha spoke crisply.

"Oh, yeah. Come out here," he said to Zehra.

She followed him to the spacious deck so many people in Minnesota treasured. It hung across the back side of the rambler and looked out on a small pond that was almost dried up this time of the fall. Lilac bushes hugged the shore. In the spring, the bushes burst with clouds of lavender flowers, and the heavy scent floated all around the deck. Now the branches were bent over, weighed down by brown and orange leaves that fell off them into the still water of the pond. Zehra smelled the fresh odor of cut grass and looked down to see a lush green carpet below the deck. Her dad loved caring for his lawn.

He opened the hood of the grill and a puff of heavy smoke came out. He waved it aside and dove into the work of rotating the shish-ka-bobs. "Tell me about your job." He used his tongs to lift out the vegetables and set them on a serving plate. They smelled delicious.

Zehra took a deep breath. "I'm involved in the murder case of that young man who was found killed in Hamel. He worked for a church there."

"Heard about it. Pretty gruesome?"

"Yeah. We're prosecuting the accused murderer."

"Tough work?"

"Really tough. In fact, I don't know if we can win. Our case is pretty weak."

"What if you don't win?"

Zehra sucked in her breath. For months, she'd avoided even thinking about the possibility. Now her father's words confronted her. She said, "I don't know. Grant can't fire me because of our union contract, but it won't be pretty. I'll probably be assigned to reviewing government contracts eight hours a day in a sealed room with only water and bread to eat. Most of them are about a foot thick of paper." She groaned at the thought.

"Could you quit and go somewhere else?"

"Depends on the fallout. If my reputation is ruined badly enough, no."

"So, what will you do?"

"My partner, Liz, is really good, and we've got one of our best investigators working on the case." She laughed and said, "If Mom's worried about the men in my life, or lack of them, I should bring home this guy."

"Huh?"

"He's well-respected by everyone, but he's a little weird. He's after me all the time to convert. Gorgeous guy, but Mom would take one look at him and scream."

"She's only trying to help." Joseph shut the cover and picked up the plate full of vegetables. He started for the door into the kitchen. "And as for your trial, you can do it. I know you can."

Zehra felt a sense of pride sing through her body. She wanted to hug her father again. She followed him into the kitchen and offered to set the table. "Eat outside?" she asked Martha.

"Too chilly."

Zehra set out three plates on the counter and, using a fork, lifted the grilled vegetables onto the plates. Quartered onions and tomatoes went into neat piles at the corner of each plate. The red and green peppers looked limp and puckered from the heat with darkened edges that curled underneath. The smell of the grilled oil that covered them made Zehra's stomach rumble.

She moved to the stove to watch her mother adding turmeric, coriander, and cayenne pepper to the long-grain rice. "Can you hand me the cumin, dear?"

The tea pot whistled. Zehra joined her parents. Without a word, they moved to the kitchen sink. In turn, each one washed their hands and arms up to the elbows to start the ablution process before praying. Zehra splashed warm water over her face and dried everything again.

One by one, they filed into the living room next to the kitchen. They stood next to each other and faced northeast, the true shortest path to Mecca from North America.

Zehra began to meditate to cleanse her heart and mind from her worldly cares. She lifted her hands parallel to her ears with the palms facing outward. Then, she knelt onto her knees and leaned forward until her forehead touched the soft carpeting. She made sure that seven parts of her body touched the floor. She began her prayers. She felt the tension seeping out of her.

When they'd finished their individual prayers, they all stood and folded their hands over their chests. They began the uplifting opening prayer of the Qur'an.

"All praise belongs to Allah, Lord of all worlds, the Compassionate, the Merciful Ruler of Judgment Day. You alone do we worship and to you alone do we appeal for help. Show the straight way, the way of those upon whom You have bestowed Your grace, not of those who have earned Your wrath or who go astray."

After a few minutes, Joseph clapped his hands. "Hey. I'm starved. Let's eat."

"Now, Zehra, you'll help with Shereen?"

"Oh, all right. Give me the date and time she's going to be in court."

"Uh . . ." Martha hesitated. "It's in two days. Friday morning."

CHAPTER 6

Thursday, October 20

BACK IN HER OFFICE, ZEHRA WAS TEMPTED to take a bite of the chocolate Hostess cream-filled cupcake she'd hidden in the lower drawer of her desk. In tense, difficult times, junk food provided comfort. She thought of her hips and decided against it, but didn't toss it into the garbage.

After she'd started on Liz's team, Zehra's office had moved to the present location: one window, beige metal and plastic desk, matching beige credenza, and bookshelf. If a person left her office and slammed the narrow door, the tan sheetrock walls shivered. Behind her far wall, an elevator ran continuously. The noise had bothered Zehra for the first few weeks until she got used to it.

She'd moved her colorful artwork from the public defender's office where it used to brighten up the tan, monotonous walls. Her grandfather's prayer rug lay on the floor, oriented to face northeast. Behind her on the credenza stood pictures of her huge family, all lined up like school photos.

Zehra needed help. Although she'd had plenty of experience as a defense lawyer, switching to the prosecution presented different difficulties. She texted her old friend, Paul Schmitt.

After they had stopped the bioterrorists and she'd saved Paul's life, they'd become close again. Paul was steady and handsome, a former Army Ranger who had gone to work as an FBI agent. He was older than Zehra and had much more worldly experience. They'd been serious, but it didn't work out and they had drifted apart. Probably because deep down, Zehra wanted to marry in her Islamic faith.

But in the Twin City area, that was difficult. Zehra had been born in Texas, attended college in Colorado in order to follow her love of snow boarding, and had come to Minnesota for law school. After many steamy summers in Texas, her parents had followed her north. Although both highly educated, her parents retained many of older ideas, including about their religion. The only change they'd made in years was their allegiance to the U.S. and their deep respect for the freedom in America and the Bill of Rights.

She'd gotten together with Paul when she was a public defender, representing an extremist Muslim accused of murder. Paul, with the FBI, worked the case from a different angle and had risked his career to help solve a terrorist plot that centered on Zehra's murder case. They'd become close, but Zehra still held back, unsure of how much she wanted to be involved with Paul again.

After the terrorist case was over, Paul had been offered the top position in the Minneapolis FBI office, which tempted him, but he'd turned it down in the end because he wanted to remain in the field. Now he texted back, "let's meet coffee @ dunns/river?"

She replied, "½ hour."

As she stood to leave, the phone rang. It was her mother. "Zehra, how are you?"

Her mother called every day. "Fine."

"Thanks for coming over last night. I'm still worried about you not being married. And you're not getting any younger."

"I'm okay, Mom. I have to run. I'm meeting Paul to help me on this new case."

"The murder of that man in Hamel? I told all my friends my daughter's going to get that animal off the streets. You be careful. I'm sure he's quite dangerous. Don't forget Shereen's case."

"Got it. Bye, Mom."

"Oh, and say hi to Paul for me. Is this serious with him?"

"Bye, Mom." She hung up.

The low clouds left only a weak sun that colored the sky pearl. Zehra threw on her coat and decided to walk the few blocks to the Dunn Brothers coffee shop. It sat on the corner of Third Avenue in an old remodeled train freight house, surrounded by a complex that had been renovated into hotels, a convention center, and even an outdoor skating rink. The freight house was a small, two-story limestone building. Inside, the warmth and smell of roasting coffee behind the counter made her feel comfortable and secure.

In a few minutes, Paul rushed through the door. "Hate to be late," he said when he came over to her. "Even though I'm not in the top spot at the FBI, I still have endless meetings." They hugged tightly. Holding her arms with his hands, he leaned back to look at her. "You're still way too thin."

"About the only good thing to come out of our 'adventure' was losing weight."

He leaned close to her face and kissed her cheek lightly. She could smell fresh soap on his face. After Paul got coffee and Zehra green tea, they climbed the narrow stairs to the second floor. They found a secluded area in the far corner and sat next to a bag full of coffee beans resting on the oak floor.

Paul took a long sip and said quietly, "Any more panic attacks?"

She sighed, not wanting to get into all this. "Had another attack. It's getting better, but it's so frustrating. I've lost all my friends, and I don't seem to care. That's not like me. I'm depressed all the time. Everything feels flat to me. You and my family are the only ones I can hang onto because you 'get me.'"

A flush rose in his face and he looked down at his coffee. "We should get together more often."

"Oh, Paul . . . I don't know what to do. You know I think the world of you. But give me time."

"I'm not going to force anything, but you know how I feel about you. We've had time. What about my feelings?" He raised his voice.

"I'm the one who had to kill him," she snapped.

"I got shot myself. You'd think our shared experience would push us into each other's arms." He stared at her. "I'm tired of waiting."

Without saying anything, she nodded. Part of her would love to let go and merge into this wonderful man's life. But until she recovered fully, Zehra didn't trust her own judgment. "Maybe later."

Paul took a deep breath. "What's up?"

Zehra shifted her legs on the chair. "You know Liz Alvarez asked me to second-chair her on the murder case involving the young guy shot in Hamel."

"Heard that. How's it going?" Frustration still curled around the edges of his words.

"Glad I'm just the second chair. Don't know if I could handle it on my own." Zehra looked around them. No one else had come upstairs. She leaned forward. "Between you and me?"

"Of course."

"The case is turning to crap."

Paul's lips thinned. "Been there before with the Bureau. I told you about the case in Milwaukee I screwed up. Almost got myself fired. Gonna dump your case?"

"Can't, really. The sheriff's department went public with it so now we're kind of stuck. That's why I need your help. See it from a fresh set of eyes."

"I'm all eyes."

Zehra looked up at his eyes, dark brown and, although not particularly large, they shimmered with moisture that revealed charm and depth. They always melted her.

Zehra started to review the case with him. "The sheriff's detective is still investigating the church." She lifted a Dell laptop from her briefcase, perched it on the front corner of the table, opened it, and began tapping on the keys. "That's where the victim was working before the shooting."

"What about it?"

"It's not mainstream. They're 'end of the world' people. Think that Armageddon is just around the corner. The detective, Chesney, also suspects they're a front for a dangerous militia group of some sort."

Paul's eyes opened. "Huh. If so, that could be FBI jurisdiction or maybe for the alcohol, tobacco, and firearms guys. Let me poke around. Talk to some people."

"It's gotta be right now, Paul. We're up against the wall and out of time." Zehra tapped on the keys. Then she opened the paper file and pulled out reports. "Victim was a single guy, no family."

"Have you seized the files and computers from the church?"

"Yeah, but nothing unusual's turned up." Zehra spoke in short, clipped sentences while she leafed through stacks of police reports and long yellow pads of notes. "What's odd is the victim. Even though he worked at the church, looks like he was trying to escape when Menendez shot him. Why?"

"You've checked the criminal data bases for Menendez?"

"Yeah, state and federal."

"Anything?" he asked while looking at her.

"He's illegal, and I found a prior conviction from Texas."

"Homicide?"

"No."

"You're right; you need more." Paul frowned and shook his head.

"Yeah . . . maybe I could try to use the Texas case against Menendez as a 'Spreigl' here in his murder case."

"What?"

"Oh, that's right. You work with the federal courts. It's a Minnesota supreme court case that allows us to use prior convictions against a defendant, if the judge agrees."

"How about this? If you can get more evidence against the perp, maybe you could squeeze him to talk prior to the trial. See if he knows anything about the church or any ties to a militia. That's the main way the FBI gets evidence."

"Uh . . ."

"You haven't offered a plea bargain yet?" His head shook from side to side as he stared at her in surprise.

It offended Zehra a little. "Of course we offered one. Mezerretti says his client doesn't want any deals. If Menendez walks, we lose everything including the chance to squeeze him into talking about anything else." She shrugged.

Silence clouded the space between them.

Paul stretched out his long legs, crossed his feet, and tilted back. "Can you get me Detective Chesney's number?"

She felt tightness in her chest. "Sure . . ." She hesitated. Zehra worried about how much to lean on Paul. One of the toughest guys she'd ever met, if he started to help, that would certainly pull them closer together—something Zehra wasn't sure about right now.

On the other hand, after what she'd been through, Zehra doubted that she could do it without his help, and particularly, his support.

Finally, she said, "First thing I need is a delay in the trial. The judge turned us down today, but we're going to try it again in front of the chief judge. Probably won't do much good, even though the chief knows the first judge's an idiot."

Paul nodded. "Any law on your side?"

Outside, the sun broke through the lumbering clouds. A narrow shaft of sunlight slanted into the room, warming the area it struck.

"No." Zehra watched the dust swimming in the slant of light like dozens of goldfish paddling aimlessly. Years ago, she would've hustled through this trial prep effortlessly. Now, she paddled. It was slower and required a more concentrated focus. Still, the fact that the process felt familiar reassured her.

She looked back at Paul. "If we get forced out on Monday . . . we're sunk." She felt better with his help. At this point, he was the only other person Zehra felt like she could trust. "I appreciate anything you can do."

"Sure." He lifted his cup for another drink, then set it down. "What else have you got on the victim?"

"Let's see . . ." Her watch beeped a few times. Without looking, she reached over her wrist and stopped it. It was designed for Muslims to remind them to pray five times a day. Her parents had given it to her for Ramadan a few years ago. Her eyes flicked up to his. "Never mind, it can wait for a while."

Zehra scanned her computer screen. "Not much. The picture I have is a lonely guy whose main social group was the church. Members who were interviewed were all shocked by the killing."

"What'd they say about Menendez?"

"No one knew him. Seems he always came in at night to do janitorial work. Wasn't a part of the congregation."

"Said you had a witness?"

"Our 'reliable' eyewitness," she sniffed. "Another illegal. Young woman from Russia. Yelena Mostropov. Stage name was 'Sparkle.'" Zehra rolled her eyes. "Can you imagine how reliable she is?"

Paul shook his head. "Okay. Let's look back at the defendant's history. Sounds like there's something in Texas."

"Right. Could you help me with your old FBI contacts?" At the thought, a prickly feeling crabbed up her back.

Paul cleared his throat. "Might have even more for you."

"What?"

"Got an email yesterday from an agent at ICE, Immigration and Customs Enforcement. Wants to meet with me. Wouldn't say what it was about, but if you get me the name and date of birth of the defendant, maybe they've got something on him to help with your case. I'll try to get you into the loop."

"Great. We could use all the help we can get."

"You told me earlier the police picked up some cell phones."

"Yeah. One belonged to the defendant."

"Have you recovered all the data?"

"Hennepin County Sheriff's forensic lab did. They ran a computer scan and didn't come up with much."

Paul's brows furrowed low over his eyes. "They probably ran the usual scans."

"Routine, isn't it?"

"Sure, but I've got an expert we contract who might be able to retrieve all the data, even the stuff that's been deleted. Messages, addresses, videos, photos, maybe more. I'll order him to do it with top priority."

"We hadn't even thought about that. Can you help?" She looked up at him and felt lightness in her chest. Paul offered even more ideas.

"We'll need the phone, of course. Dr. Leonard lives in Minneapolis."

Zehra tapped in a note on her laptop. "I'll check it out of the sheriff's locked property room."

An hour later, Zehra folded her computer and slipped it into her briefcase. "Gotta get back. Thanks so much." They both stood.

"Zehra . . . we should see each other for more than talking about our cases."

"Don't push me," she snarled and immediately felt bad. The stress made her irritable.

Paul's eyes softened as they probed Zehra's face and circled it. "I want to help."

"I know you do." She wanted his help in the worst way. Knowing he was there would give her the strength to push forward. When he reached his arms around her and dipped his face toward her, Zehra didn't move back. He kissed her on the lips, soft and firm, and he lingered longer than she'd expected. But that was okay.

 # CHAPTER 7

Thursday, October 20

KATHY JOHNSON CAROMED AROUND the corner of Minnehaha Avenue as she drove the final blocks to the meeting of the NorthStar Group. She was going to be late. Her blue Prius rocked to a halt behind the four story building where the meeting would be held. A few remaining red and yellow leaves hung from the vines that grew across the brick façade and wrapped the building like a shawl for an elderly woman. She worked close to here as a nurse in a local Allina clinic.

The NorthStar Group was a national nongovernmental organization dedicated to exposing and stopping dangerous militant militia groups in the United States. The Minnesota chapter was headed by Kevin Stout, a law professor in St. Paul. Kathy had volunteered to help with public relations for the group.

She heard rain dripping from the overhanging trees outside the building. The air smelled pungent and decaying. Yellow lights jiggled in the puddles in the street, reflected from street lamps and windows of office buildings. Climbing out of the car easily, she was glad she kept herself in good shape. And since she was single and had never had children, her waist and hips looked like a woman ten years younger and gave her pride.

Tonight Kevin and his partner, Jamie Solomon, would face the board of directors about funding requests. With the slumping economy, it would be a tough night for everyone. Turning into the hall to hang her tan Eddie Bauer raincoat, she shook off the dampness, placing it evenly on a hanger.

It had been a terrible day. She'd gone into nursing to give something to others, to the community. After all these years, Kathy had realized that a lot of her work resembled babysitting, and that the opportunities to do important work seemed few and far between. The NorthStar Group offered her something larger and exciting to do.

She straightened her back, tucked her blouse into her skirt to make it fit tighter on her body, and started for the meeting room. She looked forward to seeing Kevin again. He was disorganized, but he had energy and enthusiasm and a sexual heat that she couldn't resist.

To her surprise, the small room was full. Taking a chair next to Kevin Stout at the table, she smiled at him.

No one had called the meeting to order yet, and the voices swirled around the room like wind before a summer storm. Kevin had joined the group a few years ago. After earning a master's degree in law, he taught law school but had never actually practiced. She remembered being surprised when he'd first attended a meeting.

He had lectured her, "The system's still not responding to these nut cases. Survivalists and armed militia pose a dangerous problem. Most people assume they aren't a big deal. But they're one of the fastest-growing fringe groups in the country, many tied with illegal weapons smuggling." He sniffed with confidence. "Besides, I know all the gun rights groups and how politically powerful they are. They give cover to the illegitimate groups. Someone's got to expose the danger. I'm that person."

Kathy had marveled at his self-assurance. Along with his disheveled looks, it made him attractive.

Of course, it didn't hurt that the press seemed to show up whenever Kevin appeared. Obviously, he liked the attention.

Kevin was a little younger than Kathy and the parent of a young child still in school. She knew he was married, but unhappy. His craggy features and thick gray eyebrows suggested his personality--rough around the edges and anxious to take some risks. Still, she saw through his bluster. He mostly posed in his role as an activist.

His eyes took her in as she sat down. Coming from other men, it infuriated her, but with Kevin she didn't mind. Just the opposite. She felt an electric tingling whenever he studied her. He was also very kind to her. And she knew that she still looked attractive.

Kathy had recently picked up on his hints. Unhappy with his wife, he toyed with Kathy. Should she respond? A big part of her wanted to. She'd never had an affair with a married man before, and the thought of it bothered her.

But Kevin was different. In spite of being self-absorbed, he had brains and was passionate about exposing the dangerous groups. And his rough edges intrigued her. She didn't know what to do.

She noticed his beard. Normally, it was an attractive feature. Tonight it looked so ragged. "What the hell happened to you?"

He grinned in the self-confident way he did everything. "I know. Just got up this morning and tried to use my kid's hair clippers, and well, you see the results. Not pretty."

"You're so full of it. I don't believe you." She asked, "How're things going here?"

A small woman bustled in from the side door. Jamie Solomon, the other executive officer of the NorthStar Group, hurried to a seat next to Kevin. As she sat, Jamie peeled off a stylish leather jacket glistening with rain. "Sorry," she said to the board members who were assembling on the other side of the table.

Kathy didn't know her well but always chuckled at the fact that Jamie saw through Kevin but still supported him. Kathy slipped away from Kevin and took a chair near the corner.

The noise and chatter died off to perfect silence. Chairs scraped over the floor for a better view around the table. Others settled into chairs clumped behind Kevin and Jamie.

"Let's come to order, people," the chairman of the board said. "We've got a lot of things to cover."

Kevin nodded and smiled broadly as if he owned the board. He had a habit of shaking his head so that the long gray curls of hair ruffled like a wind had lifted them off his shoulders.

The chairman was an older man with long white hair down to his shoulders. He'd once been a liberal Democrat in the state legislature. His entire life had been a crusade against guns and laws that allowed people to possess and carry guns. He cleared his throat. "As you all know, the board called this meeting to review our funding, which is down considerably from last year. We may have to curtail our efforts."

A loud murmur grumbled from the crowd.

The chairman held up his hands. "I know. I'm as devastated as anyone else. I've fought for our principles my whole life. But with a weak economy . . ."

"Bullshit," Kevin said and grinned.

The chairman frowned as if he'd heard this before. "Where do you think you'll get more money?"

"We go public. When the public finds out what's really going on right under their noses, they'll get scared, and we'll see the money flow."

Shaking his head, the chairman said, "Too late for that."

"We're at a critical point. It's more than just about money."

"Sorry, Kevin. Maybe next year."

Jamie adjusted herself in the chair and, glancing at Kevin, said, "Maybe if we had a public relations blast. We've found something really creepy that will scare people, like Kevin said." She turned to him as if to hand off the point she was making.

He picked it up. "I've got heavy stuff to run with."

"No. We're out of money."

"Listen. You know that guy who was shot in Hamel a month ago, Marko Sundberg?" Kevin looked across the line of people at the table. "Well, we've got some good intel that he was involved with an extremist church there, and they, in turn, are tied in with armed militias around the country who are preparing for the end of the world." He smiled and waited. When no one responded, Kevin continued, "Don't you get it? Think of the public relations bonanza. We got murder, a strange church that's preparing for the Rapture, an armed militia to back them up . . ." Kevin tilted his head back and grinned in what he'd told Kathy was his "Franklin Roosevelt" look.

The chairman glanced back and forth across the table. "When we've supported some of your ideas in the past Kevin, they've turned out to be wild goose chases. What's different this time? Why should we believe you?"

Kevin looked down for a moment to add suspense to his words. "As you know, we've got a huge volunteer group who monitor blogs, chat rooms, and AM radio talk shows that focus on destroying the government or the 'end times.' In the past few months, the chatter has increased more than we've ever seen it before."

"So what?" the chairman shrugged. "These nuts have been around forever."

"I know, but with the Internet these lone, isolated groups have found each other. They connect in various ways, and the Internet becomes an echo chamber to unite all of them and offer encouragement to act."

"In dangerous ways we haven't seen before," added Jamie. "These home-grown extremist groups are unknown, for the most part, and that's what scares us."

"They're terrorists who live just 'down the street' from many of us. Unknown and unsuspected until they expose themselves on the Internet." Kevin leaned over and reached into a worn leather briefcase that had flopped next to him on the floor. He retrieved a stack of paper. "Here. I've made hard copies of a recent chat room conversation we picked up from a member of the Church of the Rapture." He passed them around to the board. The paper read:

Hey, X-Boxx.
Whas up
Big shit coming down
Hometown?
Roger that but across country—finally we act!!!!
Remember Nam? Waiting to take it to Charlie Felt scared but ready
I'm right there Bro
Who's the commander
Horseman here in Minnesota
Bring on the chaos!!! Bring down manna from heaven
Apocalypse Now!!!

The chairman looked up, his face pale. "See what you mean. Have you taken this to the FBI?"

"Sure, but they're so busy tracking down foreign terrorists, they don't have the manpower or money to do much about it until one of these groups does something violent."

Jamie spoke again. "I got an idea. We can put pressure on the local law enforcement to check into our concerns."

"How do you propose to do that?"

"Well, the county attorney has charged a guy named Roberto Menendez with the murder in Hamel. The victim worked at the church Kevin's talking about. See the connection? We've already called a press conference to grill the prosecutors about their case. Expose them for what they're not doing to really investigate the murder and the church."

"I don't know . . ." the chairman said, but his eyes glittered.

People applauded and whistled.

Kevin said, "We'll nail those idiots to the wall in front of the press. Create enough questions in the public's mind to get a wider investigation started. Our group will lead the way, but the county attorney and their investigators pay for it."

The chairman tightened his lips. "Might work."

Jamie Solomon added, "Ulysses Grant and Elizabeth Alvarez, the lead prosecutor who's trying the Menendez case, will be there. Any of you are welcome to come." Her fingers, circled with turquoise rings, curled into a fist and pounded the air above her head.

People clapped. Someone shouted, "Go for it, girl."

Kathy glanced at Kevin and she knew how excited he was. "We gotta move on this. These creeps are gonna strike any time now," he shouted above the rising noise of the crowd.

"Right on, bro," a white man in the front row called back.

Kathy had always admired the fact that Kevin tried to do something good for others. At the same time, Kathy knew how much Kevin needed the spotlight and the attention. That probably motivated him the most.

The noise and agitated rustling quieted. The board members had huddled together. The chairman sat up and faced the audience again. "Our mission is to expose these extremist, dangerous militia groups. If you think this could get us some attention and money, go for it."

"All it takes is for one man to stand up. It takes courage, not money."

Kathy almost laughed out loud at Kevin. As long as there was the promise of media attention, Kevin was always brave.

The meeting broke up. People shoved their chairs back to stand and stretch. Kevin moved closer to Kathy and looked into her eyes. "You look wonderful tonight, babe," he said. He still radiated infectious energy from the meeting.

Kathy coughed a laugh. "You're an idiot."

He moved behind her, rested his hands on the middle of her shoulders, and stroked in circles. "Let me help you relax." His mouth was inches from her ear. Starting to leave the room, the crowd swirled around them.

Kathy held her breath for a moment. "I don't know . . . we need to talk." She backed closer into his moving hands. They felt warm and strong. "This sure is exciting stuff. The plans you have to confront the prosecutors."

"I've never seen chatter as violent as the stuff we're getting. It scares me." He leaned forward and brushed his lips against her neck. She shuddered and felt a wave of warmth course down her body. She sagged closer to him.

"What're you doing later?" he whispered into her ear.

"I don't know, Kevin." Her body wanted to stay with him, but her mind jerked her back into the room. She looked to see if anyone was watching.

Later, as Kathy helped put the chairs back in place, Jamie and Kevin disappeared into a back room. When Kathy followed them, they were arguing.

"I won't put up with this shit, Kevin," yelled Jamie. "There's an issue of our reputation here."

"We've got to be prepared, just in case."

"We don't get messed up with anything illegal, and never, never with people like that. I'm not going to let you jeopardize all we've worked for."

"Aw . . . that's bullshit." He shook his head. "You think these networks, these 'sunshine soldiers' play fair? No. They're all about force and violence, and we've got to be prepared to fight back."

"There must be other things we can do. Don't fuck this up, Kevin."

Kathy interrupted, "What do you mean, 'fight back'?"

The two looked at each other, then at Kathy. A guilty grin broke over Kevin's face. "Maybe you shouldn't know . . . to uh, protect you. Don't worry, but we're taking some other . . . uh, steps to figure this out. Like, if we need help, we can access national resources and other movements."

"Huh?" Kathy backed up a little. "What the hell are you talking about? Nothing illegal?"

"Don't worry," Kevin reassured her.

She didn't believe him for a minute.

Jamie said, "Kevin, you gotta focus. Our goal is to confront the prosecutors about the murder case. Take 'em apart on live TV if we have to. Remember, Kevin, no mercy."

Kevin sneered. "I'll crack their fuckin' heads open if I have to. Just watch me."

After Jamie left, Kevin moved closer to Kathy. "Not now," she warned him. Her emotions collided with one another and left her uncertain about how to respond to him. She realized the glow inside her came from the fact that for the first time in many years, she felt wanted, and it conflicted with her questions about him. He could become unhinged at times.

Kevin nodded his head and ran his eyes over her body. He grinned and said, "Later, babe." Then he left.

Kathy wandered back to the deserted hallway. She turned the corner to see the long coat rack, empty except for her limp coat hanging all by itself. Kathy put it around her shoulders and walked out alone into the night.

CHAPTER 8

Friday, October 21

RIDAY MORNING AT NINE O'CLOCK, Zehra walked down Sixth Street from her office to the Juvenile Justice Center. A modern, two-story building, it had several courtrooms, a probation department, and attached to the north side, a four-story detention facility for the most violent offenders.

Zehra didn't want to meet her cousin. She'd make it quick and get back to work on the trial.

A light rain drizzled on Zehra, who'd forgotten an umbrella. As she rushed into the courthouse, she could almost feel her hair curling even tighter than usual. Besides that, her new shoes were wet. It was going to be a bad morning.

At least she'd remembered to wear a coat, which she removed and shook out on the main floor of the courthouse. To her right, the public service area was already crowded with people trying to find the correct courtrooms for their children's cases.

After she went through the metal detectors on the second floor, the lobby opened ahead of her. Between large windows that overlooked Sixth Street, several low couches sprawled along the walls which were too uncomfortable for sitting, so most people stood along the walls, leaning on one leg, waiting for their cases to be called. An occasional public defender walked through the tangle of people, calling names out loud., searching for their clients, whom they'd never met before the court date.

Zehra found her aunt and cousin easily. Her aunt, Salah, came up to Zehra and hugged her, kissing first one cheek then the other. She was fully covered with *hijab* and had a thin sweater on that came all the way down to her wrists. Salah also wore loose pants that reached to her feet. She was a pretty woman with dark features, but Zehra hardly knew her since the family had only been in the United States for about two years and lived on the opposite side of the Twin Cities.

"Thanks to Allah you've come. I am so worried about her. She is with the bad kids and they stay at the Mall of America, getting in trouble. I am so embarrassed. My husband is planning to punish her severely. It will not happen again. She is acting like . . . what do Americans call it . . . a slut?"

"I'll talk to her."

Her cousin stood several feet away. She slouched against the wall dressed in tight black pants, sandals, and a low-cut top with long sleeves that clung to her shapely body. No wonder the parents were worried.

Zehra separated from her aunt and moved over to Shereen. When she introduced herself, Shereen turned slowly and cocked her head to the side without responding as she studied Zehra.

"You got arrested and charged at the Mall of America," Zehra said. "Want some help?"

"Like, what could you do for me?"

"Well, your mother asked me to help. So here I am."

"Whatever." Shereen cracked the gum she chewed and turned away. She texted something into her phone. Two buds grew out of her ears with thin cords hanging down to her iPhone.

This is going to be a big waste of my time, Zehra thought. Her own trial work was piled on her desk at the office, and she wanted to get back to it. "Hey," she raised her voice at her cousin. "I don't want to be here any more than you. In fact, I got a lot of my own work to do."

"Yeah? So do you have any idea of how uninterested I am in this?"

Zehra studied her for a moment. Beautiful, large liquid eyes slanted at angles across her pretty face. Beneath the thick make-up, Shereen was very attractive. She had a long nose, like they all did in the family, and prominent cheekbones. "You wait here. I'm going to talk to the prosecutor and get the file and see what's going on."

In ten minutes Zehra returned. Her cousin hadn't moved. Zehra said, "How about if you and I talk in an interview room alone? Without your mother."

Shereen shrugged. "Yeah. I got like nothing else to do here." She texted more on her phone, popped out the buds, and put them back into a large leather bag that she carried. She followed Zehra around the corner to a small room with two chairs and a plastic table in between.

When they were inside, Zehra shut the door and laid a file on the table. She opened it and sat down. Shereen slouched in a chair. The room felt stuffy and hot and smelled a little rank from the previous occupants.

"Okay. This is the prosecutor's file and the police reports. Looks like you and two other girls were hanging around the mall. Some guys were following you, and all of you created a disturbance," Zehra read.

"Stupid cops."

"Anyway, security told you to leave, so you and your friends went to the cosmetic store."

"Like that's a crime?"

"Security cameras in the store caught you stealing make up and lipstick."

"Big deal. Like, we gave it all back."

Zehra sighed. She didn't have time to babysit this child. She closed the file. "I really haven't got time for this. You should talk to a public defender. I know most of them here, and they're the best."

"So, why're you here? Sucking up to my mom?"

"It's called a family, Shereen. And no, I'm not sucking up to her. I'm trying to help you get out of trouble. What's going on?"

"What do you mean?"

"Why are you getting into trouble?"

Shereen paused and looked up at the corner of the ceiling. Her eyes blinked and Zehra could tell she struggled with her response. Finally she said, "My parents are like so weird. They still think we're in, like, the prison camp."

"Huh?"

"Saudi Arabia. This is the United States. I'm finally free here. I'm enjoying my life and my friends. They can't seem to get it, that I'm an American woman now."

Hardly a woman, Zehra thought. But she'd experienced the same attitudes with her own parents to some degree and found herself empathizing with Shereen. Although Zehra had never been arrested, many times she had clashed—still did for that matter—with her parents over many social and cultural differences between the generations. Zehra softened her voice. "Hey, I think I kinda understand. My own parents were really tough on me when I was growing up. Wanted me to wear *hijab*, and I refused. Told me I had to get married to a nice Muslim man. I still hear that stuff from my mom."

"You do?"

"You wouldn't believe all the horrible dates my mom's found for me. Guys who were so boring, I almost dropped my face into my food as I fell asleep listening to them."

Shereen chuckled. "That's the thing. Like, my parents don't get it. They keep pushing me to date Muslims, but there aren't many in my school except Africans from Somalia. That's like, from the moon. And they smell funny."

"I know."

"You do?" Shereen straightened in her chair. "And being Muslim is a drag too. When I tell people that, they're like, 'Dude you're a terrorist.' Like we're weird."

"I know. I've gotten more odd looks than you can imagine. Most people don't say anything to my face, but I feel them staring at me. Sometimes in stores, I have a hard time getting waited on. One guy even came up to me and told me to go home. People have a pretty narrow view of Muslims. It's because they don't really know us or what we believe, so they're afraid."

"Yeah. It's like this feeling of always being a little different from everyone else. But I'm not."

Zehra nodded.

"And then my parents are like, they're pissed at the way I dress and the friends I have. But I'm proud and like my friends." She pushed up the sleeve on her right arm, exposing a tattoo of a name that ran up to her elbow. Her face reddened. "Don't worry. It's not permanent."

"What's that?"

"Huh?" Shereen glanced at her arm. "Uh . . . friend of mine. We hooked up at the food court." She pulled her sleeve down quickly.

"How about your friends? Maybe you should change some of them if you're getting into trouble with these." Zehra pointed to the closed file.

"Yeah . . . like, I got lots of friends."

"At school?"

"School sucks. No, at the mall. There's all those guys there, too. Hot ones compared to the bores in school. Dudes at the Mall of America have money and bling. They're going someplace." She dropped her head for a moment.

Zehra could understand how the glitter and flash of the dream the retailers tried to sell people at the mall could attract a young girl. "I'll talk to one of the public defenders and have them interview you. It's important to keep this off your record."

"Whatever."

Zehra stood and picked up the file folder. She paused. "Shereen, I'm sure you don't care what I say, but I think I can understand what you're feeling."

"No way."

"Okay. But nothing good's going to come out of hanging around the mall. You should get back in school. You seem smart."

Shereen waved her hand. "I can't stand to be around my parents. I can't stand to breathe the same air. They've got an old-fashioned religion and they don't know shit about what's going on in the world. I got friends out there who, like, really understand me."

"The name on your arm?"

"Maybe."

"Maybe your parents are old-fashioned, but they still love you. I can guarantee you that none of the mall rats out there truly feel that way about you." Zehra opened the door to step out into the hall. Shereen stood and put her hand on Zehra's shoulder.

"You're okay."

Zehra shrugged. "I'm trying. Even at my age, I still haven't figured out everything."

Shereen reached forward and hugged Zehra tightly for a moment, then let go to move past her into the hall.

 # CHAPTER 9

Friday, October 21

SINCE ZEHRA HAD ASKED HER SECRETARY to hold every single call, when she was back in her office and the phone rang, it irritated her. As Zehra began to raise her voice on the phone, the secretary cut her off.

"Zehra, shut up. You need to talk to these guys." Her voice rasped in an unusual way. Something was wrong.

"Who are they?" she asked.

"Office of . . . I wrote it down . . . the Bureau of Alcohol, Tobacco, Firearms, and Explosives out of the United States Justice Department. Some guy says he's a special agent and has to talk to only you. There's another dude, too. From Immigration or something. You know . . . yadda, yadda with these dicks."

Zehra frowned and sat back from studying the forensic reports on her desk. This must be the group Paul had mentioned. "Okay. Let me talk to them."

"Ms. Hassan, this is Special Agent Mike Mansfield from Homeland Security, the U.S. Immigration and Customs Enforcement, ICE . . ."

"I know what the office is."

"I'm out of the San Antonio field office, but I need to talk to you alone, ASAP."

"Uh . . . sure. Is it about the case we're prosecuting against Roberto Menendez?"

"Precisely. That's why we need to talk. It can't wait."

"Why me? Elizabeth Alvarez is the lead . . ."

"You're a close friend of Paul Schmitt, aren't you?"

"Yes."

"Our agents have contacted him in the local FBI. We'd like to talk with both of you, actually."

Zehra felt her stomach tighten. "If it's about our case, you should include Elizabeth Alvarez."

"Fine. No one else."

"Meet in my office?"

"Definitely not. We need to meet outside your office in a safe area."

"Safe?"

"How soon can you meet?"

* * *

Two hours later, Zehra and Paul sat in his new car, a four-door Infiniti.

"Come up in the world, huh?" Zehra kidded him.

"With my new position, I get a leased car. Nice, huh?" he said. They were parked beside an office building in Golden Valley, a suburb west of Minneapolis. They had received specific instructions to drive west out of the city on Highway 55, past the park to the intersection with Meadow Lane. A four-story, tan office building stood at the corner. They were to wait in the south parking lot, then, at two o'clock exactly, drive into the underground parking garage to meet the agents. With the recent recession, the office building was almost totally vacant.

Liz finished her cigarette and got back into the rear seat. A cloud of stale smoke clung to her. "How's our time?"

"Got twenty minutes."

Liz, who knew Paul from around the law enforcement groups, asked him, "How come you're here?"

"I worked with ICE during the bioterrorist case."

Liz shook her head. "You guys with the feds . . . I don't know. At the county, we haven't got enough money for all this cloak and dagger shit."

While they waited, the conversation moved to tough cases Liz had tried. Zehra was fascinated with stories of former trials and the people involved—Grant, Brown, cops, and other defense lawyers. She stopped Liz and asked about Brown.

She sniffed. "Gotta admit, I like that guy's buns."

"I've heard you like a lot more than that," Paul said.

"All right, I guess I do. Many years ago, he'd separated from his wife and we had a 'thing' going. Well, if you call a couple months a 'thing.' Then it got kind of weird."

"How?"

"Well, he felt guilty. But then it was like he got religion. He started trying to convert me. Born again, speaking in tongues. Finally, he went beyond the radar." She looked down at her paper cup of Starbucks coffee and shook her head. "Great bod, though. He's a body builder and still keeps himself in great shape. Disciplined, a zealot. One of the most decorated cops ever. He's on every government board you can imagine, goes to Twins games with the governor's staff and is well-respected." Liz's face softened. "He's smart and damn persistent."

"I know. He hits on me all the time," Zehra said.

"Bother you?"

Zehra waved her hand in front of herself. "No, not sexually. I mean about religion. It's obvious he thinks, as a Muslim, I'm going to hell. He makes me uneasy. And you're right, Liz. He's kind of weird."

Paul grinned. "Then you need to spend more time with me. I like you the way you are."

"Sure." Zehra laughed, but from the glance Paul gave her, she knew he meant something more serious.

Liz added, "But he's become bitter, thinks the country's become a cesspool of low morals and sin." She blew out a breath. "He's not the guy he used to be." She sipped her coffee. "I'm just glad he's helping us."

Liz continued, "I remember a funny case. Brown was on the street then, early in his career. Got a report from a woman that someone had left a baby carriage on the sidewalk in front of the house next to the caller's. She was worried about the baby."

"What happened?"

"Brown and his partner arrive, thinking they were on a rescue mission. Turns out, the mother and her partner were burglarizing the house where they had parked the carriage."

"What?" Zehra said.

"Yeah. Must have decided on the spur of the moment to burgle the house and didn't have time to take the baby home."

"Hey, you can't make this stuff up. I believe it." Zehra laughed.

"Time to go, guys." Paul started the car and turned it into the underground lot. He circled down a ramp to the "C" level and straightened out in the farthest corner from the elevators. No other cars shared that level of the ramp with them. Dim fluorescent lights cast the interior of Paul's car in shadow.

In three minutes, a black Suburban pulled up next to them. The driver's window drained downward until a man's face appeared. He looked at Paul and the interior of the Infiniti, nodded and said, "Get in the back. All of you."

With two huge bench seats, the three of them had plenty of room to stretch out.

The driver was tall and wide. His neck rolled over his white collar, held together with a blue necktie. He looked in his early thirties. A thin cord fell from his ear. Sandy hair cut short matched his full sandy eyebrows that flattened over blue eyes.

The other man was smaller, thin. When he turned around, unlike the first man, he wouldn't look directly at Zehra. He'd point his long ski-jump nose in one direction while his eyes swept back and forth over it.

Badges flipped open across the seat. They glittered gold in the dome light from the roof of the Suburban.

"Folks," the large man started. "I'm Special Agent Mike Mansfield." He popped a bud out of his ear. "I'm assisting Special Agent Dixon Long. He's from the Bureau of Alcohol, Tobacco, Firearms, and Explosives." Mansfield reached over to shake Paul's hand and say hello. He looked past Zehra and his eyes roamed over Liz. She glared at him.

Zehra sipped from her coffee cup, set it down on a holder between the seats, and picked it up again. Long glanced at his partner. Something passed between them.

"Okay. Guess it's all right," Mansfield said. "How much do you know about the defendant in your case?"

"Menendez? Not a lot. We know he's got some kind of a record in Texas that our investigator is chasing down. Why?" Zehra said. She felt uncomfortable in this position. She was only the second chair. Knowing Liz, it wouldn't take long for her to butt in.

"What's this about?" Liz said.

"Just answer, please."

"No . . . no, I'm not going to answer. Tell me what this is about first."

Mansfield lifted his right arm over the top of the seat, and rested it there. Snow white cuffs poked out from the end of his suit coat. Long kept looking around the parking lot. Mansfield waited awhile, thinking. "I suppose if we want your cooperation, we'll have to give you a little." He smiled.

"That's a novel idea," Liz said.

The aroma of new leather filled the interior.

Mansfield sighed. "How much do you know about the Department of Homeland Security?"

Liz couldn't help but laugh. "I know it's big. It's a bureaucracy, and knowing government, it's probably a big mess." She grinned at Zehra.

Mansfield didn't. "The Immigration and Customs Enforcement, ICE, is the largest investigative arm of Homeland Security, which is DHS. One of our most critical assets in the ICE mission is the Homeland Security Investigations, HSI."

"Never heard of it," Liz said.

Mansfield raised his eyebrows. "You should. Their mission is the investigation of domestic and international activities arising from the illegal movements of people or goods, including guns or explosives, across our borders. That's why I've pulled in ATF." He nodded at Paul. "We've liaised with you before at the Bureau."

"What do you mean about the illegal movements of people and guns?" Zehra asked.

"Another critical asset is Homeland Security Investigations Intelligence, or HIS-Intel. They use cutting-edge technology to assess threat levels and unusual activities that may lead to threats. The HIS-Intel reports to the director of DHS and, in turn, assigns us leads."

Paul shook his head and took a deep drink of his cooling coffee. "So what?"

"Our technical people are tracing the movements of Menendez over the past few months as we talk. Don't have a complete picture yet." Mansfield held his head stiffly while he talked. "We know for certain he's more than a local thug who killed some guy."

"What do you mean?"

"Not sure yet." He paused. "We would be willing to liaise with you to share intel." His eyes bounced around the small group. To further sweeten the deal, he said, "Agent Long and I are here because the investigation is leading to Texas, specifically El Paso. That's our territory. Menendez has been very active there, and we think he is the opening to taking down whatever networks he's plugged into."

"Why is ATF interested?"

Long spoke. "We investigate anything involving illegal shipments of guns or explosives. There are some, uh, connections here that disturb us." He sounded like a college professor giving a lecture. He glanced at Mansfield. "Since 9/11, we work with all agencies like ICE and the FBI to help us."

"So, you think Roberto Menendez is trafficking in guns and explosives?" Paul said.

"We don't 'think,' we know it." Long waved his hand over the open space between them. "Just before he was arrested, Menendez's actions and communications indicated an upcoming, huge transfer of something into Minnesota. We don't know where or when, but we have to stop it. That's why we thought your intel could aid us in putting together a case against him to crack open the network of traffickers before this big move."

Paul interrupted, "And you want the resources of the Bureau at your disposal?"

"Your jurisdiction, too. With the Patriot Act, all of us have to be nice to each other and work together." Mansfield laughed in a short bark.

"Until you agree to share your information, I won't cooperate. I've been through this before." Paul spoke with clipped words. "On the other hand, I want to be prepared to go active if we need to." Paul leaned forward. "You're going to work with us? Or do I have to conduct my own, separate investigation?"

"No, of course not."

Paul frowned. "Don't know if I trust you. Mansfield, if you turn on me and make it look like I sat on my ass, I'll fry you." When Paul leaned back in his seat, silence surrounded them all.

"What can we do?" Liz asked. "Any help we can get to nail Menendez on the murder charges will be great. Right now, we've got some, uh, problems with the case."

"Our intelligence leads us to suspect the Church of the Rapture is tied into this."

"So do we. What else have you got?" Zehra asked.

"I'm not sure we can share . . ."

Paul raised his voice. "I'm sick of this shit. Either we all cooperate, or as far as I'm concerned, I'm out."

Mansfield patted the air between them with his palms. "Okay, okay. We're interested in Menendez. A variety of irregularities in our intelligence data led us here."

"Can you say it in English?" Liz said.

"Let me say this carefully." Mansfield leaned forward and lowered his voice. He looked directly into Liz's eyes. "Menendez became the subject of our investigation. You are all prohibited from repeating anything to anyone about our conversation. If you do, you may be putting yourself in violation of national security and several federal statutes. I probably don't need to tell you all the laws you could be prosecuted for." He looked at Zehra for a long time. Back to Liz.

Zehra couldn't believe what was happening. She looked away from Mansfield. The parking ramp remained silent and dimly lit. Zehra noticed Liz's finger tapping furiously on the side of her coffee cup.

"You're serious?" Liz asked the agent.

Mansfield nodded but didn't add anything.

Zehra looked at Liz again. In spite of her toughness, she looked upset. For a moment, Zehra felt a tightness grab her chest, and her breathing came hard. Claustrophobia closed around her from the four corners of the vehicle. Through squeezed lips, Zehra blew out a woosh of air to ward off a panic attack. It worked. "All right. What do you want from us?"

"This investigation grew out of a task force, appointed by the director himself, and led here. Our intelligence office mines data from all over the world. We use a program called the Pattern Analysis and Information Collection System, or PAICS. You don't need to know all the details of that. Roberto Menendez has been on our radar for awhile. But recently, we harvested calls from his cell phone and a computer at the church."

"Yeah?" Liz asked.

"There was traffic about weapons and explosives."

"He's a killer. Maybe he needed to get the weapon he killed Sundberg with."

"I'm not interested in the murder."

Zehra stared from one agent to the other. She glanced at Liz, who looked worse.

"What the hell are you getting at?" Liz yelled.

"That's not all, Ms. Alvarez. Cash was mentioned. Very large numbers. More than this loser could possibly have. And the amount of weapons and explosives was enough to start a war."

Zehra couldn't speak. On top of the shaky murder case they were trying to win, now these new problems faced them.

Long twisted around and leaned over the seat and interrupted for the first time. He had a soft voice and lisped. "What really pulled us in, and why we want your cooperation, was the confluence of the most recent words mined from the computer and his phone."

Zehra raised his eyes to him and held her breath.

With a lisp, Long said, "Paraguay and the Horseman."

CHAPTER 10

Monday, October 24

Y OU'RE NOT GOING TO GET YOUR DELAY." Jack Mezerretti pushed his bulging stomach into Liz' arm.

"Back off, Jack. Save the theatrics for the jury."

"They're plenty of judges available today. The chief will find someone and won't give you the continuance." The scent of Mezerretti's pungent cologne lingered.

Liz and Zehra had come down from their office to the sixteenth floor of the Government Center on Monday for the trial calendar call. They both crowded into the area of the courtroom in front of a low wooden barrier facing the raised bench of the judge. Following them was their law clerk, Barry Wozniak, who'd done the bulk of the research in preparation for their request to delay the trial, which they needed badly.

Dozens of other lawyers, all dressed in dark suits, mingled in the same area. Some laughed and greeted each other like long-lost friends. The majority were public defenders since most criminals lacked the money to hire private counsel.

Liz pushed a metal cart filled with the contents of the file, trial notebooks, and the heavy Minnesota Criminal Law Handbook. Zehra slung her tote bag over her shoulder with her laptop. Several members of the press huddled around the edge the courtroom. They tried to intercept Liz and Zehra for questions. Liz brushed them off.

Mezerretti put his arm around the blonde reporter from TV Channel Six. "Carolyn, when're we getting together for cocktails?" he said. "Stick around, folks. You're gonna see plenty of fireworks from me." He laughed and waved to them as he stepped back into the middle of the courtroom. He opened his briefcase to reveal a stack of papers and a bottle of Polo cologne.

Barry hovered next to Liz and Zehra. Inexperienced in the courtroom, he was a third-year law student at the University of Minnesota. His blue shirt was a little too big around the collar and made him look thin and hungry, even with his tie pulled up tightly. Heavy, horn-rimmed glasses over his nose gave him a Buddy Holly look.

Mezeretti strolled by and towered over Zehra. He was dressed in a three-piece blue suit. A white shirt and bright tie sprouted from his chest. He looked down at Zehra and smiled. Since he was a private defense lawyer and worked mostly on drug cases in federal court, Zehra had never met him. He stuck out his hand toward her. "John Alfonso Mezerretti . . . the third." He chuckled at himself and shook her hand. He held on for a long time and pulled her a little closer to himself. While still staring at her, he said to Liz, "Your girl's very attractive. Good choice for a law clerk."

"She's second chair. Back off," Liz said.

Mezeretti shrugged, then ambled off to the side of the room to greet other lawyers he knew. He laughed with an over-emphasized arch of his body.

"He's a charmer," Zehra said while she helped Liz unload some of the contents of the cart.

"Forget it. Focus on what we're doing here."

"Easy for you to say . . . he wasn't looking at *your* chest the whole time."

Liz sighed. "That's 'cause you got more than I do. Don't worry, we'll beat him." She changed the subject. "I checked, and Chief Judge Robards has a vacation coming up. Today, when he starts calling all the cases set for trial, he'll have six judges available to hear trials."

Barry looked around the room. "There are a lot more cases scheduled than judges."

"Most will settle, but it's Robards's job to deal out the cases like he's playing cards," Liz said.

"So, he has to send more than one case to each judge?"

"Right. He'll decide what the chances are for settling instead of going to trial. That way, he can send several cases to one judge, knowing that at most, only one may go to trial and the others will settle."

Barry snugged his tie against the loose collar. "We don't have a lot of law on our side."

"Barry, we're not relying on the law today. I'm relying on human nature."

He looked at Liz and frowned.

"Watch," Liz ordered. "We're going to talk with the person who really runs the courtroom." She walked over to the clerk sitting next to the judge's bench who stacked papers into piles. Zehra leaned into the conversation.

The clerk, Rita, lifted eyes which traveled up through her Coke bottle glasses and peered over them, and she smiled. Liz continued, "Zehra, Rita and I have known each other for years. Back then, we both had our real hair color." They laughed together. "Would you put us at the bottom of the calendar? We're not quite ready."

"Sure, Liz. As you can see, we're swamped. 'Course, what's new about that?" Through the glasses her brown eyes looked immense, and each of her lashes stood out in detail.

Back at the counsel table, Liz grabbed the cart and turned it toward the swinging door in the low barrier that separated the audience from the jury and lawyers. "Come on," she told them.

Through the immense wooden door to the hall outside, they moved against the tide of people streaming in. She led them to a quiet corner and stopped. On the side opposite from the courtroom, a floor-to-ceiling glass wall separated them from the atrium inside the Government Center that rose in an open space twenty-four stories between the twin towers.

"What's going on?" Barry said.

"You're about to get your first lesson on how to be a lawyer."

"Standing in the hall?" Balancing his weight on one leg, arms and palms out to Liz, Barry asked, "I don't get it. And what did you mean about a vacation?"

Zehra could see the frustration on Liz's face. Normally, she was generous with the law students, but today the pressure of the trial had wound her up tightly. She snapped at Barry, "You'll see."

Four public defenders came out from the courtroom, all shouting names as if they'd never met their clients before. "Deavion Wilson?" The PD walked further down the hall. "Deavion Wilson?"

A slumbering black man who'd been lying on the low bench along the wall sat up slowly and raised his hand as if his take-out order of chow mein was being called.

A tall, scraggly man approached them, followed by a middle-aged, attractive woman. He introduced himself. "Kevin Stout. Kathy Johnson, my administrative assistant. We're from the NorthStar Group." He raised his hand to shake with Liz, who glared at him.

"What're you here for, Stout?"

"Keeping an eye on our public officials. As you can imagine, we're concerned about your murder case against Roberto Menendez. What can you tell me about it?"

Liz took a deep breath and sighed. "You've fucked us over in the press too many times on other cases. I'm not talking to you."

"As a lawyer myself, I'll be watching carefully."

"It would be a good idea, Stout, if you actually came into a courtroom as a lawyer rather than as a pain in the ass."

Stout snorted and walked away. "I'll see you at the press conference we've set up."

While they waited, Liz turned to Zehra. "Hey, almost forgot to ask you how you've been lately. Panic attacks?"

"I'm better. I've gotten to the point now where I can stop the attacks when I feel them coming on. Couldn't do that before. Besides, I think all the work on this case has distracted me from my problems."

"Good."

Twenty minutes later, Barry looked at his watch and said, "When are we going back?"

Liz nodded and led them inside the courtroom. The crowd had thinned as most people had left to their judicial assignments. A young lawyer wearing khakis and a worn blue jacket argued with Robards. His bright red glasses contrasted nicely with his black skin.

"I'm just asking the court to consider reducing the bail," said the public defender, Elliot Jackson.

Robards sighed like he'd heard this story a million times before. "This is a murder case. Accused of killing his wife, isn't he?"

"Yes."

The defendant stood behind a low wooden wall with his shaved head thrown back and his arms crossed over his crotch. He had "Lunatic" tattooed along the side of his neck. He wore an orange jumpsuit from the jail wardrobe.

The judge studied the file. "Says here that when he was arrested in his truck, it had a bumper sticker that read: 'Take Your Wife Out Tonight—One Bullet Should Do It.'"

"I know, Your Honor, but that doesn't show that he'd be a flight risk. He's lived in the community all his life."

"I'm innocent," Lunatic interrupted.

The judge leaned his face into his upraised open palm and sighed again. Without looking up, he said, "I don't think so. Motion to reduce bail is denied."

Within a few minutes, Rita called the case of Roberto Menendez.

Mezzeretti approached them. Out of the corner of his mouth he said, "Where the hell've you been?"

Liz ignored him.

Together, they moved to stand in front of the huge walnut bench. Over the marble top sat Chief Judge A.D. Robards. An older man, his balding head was still tilted forward. He spoke without lifting it. "How about it, counsel?"

"It won't settle, Judge. This is the murder case of the young man . . ." Liz began.

"Umm." Robards nodded and looked up. "Let's see . . . I'm out of judges. I guess I'll have to take it." He jerked his head and peered at them. Small eyes bounced from one lawyer to the other. "In my chambers, folks," he ordered.

Liz walked back to where Zehra and Barry waited. She smiled. "Good. We got Robards."

They hurried after Liz and Mezerretti to the judge's chambers. A greenhouse of foliage—hundreds of plants—hung in the cavernous, quiet room. The judge flopped into a chair behind his desk.

The judge looked at Zehra. "Haven't seen you for quite a while. Not since you became a hero. Or is it a heroine?"

Zehra felt her face warm. "Nice to see you again, Judge."

Robards chuckled. "By the way, I always wondered, where do you come from?" He looked up and down at Zehra.

Zehra stepped back, glanced at Liz, and said, "Excuse me?"

"Where are you from? My family's from Sweden originally."

"Uh . . . Iran."

"You're Arab, huh?"

"No, Iranian. We consider people from Saudi Arabia to be Arabs."

"Of course, of course. And I bet you're Muslim, huh?"

"Yes."

"Had a friend in law school back east. Think he was one, too." Robards cleared his throat and turned to the lawyers. The judge tried to tell a joke. He was a pleasant man, but it was obvious he was uncomfortable around people. Soon, he focused on the Menendez case.

"The young man killed in Hamel. Grand jury came back with murder one," Liz said. While the judge continued to study the court file, Liz went on, "We've moved for a continuance. Our brief should be in the court file." Liz pointed at the folder in front of him.

Reaching into his vest pocket, Mezerretti pulled out a box of Altoids. He opened it, offered it around, and popped a white tab in his mouth. He slurped, "We're opposing it, of course." He clicked the box shut.

"You say there's no way to settle this?" He looked from Liz to Mezerretti. They shook their heads. No one spoke. They waited for the judge.

Robards rose from behind the desk, strolled to the corner of the room, and retrieved a watering can. Like a hummingbird, he hovered over plant after plant, splashing water in each pot, darting from one to another.

Zehra probed Liz's eyes. She winked.

"Even if I grant your motion to continue—and I see my colleague's denied your first motion—I would still keep the trial, I guess."

Liz responded, "Right, but we'd only need a few days for the continuance."

Robards called over to Mezerretti, "Your client's willing to roll the dice with a jury? They'll decide the sentence, as you know, and they might be pretty tough on the guy they found guilty of killing an innocent young man." He pushed the defense lawyer to settle.

"Tried to talk sense to him, Judge. Insists he's innocent."

Robards turned to the prosecutors. "So you're willing to risk losing everything on this one?"

Zehra thought of Grant's order to dismiss the case and the potential personal consequences. Before she could think for long, Liz said, "We have a duty to try and convict this guy. It's a cold-blooded killing."

For the next ten minutes, the judge pushed each side to compromise in some way that would avoid a trial. His judicial clerk came into the chambers again and reminded him to check the schedule on his computer.

Mezerretti waited a few minutes. He began, "To go back to my objection to the continuance . . ."

The judge waved his small hands in the air. "Sorry, folks. I just noticed my schedule, and I'm out of here next week. I'm on vacation. You know I'd love to try a murder case. But under the circumstances . . . well, I can't." His eyes pleaded with each lawyer.

Then a frown creased his forehead and he stuck out his arm, pointing at each of them with a pale finger. "But I'm only giving you a week continuance, Liz. No more," he shouted in warning. "You'll be assigned to Judge Von Wald. Absolutely no more delays!"

Outside the chambers after Mezerretti left in a huff, Liz started laughing. Zehra joined her.

"What?" Barry said.

Liz looked up into the air. "Just what I hoped for." She looked back at Barry. "A good lesson today. I checked earlier and knew he couldn't possibly start the trial. That's why he squeezed us so hard to settle. "

"But . . ." Barry's eyes opened wide. "You purposely delayed getting the case called so we'd be sure to get Robards as the last judge, didn't you?" Barry smiled and nodded in understanding. "Sweet."

"Thought it'd probably work."

Zehra laughed in an uninhibited way, her entire body leaning backwards in a deep guffaw. It felt good after the months of despair she'd felt.

"So, how's Judge Von Wald?" Barry asked.

Liz stopped laughing and cleared her throat. "Good news and bad news."

Barry waited.

"The best God damn judge on the bench. And the toughest. We're in trouble."

CHAPTER 11

K ATHY WATCHED ELIZABETH ALVAREZ perspire, and she almost felt sorry for the prosecutor. The woman was a jerk. She seemed arrogant and self-righteous. Besides that, she looked sick. Kind of gray across her face. Why had Grant put this woman in charge of such an important case?

Next to her sat her assistant, an attractive young woman. She looked Middle Eastern, with big eyes, a little too much make up, and enviable long lashes. By the way she moved, Kathy guessed the woman might be an athlete. She looked intelligent. The two women laughed with each other.

The elected county attorney, Ulysses Grant, had agreed to a meeting with the NorthStar Group. At the last minute, instead of Grant showing up, he had sent Alvarez and Hassan. That was exactly why NorthStar had staged this "show." Irresponsible public officials needed to be exposed, and Kathy wanted to humiliate them today.

Jamie and Kevin roamed around the large round conference room in the county attorney's office, called the "Grand Jury" room. Rows of seats circled the outside edges and faced two tables in the middle. Like an operating room, everything focused in the center of the room.

Alvarez and Hassan sat alone at one of the tables. Kevin was disappointed because he wanted the "big guy" Ulysses Grant there, but Kevin had some ideas he hoped would work.

While they rode together to the meeting, Kathy had thought about the sparkle he brought to her life. They'd talked strategy about the upcoming meeting. Kathy was startled at the degree of planning he'd prepared. It wasn't like him, and it included some rough aspects for the county attorney. Kevin rambled on again about other help they could get. When she questioned him, he became vague and told her to forget it. They parked in the ramp on the east side of the Government Center and took the skyway across Fourth Avenue.

In the Grand Jury room, dozens of people from NorthStar sat quietly. The meeting began. Jamie began by tossing out easy questions. The two prosecutors stopped laughing and composed themselves. Alvarez seemed annoyed by the questions and didn't volunteer much by way of answers. That'd change when Kevin ramped up the attacks.

Kathy couldn't figure out if Alvarez was in control of the prosecution or in over her head. She certainly looked experienced. Her dark suit looked baggy, and her white blouse and dull scarf made her look a little rumpled. She gave the impression of being tired or bored, but Kathy had caught several instances when the woman's brown eyes flashed at them. There was something deeper inside that made Kathy uneasy. Maybe they had underestimated her.

Kevin cleared his throat. "So, Ms. Alvarez, has Menendez made any kind of statement?" He glared at her with fake intensity.

"No."

"Do you think he'll testify?"

"Don't know. Any good defense lawyer will tell his client to shut up."

"We understand that he's got a record from Texas. What is it?" Kevin swaggered back and forth at the edge of the room.

"I can't tell you that at this time. It will be argued at trial."

"Is he connected around the country to other violent groups?"

Alvarez paused, ignored Kevin, and then wiped her forehead. "We'll be ready for trial."

Kevin said, "We're just citizens concerned about trafficking in weapons for militia groups. I'm sure an investigation into this trafficking ring is part of your case. Especially *why* they need weapons. What are they planning to do?"

"Our first priority is to get a conviction of Mr. Menendez. Beyond that, of course we're concerned as anyone about the larger aspects of the crime. But some of those are federal issues under the jurisdiction of Homeland Security and the FBI. We're county government with limited resources."

"But we understand you can't determine the reason for the homicide. Is that true?"

"That will be developed at trial."

"You mean to tell me with all the expensive resources you have, you can't even figure out the motive for the killing?" Kevin spun around quickly and pointed his finger.

Kathy loved Kevin's self-righteous tone. She knew he was full of shit, but that wildness was one of his most attractive qualities.

"As I just said, that will come out in trial. We have our theories."

Kevin leaned back and flapped his arms. "Theories? This sounds like a biology class, not a criminal prosecution." When he turned to the people grouped around the edges, they applauded as if on cue. Kevin grinned at the response. He turned back to face Alvarez.

She said, "We're troubled by the fact that no one from the community has come forward to aid in our investigation . . . to tell what they know as witnesses. Why not? Maybe NorthStar could help us." Alvarez looked up into the rows of people who quieted and now sat mutely. She raised her hand and swept it across the back of the room. A look of pain creased her face, then disappeared.

Kathy's stomach grumbled. This wasn't going the way Kevin had said it would be. The prosecutor hadn't collapsed at all. She was fighting back for favorable public opinion.

Suddenly, the door on the far side of the room burst open and Ulysses Grant entered, followed by two young assistants. He walked confidently to the middle and stood in front of Alvarez, facing the group. "What's all the noise?" He spread his legs and crossed thick arms over his chest. He wore beautiful blue glasses.

Kevin stopped and looked Grant up and down. "We're from the NorthStar Group and are dedicated to educating and monitoring—"

"I know what you people do. What do you want to know?"

"We want to know why you haven't followed up on the connection between the victim and the Church of the Rapture." Kevin glanced at Jamie and nodded once. She left the room.

"This is a murder case. We've got a victim and a defendant. With our witnesses and forensic evidence, we're confident of a conviction." Grant snapped off his words.

"Why weren't you here when we started this interview?" Kevin demanded.

Grant's face darkened. "I don't work for you, Mr. Stout."

"Oh, yes, you do. I represent the public right here before you. We pay your salary and you work for the voters of this county. Why aren't you being honest with us about the murder case of Roberto Menendez?"

"I trust Ms. Alvarez with the case. She and Ms. Hassan have been working on it around the clock. I decided they should talk to you."

Kevin furrowed his brows and said slowly, "That's very unusual . . . rumor has it this case is so weak, you may have to dismiss it. Is that true?"

"Not at all. We've got a team of our best people working on it. I'm behind them one hundred percent."

"Which proves my point." Kevin pointed his arm at Grant to emphasize his words. "You're not personally responsible anymore. The case is in the hands of your assistants."

At that moment, the front door of the room opened and two large men carried TV cameras into the room. They posted themselves on either side of Grant and focused on the people in the middle. Then several participants from NorthStar pulled cell phones out, held them at arm's length, and started to record.

"What the hell is this?" Grant shouted. He turned around to Alvarez. "What's going on here?"

She shrugged her shoulders.

"The public has a right to know," Kevin yelled above the noise in the room. "We're not powerful, but we can expose ineptitude when it exists in government. So let's get serious about stopping these crazy, dangerous militia groups who live amongst us and are the real terrorist threat to this country."

Grant lowered his dark head. He reminded Kathy of a charging rhino. "This is a murder case, nothing more. We've prosecuted thousands of murder cases successfully." He scowled. "And I resent this cheap trick."

"We understand the trial was supposed to start today, but you asked for a delay. Why can't you get going and convict the killer and find out what's really going on? Is there a problem you won't tell us about?" Kevin chipped away with his questions, poking the air with his finger at each accusation.

Grant frowned and looked around him. He seemed to be thinking about what Kevin had asked. He leaned down toward Alvarez. They talked between themselves quietly. Then Grant turned back to the group. "Alvarez and Hassan are in charge of the case. They're more familiar with it, so they'll take over here."

Kathy laughed to herself. Typical politician to duck out. She saw the anger cross Alvarez's face as her boss hurried out of the room. Kevin was right: these politicians were all alike—gutless and lazy. No wonder he didn't respect them.

Alvarez took her time. She stood up and actually smiled at them. "It's really simple. The delay we asked for is part of our strategy. We're following some leads that developed recently. You wouldn't want us to miss anything and risk Menendez walking free, would you?" She swayed to the side as a gray color washed over her face. A layer of sweat moistened her face.

"What are those leads?" The camera swung onto Kevin, and he frowned in a serious expression as he looked directly into the lens.

"You know as a law professor that I can't tell that, Mr. Stout." Alvarez smiled in a reassuring way.

The camera on the left moved closer to Alvarez. She glanced at it without changing her expression and smiled at Kevin. But she remained turned at an odd angle, playing to the camera while talking to Kevin. She was more savvy than Kathy had originally expected, and much tougher.

"Well . . ." Kevin demanded and stepped back, a little deflated. Kathy wanted to help him. He looked over at Alvarez. "With a case this big, how come it's just you two? You and a . . . law student? That's it?"

"Of course not." Alvarez crossed her arms over her chest. "There are dozens of police and investigators involved." Alvarez paused and looked down at the young woman next to her. She said, "And Ms. Hassan is the best lawyer I've ever worked with in a trial." She waved her hands toward the camera dismissively. "You must not remember who this is." Alvarez paused. "This is Zehra Hassan, who solved the Somali boys' disappearances."

A murmur bubbled around the back of the room. Some people leaned forward and nodded.

Kathy was impressed. She remembered the media coverage of the Somali boys several months ago and how this woman had killed the mastermind terrorist. Kathy worried. Had they picked on the wrong prosecutors to attack?

The interview started to lose steam. Kevin tried vainly to pump it up, but he must have sensed the time had passed. The "show" that NorthStar had planned didn't have the punch they all had hoped for. Still, there must be great footage of the county attorney himself, ducking the whole thing and dumping it on Alvarez. Kathy felt like they'd scored a few points.

She saw Alvarez start to say something until the gray color crossed her face again, pinching it in a painful expression. In a moment, it passed and the prosecutor took a deep breath.

Kevin switched tactics and nodded toward the woman he'd planted in the audience. "We've got someone who would like to make a statement."

"I am Lola Savage. I live near Hamel, and I'm worried about these crazy survivalist groups that seem to be proliferating. Why aren't you looking into the connection between the murder and these groups? I'm scared because they live all around us, next door to many of us. They seem normal but you just don't know . . ." Her words carved through the air like a sharp knife.

No one spoke for a long time.

Alvarez nodded and cleared her throat. "I'm sorry. We're doing all we can to convict Menendez. Believe me, we want this stopped as much as you and everyone else does."

Kevin finished up. "Ms. Alvarez, are you confident you can win this case?" He spoke in sonorous tones.

Alvarez blinked, chuckled, stood up straighter, and answered immediately. "Mr. Stout, I've tried hundreds of jury trials. I can guarantee you that we will fight like hell for a conviction. At the same time, there's no way to predict what a jury will do. But then . . ." she paused and glanced at the cameras before she spoke again. "I'm sure you've had lots of jury trial experience, haven't you?" Her words stung him in the uncomfortable silence.

Kathy knew Kevin had never entered a courtroom in his life. This wasn't going as well as they all wanted. Kathy saw Kevin struggle to find something to say. Elizabeth Alvarez remained standing, staring at Kevin.

"We'll be watching." Kevin stopped talking, lowered his head for effect, then raised it slowly and looked into the running cameras. "We will never let you rest until we're satisfied you can protect the people who are so needlessly victimized and exploited." He pointed his finger at Alvarez for the final, dramatic touch.

The room emptied quickly. Kevin slouched toward the door and walked out. Kathy saw that Hassan and Alvarez remained in the center. Alvarez had sat down with her face on the table. Something was wrong.

Kathy walked down from the raised edge of the room to see if she could help.

Alvarez rolled off the chair and flopped onto her back across the floor. Kathy slid down to her side. Alvarez's face looked pale and sweaty, and her breathing came in short gasps. Cardiac arrest. "I'm a nurse," Kathy told Hassan. "Call 911 while I start CPR." She adjusted Alvarez' body and worked on chest compressions at a rate of 100 per minute compressed at least five centimeters deep. Kathy could smell the smoker's breath and shook her head in frustration at the risks people took.

Within seven minutes, emergency medical people from the Government Center responded to the call. They came in with oxygen, a stretcher, a blood pressure monitor, and a defibrillator. With practiced efficiency, they took over from Kathy and strapped Alvarez onto the stretcher. On a radio attached to her shoulder, the technician called in to reserve an emergency room for Alvarez at the Hennepin County Medical Center four blocks away.

Kathy waited until the emergency team left with Alvarez. She started to gather her purse and a bag with NorthStar Group literature stuffed in it, when she noticed Hassan sitting by herself, her head bent. "I'm Kathy Johnson." She offered her hand. "We met outside the courtroom."

At first Hassan didn't respond. Her head came up slowly. She looked at Kathy but refused to shake.

"I'm sorry about your colleague."

Hassan's face turned red. Large brown eyes seemed to pop out of her face, contorted in a rage. "Get out of here," Hassan shouted. "Look what you jerks did." She swung her arms wildly.

Kathy felt the intensity of her anger like the blast of hot air when stepping out of an airplane door on a vacation from Minnesota in January to a tropical climate. "Sorry . . . We didn't know she had problems."

"Thanks to you, Liz has one hell of a problem now."

"If this makes you feel better . . . as a nurse I think we got to her in time. She'll probably survive." Kathy thought of what Kevin would do in this situation. She softened her voice. "What about the Menendez trial? Will you delay it again?"

Through clipped words, Hassan said, "No. I was second chairing it. Now I'll try the case myself. We're going ahead."

CHAPTER 12

A FTER RETURNING TO THE TWIN CITIES, Jeremy Brown checked in immediately with Paco, his best fix-it man. He had been converted to a true believer, thanks to Brown. It also helped that he was deadly with a knife and enjoyed violence. The Bible demonstrated how God often used strong men to carry out His will.

Strong men like Jeremy's distant relative, the abolitionist John Brown. Jeremy had read everything he could find about the great man. For years before the Civil War, John Brown was possessed with the holy mission of destroying slavery. He felt that not only were southern slave owners going to eternal damnation, but also the northern people who allowed the institution to continue. Brown was convinced that God would punish the entire country for this sin. A few years later the Civil War started, proving Brown right in his prediction.

His opposition to slavery grew from his religious fervor and made him into a strong, uncompromising, unwavering extremist in the fight to end it. In his holy war against slavery, Brown justified the use of any amount of force, violence, or even terror to accomplish the end result. He formed a militia that included some of his sons in the crusade against the institution of slavery.

Brown's plan at Harper's Ferry had been to use his militia to raid the federal arsenal, steal weapons, and move into the south, where they would be met by a spontaneous uprising of slaves, motivated by God and freedom, to start a reign of terror against the white slave owners, thereby overthrowing the system.

Today, Jeremy Brown felt motivated by the faithful and courageous example of his relative. He carried a reproduction of an old photo of the abolitionist inside the cover of his Bible. Looking into the intense eyes of John Brown, Jeremy felt a sharing of the old man's spirit and willingly accepted the blood and sweat of the struggle to do God's will today.

"Man, you got a problem," Paco insisted, breaking into Jeremy's thoughts.

Over the phone, Brown could hear the clinking and loud chatter in the background. "What? Something at the power plant?"

"No, the problem's here."

"What? I thought you were on top of things." Brown raised his voice. Ever since he'd busted Paco as a juvenile, Brown had followed the kid into his early twenties. After leaving the police department, he'd quit busting Paco and started getting him off of charges. Then it was easy to hire Paco cheaply and convert him to a Christian. He wasn't too bright but was tough and loyal.

"It's our guy in jail. Menendez."

"What about him? You got the message to him?"

"Of course. His sister is so scared, she was shittin' bricks the last time I even looked at her. 'Member her? Worked at the church a few times?"

Brown sighed. Menendez knew everything. He was smart, but he could easily give in to temptation and sin. "Okay. We'll have to get another message to Menendez to keep him quiet. Where's his sister?"

"North side."

"Hope you weren't too rough." Brown shook his head. What should he expect when dealing with guys like Paco? "Meet me in a half hour."

Brown drove through the Warehouse District at the edge of downtown Minneapolis along Washington Avenue until he came to Broadway. He turned right and pulled into the lot of Broadway Pizza. Set on the spot where the railroad tracks used to run, the restaurant resembled a railroad car and still overlooked the Mississippi River.

Brown spotted Paco's late model Cadillac next to the door. Brown pulled his Ford pickup behind Paco's immaculate car and saw him bent over in the driver's seat. For a minute, Brown thought something was wrong until he saw Paco straighten up, his jaws working wildly on a slice of pizza. Brown tapped his horn.

The slim man slid out of his vehicle and nudged the door shut with his foot as he turned toward Brown's truck. A huge slice of pizza folded over his hand as he lifted it high in the air above his open mouth. He looked like a baby bird waiting for some slop from the mother. Paco caught the corner of the slice with his mouth and gnawed it off, swallowing it with a few muscular chews.

When he got to the truck, Brown said, "Finish that crap and wipe your hands before you touch anything."

When Paco crawled in the passenger side, Brown noticed he hadn't shaved for a few days and his black hair hung shoulder-length in a glossy pelt. The girls loved it.

"*Que pasa?*" Paco said.

"Shut up. We need to find the sister right away." Brown glared at Paco and pulled from the curb. "You check out the weapons?"

"Hey, chill, man."

Brown swerved to the side of the street, slamming on the brakes so hard that the pizza slobbered against Paco's chest, and Brown yelled at him. "You stupid idiot. This is the Lord's work. I've told you a hundred times. We're scheduled for next Sunday. Once we lead the way with our attack, all the others will attack their targets across the country. If we fail, the others will probably get scared and not act. We've gotta keep the lid on everything, including Menendez, or we'll face the wrath of God. You want that?"

"Naw, man."

"When our team arrives, we must be ready with the weapons. What good is it to have an army if they're not armed? The Lord can work miracles, but we have to do our part also. The weapons must be ready."

"Okay, okay. I ordered all of 'em. They're the same types used by the A-rabs in the Middle East. Just like you wanted."

Glaring at Paco to emphasize his point, Brown said, "Good. It won't hurt to make the take down of the nuclear plant look like Muslim terrorist rag-heads caused it in order to help start the holy war."

"Right."

Brown let out a lungful of air in frustration. He pulled off the curb again. "Show me where she's been living." He followed Paco's directions as they drove north on Washington Avenue.

Brown glanced at his partner and thought about him. The best use of his time occurred at the Mall of America. Paco proselytized for the church there. Over 100,000 people came through the mall every day, especially young people who were looking for answers to life's questions. All of them had cash—which was the main reason for Paco's presence there.

Hundreds of young girls hung out at the mall, lured by the noise, activity, boys, and the shops that sold everything imaginable. Brown knew the place was proof of the rapid descent of the United States into total, twenty-four-hour-a-day mindless entertainment through consumerism. Godless and sinful. That made them vulnerable to the message of the Lord to repent and serve the church.

Brown had trained Paco well. He cruised the mall in his languid stride, dressed expensively but in casual clothing with lots of bling. In many ways, it was simply a numbers game. Paco approached pods of young people and talked them up. Most of them weren't interested and ignored him. But then, every once in a while, he came across a lonely girl or boy. The girls were the easiest.

Brown wasn't sure how sincere Paco was about his religion and suspected that he enjoyed the flash more than the serious business of converting people. It didn't matter to Brown so long as Paco brought in new people and money to the cause.

At the mall, Paco found that kids came from all over. Inner city, suburbs, small towns, farms. The key to winning them over was the same: finding lonely kids who lacked self-confidence. Maybe they didn't have any friends. Most often, the girls were mad at their parents, running away, looking for someone who pretended to care about them.

They were easy to manipulate. Paco assured them that God intended them to be happy, successful, rich, and to give their lives in service to the church . . . and Jeremy Brown. They didn't always accept everything Paco told them, but they did give money. Loaded with cash, the kids easily gave their money to the church and Jeremy Brown.

Thanks to Brown, Paco had finally made something of himself in life. Before, he was involved in petty shit, bar jackings where he'd do a lick on a drunk to get a few bucks, beating up pimps for their stash, or purse grabs on busy Hennepin Avenue after the bars closed at two in the morning and the rich suburban chicks were drunk and loose. Tough life, since the risks of getting busted were high for little gain.

Now he made lots of money, did the Lord's important work, got laid occasionally—although he never told Brown about that sin—and was a success.

Occasionally, the kids didn't come through as he expected, and Paco had to get tough. "Holy discipline," Brown had told him. Sometimes necessary. God demanded absolute obedience.

In Brown's truck, Paco listened to a long list of orders. "We're on a holy mission, Paco." Brown smiled, like he did a lot, and that made Paco feel proud to be part of such a holy endeavor. "The whole game starts next Sunday, so get the weapons ready."

"Man, I'm getting tired. You're pushing me too hard."

The smile disappeared from Brown's face. His eyes hardened, and swollen red veins bulged along his neck. "You questioning what the Lord has ordained? The truth has been revealed only to us believers. Don't you remember the conflagration must begin before the Rapture will occur? Once Armageddon has started, that will usher in the new millennium and the reign of the Lord. The unbelievers will be left behind, but not us."

Paco backed down immediately.

"Prophecy is being fulfilled faster than ever."

"Yeah." Paco's tone indicated that he'd forgotten about prophecy.

Brown reminded him. "Scripture. It's all in there. Before the end times, there will be the rise of Russia as foretold by Ezekiel in chapter 38, verse two. Remember Daniel twenty, verses 40 through 43 and the rise of the new Roman Empire."

"I thought Italy was almost bankrupt?"

"You idiot. The new Roman Empire is the European Union. It's as large and powerful as the old Roman Empire."

"Yeah."

Brown blew out a breath of air. "I haven't got time now to teach you again . . ."

"Wait a minute." Paco's face lit up. "Like that verse in Matthew about how all the earthquakes will happen, then the famines and then Armageddon, the big battle will happen and—"

"First, there will be false prophets and the antichrist." He corrected Paco. Brown's eyes punctured into Paco's slow brain. "Watch for the mark of the beast. Six, six, six. These signs are here already."

In North Minneapolis at Emerson Avenue they turned north and sped along the street, ignoring the stop signs and kids that crossed the corners. In five minutes, Brown pulled to a stop in front of a frame duplex painted light blue.

When they got out, they headed for the ground level front door. A chain-link fence surrounded a yard that had little grass in it. A child's bicycle lay near the sidewalk, missing the front wheel.

Before they got to the gate, five black kids approached them.

"Wha's up, bro?" one called.

Brown glared at them and fiddled with the broken latch on the gate.

"You in the wrong hood, bro. This here belongs to the Tre-Tres."

Paco crowded a little closer to Brown. Finally, the latch popped and Brown pushed it open. Just as he was about to step through, the biggest one of the group put his hand on the gate to hold it closed. He wore a long t-shirt that reached to his knees. A baseball cap tilted across his head, turned at a precise angle, with the sales tag still attached. His right hand started to lift the front edge of his t-shirt. A gun butt poked out. "I's talkin' to you from jump street." He leaned toward Brown and smiled to show a large gold tooth that glittered in his dark, dirty face. He smelled of alcohol.

Brown debated whether he should just shoot him right on the spot. He glanced up and down the street to see if anyone was watching. No one. Here was a holy opportunity to rid the world of trash before the Great War began. Make things easier. Then rational thought took over.

Brown raised his eyes slowly and looked the young man directly in the face. When he had the kid's attention, Brown jerked out his Ruger from the shoulder holster hidden under his jacket. In one swift, practiced motion, he raised the gun, jammed the barrel into the punk's nose, drew lots of blood, and spoke to him softly. "Get out of my way."

The kid's "homeys" merged closer until the first kid fell back, and Brown walked through the gate to the door, followed by Paco. At the door, Brown sent Paco around to the back side. "Find her," he ordered Paco.

No one answered the knock. Brown replaced the gun in its holster. He lifted his leg and kicked the door in. He heard a scream from children and a woman. Brown burst through the opening in time to see a dark woman scramble through the kitchen and out the back door.

In five minutes, Paco came back, dragging the woman with a hand under her shoulder. She struggled to get up and walk, but Paco moved quickly and threw her down in a heap. More kids screamed from the room off to the side.

She cried and slithered toward the living room until Brown cut her off with a kick to her butt. "Get up. I haven't got time for this."

She gathered herself to rise to her knees. She wore a loose tank top and jeans. Her ribs showed along her chest where the tank top gapped open. Curly black hair was matted over her forehead, and she cried. "Forgive me. I've sinned."

"That is correct. You have sinned before God and man. You must atone for those sins." Brown kneeled down next to her. "You get back to the jail and talk to your brother. He has lost his faith. Tell him to keep his mouth shut."

She sobbed. While nodding her head, it struck his left hand. Pain shot through his damaged little finger, and it cracked open to bleed slightly. Brown grunted but shoved the pain down inside of him. There was a job to finish.

"Tell your brother I'm fixing it and he will be set free, just as Daniel was from the lion's den. The Lord is with us."

"Okay."

"He doesn't follow orders, here's what's gonna happen." Brown put his foot on her upraised butt and shoved her across the floor. He nodded to Paco.

Picking her up under her arm, Paco dragged her into the living room, where he hefted her up onto a sagging couch. He pushed her into a sitting position and adjusted her shoulder and head just so. "I'll make it quick."

Paco put on a pair of leather gloves and turned his body to the side in front of her. He spread his legs about shoulder width apart. Starting with his left hand, he swung hard into her face. Then he popped with his right. Wet, smacking sounds that ended in dull thuds.

Brown waited near the front door. When Paco was finished, he removed the leather gloves, wiped off the blood and sweat from them, and came to the door. "Should leave some good marks for Menendez to look at."

"The laws of the Lord are difficult sometimes. But we must all remain faithful," Brown sighed.

CHAPTER 13

Wednesday, October 26

ELIZABETH ALVAREZ WOULD LIVE. Although thrilled, Zehra knew that meant she would take over the Menendez murder trial, scheduled to start in five days on Monday. It scared the hell out of her.

Zehra sat in Grant's office with Jeremy Brown and the law clerk, Barry Wozniak.

Grant had paced behind his desk for several minutes without saying anything. He stopped and in a loud voice said, "God dammit, I told you to drop it, and now we're all stuck with the case to the bitter end. I won't risk my career over it." He rubbed his hands together as if her were washing himself clean of the case.

While Grant fumed, Zehra calmed herself with breathing, images of beaches, and the thought that she and Liz had already done a lot of the trial prep. It worked, and the panicky feelings subsided. They still didn't have the strongest case. "After their grandstanding trick the other day and Liz's problem, NorthStar has been quiet."

After a moment of silence, Grant threw up his hands in the air. "All right. Get me a conviction." It was a signal that he was done talking. They all left.

Jeremy pulled her aside. He looked into her eyes. "I've got your back. Don't worry."

It made her feel better. Zehra paused, wondering if she should even ask him about this. "Uh, there's something that's bothering me."

"Huh?"

"My niece Shereen is hanging out at the Mall of America and getting into things. Do you think there's any real trouble she can into out there?"

Brown's eyebrows hooded over his face. "It's not a healthy place."

"I know." She reached into her purse and removed a snapshot of Shereen. "See? Isn't she beautiful? I'm worried she's a target out there."

"I can see why. What can I do?"

"I'm just concerned about her, and I thought with your law enforcement background . . . well, I don't know why I even brought this up."

"Because you're worried. I know people out there from my days as a cop. If you ever need any help, let me know."

Back at her office, Zehra collapsed into her chair, glanced at her watch, and saw it was time for prayer. She hesitated because of all the work left to do, then decided she needed the break. In ten minutes, she'd bent down on the floor of her office, said her prayers, and felt refreshed as she stood full of new strength and peace.

Zehra turned on Minnesota Public Radio. The announcer said, "This is Science Wednesday, and today we have Dr. Jacqueline Fontaine to comment on the medical risks associated with the nuclear reactor in Fukushima, Japan. Luckily, the Japanese have been able to contain the release of radiation, doctor. Tell us what would happen if humans were exposed to high levels of radiation?"

"Not pretty. At first, a patient of radiation sickness would feel fatigue and weakness, leading to hemorrhage and infections. At higher doses, they would experience fever, diarrhea, and vomiting. Probably the worst symptom would be the effects of beta and gamma burns, with gamma being the deeper burns. Initially, the skin would turn red, then blister, and then ulcerate. It's horrible to look at and is extremely painful for the patient. Death could occur anywhere from one day to a couple weeks, depending on the level of exposure."

Too depressing for Zehra. She turned if off and called in Barry. When he slumped on the couch before her desk, she laid out the work they still needed to do before the trial started. She gave him several assignments to complete. "You can handle this?"

He nodded. "I miss Liz . . ."

"You're doing a great job. I'll see if I can get you a permanent job here. That is, if I still have a job here." She laughed to lighten up the tension they both felt. She answered her cell phone when it rang and lied. "The case is going well," she said to Special Agent Mansfield's question.

"Sorry about your partner, but we may be able to help you. We've received authorization to fly you to Texas. We've got some contacts that can help you trace Menendez's activities and background. Can you leave late this afternoon?"

"Uh . . . yeah, I guess so." She glanced at Barry. "I'd like my law clerk to come with me. And my investigator would be essential, too." She felt a surge of energy at the turn in the investigation.

Mansfield paused. He covered his phone and must have asked someone else for permission. When he came back, he said, "Okay. But that's it. Luckily, the plane's just big enough 'cause we have to include Paul Schmitt on this." He ended by giving Zehra the details of the departure. She called Jeremy Brown's cell. He agreed to accompany them.

Zehra turned to Barry. "Will you have time to work on the Spreigl motion?"

"I'll bring my laptop on the plane. I need to make sure I understand what you want." He paused and looked at her. "We haven't covered this in school yet. But the rules of evidence in Minnesota allow us to, like, offer proof to the jury of crimes other than the murder Menendez is charged with?"

"Right. Rule 404b. But only if the other evidence goes to show a 'motive, opportunity, preparation, or plan.' I hope his conviction in Texas may be similar, and that would satisfy the requirements. Also, witnesses to the other crimes have to actually appear here, in court—that's the tough part. The defense will fight like hell to keep it out of the trial."

"If we can't find the witnesses?"

Zehra looked up at the ceiling and frowned. "We're sunk. So, I'm hoping we can find them in Texas in time to get them up here. Hollywood can help on that." Packing her briefcase with the file folders and notes for trial, Zehra rushed out of her office as Barry ran to catch up.

* * *

AT HER CONDO IN DOWNTOWN Minneapolis that overlooked the winding Mississippi River, Zehra opened the door carefully. Larceny always tried to sneak out. She found him at the sliding glass door that led to the small balcony. He sat beside the window, composed, silent, and staring.

"Hoping for warmer weather?" she called to him. "You're in the wrong state." She walked to the door, unlocked it, and slid it open a crack, enough for both of them to go out onto the balcony. In the two far corners, her potted plants struggled to hang on in spite of the increasingly chilly nights. Three arrangements of mums. Large yellow puffs. She looked across the river along the Hennepin Avenue Bridge with its suspension cables quivering in the brisk wind from the north. The struggling flowers represented her defiance toward the coming winter.

She grabbed a small suitcase, assembled enough clothes for a few days and picked up her laptop, briefcase, and purse. She tried to decide on shoes. As always, she waffled between sensible ones or the stylish. She opted for her new running shoes to wear with jeans and a pair of khakis. Then, at the last minute, she squeezed in the stylish red leather ones. At least they had low heels.

It felt good even to care about how she looked again. She'd spent time fixing her hair, which now shone in shiny folds of ebony. For months it hadn't made any difference to her. It was a sign that she was healing and growing out of the PTSD.

Zehra stopped to make sure the cat had water and food. She knelt down beside him, stroking his soft, long white hair. For a moment, Zehra envied Larceny's life: peaceful and calm, with someone who took care of him all the time.

"Okay, gotta run. I'll have my mother look in on you, don't worry." That reminded her to call Martha.

"Going to Texas? I thought you hated that state and couldn't wait to get away?" her mother said.

"This is part of the investigation. It's business."

"Be careful. Oh, by the way, my sister is so thankful that you helped in court the other day."

"She's a nice kid."

"I'm sure, but she's hanging around with a bad crowd."

"She'll probably outgrow it. Gotta run."

Zehra and Barry drove east on Highway 62 to the Air National Guard station in Richfield. The military used it along with many federal agencies. At the security gate, Zehra leaned across the seat and showed her Assistant Hennepin County Attorney ID to the sergeant on duty and told him the code words the ICE agent had given to her.

Passed through, they came to a small, one-story limestone building with a second story patched on top like the hump on a camel. Low clouds shifted across the sky. When they reached the terminal building, Zehra pulled into a spot designated as long-term parking. They got out, lifted their suitcases and briefcases out of the trunk and walked toward the terminal.

Three gray-green military planes hulked on the runway. They were propeller-driven, and the wings stretched across the top of the plane with fat bodies hanging below them. How could they get off the ground?

Bare fingers of tree branches grasped at the corners of the air terminal, like they were trying to get in to avoid the coming weather. As she walked toward the metal door, Zehra crunched over dead leaves. Then she noticed, all alone by the sidewalk, a patch of defiant green grass. It comforted her.

Maybe they'd get their answers in Texas.

As she walked more quickly, the low door squealed sideways across concrete to allow their entrance. Zehra met the two agents and found both Paul and Brown already in the hangar. Zehra could feel the tension. Brown, usually smiling, scowled and looked at the floor. Paul's eyes sought out Zehra's. They were soft and reassuring, but he kept looking away. *What's wrong?*

Paul pulled Zehra aside. "Uh . . .I've been meaning to tell you this, but I can't go."

"Huh?" She felt her back stiffen.

"I've got last minute 'visitors' from Washington. The deputy director. I have to hold hands." He smiled at her. "Besides, you've got plenty of help." He nodded his head toward the three men who stood in the line before them. Paul paused for a moment and looked down at her. "You'll be okay, and you'll do great." Quickly, he kissed her on the cheek before the others could catch it.

They boarded a small government jet that had ten seats and lifted off into the cold sky. Mansfield sat across the narrow aisle from Zehra. He popped the bud from his ear. "Nice change from waiting in lines at the civilian terminal, huh?" He smiled with pride. He stretched out his legs and showed a new pair of expensive wingtip shoes.

"This wouldn't be hard to get used to," Zehra said. She pointed to the bud lying in Mansfield's lap. "What are you always listening to?"

"Ah . . ." He blushed. "I like to listen to the theme from *Rocky*." Mansfield leaned closer. "Have you had any more contact with the NGO?"

"NGO?"

"Non-governmental organization. NorthStar."

"Not since they caused Liz's heart attack."

The jet arched up into the surrounding clouds that made the interior of the cabin as dark as dusk. In a few minutes, they broke through the top to see the orange fireball of the sun dipping into the west.

Mansfield's eyes locked on Zehra again. "You haven't mentioned anything about this to anyone, have you?" He spoke sharply.

A picture of her parents flashed in her mind. Zehra took a deep breath. "No." She found it harder to breathe and wanted to change the subject. "How'd you get into ICE?"

"Me?" Mansfield chuckled a little. "My old man was a Marine, twenty-five years. The Marines wanted everything about me 'cept my eyes. Couldn't pass the test. So . . . what could I do? This is the closest I can get to fighting for my country. My dad died just before I was sworn in, but I know he'd be proud." Mansfield turned in his seat. "What do you know about Menendez's criminal record in Texas?"

"I found out he's been convicted for fleeing police and assault."

"Tip of the iceberg. We've been following this punk-ass creep for years but haven't been able to nail him for federal offenses. He's a snakehead, bringing in all kinds of illegal things from Mexico. People, guns, drugs, rare animals, anything you can't buy at Walmart. Unlike the others who operate on a shoestring, Menendez has always been well-funded. He's got money and good cover—that's unusual."

"So we're going to check on that?"

"We've got contacts in both the local law enforcement and the border patrol. Since you're closer to the murder case, we thought you could ask better questions than we could."

"Where do we start?"

"First thing tomorrow, we've got a meeting with the local sheriff that caught your boy. We'll also make contact with our agents on the border. Your investigator can follow up if he wants to."

"You keep talking about NorthStar . . . an NGO? What's that?"

"Non-governmental organizations. They're all over and are usually formed for a specific mission. Some are charitable, some are 'whistle blowers' who expose human rights violations, or they fight diseases like AIDS. They get their money from many sources. They can operate in theaters where formal government agencies can't work, and they don't have to respect political borders like our agency does, for instance. Or wait for a bureaucracy to okay their actions. In that way, they're much more flexible than we are."

"But they can't use force like you can, huh?"

Mansfield chuckled and shook his head. "You got a lot to learn. They can hire any private security organization in the world. Just like we do."

"What does it have to do with NorthStar?"

"You really don't know, do you?" Mansfield leaned back. "There's the local branch in Minneapolis. They're tied closely to an international group that says its mission is to monitor armed militias who could pose a danger to national security."

"They just monitor it?"

"Zehra . . ." Mansfield sounded like a patient father correcting his child. "As far as we can tell, they've got access to some of the most heavily armed and aggressive mercenaries in the world."

The plane banked over a huge white cloud. Zehra turned away, looked out over the puff-balls of clouds, and heard the steady whine of the jets. It seemed so peaceful up here. Why couldn't she stay here, cocooned in this quiet, sleek tube away from everything on the ground?

Without Liz, could she do it? Zehra worried.

Zehra knew that she possessed the technical lawyer's skills. Trying the case in the courtroom and fighting with Mezerretti would be tough. Still, she felt confident in her ability to handle the basic steps—questioning of the jurors, direct exam of her witnesses, objections, cross-exam, and the closing argument. Experience and many trial schools had prepared her.

It was the larger problem that really worried her. Would she have enough evidence to convict Menendez? As the case stood now, the answer was still no.

Hopefully, this trip to Texas would give them more ammunition to use against the defendant. Zehra felt good with Brown along. He wouldn't miss a thing. She'd have to depend on him.

She thought of her career. Was this case the right one to risk everything on? Zehra knew Grant would fire her in a minute if she failed. Her dreams of becoming the first female Muslim judge in Minnesota would be gone. Her work to prove that American Muslims were normal, moderate, and patriotic people in the U.S. would be set back. The media would exploit the case relentlessly. Zehra also thought of her family and the cloud of dishonor that would hover over them if she failed.

Looking out the window again, she sipped at her bottle of mineral water and thought of the victim. Zehra felt sorry for him. All lawyers were taught not to become emotionally involved with their clients. Zehra couldn't help it. He had been running, trying to escape something so terrible, it had cost him his life. What was it?

Zehra felt in her gut that Menendez was guilty and she thought of the bio-terrorist, Mustafa, and all the brutal criminals that preyed on less fortunate or weaker people. Suddenly, her rumbling stomach changed to a low burn that spread up into her chest. Zehra's breathing deepened. She was mad. Angry and furious at people who'd used their power to victimize so many others. It was an old, old story.

Would stopping Menendez and the criminal network he was part of change much? No, but it offered one point, one opportunity to make a difference. Zehra would run with that and try her best. She settled back into the narrow seat and felt the jet tilt on a higher trajectory. The engines whined in a louder pitch as they all rocketed up through the thin air.

CHAPTER 14

Wednesdy, October 26

EVEN THOUGH CIUDAD DEL ESTE IN PARAGUAY had a reputation for harboring terrorists like Al-Qaeda, it didn't bother Mr. Han in the least as he flew over the jungle to reach it.

He was not a terrorist. He worked for the Chinese government, and he wanted to get his business done quickly. With a little luck, he'd get time to view the world famous Iguazu Falls at the Brazilian border.

The Chinese government provided clandestine financing for a variety of extremist political groups within the United States in an effort to destabilize the country. They certainly didn't want to destroy the U.S., only to cause it internal problems, forcing them to borrow more from the Chinese.

Months earlier, Mr. Han had found a contact in Minnesota, a church, with a member who identified himself with the ridiculous moniker of "Horseman." Now he needed cash again for his "mission" in one last, large transaction. As usual, Mr. Han was asked to provide it in a way that would be impossible to track and identify. He'd do it, of course, but Han wanted to get out of this shit hole of a country fast.

At the tiny airport outside of Iguazu Falls, the rain forest reached out from the edges of the runway toward him as he crossed it. The air smelled damp and warm. He removed his tropical tan suit jacket to avoid wrinkling it. He folded it with care, glad he hadn't worn a tie.

After he'd flown over the expanse of more than twenty million people crowded around Sao Paulo and worked his way through that surprisingly quiet airport, Iguazu Falls was refreshing in its simplicity. It sat at the intersection of three international borders: Argentina, Brazil, and Paraguay.

Before he could enjoy anything, he had to find a ride across the border into Paraguay. Collecting his small suitcase, he searched for a cab.

Though he was the only Asian in the airport, no one seemed surprised when he asked for transportation to Ciudad del Este. The Asian population of the city, particularly Taiwanese and Korean, was large—so large and financially strong that they had provided funding to build the town hall, gaining the gratitude of the impoverished Paraguayans. The Taiwanese flag flew over the building next to the flag of Paraguay.

Neither did it surprise Mr. Han when several drivers insisted on double the rate to take him there.

"*Es peligroso.*" Dangerous, many said.

Finally, he struck a deal. The exorbitant cost was not important. He placed his suitcase inside the door, arranging it square to the edge of the seat. Next, he draped his folded suit jacket over the suitcase. He had to reach the city and finish his business.

The old cab turned from the front of the small airport and drove out to the two-lane road. Turning onto it, the cab scattered a cloud of yellow butterflies hovering over wet ground.

Han stretched his hand over to rest on the suitcase as if to reassure himself it was there. Everything depended on getting its contents to Ciudad del Este. And it had to be done personally. Once his business was completed, he had no intention of staying there. He had Googled for "Things to do in Ciudad del Este." He hadn't found any entries.

In a short while, the cab approached the Friendship Bridge that spanned the Rio Parana between Brazil and Paraguay. In the late afternoon tropical sun, the bridge shone in tan stone colors. Below flowed the thick and muddy river. Across the bridge flowed hordes of Brazilians. As they crossed into Paraguay, not one immigration or customs officer stopped them, as Mr. Han had expected.

Ciudad del Este sprawled over many blocks. At the edge of the town, the rain forest poked fingers of green into the urban areas. Birds cawed incessantly and monkeys chattered. Buses, cars, and scooters jammed the streets, all moving at top speed. They drove from the river up a steep slope into town.

As they approached the downtown section, buildings were jumbled on top of one another. It reminded Mr. Han of Shanghai's crowding, without the prosperity and new construction. Even though Ciudad del Este had been founded in 1957, it already looked worn out. Electric wires sagged in deep curves, looking as tired as the city sweltering in the humidity and heat.

He had learned that one of the largest dams in the world, Itaipu, blocked the Rio Parana upriver. Both Brazil and Paraguay shared equally in the electric production. Brazil's share generated enough power to run the city of Sao Paulo. But Paraguay sold ninety-five percent of its share back to Brazil, because Paraguay had no use for the power.

They turned at a corner where one of the new mosques rested. Robed men in turbans rested along the walls and watched everything that passed. The Arab population was second only to the Asian, after the Paraguayans. Rumors said the city was a staging point for al Qaeda.

Buffeted by the smell of cheap gas, the cab threaded its way through the traffic to reach what the city called their financial district. In comparison to China, Mr. Han almost laughed. But what he was going to do must be done outside of China to avoid suspicion. The network Mr. Han worked in really didn't exist anywhere except on the Internet.

Thanks to globalization, most products, labor, and capital could move easily around the world. Unfortunately, political and military borders remained, and their rules made his business difficult. Mr. Han's main skill was his ability to find cracks in the myriad rules and laws of many countries and exploit them. He'd chosen Ciudad del Este to help open those cracks he discovered in other parts of the world. But that was the nature of the new capitalism—one looked for the inefficiencies in order to take advantage and keep costs down.

Ten minutes later, they stopped in front of the Banco de Paraguay on Calle Pa'i Perez. First Mr. Han got out. He unrolled his sleeves and buttoned the cuffs. He lifted his jacket out and put his left arm in, then his right. He looked from the suitcase inside the cab to the crowded street in front of the bank and studied it. Finally, he lifted the suitcase out and paid the driver half the fare. "Wait for me. It won't be long," Mr. Han said.

On the crowded sidewalk, a small man with a greasy beard stepped in front of him. "*Tu quieres drogas?*" He opened his palm to show something that looked like a white golf ball—cocaine.

At the far corner of the bank, several AK-47s stood at attention on the sidewalk awaiting sale. The teenage vendor who looked about thirteen waved at Mr. Han to come over and buy.

Inside, the bank the air conditioning smelled metallic. Marble covered everything, making it look like a cheap stage design from one of the old theaters in Shanghai. A small, dark woman with reddish-black hair piled on the back of her head greeted him. Her skin was flawless, the color of tea mixed with milk. In contrast to the light skin of his people, she intrigued him. Her skirt hugged the shapes of her body closely. Unlike most Chinese women, she was full-figured and made sure he became aware of it. Maybe if he had time, he'd buy her, too. Like everything else here, she was probably for sale.

"*Buenos tardes.* Good afternoon, sir."

He spoke English. "I'm here to see Vice-President Julio Suarez."

She nodded and led him immediately into the man's office. After introductions, she leaned forward to expose most of her breasts and retreated reluctantly.

After the polite preliminaries, Mr. Suarez turned the conversation to business. "We have prepared the account as you requested last week. As you know, we are a correspondent bank to many others all over the world, including many in the city called Minneapolis in the United States. You saw our list?"

After Mr. Han nodded, the man continued. "We see ourselves as the Switzerland of South America." He propped silver wire-rimmed glasses halfway down his long nose.

Mr. Han smiled to himself. They had a long way to go.

"Everything is confidential, and we don't subscribe to the overly restrictive banking regulations of our correspondent banks, or those in Switzerland, for that matter. So no one can ever obtain access to your private information. Guaranteed." He smiled, revealing a gold tooth on the left side of his mouth. "We can open the numbered account right now. How much would you like to deposit?"

Mr. Han lifted the suitcase from beside his foot and set it on the desk. Clicking the locks open, he reached inside and retrieved bundles of checks drawn on Barclay's Bank of Shanghai and bricks of cash. He would be happy to get rid of them and put them safely into the bank.

"Actually, I want to open one hundred accounts."

Chapter 15

Thursday, October 27

Zehra thought she might die. When she awoke on Thursday morning in the two-story motel in El Paso, wind shrieked around the corners of her room. The glass seemed to bend inward as if the wind were a large hand pressing on the panes, trying to get at her. She heard groans from deep in the motel as it fought the gusts.

She jumped out of bed, took a quick shower, dressed, and hurried down to the small coffee shop on the first floor. Outside, she could see the desert stretch out from the motel to the west, brown and flat. Wind kicked up dust that swirled away from the motel until it was lost in the tan horizon, where it was difficult to distinguish sky from soil.

Long and Mansfield sat at one end of the table, Bluetooths plugged into their ears. They talked softly to themselves. Hopefully, their phones were turned on.

Jeremy Brown looked fully awake. He was drinking water. He read from a well-worn brown leather Bible on the table in front of him, almost caressing the pages as he turned them. Barry slumped into the chair next to Zehra. He still looked half asleep.

"Quite a storm, huh?" he said to Zehra. "Reminds me of some of the lawyers I've seen in court." Both of them turned when Mansfield started to talk.

"We got a full day planned. First, we're going to see Deputy Sheriff Joe Gomez of the EPCS. He's the one who worked on Roberto Menendez's cases. He'll liaise with you about your murder case. Then we'll go to the border itself. See where the illegal products are brought in and how it's done."

Zehra thought she should thank Mansfield, but his patronizing manner offended her. She nodded and finished her tea.

In ten minutes, they all stood under an overhanging roof at the front of the motel. Scrub bushes and weeds clung to the edge of the motel's walls in the shade. Around the entrance, four large planters held various types of cactus. The colors ranged from gray green to bright yellow-green.

Zehra approached Brown. "What should we be looking for here?"

He raised his eyebrows and shrugged. "You're going to try and use his crime here as evidence in the trial in Minneapolis, right?"

She nodded.

"We should be finding the witnesses that were part of his case here. Gomez should have contact information for them." He raised his hand over his eyes to shelter them from the glare. The pink bracelet dangled from his wrist.

"But that was a few years ago. Can you still find them?"

"That's why you've got the best." He smiled so beautifully that Zehra would believe anything he said.

"Do you miss your wife and kids?"

He nodded. "Lots. The Bible says we are to procreate and inherit the Earth. I'm just sorry we could only have two children. I wanted many more. Twelve is a good number."

Zehra thought he was kidding. "What about your wife? She wasn't too excited about that, was she?"

Brown's face clouded over. "She defers to me in those matters. Medically, she can't bear more children. God tests us in many ways." The wind pulled at his words and scattered them out across the desert.

Zehra felt uneasy. She backed away.

"You're from Texas, aren't you?" Brown said.

"Dallas. We always thought this part of the state was like going to the moon. Reminds me, I've got a college friend who took a job down here with the county government. I think she works in child protection. If I get a chance, I'll call her."

They all looked up as a large blue-and-yellow van appeared from around the corner. Rolls of dust trailed it for a long distance. It curved around the parking lot and stopped before the motel. Lettering on the side said, "EPCS" and below that, "El Paso County Sheriff."

They all climbed into a spacious, plush interior. The seats were soft and curved to fit a body. A cooler rested behind the driver's seat. As they filed in, Mansfield opened the top to reveal icy bottles of mineral water and Coca-Cola.

"Wish we could offer you chilled white wine," he laughed when Zehra passed by him. "But it's against the regs."

A half hour later, they turned onto Justice Street in El Paso and drove up to a two-story, blocky tan building with tall glass windows. A large sign in the front said "El Paso County Government Center." When they got out, Zehra felt the hand of the wind pushing her toward the front door.

Inside, the air felt cool. Besides a few phones ringing, it was silent and calm. They checked in through a metal detector, showed their ID's, and were passed through. Following the federal people, they filed down a long hall, turned right and kept walking. Zehra heard their steps echo off the polished floor and the closed doors along the way. She saw signs on some of the doors. They read: "Courtrooms," "Warrants," "Civil Investigation," and in the corner, "Crime Lab."

Mansfield led the way to a conference room at the far end of the hall. They entered and circled a table to find seats. Large windows, covered by thin open blinds, looked out over the desert. In the corner, a coffee machine spit as it finished brewing a pot of coffee.

Before they could get seated, a deputy sheriff came into the room. He was dressed in a tan uniform with yellow piping along the edges. He was dark skinned with a haircut that looked like a black shoe brush upside down. A matching moustache was trimmed to the sides of his mouth. He smiled quickly and said, "Welcome. I'm Deputy Joe Gomez." He didn't sit.

On his chest, Zehra saw three medals of some sort. A small radio was clipped to the epaulet on his shoulder. Occasionally, it squawked in words that were not clear.

He shook hands with the two federal men and nodded at the rest of them. "How about the weather? Usually not quite this windy. I understand you're here because of a case we handled a couple years ago. Roberto Menendez."

"That's right," Mansfield began. "I briefed you on the phone, so we can get right down to business. Tell us about the illegal trade here."

Gomez's chest lifted as he took a deep breath and let it woosh out. "Guys like Menendez, they bring in lots of illegal goods. Drugs, stolen stuff, guns. Worst problem is trafficking of young girls. It's up in numbers. We estimate over 100,000 girls come across each year."

"Are you stopping them?" Long said.

"We're getting higher arrest rates. Trouble is, as we tighten the border here, the risk gets higher, so the traffickers go to different borders that have less resources to stop them. Up north, I hear. We call guys like Menendez *polleros*."

"Spanish for chicken farmers," Brown said.

"Right. Because that's the attitude these dudes have about the girls. They just animals to be transported and sold. They lay out routes through the desert that are safe from our detection that they call 'chicken runs.'"

Zehra asked, "How do they actually get the girls in?"

Gomez swept his arm toward the windows. "Look out there. Impossible for us or Federal Border Patrol to patrol everything. The *polleros* know that. They bring the girls up through Ciudad Juarez, across the Rio Grande, wait 'til dark, then walk 'em across border to pick-up points on this side. Once they get past us, they use El Paso as staging point for distribution around the country. Using the same routes, Menendez was distributing lots of illegal things to your state."

"Do they always come across at night?" Long said.

"No. Lots of times, they try to smuggle in vehicles. I remember one time the false bottom of a van fell out just as it left the border checkpoint. Girls rolled across the road like loose bowling pins."

"I've learned Menendez had an assault conviction and fleeing police. Who'd he assault?" Zehra asked.

"He assaulted his woman, his kids, and the cop. Neighbor called police when he start beating his woman and kids, police arrive, Menendez run, and when caught, he fought with police. We prosecuted him, but at the last minute, his woman refused to testify against him. So, only conviction was for assault on cop." Gomez' face reddened.

"Was there any kind of pre-sentence report made about him?" Zehra said.

"Sure. I can show you copy."

Zehra asked, "With the drug wars going on in Ciudad Juarez, isn't it dangerous here?"

Gomez seemed surprised. "Not at all. The relationship between the two cities is complicated. It is symbiotic and, at same time, parasitic."

"What?"

"The drugs and young girls and illegal stuff come north, and the bricks of cash and guns go south. Economy of El Paso is booming. Why?" He sighed.

He leaned his head to one side and answered the squawk from the radio on his shoulder. He looked back at Zehra and said, "You can use the room next to this one. My assistant brings the reports."

Zehra was impressed at the crisp efficiency of the sheriff's office and how helpful they were. Before he left her and Barry in the next room, Gomez said, "We want you to get this dude. Guys like Menendez prey on the vulnerable. Doesn't show up in the reports, but he's tricky . . . and evil. That's what makes him dangerous." His face contorted.

Zehra and Barry split the paperwork in half.

When Zehra came across a psychological evaluation, she brightened. "Hey, Barry. We struck gold here."

"Huh?"

"Psych evaluation. I may be able to get into Menendez's head. Let's see what it says."

The psychological evaluation started with a description of Roberto Menendez. A twenty-nine-year-old Hispanic male, possibly married, and living with a family. He says he has fathered twelve children in all. The present family has been the subject of a child protection matter, although that information wasn't available to the author of the report.

Sources of Information:

1. Beck Depression Inventory – 2nd Edition (BDI-II)
2. Interview with Mr. Menendez
3. Minnesota Multiphasic Personality Inventory – 2nd Edition (MMPI-2)
4. Wechsler Abbreviated Scale of Intelligence (WASI)

After preliminary information, the report continued: Mr. Menendez was administered the WASI, a measure of general intellectual functioning. His overall performance places him in the below average range when compared with a national sample of adults his age. There was no significant difference between his performance on verbal items or non-verbal items. Mr. Menendez test scores are as follows:

Verbal IQ	89 (23rd percentile)
Performance IQ	82 (12th percentile)
Full-scale IQ	84 (14th percentile)

Mr. Menendez's clinical profile is consistent with those of individuals who demonstrate a marked disregard for social standards and values, exhibit antisocial behavior, and have poorly developed consciences. A wide array of antisocial acts by such individuals might include fighting, stealing, and sexual acting out. These individuals are usually viewed by others as selfish, impulsive, and self-indulgent. They typically cannot delay gratification of impulses. They fail to learn from punishment experiences and are likely to repeat antisocial behaviors. They typically have little tolerance for frustration and often show intense feelings of anger and hostility, which are often expressed in negative emotional or behavior outbursts when triggered. Diagnosis:

Axis I: Major Depressive Disorder, Physical Abuse of an Adult, Neglect of a Child, Physical Abuse of a Child

Axis II: Antisocial Personality Disorder

Axis III: Client does not report any physical illness.

Axis IV: Childhood experience witnessed his father physically assaulting his mother on numerous occasions, lengthy history of legal problems and arrests.

Axis V: GAF = 52.

When Zehra finished reading, she thought to call her friend Chris Wilson. Zehra wondered if the report could be used against Menendez in some way. She wasn't a shrink, but a few things stood out for her. His IQ was low, and his criminal behavior was explained by the testing. The diagnoses on the axes revealed a depressed person with an antisocial personality. Not unusual for many criminals. She focused on the sentence that said he had a low tolerance for frustration and could blow up in emotional outbursts when triggered. Could she use that somehow?

After lunch at the sheriff's canteen, they all climbed back into the van and drove toward the border to view some of the smuggling routes used to bring in all the illegal items. Zehra had forgotten how dry the country was in the south of Texas. Low mountains surrounded them, bleached white in the sun and blown clean of all visible vegetation by the wind. She saw oak, juniper, and mesquite in the flat areas. Perched in the mountains, she'd see some magnificent homes. But down where she was, the flat land rolled off into the endless horizon.

The sun pierced straight down. In the desert there was no gray. Everything was either brightly illuminated in the sun or shrouded in dark shade.

The driver of the sheriff's van cruised up the side of a low hill and turned at the top to face across a low valley. Dirty water seemed to stand still in it. The Rio Grande. Stopping, they all got out. Zehra walked around the far side of the van.

When she first saw the bare tree, tossed by the shifting winds, she thought it was a Mexican version of a Christmas tree. Hanging from the branches, colorful objects fluttered in the wind. Red, pink, white, black, and light blue, they looked like ornaments to her. Maybe it was used for a fiesta of some sort. As she came closer and circled the tree, she stopped at the base.

Startled, Zehra noticed the ornaments were women's underwear, panties. They hung haphazardly from many spots in the branches. Dust puffed up around her and made her legs itch. Uncomfortable. She circled the tree and saw more panties on the back side. Why? she wondered. *Why decorate a tree out here in the middle of nowhere?*

Crows from the adjacent bare oak tree cawed at her intrusion.

Gomez had worked his way over to her. He stood next to her and looked up. Finally, he said, "Rape tree."

Zehra jerked her head around toward him.

"When *polleros* get done rapin' some of the women, they leave 'em for dead and toss their panties up there. The good ones, they take with 'em to send north." His eyes squinted from the glare of the sun.

Suddenly, the wind seemed to suck the breath out of Zehra. Her legs became so weak she felt like falling to her knees, stunned. She refused to look up again. Like a person passing an accident on the freeway, she couldn't help but search the ground under the tree for evidence of what had happened here.

Zehra forced herself to take deep breaths, to imagine a beach, take control to avoid a panic attack. This was too close, too painful.

Gomez looked down at her. "You okay?"

Zehra sniffed and nodded, smelling the dust clinging to her and the dry heat that enveloped her like a dirty blanket.

Back at the van, Zehra got a cold mineral water, drank half the bottle, and recovered somewhat. Gomez had followed her back. He pointed south across the shallow valley of the Rio Grande with his arm.

"Look over there." At the foot of the immense Juarez Mountain range squatted a low, dusty, sprawling jumble of buildings, one story, brown and gray like the mountains. "Ciudad Juarez. If there was ever a town of sin, that's it. Between drug wars and trafficking in everything illegal you can imagine, it's the most dangerous town in Mexico. They say the sheriffs there last less than a month before they get shot or they disappear."

"What does their government do?" Zehra said.

"No government. It's a slaughterhouse over there."

"Huh?"

"Think about this: this is one of the poorest regions along the border, but El Paso's got some of largest cash transactions in the country going through our banks. It's also one of the safest cities in the U.S. Makes ya wonder, don't it?"

An hour later, Zehra stepped out of the van in front of the motel. After what she'd seen, her doubts about the case, herself, and the trial had evaporated like water in the desert. Her sense of anger and rage about men like Menendez and how they preyed on innocent people fired her resolve to do what she could.

She thought of Paul, missing him. Not only because of his position with the FBI, but also because of his strength and support. She needed him now. Maybe her hesitancy to see him more often and become more intimate with him should change.

Zehra longed for a solid relationship with a man like Paul, but she still wanted the man to be Muslim. Her family's attitudes weighed on her, knowing they preferred the same thing. Unlike a lot of her friends, her family's attitudes meant a lot to Zehra. Any man would have to fit into that family—a Muslim family.

She turned on her cell phone for the first time all day. Scrolling down, she saw her mother had called four times in the last hour. Something was wrong.

Zehra reached her on the second ring. "What's up, Mom?"

"She's missing," Martha said.

"Who?"

"She's missing. Shereen."

"What happened?"

Martha took a deep breath and calmed herself. "She went to the Mall of America like usual, but this time, she didn't come home."

Zehra felt her stomach tighten. "What'd Salah do?"

"Called all Shereen's friends. No one knows where she went."

"Police?" Zehra gripped her phone harder.

"Yes. Wait for twenty-four hours."

"We can't."

"What should we do, Zehra?"

Her mind spun. The trial would start in four days, on Monday, and she'd be swamped with that effort. But this was family. What could she do?

"Zehra?"

"I'm thinking." Zehra saw Jeremy Brown get out of the van. *Why not?* She thought. He was the best investigator she'd ever known. Maybe he'd help. "Mom, we're done with our work here. We're coming home today. I'll talk to our investigator. Maybe he's got some ideas to find Shereen."

CHAPTER 16

Friday, October 28

K EVIN, GET YOUR HANDS OFF MY ASS," Kathy Johnson hissed into his ear.
"Nobody can see," he protested. "I need you."
"I don't care. Not here."

"All right. Where? Your place? Can't go to my place." He laughed too loudly and lifted the martini up to his lips again. He slurped about half of it out of the shallow, stemmed glass.

"Slow down. You're getting drunk."

"I should. Our guys in Seattle just forwarded another blog that's linked to the blog from the Church of the Rapture. It scares the shit out of me." He turned in the booth to pull a crumpled hard copy from his leather briefcase and hand it to her. "Read it."

They sat in the back at the newest bar and restaurant in Uptown, a trendy area just south of the downtown area of Minneapolis. Besides young people, it attracted lots of suburban people who wanted to experience the grit of inner-city life—so long as it offered clean bathrooms and lots of food and booze and free parking for their expensive cars.

Kevin and Kathy were at the Take Five. Besides the bar, it had live jazz music on the weekends. It was just down the block from the Lagoon Theatre that also assured them an after-movie crowd.

Two nights earlier, after another NorthStar meeting, Kathy had taken Kevin back to her house. She remembered how his body looked in the dim light from the bathroom door, cracked open just enough to make things romantic. Her CD player purred softly in the corner with a Miles Davis track playing.

He was skinnier than she'd imagined when he finally got all his clothing off. Gray hair curled off his chest, itself still bunched with muscles. His long legs rose to meet at his buns, firm and smooth and white from where he must have worn his bathing suit the past summer.

Kathy had been nervous at first, but soon relaxed into his arms when he lowered himself into the bed next to her. It seemed to go on forever, slow at first, building with intensity and speed, until the end. Although she felt totally naked, inside and out, he accepted her as she was and she had not felt so relaxed and happy for a long time.

They lay together in bed, touching each other, and Kathy heard soft thunder off in the distance which rumbled into the bedroom through the fluttering curtains. Later, gentle rain came, blown on the wind from the west.

Kathy flattened the crumpled paper on the table so it was under the Tiffany lamp that left only a small cone of light for her to read the blog from Seattle:

ONWARD CHRISTIAN SOLDIERS

MARCHING . . . TO WAR

Soldiers and True Believers!!! In other posts, I've warned you the TIME IS HERE! Read Revelation 13:16-17: "Also it causes all, both small and great, both rich and poor, both free and slave, to be marked on the right hand or the forehead, so that no one can buy or sell unless he has **The mark**, that is, the **name of the beast** or the **number of his name**."

Loved ones, prophecy is fulfilled today and we are truly living in the End Times. Recently, biochip implants called Verichips, which are the size of a piece of rice, have been implanted in the right arms of many people, containing personal identification information.

How much more obvious can it be??? This is the Mark of the Beast and it's happening right now!! 666.

Rise Up!! Throw-off the antichrist of government the United States!!

We must all act now. Keep your eyes on the holy work done by our anointed and chosen commander in Minnesota—The Horseman of the Apocalypse.

Wait for his sign and then attack as planned!! 18!!

Nuclear=chaos.

In the words of our Savior: "Be ready for you will not know the hour . . ."

Kathy sat back and took a deep breath. She gulped her cosmopolitan. "I see what you mean."

"I've been following this junk for years. They're gonna do something big, really big."

"Nuclear weapons?"

Kevin's lips tightened and he nodded.

"Have you gone to the FBI?"

"Tried. They're 'looking into it.' By the time their bureaucracy gets moving, it'll be too late."

Kathy realized why he'd mentioned something that NorthStar was doing with a larger, national group. It worried her. She asked him, "That's why you're getting help from the national?"

He snorted. "These chat rooms are at an all-time high with chatter. We gotta get going to fight it."

"Get going on what? You've never focused on anything long enough to complete it, except for sex."

Kevin drew himself up and looked around the back of the restaurant. Satisfied no one was listening, he leaned closer to her. "Don't you see?"

"What?"

"I gotta explain something." He threw his head back and shook out his long hair. He sipped his drink once more. "We're allied with some international groups to stop these militia groups. We get muscle from 'em. When the bad guys are armed, we need to be also."

"Kevin, what the hell are you babbling about? Is this going to be dangerous?" A twinge of excitement rippled through her body, but she hid it.

He shrugged. "The big boys at national tell me there's some heavy shit gonna come down right here in Minnesota soon."

"What?"

"Not sure. But it's something big and is connected with the militia group and the church and a national movement that must be dealing with nukes. Wouldn't surprise me if Menendez was smuggling in a nuke. He's got a history of trafficking all kinds of shit."

She held her breath.

"These crazies need weapons and explosives to arm themselves. But a nuke? I don't know, but there's something about ready to break."

"Yeah?"

"We shadowed the militia group and its connection with the Church of the Rapture. You know what they believe, don't you?" He sat back and listened to an alto sax solo on the sound system. Kevin leaned forward again.

"Something about the 'last days'?"

"Right on. They believe we're all living in the 'final days' as predicted in the Book of Revelation. For years, most of the militias were sourced through Mexico. The traffic of illegal immigrants and drugs gave the militias cover and distribution routes. They also hired the same guys to bring in the stuff they needed."

"Guys like Roberto Menendez?"

Kevin nodded. "Guys like him are at the top of organized syndicates who traffic in illegal goods. They piggy-back on existing supply routes."

"So what's changed?"

"The border. The U.S. government has tightened the security on the southern border. It's working to some degree. The risk of getting caught is higher, so guys like Menendez charge more to get the stuff into the U.S."

"So where do they go now?"

"These thugs are real smart. They study the borders of many countries to figure out where the cracks and weak points are. They change all the time. The criminals can switch ingress routes quickly, depending on how porous the borders are at certain points."

"And that's now Minnesota?"

"Right. Think about northern Minnesota. What comes to your mind?"

"Lots of lakes, woods, and wilderness."

"Exactly. We've got border patrol up there, but come on . . . Canada? What threat are they? That means we're vulnerable from the north. That's where the smugglers are going."

"How do they work?"

"Like any modern business. The syndicates have a variety of contract employee functions: transportation logistics, human resource management, distribution, financial control, not to mention secrecy and security. The top guy has to be brilliant to make it all work."

"Doesn't the government do anything?"

"They try, but government is slow and bureaucratic, so they aren't flexible enough to combat the networks. These new trafficking organizations can move incredibly fast and can change overnight. Besides, consumer technology has boosted the trafficker's abilities. Encrypted radios and email, disposable and encrypted cell phones help immensely."

"How do they get money for all this?"

"International financing. They assemble investors from all over the world in project financing—which isn't hard since the profits are huge. Once the money's assembled, they spread it into hundreds of smaller accounts to avoid reporting requirements by the banks and hide the money."

"But can't our government stop them at some point?"

"It's tough. These new syndicates are like a wheel. The main operator is the hub, and whenever he needs something, like financing, he plugs into an international network. They are in contact, never face to face, just to set up the deal. Once it's done, they unplug. No one in the net knows anyone else."

Kathy drank from her cosmopolitan. Her mind knotted with the intricacies of traffickers' organizations. She admired Kevin. Goofy sometimes, but was smart enough to be able to do something about stopping them.

As the vodka trickled into her brain, her thoughts spun off in fantastic images. She and Kevin battling the traffickers, traveling internationally, excitement, regular sex after they won. Would she have to carry a gun? That thought made her laugh. Either of them with a gun? That was a little too far out there.

She faced Kevin. She let her eyes walk through the tangle of his beard and saw the curls of gray hair amongst the brown. She watched as his lips opened to sip from his drink. He had the most beautiful, full lips she'd ever seen.

A tingle went through her body as she thought of all the excitement they'd have together. Her dull life would be transformed into something so much more exhilarating. But what about Kevin's wife? He'd insisted they were getting a divorce. A deeper part of Kathy warned her not to trust him entirely, but after all, how many times did an opportunity like this come along? If she didn't grab it now, she'd sink back into her lonely, boring life.

Suddenly, Kevin stood and walked to the TV that hung over the bar. It was turned on to Fox News. Kevin waved her over.

An announcer with silver-gray hair introduced Marion Bennett, a candidate for the U.S. Senate seat in Minnesota. "We covered your speech last night at the Living Word University, a Christian college here in the Twin Cities. As usual, you were unequivocal in your support for your Christian voter base and, in turn, they make up your largest cash donors."

Bennett smiled, her eyes glittering. "That's because we agree. Christian moral standards, if applied in our country, would save us from the problems we face. "

"You've often said that. But last night you went further and stated we are living in the 'last times.' This is new for you."

"Not really. I think it's obvious to anyone who studies scripture and follows the signs that we're definitely in the End Days when we should be expecting the Rapture. The Elect will be the only ones who survive, so we must work to show people the true way."

"Don't you think it's irresponsible to scare people like this? To draw a line between the 'Elect' and all others in a democracy?"

"No. A democracy means that, free of government control, anyone can choose what they believe and . . ."

Kevin spun around and stomped back to the booth. "This is the proof of what we're fighting against."

"What are we going to do?"

"Like I was saying, our national intel says they've chosen the northern border of Minnesota to bring in something. I'm afraid it's a nuclear weapon of some kind. We'll organize to expose them and stop 'em."

Kathy said, "You really think they can bring in a nuclear weapon? Really?"

Kevin lowered his head and voice. "What scares the shit out of me is that they're gonna try. Who knows what crazy plans they have? These militias and 'end of the world' people are way out there."

"When will it happen?"

"The blogs and chat rooms all point to next weekend."

"I want to help."

"Of course. We're in this together."

Kathy wondered what she could really do. Kevin seemed so much in control, what was left for her to help with? Kevin would be the one informing the government agencies and the press. What could she do?

She thought of Zehra Hassan, the prosecutor in the Menendez case. Kathy remembered how furious Hassan had been when the other woman had the heart attack. But Kathy also remembered something she'd seen in the prosecutor's eyes—determination and courage.

Maybe Kathy could make contact with Hassan and tell her about Kevin's information so she could use it in the murder case.

CHAPTER 17

Monday, October 31

THE DAY THE TRIAL WAS SCHEDULED TO START, Larceny caused the first problem for Zehra. She'd gotten up at 5:00, eaten an English muffin with peanut butter, drunk two cups of hot tea, eaten a peach, prayed, and tried to orient her cat to the strange time. Usually, Zehra got up about 6:30 and fed the cat by 7:00.

He wandered in circles, nibbling occasionally at the wet cat food he normally dined on later in the morning. When he stopped padding around the kitchen, he'd look up at Zehra with soft, pleading green eyes. *If only I could use him with the jury,* she thought. *No question I'd win.*

Her mother had already called about Shereen. She said the Bloomington police were now investigating the case. Zehra promised to do what she could, but cautioned Martha that all of Zehra's attention and energy would go into the trial.

The night before, Paul had come over with pizza and a small bottle of Italian wine. As a Muslim, Zehra usually didn't drink, but a glass of wine had sounded good. Together they'd gone over the case start to finish, covering witnesses, legal motions, jury selection, strategy for fighting Mezerretti, and the legal research Barry had prepared. Since Paul wasn't a trial lawyer, his view of the case differed from hers. The difference helped flush out gaps in her case.

Besides, she liked having him there.

They purposely put off eating until all the hard work had been done. By eleven o'clock, the case was as prepared as it ever would be. Zehra felt a low hum of nervousness buzzing through her that she knew wouldn't go away until the trial was finally over. She could live with that.

One thing Paul insisted on doing for her was testing the cell phone found at the murder scene. "The expert we use is slow. I called Dr. Leonard yesterday and ordered him to finish it by tomorrow. We can meet him after you finish with the trial for the day."

The tough part of waiting for a trial to start was all the second guessing she went through. Did she have enough witnesses? Were her motions researched fully? Had she forgotten anything? The doubts could go on forever. Paul's opinion and presence calmed her down.

After they finished working, she slipped the pizza into the oven to warm up. They both poured a small glass of Valpolicella. Zehra sipped and enjoyed the dusty aftertaste. It helped her to relax.

"Wish I could be there to second-chair you," he said.

They sat across from each other at her small kitchen table, elbows propped on the top and leaning toward one another. She looked up into his brown eyes and traced around his dark eyebrows, over his cheeks, and found his white teeth smiling out from his face at her. She felt warm and content. A strong urge to stand and hug him tightly coursed through her. Why not?

She got up from the table, pulling his hand behind her, and turned to lean into his strong body. She pressed herself into him and felt his arms go around her shoulders, rub down her back, and descend into her lower back. She nestled her head under his chin and simply swayed together with him. Neither spoke.

His hand dropped lower to reach her butt and to curve underneath. An electric current switched on, and she felt heat rising from her stomach. His hand caressed the cheek of her butt and gave a gentle, sensual squeeze.

She lifted her head and found his lips, full and warm. They kissed deeply and Zehra felt him touch closely along her entire body. Her legs were a little wobbly. Their heads shifted position and they kissed again. She could feel his hot breath brush across her neck.

How wonderful it would be to give in to her urges. To rest with him and never have to get up the next morning. Maybe she'd get up long enough to make tea and serve it in bed, then go back to sleep.

"Zehra . . ."

"Not now, Paul."

"I know you're interested. Why not let go? We're good together, aren't we?" Frustration shot through his voice.

"Yes." She dropped her head on his chest. "Just not now. Let's talk after the trial is over." Zehra knew she was falling in over her head, but it sure felt good. Reluctantly, she pushed away from him.

His face clouded over in anger. "I know how important and difficult this is, but think about my feelings sometime. I'm not always going to be here." He grabbed his jacket and rushed out the door.

At 6:00 in the morning, Zehra put Paul out of her mind and tried to assure Larceny it would be okay. By 6:30 she sat in a large conference room with Barry and the victim/witness advocate who had been assigned to the case and had worked with the witnesses. Zehra had a checklist she reviewed with them.

"Barry, you've got the Spreigl motion researched fully?"

He lifted a thick folder off the table. "The motion's finished and all the supporting cases are attached. I even added the court of appeals unpublished opinion that came down last week."

"Great work." She turned to the advocate. "All the subpoenas served?"

Detroit—she pronounced it "Detwah"—looked down through her list. "Yeah. Got the witnesses from the church, the forensic people, all the cops . . . even the one called, 'Father O'Brien,' who tried to get a confession out of Menendez." She flipped the page. "And depending on what your friend at the FBI gets off the cell phone, I got the expert, Dr. Leonard, subpoenaed in case we need him."

"You didn't forget the main witness?"

"Chill, Sister. Called Sparkle myself on Friday. She's cool."

"Thought she was scared?"

"She is, damn sure. That's because of the business she's in and the fact she's illegal. But I worked with her, and she's cool. You know what I'm saying?"

Barry asked, "How we gonna handle the facts of her background? She's not the most credible."

"When we question the jury, I'll bring it up and prepare them as best we can," Zehra said. "The defense is going to focus on her and try to make the case rise or fall with her alone. We've got to teach the jury to look at *all* the evidence."

"What order do you want the witnesses in?" Detroit asked.

Zehra scanned through her trial notebook, a large three-ring binder with each phase of the trial included in sections with supporting documentation. "We'll start with the routine witnesses and build to the more critical ones. I want a sense of drama, if we can."

Detroit looked at the large red watch on her wrist that matched her bright red glasses. "I'll start calling them at nine o'clock."

Jeremy Brown hurried through the door of the conference room and took a chair at the end of the long table. "Sorry I'm late. Busy."

"That's okay," Zehra said. "At this point, most of your work is done. How about Menendez's wife in Texas?"

Brown opened a tan file folder he carried. "Found her outside of El Paso and interviewed her myself. Here's her statement. She hates Menendez. You'll see all the damaging stuff she told me in there." He handed the papers to Zehra. He sat back, crossed his foot over his leg, and bounced the foot nervously. "Dropped a subpoena on her, too."

They worked through other details. At 8:00 Zehra sighed, indicating the meeting was over. Barry would sit with her in trial as her second chair. He'd have his laptop and be able to access legal research data right there if the defense came up with arguments that were unanticipated. Detroit would work with her staff between the office and the courtroom, prepping witnesses and escorting them down to testify. They also had another law clerk to help if needed.

With their marching orders, everyone left the room except Brown. He got up and moved closer to Zehra. "I'll get out to the mall this morning."

Zehra leaned back in her chair, ran her hands through her curly black hair, and slowed her breathing. She was winning the battle against the panic attacks. *Just keep at it.* "Thanks, Jeremy. You don't know what a big favor this is to me and my family."

He grinned. "So, we can talk? Believe me, there isn't much time for you to get straight with the Lord."

Zehra understood his tone. He never gave up. "Later. What have you found out?"

"Well, I know that the Mall of America is one of the biggest recruiting spots for all kinds of criminal activity."

Zehra sat forward. "What does that mean?"

"Uh . . . well, there are guys out there who pick up young girls and use them for shoplifting rings, burglary operations, and things like that. Since they're juveniles, if they're caught, the system goes easier on them."

Zehra felt her chest tighten. "Shoplifting? You mean they *train* them to be criminals?"

"Right. Or even prostitutes."

She moaned at the thought of Shereen on the streets. She was so young and naïve. The potential danger made her sick to her stomach. "So, you're going out there this morning?" She pulled on her hair. "Shereen's been missing for days."

"I know some of the security there from when I was a cop. I'll check out your cousin. I've got the photos you gave me and a description. Don't worry. I'll find her."

Her chest loosened and she felt better. In spite of his constant proselytzing, he was smart and tough. She could depend on him while focusing on the trial. "Let me know, first thing, what you find out. My whole family's worried sick."

His eyes softened and he stood to walk next to her. Brown rested his hand on her shoulder and gave it a tight squeeze. "You concentrate on convicting that slug Menendez." He started to walk out of the conference room. Turning at the door, he said, "I'll be in contact by text or phone. But don't worry. I'll find your cousin." He smiled his beautiful, killer smile and left.

At 8:45 Zehra loaded up all her files, the heavy Minnesota Rules of Court book, her laptop, and everything else she needed into a metal cart with wheels. She noticed the lower right hand drawer of her desk and thought of the chocolate cupcake inside. It was tempting to take a bite, but Zehra refused and felt proud of her discipline.

Before Zehra left her office, she called Liz, and found her resting at home.

"Wish I could be there to cheer you on," Liz said.

"Wish you were here to try the case yourself."

"I've watched you over the years, Zehra. You can do it. Just don't let things overwhelm you. Keep calm and don't let Judge Von Wald push you around. She's a former prosecutor and she loves to give us a hard time." Away from the phone, Liz coughed and then came back on. "You know we're doing the right thing here. Good luck."

Zehra left her office, pulled the cart toward the elevator, and met Barry there as they waited. Detroit came out to make some last-minutes checks with her.

"Mmm. You're stylin', girl," Detroit said.

Zehra looked down at the suit she wore with low-heeled shoes. It was her most expensive designer suit in an unusual, rich shade of blue. Instead of a white blouse, she'd decided on more interest and picked a salmon-colored one. It accentuated her dark skin. She had also pulled her hair back off her face in a more formal manner. Zehra knew the jury would study every single thing about her. Might as well try to impress them in any way she could.

She had felt more confident lately. She was surprised at her renewed interest in clothing and makeup. She healed more every day. The PTSD was receding.

She rode the elevator down to a courtroom in the Government Center where Judge Judy Von Wald presided. People jokingly called her "Judge Judy" after the TV program—but never to her face. Smart, tough, ambitious, and pushy, the judge had been on the bench for over ten years. She ran the courtroom with a rigid hand and demanded a lot out of the lawyers who appeared before her. Of course, she demanded equally as much from herself and usually produced it.

Although attractive, she'd never married, didn't have a family, and had devoted her life to her career, and now, to serving on the Hennepin County bench. On the surface, she was pleasant to everyone but if people didn't have business before her or couldn't help her career in any way, the judge didn't have time for them. So Zehra was surprised to learn that outside of her judicial work, she spent a lot of time on a pre-school reading program that she had founded and supported with her work and money.

Zehra met Mezerretti outside the courtroom at five minutes to nine. Judge Von Wald demanded the lawyers show up on time. Zehra appreciated the firm way the judge worked. Too many judges wasted time on small talk and courtroom gossip.

Two tall blonde women followed Mezerretti and carried his briefcases. "My law clerks," he winked at Zehra when he introduced them. When one of them opened the briefcase, Zehra saw another large bottle of men's cologne inside.

Before the defendant was brought up from a holding area for prisoners in the basement of the Government Center or the jury, the judge wanted to see both lawyers in chambers to review the case. In her large office or chambers,

Von Wald studied some files and didn't seem to notice when they sat down. In a few minutes, she looked up and said hello. Setting aside the file she'd looked at, she picked up a new one that her clerk had set on the desk. "State versus Roberto Menendez, huh?"

"Murder One," Zehra said.

"I can see that. I read the complaint on Friday." The judge turned to Zehra. "Tell me how you're going to prove this, Zehra."

"Uh . . . well, I've got the witnesses from the crime scene, the forensic people—"

Von Wald cut her off. "I don't need a recitation of your case. What I mean is, do you really think you can prove it beyond a reasonable doubt? I'm not so sure you can."

Zehra felt moisture pop out across her forehead. Her stomach rumbled. Maybe they should have dismissed the case. Maybe this was going to be a disaster. If the judge had questions about the case now, what would a critical jury think? She started to try and answer until an image of Liz poked into her thoughts. Zehra realized the judge was pushing her to settle the case short of going to trial.

"It's a circumstantial case, I know."

Von Wald peered at her.

Zehra started to get angry. She fought back. "We have a duty to the citizens to prosecute criminals in this county. And this guy is one of the worst. We're convinced he's guilty, and I plan to convict him."

Apparently satisfied, Von Wald turned to Mezerretti.

In the corner of the chambers, Zehra heard a clacking noise. While Von Wald started in on Mezerretti, Zehra looked back over her shoulder. It was a clock of some sort. It had horizontal tubes that held a steel ball. As time passed, the ball would clatter down one of the tubes to tip it onto another lower tube. When the ball hit the bottom, it rang a soft bell for the hour. Mechanical and predictable and made of steel.

"Jack, I'm sure you've fully advised your client of the penalties if he's found guilty of murder in the first degree? Any offers from the government to settle?"

Mezerretti clicked open a can of Altoids and said, "No."

Von Wald turned back to Zehra, who said, "We can't offer anything. We suspect Menendez of participating in a network of criminals who are smuggling guns and explosives into the state. We want him put away for a long, long time."

Mezerretti exploded, "I'll object to any mention of that. It's pure speculation on the prosecutor's part. No proof."

The judge smiled at each of them, then paused, seeming to consider it. Finally, she said, "Okay, folks. We'll start the trial."

CHAPTER 18

Monday, October 31

WHEN JEREMY BROWN LEFT the meeting with the prosecution team, he stopped at his home in Maple Grove, a northern suburb of Minneapolis. A newer city of rolling hills and thousands of ramblers perched on numerous lakes, Brown had bought out there to be as far from the evils of the city as possible. It was a neighborhood where his children could play safely in the streets and people could still have backyard barbecues without hearing gunfire.

As he came into the kitchen, his wife Ruth came from the dining room. At a large, round table, his two children sat in narrow chairs with kid's books in front of them. Ruth was methodical and organized. They were probably going over math assignments for their home schooling.

She reached up to peck a kiss on his cheek. "Are you ready?" Her blue eyes searched his face, trying to help in any way she could.

Brown sighed with bulging cheeks and a puff of breath. "So many details. I've got the team coming in, and we have to meet the shipment at exactly the right time up north. The power plant will shut-down for only a short time. We have to get the supplies distributed across the country, and everyone else in the network that is waiting for my move will start their own attacks or everything fails . . ."

Ruth stroked his shoulder. "Commit your way to the Lord, trust in him, and he will act," she quoted from the Psalms.

Brown frowned and sat heavily in the chair by the kitchen table. "We're right about this, aren't we?"

"Of course."

"I know that Satan plants doubts in our minds to separate us from the will of God. And I'm so unworthy, so sinful to be given this mission."

"We all are. But there's no doubt that prophecy is being fulfilled as we speak. Look at the prophecy in Matthew, chapter 24, verse 6. 'You shall hear of wars . . .'"

Brown nodded in agreement and finished the verse, "'There will be famines and earthquakes in various places: all this is but the beginning of the sufferings.'"

"'Immediately after the tribulation the sun will be darkened and the moon will not give its light . . . and they will see the Son of Man coming on the clouds of heaven with power and great glory.'" She continued to stroke his shoulder. "You are a soldier of the Lord to make that come about. We chosen have been given the truth and the responsibility to act on it."

Brown walked into the dining room and thought about John Brown, how he too had felt unworthy. He would often flog his bare back with a sharp whip until he bled to atone for his sins. But he'd remained uncompromising in his mission. Jeremy took strength from that knowledge and in his lowest moments there came times when Jeremy could almost feel the presence of his relative, comforting him. And he thought also of his family. Above all, he must save them from the decay and evil of the present world. God had made him a steward of two precious gifts, his girls. Jeremy could not fail to protect them.

He stood for a moment, looking at his girls. Mary, the older one, twirled a pencil in her tiny fingers. He was doing this for them and all the young believers who would be saved and brought into the glorious millennium of light and peace.

* * *

An hour later, he met with Paco. To avoid detection, they met in Brown's truck again.

"Chill, dude. You're too stressed."

"I've got a lot on my mind. In El Paso I found Menendez's ol' lady and made sure she'll never cooperate. In fact, she may even disappear for a few months. 'Course, the prosecutor doesn't know that. When they realize she won't testify, it'll be too late to delay the trial."

"Why's that important?"

"Because the prosecutor wants to call her as a witness here in Minneapolis because there's a provision in the law that allows the prosecutor to bring in evidence of other crimes to try and . . . forget it."

"Won't happen, huh?"

"No way. But we've got work to do here. Remember the other whore that was in the street when Menendez shot Sundberg? The one who told the cops she could ID Menendez?"

"Sparkle?" Paco laughed.

"She's their main witness. They have to call her."

"We gonna change her mind?"

"Yeah," Brown chuckled. "We're going there right now."

"So, what happens when the prosecutor's case falls apart?"

"Something called 'double jeopardy,' you stupid. Menendez can't be tried twice for the same crime, so if the case collapses and the prosecutor has to throw it out, story over. Menendez walks . . . all the way back to Mexico, I hope."

"Think the prosecutor will catch on?"

"Don't think so. She's bright, but she's all alone and she doesn't have a strong case. I think she'll panic and dump the case. We win." Brown looked out the window and thought for a moment. "Too bad. I've gotten to like her, but she's a Muslim. She'll be left behind."

They merged onto Highway 35W headed south out of downtown Minneapolis. At the Thirty-sixth Street exit, Brown edged off the freeway and turned to the east. They passed by small frame houses with chain link fences surrounding the front yards. At one corner, a black man stood behind his fence with two pit bulls sniffing his leg.

As they drove further east, the population changed from African American to Latino. Large, older cars lined the curbs with the back ends jacked up. In various bright colors, the cars gleamed with polish and looked like jack rabbits poised to jump forward. A stone church had a blue sign that read: MASS EN ESPANOL.

Paco guided Brown through a series of turns. "Did you get things done at the mall like I told you?" Brown asked him.

"Yeah. It's a big place, but she was easy to find. The photo you gave me was good and it didn't take long to get Shereen outside and into my car. "

"Put her at the house in Crystal?"

"Yeah. I gotta make sure she's got food and water. I turned the TV on for her so she could watch the game shows." Paco chuckled. "Should drive her nuts."

Brown nodded in agreement. "Good. Get some people from the church to help. We must witness to her and at least give her the chance to convert and become a believer. "

Out of the corner of his eye, Brown watched for Paco's reaction. Brown needed him to remain faithful and carry out the mission. The thought of it caused his breath to catch in his throat. He'd dreamt of this for years.

Paco smiled with confidence. "I'll get it done."

Brown ran through the upcoming plans again, even though he'd thought it through hundreds of times before. They'd meet the shipment of explosives from Mexico at the Canadian border on Sunday morning. It would be a quiet time of the week, and security should be minimal. Besides, the area they'd cross at was so remote, it'd be hard to detect them—even with the large load they'd bring over.

Together with his team, they'd distribute the explosives around the country and bring some back to the small town of Monticello located on the Mississippi River less than thirty-five miles north of the Twin Cities. They would be just in time to deliver the product to their man on the inside to set the charges and blow the plant, spreading radiation high into the air and wind and also into the Mississippi River to be carried through the heart of the country. As the Bible prophesied, kingdom would rise against kingdom, and the fighting between unbelievers would usher in the millennial kingdom.

All the dozens of details in preparation had been worked out. Transport, vehicles, financing, security, food and water and clothing in case it got cold up north. All had been planned down to the smallest detail.

The weather was the only factor Brown couldn't control. The predictions were for snow in northern Minnesota. Brown would have to adjust for that if any storms hit.

In the meantime, he had to stop the prosecutors in the Menendez trial, which he would do for good, right now.

They crossed into a neighborhood of small Tudor-style homes with tan stucco siding and brown trim around the roofs. The lawns were cut neatly, and a few rakes leaned up against front doors. They crossed Minnehaha Creek and took a left.

As he drove, Brown glanced at Paco. "You got the stuff for Sparkle?"

"Right here." He patted the side of a black leather purse that he usually wore over his shoulder. "Enough to do an army." He frowned at the thought. "Sure this is the only way?"

"I know it's not pleasant. The work of the Lord can be troubling. Our job is not to question, but to obey. Sometimes violence, Godly violence, is necessary."

They pulled up in front of a three-story apartment building. It had stucco siding like the homes nearby, and in the front each unit had a sliding glass door that opened onto a narrow deck. They were too small for furniture, but many people left their bicycles on them. Some had pots of plants and others had old grills. Most of the windows were covered with hanging sheets.

Brown cruised by once and pulled to the curb one block beyond the building in order not to attract attention to the truck. They got out and met at the sidewalk. Brown glanced at the other apartment building across the street and toward the houses beside it. Middle of the afternoon, things were quiet.

A cool wet wind gusted down the street directly at them, threatening to bring snow storms.

Brown turned up the collar of his jacket. They walked quickly and reached the front door of Sparkle's apartment building. With one last glance behind, Brown and Paco entered the lobby. A plate-glass door opened into a small area. The floor was covered with brown indoor-outdoor carpeting. Near the door a long metal panel had name tags and buttons to press for an intercom. Brown pushed on the button to Sparkle's unit.

"Who's there?" she answered after a long wait.

"Jeremy Brown. Remember, I'm the investigator from the county attorney's office?"

"I haven't got anything else to say."

"I know. But I have to talk with you to prepare for your testimony."

"Go away."

"Yelena, you want maybe I break the door down? You know you gotta come out of there sooner or later." Brown leaned his face close to the microphone.

Yelena didn't answer, but the far door buzzed. Brown and Paco jumped through into the hall. They climbed to the second floor and walked down the long hallway. An empty beer can lay along the wall. Brown could smell something fried and greasy. Through most of the doors, he could hear the soft murmur of TVs.

Yelena Mostropov was like so many of the illegal girls from Eastern Europe. Brokers in those countries offered trips to the United States where they were promised contacts in Hollywood. That usually got them because all the girls yearned for fame and money. Once in the United States, as illegal aliens, these girls were easy prey for pimps. It must have been the same for Yelena. She'd been forced into exotic dancing and prostitution to make enough to live on.

Brown had learned that the problems had started when she got hooked on heroin. She couldn't really be taken to a legitimate treatment facility, so her pimp had tried to get her to kick the habit on her own. Several times. Then she'd go back to work.

Brown and Paco came to unit number 201. They stopped and glanced to either side. Brown waited a moment and listened. He nodded at Paco, who knocked softly.

"Remember: don't touch anything," Brown said.

"Yelena, open up," Paco called through the door.

Brown heard a chain scrape across the back side of the door, a lock clicked, and the door opened slowly. Behind Paco, he pushed in quickly and shut the door behind himself. He locked and chained it and turned around to face the room.

Yelena stood in a black bra and panties, covered by a thin robe that looked like silk but was probably polyester. It gaped open to show that she still had an impressive body. Barefoot in spite of the chill, she cocked one knee in toward the other and put her hand on her hip.

In the month since Brown had seen her, what had once been alabaster white clear skin was now dry and lined. Although the features were still stunning, her eyes were sunk deeply into her head and moved from Paco to Brown slowly. She tried to smile but it looked like an effort for her. One tooth on the left side was missing. The wages of sin.

"I just talked to De-twa couple days ago."

"We know," said Paco. "We've got a present."

She turned around to walk into a small kitchen. "Want drink? Vodka?"

"No. Sit on the sofa."

"What for?"

Paco grabbed her thin arm and jerked her so hard she almost fell over.

"Hey," she protested.

"I told you to do something," he said.

She sat on the sofa and leaned back, her robe falling open. She crossed her long legs and rested her head on the back of the cushions. "What?"

"I got some blow for you."

"No. I kicked. You know."

"Don't bullshit me," Paco yelled at her. He crossed the room and grasped for her arm. Twisting it over, he pointed at the red sores on the inside of her elbow.

"Okay. Little bit. Keep my weight down."

"I got some good shit for you right here." Paco tapped the leather purse hanging over his shoulder.

"No." She blinked at them, trying to figure out what they really wanted with her.

"You been working so hard, Mr. Brown, he says you need a break. Right, Mr. Brown?" Paco turned to Brown, who nodded.

"Thanks, but no." She waved her hand in front of herself.

Brown stepped up to her and with his hand, grabbed her hair to lift up her face. He pulled back and slapped her, and the sound cracked off the walls. "You're gonna cooperate."

Her entire body quivered from the blow, and she nodded slightly but couldn't talk.

Paco went into the kitchen and came back with a spoon. He reached into the leather purse to lift out a thin plastic baggie. He set the spoon and the baggie on the low table before the sofa. Paco dipped the spoon into the baggie and scooped out a rounded pile of white crystals. He flicked a lighter and put the flame under the spoon until the heroin melted.

After waiting a while for it to cool, Paco took out a syringe in a crinkly plastic wrapper. "Paco's taking care of you, baby. This here's from a hospital. Clean. This'll send you to heaven, I promise." He grinned at Brown while he spoke. She didn't protest. Her head still wobbled from Brown's blow.

Paco stretched out her arm, stabbed the needle into her skin, and slowly drove the plunger down until all the heroin had entered her. "Pleasant dreams," Paco said. Her legs came uncrossed and fell apart.

Brown pulled back the sleeve of his jacket to study his watch next to the pink bracelet. "How long?"

"Ten minutes, maybe more. I gave her one hell of a hot shot."

In five minutes, Paco stepped forward to wiggle Yelena's head. She didn't respond. Brown leaned down and put his ear next to her mouth and listened. He straightened up.

"Still breathing, but not much."

"Trust me, bro. She's gone."

While they waited to make sure, Brown wiped down anything they might have touched to avoid leaving fingerprints. Paco washed off the spoon, dried it, and made sure everything else went back into his purse. Twenty minutes later, Yelena had stopped breathing. Her head lolled forward, and blonde hair hung to either side of her face. Brown reached forward to lift her face up. He rested it gently against the cushion. Paco arranged her legs, re-crossing one over the other.

"She should be smiling. It would make me feel better about this," Paco said.

Brown nodded as Paco reached out toward Yelena's mouth. Using both hands, he pushed the edges of her dead lips up into a weird smile. He stood back to study her from a different angle. "There. She looks good, don't she?" Paco said.

Brown sighed and shook his head. "Sometimes, doing the work of the Lord is so difficult, but we must remain faithful to our calling."

CHAPTER 19

Monday, October 31

BEFORE THE TRIAL WITH THE JURY AND WITNESSES COULD START, Judge Von Wald ordered any pre-trial motions or requests from the lawyers to be argued. While the lawyers waited in the courtroom for Robert Menendez to be brought up from the holding area, the judge squeezed in another quick appearance on a different case. Jim Patterson, a public defender that Zehra used to work with, stood up before the judge and waited for his client to come from the back.

Slowly, a woman worked her way forward. Over her head she wore something that looked like a clear plastic bucket that had a kinked hose running down her back to a tank of oxygen. She labored to walk the short distance to the judge's bench. Her breathing sounded like Darth Vader when she moved past Zehra. Obviously, she had a lung problem.

When the woman finally reached her lawyer, Jim turned to the judge and announced they were ready to set a trial date. "My client must wear her breather all the time, so we should to be sensitive to her needs in setting the date."

The prosecutor rolled her eyes without trying to conceal it.

After reading the file, the judge said, "You're accused of felony theft, and the state seems to have several witnesses who said they saw you do it."

From inside the plastic bucket, the woman echoed, "Wasn't me. I'm innocent. This is a case of mistaken identification."

The judge raised her eyebrows, agreed to the new date, and left the bench.

A ragged murmur rippled through the courtroom as people tried to be polite but laughed at the same time. Zehra felt sorry for her friend Jim. He'd been appointed by the court and had to defend his client as best as he could.

Mezerretti took a chair at the defense counsel table and grinned at his assistants and then turned around and grinned at the audience, including several media people sitting in the front row. Every seat was filled.

Zehra felt a nervous energy buzzing through her. Scattered thoughts and nagging questions that maybe she'd forgotten something. She pushed them aside.

In ten minutes three deputy sheriffs escorted Menendez into the courtroom, where he sat next to his lawyer. Zehra and Barry sat at a long table next to the defense, both facing the high bench for the judge. Zehra hadn't seen Menendez since early in the case. She was shocked at the change. And worried.

Zehra remembered Menendez as a scruffy, small man who looked like he hadn't slept in a few months. And although she had envied his shiny, thick hair, it looked greasy and too long. When Menendez had looked around the courtroom, his eyes jerked back and forth, giving the impression that he was shifty and untrustworthy and probably guilty.

All that had changed. Mezerretti had worked a miracle.

Menendez sat straight in his chair, obviously uneasy in the dark-brown suit and yellow tie, but still dressed up and looking good. His hair had been carefully cut short and combed back out of his face. He actually looked kind of handsome. Instead of appearing sneaky, Menendez resembled someone comfortable and calm.

Zehra studied him and began to worry. It was always harder for a jury to convict someone who didn't look like a criminal. Now Menendez could pass for a young employee at the customer return desk at Macy's.

Convicting him had just become tougher.

Judge Von Wald entered the courtroom. She looked up from half-rim glasses that rested on her nose. "Call the case."

Mezerretti stood first. "Your Honor, we object to the government's attempt to introduce Spreigl evidence."

Zehra replied, "The state has filed the proper motion for introduction of evidence about the activities of the defendant in Texas under the Minnesota Rules of Evidence, Rule 404b. Our brief is attached to the motion."

The judge leafed through the official court file until she found Zehra's motion. "Yes, here it is." She lifted it from the folder and thumbed through it. "Would you summarize your position for the record?"

"As the Court is aware, the state may offer evidence of prior convictions, prior criminal conduct, or even 'bad acts' under this rule following the procedure laid out in *State v. Spreigl* and *State v. Billstrom*."

"I am familiar with those cases."

"This is evidence about other conduct that tends to show the defendant acted with a motive, opportunity, and plan, as the rule requires."

"This is simply a 'back door' way of attacking my client's character." Mezerretti said. He popped an Altoid in his mouth.

"This murder case and the one in Texas involved the use of extreme violence. In both, the defendant ran to avoid apprehension. They show a common pattern of behavior of violence toward people who don't agree with the defendant."

"The conviction in Texas was an assault against a cop." Mezerretti turned toward the audience and smiled as if he'd scored a knockout punch.

The judge said, "You know that if I grant your request for admission of this Spreigl evidence, you must have a live body here in court to testify? You can't rely on the hearsay statements of some police officer."

"Of course."

Judge Von Wald removed her glasses, put the frame in her mouth to chew on, and leaned back in the high leather chair. It looked like she was seriously thinking about the issue. "Ms. Hassan, can you give me an offer of proof?"

Zehra felt elated. If the judge was going this far, she might decide to grant Zehra's motion. "Sure. If called as a witness, Ms. Esperanza Guzman would testify that she was living with Roberto Menendez and their two children in El Paso, Texas. That the relationship was stormy and filled with violence on the part of Mr. Menendez. That on several occasions, he became mad and beat them all. One time, she and the children were able to escape the house, but Mr. Menendez shot at them as they ran. That apparently caused a neighbor to call the police, who arrived and eventually arrested Mr. Menendez."

When Zehra finished and sat down, the courtroom echoed with silence. The stark and horrible accusations reminded the spectators and all others of the real people who had suffered and the reason for the trial.

Mezerretti had the sense to stop smiling.

"Give me a minute to read the complaint in the file," the judge said. Finishing, she laid the file on her desk. "I'll grant the State's motion to admit the Spreigl evidence."

They worked on other issues until it was close to noon. The judge called a recess for lunch to give her court reporter a rest. Even though all the courtrooms had switched to the "blue man," the judge still wanted a human reporter present. Technology had finally advanced into the courtrooms. Each one was fitted with digital recording systems and sensitive microphones placed at several spots in the room. When the system was switched on, a monitor high in the far wall glowed blue with an image of a man to tell the judge the recording system was active.

Zehra and Barry waited for a while. If possible, they wanted to avoid the worst of the media waiting in the hall. In ten minutes, they left through the double wooden doors of the courtroom. With a few non-committal comments, Zehra satisfied the remaining reporters' need for information about the trial. As the reporters drifted away, Zehra saw a woman standing off to the side. She looked familiar. When Zehra and Barry started for the elevators, the woman stepped forward.

"Ms. Hassan, I'm sure you don't remember me."

Zehra tried to recall where she'd seen the woman.

"I'm Kathy Johnson. We met when . . . uh, your partner had her heart attack."

Zehra stiffened. The NorthStar group. Zehra glared at the woman and hoped that would deter any more conversation. It didn't work.

"You're probably mad at us or me or whatever, but I have some information that may be important to you in your case."

Part of Zehra wanted to scream at the woman for what she and her group had done to Liz. The other part paused, intrigued by any information that may help. "What are you talking about?"

Johnson looked around and leaned closer. "Can we talk in private?"

"There's a conference room down the hall past the elevators. My assistant comes with," she demanded.

"Sure." Johnson followed them to a small room off the main hallway. Zehra pulled her cart into it and let Barry work his way around the other side. He had already brought out his laptop and was ready to take notes.

Johnson's face furrowed into seriousness. She wouldn't sit and hesitated for a moment. "First, I'm sorry about your colleague. I really am. None of us expected that, of course. We really wanted to get to your boss, Grant."

Zehra waved her hand across the table. "Forget it. What do you know?"

"Our group's connected with a larger, national NGO that's been tracking these militias for years." She paused and seemed to reconsider what she was saying. A flush rose across her face and she continued, "I have information that the man you're trying, Menendez, is part of a larger network of traffickers."

Zehra sighed. "We know that."

Kathy frowned and said, "It dawned on me that our group and you are on the same page. We want animals like Menendez put away and the dangerous groups he supplies stopped." She wrapped her arms around herself. "I'm not sure I'm supposed to be talking to you . . ."

"Okay." Zehra remembered how vicious the attack had been against Liz and herself. She remained cautious. "Let's focus on Menendez. I want to convict him. What can you tell me?"

Kathy unwrapped her arms and sat in the chair Zehra had offered. "Yeah, well. We don't think Menendez is the brains behind this network. There's someone behind him that you must find and stop. We collect blogs and chat room conversations. It's someone called 'Horseman,' here in Minnesota."

Zehra took a deep breath, looked at her watch, and thought of all the work piled on her desk upstairs that she had to get to before trial resumed in the afternoon. "Look, Ms. Johnson, I'm sure you're right, but my focus is on Menendez and my trial. We don't have the time or ability to . . ."

"We also have information that something big is going to happen this weekend. Something will come across the northern border of Minnesota." She paused. "We think it's a nuclear weapon of some kind."

"Nuclear?" Zehra sniffed a quick laugh. "Sorry, but we have to get back to the office."

"Don't you see? Menendez is the key to figuring out what is really going on. We don't have the resources you have. Money, investigators, the power of the prosecutor's office. If you could find out who's pulling the strings, you could stop everything."

"Probably. But we have to convict Menendez first."

"There's no time left."

Zehra started to pull the cart toward the door. Barry folded his laptop and came around the table. "Let's keep in touch." She handed Kathy her business card.

Kathy's face pinched tightly in frustration. "Sure."

As Zehra and Barry rode up the elevator, a thought popped into her head. No doubt, someone above Menendez was running the network. At this point it was intriguing, but she didn't have time to do anything except try the case.

Back in her office, she called Brown on her cell. She wanted to make sure all the details about Guzman's trip to Minneapolis to testify were set up. He didn't answer. She texted him and decided to have Detroit get on it and make contact with Guzman. Zehra left Detroit a voice mail.

She paused. No panic attacks for several days now. Things were getting better. Zehra felt, for the first time in months, engaged with life, interested, and anxious to make contact with old friends again after the trial was finished. Even hope poked its head up into her thoughts as she relished her victory in court this morning. Maybe there was a chance she could win the trial.

She scrolled through the messages on her cell phone. Her friend from El Paso, Cindy Wilson, had left a message. Zehra listened to it.

"Sorry we didn't have time to meet, Z. You left me the name and birthdate of the guy you're prosecuting. I checked our database and actually found an old child protection case he was involved in. A woman named Diaz was the mother. Looks like the case was opened for a domestic assault or more. Kids were removed. Call me. I might have more dirt."

Zehra sighed. Too bad she had missed her call. She'd call Cindy later tonight. It'd be nice to talk to her, and maybe Cindy had something worthwhile, even though the trial had already started.

She called her mother. Still no word about Shereen. Zehra could sense her mother on the edge of a breakdown of some sort. "Look, Mom, I've got a friend, Jeremy Brown, who's out at the mall this morning searching for her. I'll let you know what he finds."

"Can't we go to the FBI?"

Zehra looked across her desk and the pile of work on the table for the afternoon trial session. "I'll try." She hung up and called Paul. Luckily, he was at his desk. She explained the situation.

Paul didn't say anything for a while. "There's no ransom note? No one's taken responsibility yet? How do you know she didn't run off with some boyfriend? Police are already investigating?"

"I'm worried she did run off with someone from the mall."

"Zehra . . ."

"My family's going nuts. I know this isn't federal yet, but is there anything you could do?"

"Well, I suppose I could do some digging. I'd have to keep it quiet around here."

"Great." She gave Paul the details and the contact information for her aunt.

"You know I can't promise anything, Z."

"Of course. Thanks." She was about to hang up when she thought of Kathy Johnson. She told Paul about the conversation. "Heard anything from the boys at the ATF or ICE?"

"Nothing, but there are still the words 'Paraguay and Horseman' that triggered their investigation and the existence of someone who is master-minding this trafficking ring. The Bureau authorized me to become fully involved in their investigation now."

"Horseman? I'd forgotten that." Zehra told him about that part of the conversation with Kathy Johnson and the blogs NorthStar had intercepted. She listened as he promised to pass on the message to Mansfield.

"Sounds a little out there." Paul didn't say goodbye. He waited and finally said, "Zehra, be careful."

"What? I'm locked into a courtroom with deputies all over the place. What do you mean?"

"You know there's a connection between your trial and the trafficking ring. If the people running the ring think you're getting close to them . . . well, there's no telling what they might do to you."

CHAPTER 20

B EFORE DAYBREAK, JEREMY BROWN stole out of bed, slipped through the kitchen door, and walked into the cold garage. He stood alone with his arms at his sides, his legs together, and tilted his head forward until it touched his chest and the back of his neck hurt from the extreme angle.

He prayed. Quietly at first, then becoming more fervent with the thought of all his guilt. He confessed his many sins, grew penitent, prayed out loud, raised his head, and squeezed his eyes shut so tightly tears came forth like great drops of blood to stain his cheeks and drip onto the cold concrete floor.

His body started to sweat from the effort, and as he prayed he began to sway back and forth. "I have sinned, forgive me," he shouted over and over. "I am not worthy, forgive me."

The guilt stabbed him so sharply that he could feel it as physical pain. Jeremy knew what he must do next.

Wiping his cheeks, he took a few steps over to his workbench. On the corner, he'd mounted a vise grip, a steel tool that had two flat sides that could hold an object. On the end of the vise grip, he could turn the crank to tighten the grip. He took a deep breath and prayed once more, but this time for strength. He thought of John Brown, felt his presence in the chilled air.

He put his left little finger between the sides of the vise grip and with his right hand, turned the crank around and around, slowly squeezing his finger. The pain increased, but he refused to cry out. He deserved the punishment for his failings in the faith. The only thing that allowed him to keep turning the crank was the knowledge that in a moment, the pain would actually turn to ecstasy in a strange, blessed way. It was proof the Lord required this sacrifice of Jeremy.

Less than an hour later, he'd showered, dressed, eaten and prayed with his family, and left the house. Although Jeremy Brown had told Zehra Hassan he

141

would investigate the disappearance of her cousin at the Mall of America, he didn't intend to go anywhere near the mall. Paco already had the girl.

Various thoughts clambered for attention in his mind. Each of them insisted on its importance and urgency. First, he had to get north to meet the shipment. He would take the hand-off at the Canadian border. The plan had developed a couple years ago when he was on a fishing trip in the Boundary Waters. Along the narrow lakes that separated the two countries, there were always several power boats that patrolled the international border. They were all Canadian. Brown never saw any boats on the U.S. side.

Second, he felt confident the sacrificial death of the Russian girl would stop the prosecution, giving him enough time to pick up the shipment, distribute it, and get enough back to the power plant in Monticello. Timing was critical. Although they had eliminated Yelena, he sensed Hassan was tougher than people thought and relentless if she wanted to be. That's where her cousin came in—insurance in case Hassan didn't crumple.

The pressure gave him a headache. He paused to pray for strength and resolve to carry out the entire plan faithfully. The details of an operation of this size almost overwhelmed him.

He used his iPhone to keep in touch with all the players, most of whom he'd never met in person. That was intentional so that no one could connect the dots if law enforcement ever caught on to the scheme. Each of his partners was anonymous and didn't know anything beyond his small part in the plot.

He also worried that some of the network had been using blogs and chat rooms far too often. Brown knew that law enforcement cruised those regularly, looking for key words. He shook his head, hoping nothing would be revealed.

Brown keyed in the people from Mexico. He communicated with Estevez's son, since the old bastard couldn't figure out how to use a smart phone. The son assured Brown the explosives had left Juarez by truck, bound for the Caribbean ports in Mexico. They'd been broken down into small sizes and concealed inside pallets of hollowed-out Bibles. All the necessary bribes had been paid so the shipment wouldn't be stopped. They'd travel by boat to the St. Lawrence Seaway and would be off-loaded in Canada for the transfer to Minnesota. The shipment would arrive in Winnipeg, Ontario, because the security was more lax than in Toronto.

Addressed to the church in Hamel, the pallets of Bibles would be loaded into a panel truck for transport to the Minnesota border. Brown had traveled up north to make sure everything was done correctly. He'd taken Paco, Marko Sundberg, and Roberto Menendez with him each time since Brown intended for them to be part of the transfer team. They had to know the terrain.

All of them had taken ingress routes to test the border security at different points and places. The most remote area was Voyageurs National Park. The convoy wouldn't go deep into the wilderness, just far enough to shake any pursuit. They'd mapped out a line of GPS coordinates to mark the path across the water and through the wilderness to the closest road for the pick-up point.

Brown called Paco. "Pick you up on the way out of town."

"You check the weather, dude?"

"No. Why?"

"Storm predicted for up north."

"We're on a crusade for the Lord. Can't stop it now."

Brown clicked off. For months, he had recruited an enforcement team to replace Menendez and Sundberg. They came from all over the world. None of them knew each other, and only Brown was connected to all of them. In case any of them was caught or compromised in any way, they wouldn't lead law enforcement back to him.

He chuckled at the thought of how easy it was to get professional help these days.

Several web sites that operated like Craigslist offered criminal help. Of course, it was all hidden in code, but if a person had money, everything was available. When Brown needed a bomb expert, he found one. Forgers, hit men, crooked lawyers, skilled drivers, money launderers, both men and women, were all available. The Internet gave them all a place to congregate and offer their skills to the highest bidders. Ironic, he thought, because technology fulfilled even more prophecy: "Knowledge shall multiply around the world." Using the Internet, the attacks on the other nuclear plants could be coordinated easily.

They coalesced for a particular job, finished it, and disbanded just as quickly. They could come from anywhere in the world. Many of them lived in countries that ignored their work and lifestyles and didn't have extradition treaties with the United States. Even in the U.S., the law enforcement agencies were still organized as pyramids, with top management dictating orders to the heap below. It made them slow, ponderous, and unable to react quickly enough to effectively counter the new criminal networks.

For the most part, they were no match for the networks.

Various nongovernmental organizations operated in networks and could move as quickly as Brown, but these groups usually lacked the firepower and muscle to be really much of a threat.

Brown laughed to himself at how lucky he'd been to infiltrate the prosecutor's case against Roberto Menendez and even get invited down to El Paso to learn everything the government was doing. To him, it was a clear sign of the holy purpose for which he struggled. That turned his mind to the power plants across the country. His target was the one at Monticello.

Licensed by the Nuclear Regulatory Commission in 1970, the plant operated a single boiling-water nuclear reactor. Built by General Electric, it was the BWR-3 design, which could generate 613 megawatts of electric power or more, if authorized by the NRC.

Generating the power was a simple process. The fission of uranium atoms created immense amounts of heat. Water flowing through the reactor boiled to create steam, which turned huge turbine generators, creating an electric current. The reactor core held 484 fuel assemblies. Each assembly was about fourteen feet long and contained a square collection of individual fuel rods, each one about the diameter of a human finger.

Every twenty-two months, the plant operators shut down the plant. One third of the used fuel assemblies were removed and replaced with new ones. The used ones were moved from the reactor and stored in a pool inside the reactor. Brown had learned that the process created the most vulnerable point at which to blow the plant. And since it only occurred once every twenty-two months, the timing for Brown's plan had to be precise.

The Nuclear Regulatory Commission had warned of two emergency planning zones around nuclear power plants in the event of a radioactive leak. The first was the *plume exposure pathway zone,* which was estimated at a ten-mile radius and referred to exposure and inhalation of radioactive contamination. The second they called the *ingestion pathway zone* of about fifty miles in radius and referred to people ingesting either food or liquid contaminated by radioactivity.

Brown knew these emergency zones would be meaningless, because what he planned wasn't a mere leak, but a complete opening of the reactor. It would be like setting a sealed can of baked beans into a fire and waiting for the pressure inside to blow the can and beans all over in maximum dispersion patterns. It had taken him years of careful, meticulous work to set it all up.

Then Brown had found Bernie, the nuclear engineer, and things had gotten even better.

When Brown was a cop, he'd busted Bernie for sexual assault on underage girls. Three years ago, he'd found Bernie working at the power plant in Monticello under an alias and a faked identity because convicted sexual offenders were required to register with the state, which he hadn't done. Brown recognized the fragile position Bernie was in, but instead of blackmailing him Brown worked to convert him. In a few months, Bernie saw the sinful life he'd led and changed, becoming a true believer and dedicating himself to the same mission as Jeremy Brown. Jeremy felt proud. Not only had he saved a sinner, he'd enlisted a soldier.

Bernie had described the layout of the plant. After he drove through the tight security, Bernie faced two square buildings flanked by a narrow tower. The tower exhausted the spent gases and water vapor into the air high above the plant. Inside the square buildings the reactor itself worked twenty-four hours a day. Everything was painted tan or light green and was made of either metal or fire-resistant fiberboard.

Bernie had taught Brown how the explosion would do the most damage and where to place the charges. The hard part, of course, was getting the plastic explosives inside the facility and into place at the exact time. That problem had stumped them both for months. Suddenly, a blessing had occurred for Brown. In February of 2011, the Nuclear Regulatory Commission had discovered extensive cracking and material distortion in the Marathon control rod blades at the Monticello plant.

"What's that mean?" Brown had demanded from Bernie when he met Brown and told him in excited, choppy sentences.

"They're kind of like brakes on a nuclear reactor. They can slow down or stop the control rod from inserting when reducing power or shutting down. The NRC said the cracked ones had to be replaced. That's our opening."

"I don't get it."

"They have to be replaced. We can hide the explosives in packaging material to look like they're new control rod blades. They'll be delivered inside the plant. I'll intercept them and deploy the charges in the critical spots around the plant."

"How you gonna avoid security?"

"When we shut down for the twenty-two month refueling changes, the plant drops to a skeleton crew. There won't be many people around. I'm authorized to stay and work on the replacement assemblies."

Brown smiled at the blessings from the Lord. He received a text message that more cash from the church had been deposited into several accounts.

As Brown clicked-off his cell and started the truck, he allowed a brief smile and sense of satisfaction to run through him. Truly, the God of Abraham provided for the Elect like him and his family. He felt a momentary twinge of sorrow as he thought of all the people who were unbelievers and how they'd be left behind to suffer. Only the Elect would be saved. Brown sighed. It was not for him to question the wisdom or laws of God.

To make absolutely sure things went as planned, he turned to drive up to Crystal, an older suburb of Minneapolis loaded with cheap homes where Paco had stashed Shereen. If he still needed it, Brown would use her as his "insurance policy" against the prosecution.

CHAPTER 21

A BLACK MACHINE ABOUT HALF the size of a shoebox sat in the middle of Dr. Leonard's table. A short black electric cable hung by itself from the left side of the box and a zip drive poked out of the right side. The name Cellebrite was printed in slanting blue letters on top of the machine just under an LED screen.

After court, Paul had brought Zehra to Dr. Charles Leonard's laboratory, hoping he could give her anything to help win the trial. Days before, he had delivered Roberto Menendez's iPhone to the scientist.

Lifting a finger in the air, Dr. Leonard announced that he was opening the seventh can of Coke for the day. "Keeps me alert," he said. "Want one?"

Leonard's house and lab were located in an older corner of Minneapolis called Prospect Park. The streets in the area curled in circles as they climbed up to the crest of a hill, guarded by an old water tower with a roof that resembled a witch's dark green hat. Under the roof of the unsued tower, vacant open windows stared sightlessly over the bare tree tops below.

The houses in the neighborhood didn't match any consistent architectural style. Like the extensive gardens around them, the houses grew in different shapes, sizes, and colors. Some even seemed to bend to one side as if they were organic, growing objects themselves.

In the car, Zehra leaned back to try and relax. She smelled Paul's cologne that he'd worn since law school. So typical of him. Steady, dependable, and attractive. What would she do without him?

Following directions, Paul and Zehra arrived at the black cupola-domed Russian Orthodox Church. Its windows were dark. Leaves blew through the black wrought-iron fence that guarded the church. They turned right and headed up the hill to Leonard's house.

Outside his lab, the full sun shone through bare branches and drooping bushes. Without the shelter of leaves, it felt hot on Zehra's back as she walked up to the house. Small gray flocks of sparrows fluttered among the branches, playing in the sun. They chirped and chased each other around in circles. Most of the other birds had left before the coming winter.

Inside the lab, Paul told him, "Charlie, we haven't got much time, like I told you." He glanced over at Zehra. "Can you give Zehra the short version of what you're gonna do?" A stale smell of old cigar smoke clung to the walls and furniture.

Leonard slurped from the Coke and set it down on the table before him. He talked slowly. "I'll start the acquisition of data with the Cellebrite." He nodded at the black machine on the table. "Even though my old pals at the sheriff's lab have given you the data that was still on the phone, the tough part was to find the deleted material."

"How do you do that?" Paul asked.

"There are about fifty tools for extraction of deleted material," Leonard explained. "Trouble is, I don't know which one will work for this phone. Intuition helps. That's the art of this process. Sounds boring, but us geeks love this stuff."

"Why's it so tough?"

"Remember, there's over 3,000 different phones out there. Each company uses slightly different technology. There's a staggering variety of different proprietary platforms, unlike a computer, where you've got either a Mac or a PC."

"So where are we?" Paul talked quickly.

"I've narrowed this down to about ten tools for extracting deleted material from an iPhone. I can usually go back almost two years."

"Why do you need so many tools?"

"Some tools work better at extracting video or photos. Others are better for retrieving texts or emails or PINs. Takes about two days."

"No," Zehra shouted. When Dr. Leonard stared at her, she realized he didn't understand her predicament.

"I'll prepare an analysis and a report for you."

Paul blew out a big breath. "We can't wait." Zehra caught his eye and smiled at his support.

Leonard lifted his eyebrows as if Paul was the most ignorant person in the world, but he went to work. "The Cellebrite's an Israeli product. Universal Forensic Extraction Device. It's the flagship tool, but these suckers aren't cheap. Put me back $5,000—"

Paul interrupted, "Just tell us what you're doing."

Leonard blinked, sipped from his Coke, and picked up the iPhone. "Let's see . . ." Leonard popped out the battery from the phone and studied the label beneath the battery.

Lifting the Cellebrite, he plugged in a new zip drive on the right side. "Our target," he told them. From a case on the floor he fingered through a series of electric cables, all about eight inches long. "This one may work."

"What's that?" Zehra asked.

"About eighty-five cables come with the instrument. Depending on the phone, different cables can extract the data we want. I'm guessing this'll work."

"Guess?" Zehra said. Her stomach rumbled, and she wondered if all the time spent here would be worth it.

There was an edge to Leonard's voice. "The process is incredibly complicated. I don't know if I can get a damn thing off this phone. Cable A may extract text messages but only Cable B will get photos." He swept his hand to the side where Paul stood to move him away.

Outside, bare branches rapped against the window in the living room. Wind groaned along the side of the house.

Leonard attached the iPhone to the cable he'd selected and plugged the other end of it into the left side of the Cellebrite. He turned on the power and watched as numbers slipped across the small screen. A message told him to use Cable 56, which Leonard used.

In ten minutes, he said, "Ah . . . looks good so far."

"What?" Paul asked.

"I'm getting the live data. This is the same material the sheriffs got when they did their initial extraction. I know you already got this, but it's the first step in extracting the deleted data." Leonard looked up at them. "Deleted data can last for months. Sometimes I can get phone book information, calendars, texts, missed calls, what calls were incoming, email, photos, videos, and even web browsing activities—if we're lucky."

Zehra stepped back. "So, I thought everything on my phone was private . . . that's not true?"

Leonard laughed hard until a cough from deep in his chest stopped him. "Too many cigars," he apologized. "No. We think our lives are private and protected, but we're all walking around naked."

"How about PIN's or encryption protection?" Zehra asked.

"Slows me down. I've got software that can usually crack them."

Paul moved next to Dr. Leonard. "Look, we gotta get this information as soon as possible. Are you almost done?"

Leonard glanced at Zehra and looked back at Paul. "You don't get it, do you? This ain't easy." He frowned.

Zehra slumped into the dumpy chair in the corner. It stank of cigar smoke. Must be where Leonard lived all the time when he wasn't working at the desk. Paul noticed and turned back to Dr. Leonard.

"I told you I want this done right now. You want your contract with the government renewed?"

Leonard blinked a few times.

An hour later, he found them in the living room. "Got some dynamite data for you guys."

Back in his lab, he showed them his report. It read:

The following evidence was examined at the request of FBI Agent, Paul Schmitt:

1. iPhone 5310b Cellular Phone, IMEI: 537554201232951
2. T-mobile SIM Card, IMSI: 1098206280059012755
3. Unknown Brand 1GB MicroSD Card, Model: SD-CO1G

Examiner attempted to retrieve the following information from each piece of evidence:

1. Address book
2. Call History
3. Images/video
4. Stored Audio
5. Text message

The following equipment and software were used during the examination to retrieve or document data:

1. Encase 6.17

2. FTK Imager 3.0

3. Cellebrite Universal Forensic Extraction Device

4. App: 1.1.5.6 UFED

5. Cellebrite Physical Analyzer Version 1.8

6. EnScript program (To search the unallocated space—where the deleted files reside)

The contacts, call history, text messages, calendar, images, video, and phone information stored in the cell phone were transferred onto a USB thumb drive.

The results of the file system dump were placed in a zip file.

The examiner attempted to process the MicroSD card but was unable to get the Windows operating system to mount the device.

The examiner also performed a search for deleted images using the file finder EnScript to search the unallocated spaces. Information about the items such as creation date, file paths, and hash values are also included in the report.

On a table to the right, Leonard pulled the flash drive out of the right side of the Cellebrite and moved to a large desk in the middle of the room. He sat before a PC and inserted the flash drive.

"See?" He glowed as if he'd discovered a new planet in the universe. "Luck and my skill got this."

"What?" Paul asked.

Leonard paused as if to emphasize the importance of his work. "Look at this." He pointed at the PC screen. "Doesn't always work, but this time I scored."

"We haven't got any time left," Zehra insisted.

"Of course. You're aware, I'm sure, that in e-discovery technologies there are two general categories."

They looked at him with blank expressions.

"Back up, Charles," Dr. Leonard talked to himself. "One is called 'linguistic' which means the software uses key words or phrases to find data that's related. Kind of like a Google search."

"Sure." Zehra understood.

"I use software that's described as 'sociological.' This approach adds an inferential layer of analysis, mimicking the deductive powers of people. It will mine the data from the cell phone for activities and interactions of the user with other people."

"Did you get emails and address books?" Paul asked.

"Yes. But I'm going to show you something even better." He paused to raise his finger in the air. "The software seeks chains of events or discussions that have taken place across email, texts, phone calls, or even media like Facebook."

"All of that data is available?" Zehra asked. "Like from my phone?"

"Of course, but you'd need the equipment I've got and," he paused, "my expertise."

"I see what you mean when you said we're all 'walking around naked.'"

"Not only can I get the substance of the data, the software I'm about to demonstrate can pick out the networks the data flows through. Here." Dr. Leonard pointed toward the screen. After a few keystrokes, a starburst pattern appeared on the screen. It had a pink center with dense clusters of lines that radiated outward in thin black lines. "See?"

"See what?" Zehra said.

"This starburst represents hundreds of messages that have been sent or received by this cell phone over a month's period of time. Each of these tiny lines is a connection with someone else. As the frequency of communication increases, the chart starts to turn color. That's why you have this pink center. That's where the most activity occurred."

Paul traced his finger above the screen. "What's that show us?"

"It can help us identify the most important decision makers or as I call 'em, the 'movers and shakers.' Here's your key source." Dr. Leonard's finger pushed Paul's aside.

"Do you know who?"

"Not yet, but this person's clearly at the center of this network. Now watch this." Leonard grinned as he keyed quickly. Another chart that looked like a constellation in the nighttime sky appeared on the screen.

"Looks like the Big Dipper." Zehra allowed herself a chuckle.

"This is a more detailed analysis of a smaller group," Leonard explained. "The software takes the most dense patterns and draws them apart. This will give us the relationships among individuals and assess their communication.

So, in this one we see what looks like the handle of the dipper comes from the user of this cell phone."

"Roberto Menendez?" said Zehra.

"The line connects with the unknown source. Notice how the bowl part of the dipper has Menendez and the unknown. The unknown is bigger because of more activity. Although this phone, the one Menendez had, indicates he's in on the communications, the unknown is the key decision maker, as demonstrated by the number and frequency of communications."

"Let's go back to the starburst," Paul said. When Leonard had clicked back to the previous screen, Paul leaned in closer to study the pattern. "Here's another pink area. What's that?"

Dr. Leonard wrinkled his nose in order to lift his glasses closer to his eyes. He stroked the keys again. "Here we go." Another "constellation" screen came up. "Check it out. And here's dense, dense activity with someone near the Canadian border. Wow . . ." The doctor whistled.

An uneasy feeling crabbed its way up Zehra's back. She remembered Kathy Johnson's warning. She might be correct. "What's the bottom line?"

"The software also is able to pounce on something called 'social anomalies.' These are instances where the user may switch media to try to hide sensitive or illegal activities. We can see that in these patterns all the time. The software can also recognize the 'sentiment' in an email."

"Son of a bitch, that's amazing," Paul said.

Zehra edged Paul aside from the computer screen. "Amazing, but we've only got a day left . . ." Her voice carried a desperate edge to it.

Paul spun the doctor's chair around to face him and pushed his face close to Leonard. "No more college lectures," he shouted. "What other evidence do you have to nail this guy? Right now, what have we got?"

Leonard gulped several times from his can of Coke. "Okay, okay. There is something unusual."

"What?"

"There's a phone contact that's near the Canadian border. Don't know where for sure, but look at all the traffic." Leonard keyed up another screen. "Both calls and texts." He swiveled the chair to face his PC directly. "Why didn't I think of this before?" He slapped the table. "Let's look at a timeline." His fingers blurred over the keyboard. He looked up, turned the screen so Zehra could see better, and smiled. "Just what I hoped for."

"Huh?"

"Timeline. See . . . all the contacts between the network to the location in Canada increased tremendously and then suddenly stopped at this date." He squinted at the screen.

"The day Menendez was busted and we got his phone." Zehra asked him, "Can you get the identity of the unknown phone and the location in Canada?"

"Take a while, but sure. Then I'll check on the GPS signals and plot them against a Google Earth map." He turned to Zehra. "I'll let you know right away."

Outside, the wind surrounded them with cold damp air. Just as Zehra got back into Paul's car, her phone rang. She recognized the first six digits of a Hennepin County number. She answered.

"Z, this is Detroit." Her breath came in gasps. "I just heard."

"Heard what?" Something was wrong.

"Ms. Guzman, our Spreigl witness."

"Yeah?"

Detroit took a deep breath. "She won't come."

"She won't testify?"

"No, 'cause I can't find her."

"Oh, shit." Zehra felt her chest collapse as if someone had hit her. Panic rose in her body and she leaned over into Paul's arms.

"Z, I'm sorry. Feel like it's my fault."

Zehra wanted to cry. After all the work they'd done, their case in chief was still impossibly weak, and now even the evidence of Menendez's actions in El Paso would never be presented to the jury.

Paul could sense the problem and hugged her tighter. She turned her face up to look at him. "Now what do I do?"

CHAPTER 22

Friday, November 4

H
IT 'EM WITH THE BLOOD AND GUTS FIRST. I always do." Liz wheezed over the phone. She wasn't doing well. Back to more bed rest.

"I've been doing that for two days. Dr. Wong testified yesterday about the autopsy . . . with lots of photos," Zehra said.

"How's 'Chopsticks' these days?"

Dr. Helen Wong was the Hennepin County chief medical examiner, and because of her crude but excellent work in autopsies, she was called "Chopsticks" behind her back. Zehra said, "She's great. She finally got the second position as a professor at the university."

"'Bout time. Helen's certainly qualified, and the man before her got the two positions automatically. And how about Hollywood?"

"I don't know. He's disappeared."

Liz coughed. "Disappeared? Just as the trial started?" She waited. "Unusual."

"He's promised to help me . . ." Zehra decided not to bring Liz in on Shereen's disappearance. "But I really need it now." Zehra paused. "Today, I'm calling the cop who first found the body."

Liz paused. Her voice lowered. "Don't give up, Z. I thought that witness from Texas, Guzman, was a long shot anyway. We still got enough of a circumstantial case to win. Sparkle will be the key."

"I know."

"And that strange conversation you had with the woman from NorthStar . . . weird."

"Her warning about Canada? None of the feds have said anything like that to me. Besides, it's hard for me to even talk with Johnson after what they did to you."

Liz barked a rough, ragged cough. "Naw. Wasn't their fault. Was mine with all those damn cigarettes and no exercise on a fifty-four-year-old body."

"Reward yourself with some new clothes."

"How about the dicks from Washington?"

"They want to talk to me at the noon recess."

"Pricks. They always come in with lots of noise and money and swagger. Tell 'em from me to kiss my ass."

"My exact words. Gotta run."

Zehra called Jeremy Brown. Still no answer, which frustrated her. He'd promised to check out the mall about Shereen. Tomorrow, Saturday, she'd get a break from the trial and would be able to get Paul to help with the search. A thought struck her, and she called her mother.

"Hey, I've been so busy that I almost forgot. Shereen was interested in some guy at the mall that she met at the food court. Maybe they could find her through him." Her mother agreed. The thought of Shereen missing slashed through Zehra's chest in a hot flash, and she hung up.

Zehra started to shut off her cell phone. She noticed an email from Cindy in Texas.

"still checking. went back into Menendez's case and discovered a series of domestic assaults against the diaz woman, 1 time tried to shoot her. this must be different woman than the one u told me about earlier. if u still need witnesses 2 testify against him—hope u don't mind—i'll see if i can still find diaz. maybe . . ."

In ten minutes, she got off the elevator on the courtroom floor. She ran into an old friend of hers from the public defender's office, Randi Friedman, a newer lawyer in the office, her face flushed red. "Hey, what's wrong?" Zehra asked her.

Randi took a deep breath. "Just had my first experience with 'trial delusion.' You know, when you get so into the case that you lose all perspective and you actually began to believe your client?"

"Happens to all of us."

"Well, this is worse. I just got a 'not guilty' verdict with a 'kiddie twiddler.' Accused of sexually assaulting a young girl. I got so excited by the verdict that I hugged him."

"So?"

"So, until I remembered what he'd done to the girl. He'd bit off her nipple and said it tasted like Cheerios."

"Ugh. Take a shower." Zehra put her hand on Randi's shoulder. "I remember the case I had as a public defender where the judge had to specifically order my client not to masturbate in grocery store vegetable sections anymore."

They chuckled at the absurdity of it all and for support in the tough jobs they both had.

In ten minutes, Zehra sat beside Barry at the counsel table. The jury sat in their row of chairs and Mezerretti leaned back in his chair, chatting into the ear of one of his blonde clerks. Menendez sat passively next to him. While they all waited for the judge to come out, Zehra snatched a few glances at Menendez. Although Mezerretti had prepped him well and was keeping him under control, Zehra studied his eyes.

Black dots were pinned in the middle of his eyes. His flaccid expression didn't betray anything about him, but the eyes moved constantly. They probed all over the courtroom, especially at the jurors, as if he could convince them with a stare that he was an innocent man. Then Zehra noticed that his eyes jiggled. Nervous? Scared? Angry? Something behind them must be crackling through his brain.

In a swirl of activity, Judge Von Wald came out of the tall door next to her raised bench, and with robes billowing behind her, hurried up the steps to sit behind the large granite desk.

She looked at Zehra. "Is the State ready to call its next witness?"

Zehra stood. "We call Officer Bradley Pickens."

Detroit, who sat in the back of the courtroom, rose with a laptop in her hand and walked out of the courtroom into the hall. She returned, followed by a police officer in full uniform. Zehra and Detroit had agreed the uniform would be important and made sure the officer wore it for his testimony before the jury. He was young, tall, and muscular, with a shaved head and red moustache. As he walked to the middle of the courtroom and stood before the bench, the equipment on his belt clanked in rhythm to his steps.

Zehra scrolled through several screens on her laptop until she came to the part of her trial notebook which contained a scanned copy of the officer's report. She'd use that report as the basis for her direct examination, with the addition of critical questions she and Liz had put together weeks ago when they'd interviewed the officer.

After he stated his name and occupation as a Hamel police officer, Zehra gave him plenty of time to fill in his professional background. She wanted to impress the jury with the quality of the witness to increase the jury's willingness to believe him.

"On October 4th we received a call about the sounds of shooting." The officer talked in a matter-of-fact manner and was instructed by Zehra to look at the jury when he answered, not at her.

"Did you investigate?"

"My squad was the closest to the address so I proceeded to the address."

"What did you find?"

"When I turned the corner by Inn Kahoots, I saw what looked like a rolled up blanket partially lying in the street."

"Inn Kahoots?"

"Oh, yeah. That's a local restaurant. Oldest building in Hamel."

"What did you do next?"

"I stopped my squad several feet away from the object to avoid contaminating the crime scene. I approached on foot and determined it was the body of a young man."

"Was anyone else present?"

"At that time, several people had come out of the Super America across the street from where the body was found. I kept them back from the scene."

"What did you do, Officer Pickens?"

"Once I determined it was a body, I knelt down to check for vitals. I found none so I radioed in for backup and the sheriff's forensic team. I remained with the body. My job at that point, until backup arrives, was to secure the crime scene. It looked like the man had been killed by a bullet wound to the head."

"Objection," Mezerretti stood and shouted for the benefit of the media in the courtroom. "Witness is not competent to testify about the cause of death. Only a doctor can determine that."

"Sustained."

"What did you observe on the body?"

Pickens paused and his face furrowed into a serious, troubled expression. He said, "I found his body stretched out, facing away from an entertainment bar. It was positioned partially around a parked car, with the lower half of the body in the gutter of the street. Body was fully dressed. His right leg was cocked at an angle, as if he'd been running when he was shot." He looked across the jury as Zehra had instructed him to do, to make eye contact with them.

"Objection. Calls for speculation as to what the victim was doing prior to the officer finding his body."

"Sustained."

Zehra asked, "Could you estimate an age?"

"Young. Late twenties maybe. He had blonde hair, at least the little left on his head."

"Why do you say that?"

"There was a lot of blood beneath his head that had puddled onto the pavement. It looked like there was a fresh entrance wound in the back of his head, and most of the top of his head and skull were missing."

"Any other wounds?"

"Not that I observed. His face was turned sideways, as if he were looking across the intersection to the Super America."

"Notice anything about the face?"

"Yes. He had an expression of fear or terror on—"

"Objection," Mezerretti shouted. "Competence, and besides, this is being done solely to play on the emotions of the jury." He puffed his chest out and shook his head.

"Yes," Judge Von Wald said as she leaned down toward the officer. "Sustained. Sir, please limit your testimony to what facts you observed. You can't speculate what the victim may have thought."

"But, Your Honor, that's what I saw. His eyes bulged, his teeth were bared, and the skin pulled back—"

Mezerretti thundered an objection again. "Any number of reasons could have caused a facial expression. That doesn't prove the victim's emotional state at all."

Judge Von Wald scowled at the officer. "Don't make me follow up on my warning."

Zehra looked around and glanced at Detroit. Their eyes met, and without showing it, they both smiled at each other. The officer was doing a great job. The more they could "humanize" the victim to the jury, it would remind them that in spite of the official legalese and the sterile setting of a courtroom, this was about the death of a real human being.

Zehra asked, "Did you find any witnesses?"

"One that I talked to later was named Yelena Mostropov. She was also called Sparkle."

"Do you know why she was there?"

"Uh, I believe she was employed at the bar as a dancer."

"Any other witnesses?"

Pickens knew the answer to the question but paused to avoid making his testimony look rehearsed. "There was another man with Ms. Mostropov. We attempted to stop and question him, but he fled before we could identify him. We've been unable to locate him since then."

Zehra sat down and told Mezerretti he could ask questions. Wisely, he didn't have anything to ask the cop. After all, the witness hadn't linked his client to the dead body, so there wasn't much that Mezerretti could gain from more questions.

By noon, Zehra had put three more witnesses on the stand. These were routine sheriff's deputies and investigative people, including the preliminary forensic witnesses.

She led Barry back to her office, took off her shoes, and thought about raiding the chocolate cupcake in the lower drawer. Luckily, with Barry there she felt embarrassed enough to stop. She was about to give Barry a ten minute break for a sandwich when she checked her cell phone. Mansfield had called.

She dialed and heard him answer on his cell. "Hey, Zehra, thanks for the call. How's the trial going?"

"Great," she lied and started brushing white lint off her suit. She curled her legs underneath herself.

"At this point, either I or Special Agent Long could testify about the trafficking ring. We've got enough evidence to put Menendez right in the middle of it." His voice sounded upbeat and excited.

Zehra dropped her head.

Barry looked up. "What? What's wrong?"

"Zehra? You still there?" Mansfield asked.

"Yeah. Unfortunately, I'm still here with the same case . . . a murder case. Not an international gun trafficking case. Thanks, but your evidence won't help much. Besides, the trial has already started." She sighed and was about to hang up. "Wait a minute. A woman from that NGO, NorthStar Group, talked to me about some plot that Menendez is involved in to smuggle something like a weapon or nuke into Minnesota through Canada. In the next couple days. Local contact named 'Horseman.' What about that?"

"Canada? Oh, yeah, Schmitt mentioned something." Mansfield suppressed a chuckle. "A nuke? What? Disguise them as walleye fishermen?" The chuckle turned into a polite laugh. "'Fraid not. The ingress routes out of Mexico into Texas and Arizona have been used for years. One of them is even called 'the Milky Way' because of all the kids they bring in through it. None of our intel shows the traffickers altering the routes they've worked so long and built up with so much bribe money. Tell that crazy woman to quit bothering you."

"Well, maybe you're right. Paul Schmitt agrees with you, too." She hung up, frustrated that for all their promises early on, in the end they had produced nothing of help to her. Liz was right. Zehra grunted when she realized she'd forgotten to tell Mansfield what they could do to Liz.

Barry asked her, "What are we gonna tell the judge about the Guzman woman?"

"We have to let her know we probably can't get the witness up here."

Zehra was about to kick Barry out so she could do her noon prayers when she heard a knock on the door. She uncurled her legs from underneath herself and walked to the office door. Detroit burst through and collapsed in the chair next to Barry. She wouldn't look at anyone. Behind her, Homicide Detective Joel Henderson walked in. In his fifties, he was slightly overweight, had dull gray hair, and had worked his way up the Byzantine chess board politics of the Minneapolis Police Department. In spite of all that, he was a damn good homicide cop.

"Zehra," he said between clenched teeth.

What was wrong? She looked at Detroit, who still hung her head. "What?"

Henderson sighed deeply. He nodded toward her desk. She followed that look and sat in her chair. He sat slowly while propping his palms on the tops of his knees. Settled into the chair, he lifted sad eyes to look at Zehra. "Yelena Mostropov, your main witness, is dead."

For a moment, Zehra drifted far away and the sound of his voice took a long time to travel to reach her. A single word finally struck her ears. *Dead.* "Wha . . . ?"

"M.E. took a look this morning when she was found in her apartment. Thinks it's an overdose."

"Z, I'm so sorry. I talked to the girl a few days ago. She was cool with comin' in. Nervous, but she sounded real cool." Detroit almost cried.

"Who?"

Henderson shook his head slowly. "Apartment was clean. With a person like Sparkle, unfortunately it could be an overdose or almost anyone could've done her. We're hesitating to call it a homicide at this point, but frankly, who knows for sure?"

Suddenly, the office went silent except for the ringing that echoed around Zehra. She felt her chest constrict as panic started to claw its way up into her stomach, across her chest. She wished the others weren't there. She slowed her breathing and thrust her mind to her favorite beach. She tried to feel the warm sun in spite of the scene outside her window of gray clouds, light rain, and cold wind.

Zehra fought the panic, got on top of it and managed to suppress it. She took a deep breath and came back into the sound of the office around her. "Now what the hell do we do?"

No one helped by answering.

She sighed. "I guess we shouldn't have gone so far from home with this one. Bud was right all along." She looked from one person to another and ended with Barry. "After the noon recess, we don't need to tell Von Wald about Guzman. We got a bigger problem."

"We gonna throw the case out?"

"Can't see any alternative. I know we can't prove the murder now, and we have an ethical duty to dismiss if we know we can't." Zehra felt like all the air and water and weight had been drawn out of her body to leave it hollowed out. She wondered how it could remain sitting upright in the chair. Her body should collapse.

Detroit said in a quiet voice, "Should I call off the rest of the witnesses?"

Zehra roused herself and was about to tell her yes, when an image of the victim flitted through her mind, followed by an image of Sparkle and the memory of the rape tree, and all the innocent people who were preyed on by men like Menendez. The thought of Menendez walking out of the courtroom, his little eyes finding hers while he grinned, made her angry. Furious.

"No," Zehra told Detroit. "I don't know what to do, but I'm going to tell the judge everything. I'll ask her for a recess from the trial. At least through the weekend. On Monday, we'll have to make the final decision." She stood and faced them.

No one spoke, and Zehra's cell phone buzzed. She glanced at it, thankful to have the distraction. It was a call from Dr. Leonard. She answered it.

"Ms. Hassan, I've got the information you wanted. I finished the GPS mapping and thought you had time after trial this afternoon, you could stop by and we'd go through it together."

"Uh . . . I'm not sure we'll need it . . . Thanks, I'll get back to you on that."

"Also, I've got the name of the other phone that was most often linked to the iPhone that you brought me for testing. This phone is a decision maker, linked to hundreds of other communication networks across the country."

"Who?"

"Person named Jeremy Brown."

CHAPTER 23

I JUST GOT THE WORD AND WE'RE MOVING," Kevin Stout shouted.

"This is ridiculous, Kevin," Jamie Solomon said.

"You're either with us or not. This is our chance to stop these guys before they go nuclear. We can't delay," he insisted.

"I say we call the authorities. What can we do by ourselves?"

Kathy Johnson remained silent, sitting in the corner of the "executive" suite of the NorthStar Group. The suite was in the lower level of a dingy group of offices at Lake Street and Bryant Avenue. Above them, the Bryant Lake Bowl, a combination bowling alley, theatre, and restaurant, rumbled all the time from bowling balls thrown on lanes above their office space. She watched the argument grow in intensity between Jamie and Kevin. Kathy knew Jamie was probably right, but her gut urged her to support Kevin and to try and be a part of the excitement.

"I warned you that you'd screw up our whole mission if you got involved with these other thugs. That's not us and never has been."

Kevin stood and paced around the small room. He carried a stained coffee cup that advertised the law school where he taught. "You just don't get it, do you? For years, we've talked. That's all, Jamie—talked. Now we finally have a chance to act. Besides, this is the scariest thing I've ever seen from these nuts."

"That's why we have FBI and police and border guys to stop it." Jamie shook her head at Kevin's childish display.

Kathy interrupted, "Can I ask what, exactly, we're talking about? Do you mean we'd get into something violent?"

Above them, they heard a sharp crash as a bowling ball smashed into wooden pins.

Kevin stopped pacing and turned to her. "Not us, personally. But we've got contacts with other national groups that could use force to stop these guys.

We'd go along for the ride." He spun to face Jamie. "And that's my God damn point. We're just along for the ride. They do the dirty work."

"No. We shouldn't even be associated with that kind of thing. We're a non-violent group. Once we go down that road, our cred is shot. And you know that." Jamie's voice rose even higher.

"I'm not taking a van with the name 'NorthStar' plastered across it. We'll go undercover."

"Oh, my God. Kevin, you sound like the child you really are. Besides, I know you. You can't keep your mouth shut if you tried." Jamie slammed her hand on the desk. Her small body quivered with anger and her face puffed red.

Kathy had to agree with Jamie. Kevin might promise to keep quiet, but he loved the limelight. Still, the thought of the possible excitement stirred her. "What if we just went as observers?"

"See." Kevin swept his hand toward Kathy. "She's right. We go just as observers. Do you think I'll be in the front of the charge with a bayonet attached to my rifle, going over the top?" He spoke loudly. Suddenly, he spread his legs and posed in a kung-fu stance. "Hai," he yelled.

Kathy laughed. "Kevin, what the hell are you doing?"

"Trained in this years ago. For the movement in the sixties."

"Don't hurt your rotator cuffs."

"Look, Kevin." Jamie ignored his jumping around. "If you two do this, you're on your own. I'm going to the board this afternoon to make the record. I don't want you to ruin all the hard work we've done." She slid into her leather jacket. "Besides, Kevin, you've never been north of Anoka. You'll get lost up there in the woods."

Kevin shrugged. "Do what you have to. Just remember my words: when we bring down the biggest militia plot in history, we'll be the heroes."

Jamie waved her hand in front of her to dismiss Kevin and walked across the room and up the five steps to get to the street level. A puff of cold air billowed in from the open door.

Kathy commented on it, "It's getting cold too early this year."

"Storms predicted for up north."

"That's where we're going, isn't it?"

"Yeah." Kevin crossed the room to face her. He pulled her up into his arms. "It's just you and me, babe. Takin' on the bad guys."

"You're so full of shit. I don't think *we're* going to do much of anything."

He raised his eyebrows. "There'll be some rough stuff to get through. These traffickers won't be easy."

"So, what can we do?"

"I'm working with a small but tough organization that has guys who can fight fire with fire. They're ready to come with us to the northern border. We leave tomorrow morning. You're coming with me, aren't you?"

Kathy paused for a moment, worried about what might happen, but also thrilled at the idea. How many times does a nurse in a dull job get to race up to the Canadian border to stop international criminals? "Of course," she said. "Where are we going?"

"I've been in contact with some of our group who work in Canada. They've pinpointed three spots the traffickers could cross. Two involve small towns, and one is through a national park wilderness area. That's our first choice. Thing is, we don't know for sure. Best thing we can do now is pack up and get ourselves in position with the team."

"The team?"

"Yeah. The guys who can actually stop the transfer."

"Will anyone get hurt?"

Kevin shook his head. His eyes lost their focus. "We hope to hell not. Depends on the bad guys and how they're coming across."

"This is the same group that Roberto Menendez is part of?"

"He's right in the middle of this whole thing. And so is that church. We'll break open the whole thing and expose 'em all."

"I don't know, Kevin . . ."

Kevin turned on her, his face red and contorted. "Want to see more of the blogs, the chat room crazy shit?" He snapped his fingers in the air. "Reminds me. The number eighteen mentioned in that blog I showed you."

"What about it?"

"The church, the end times. If you divide the eighteen by three . . ."

"Why three?"

"The Trinity. If you divide it by three, you get six, six, six. In the Bible, that's the number of the mark of the beast. It all makes sense."

"Then shouldn't we tell someone? The police? The FBI?"

"What the hell would they do? Think they'd believe us? And even if they did, how fast would they move? By the time they 'got approval,' these extreme crazies would have done whatever they're gonna do. It'd be too late to stop them."

"Well. I don't know . . ."

"Okay, Kathy. Tell you what. If it'll make you feel better, you call 'em." He grinned. "Tell them everything and see where it goes." He set down the coffee mug. Energy coiled off him in waves. He started to dart around the room as he talked. "We'll get packed up tonight, and I'll come to get you early. Five o'clock. We got a long way to go up to the Canadian border."

"And . . . where are we going?" She shook her head.

"We'll start traveling up there, and I'll be in contact with our people on the border. They've got spotters out this weekend to try and intercept the transfer. When they find 'em, we move in."

Kathy's mind spun. Part of her realized this was a ridiculous plan. They should tell the authorities and let them take care of it. But part of her tingled with the crazy possibility that they might be able to do something. If Kevin really had a group of men who could fight the crooks, wouldn't it be exciting to be there to see what happened?

She thought of all that needed to be prepared before tomorrow morning. Then her rational mind kicked in again. Kathy really should tell someone in law enforcement. But who? Who did she know? Who would really listen to her?

Zehra Hassan. Kathy had already talked to her, and she'd seemed receptive. Besides, Menendez was involved in the plot. Maybe Hassan would be happy to learn about the plan and could use it to convict him in trial.

Kevin pushed shut the open file cabinets, finished his coffee, and started to shut off the lights. "It's the chance of a lifetime," he beamed at Kathy. "Catch you at five in the morning."

She walked toward him and grabbed onto his shoulders as he hugged her tightly. They kissed with a deeper passion than usual, fueled by the anticipation of an adventure. Finally, they separated and Kevin stepped out into the cold.

Kathy gathered her coat and slipped into it. She'd tried to warn Kevin that the forecast called for snowstorms up there, but it was so early in the season, he didn't believe it.

Picking up her purse, she dug through it for her keys and also found Zehra Hassan's business card. Kathy looked at it and thought again that she should tell Hassan about the plot. As a prosecutor, maybe she would know what to do.

CHAPTER 24

Friday, November 4, Afternoon

A STREAK OF HEAT SHOT THROUGH ZEHRA that left her gasping for breath. Jeremy Brown.

A common name. Was it the same person? It had to be. She collapsed into her chair, and the momentum of her fall caused it to twirl around. It matched the activity in her brain. How the hell could so much go wrong? Where could she hide? It seemed as if she were trapped in a silent bubble for a long time.

Finally, Zehra heard voices from outside the bubble. Detroit and Barry. Concerned, they both stood over her. She looked up and saw them peering at her like someone might look at an accident victim. Their faces appeared distorted and although their mouths hung open, Zehra didn't hear a thing.

"What happened?" Detroit's voice suddenly crashed through the silent bubble. "Are you okay?"

"Yeah." Zehra waved her hand before her. The old panicky feeling started to climb up her body. She could feel the contours of the edges as it rose. Zehra pushed her chair back to get some room from Detroit and Barry. She thought of a beach, listening for the call of gulls and the smashing waves.

It worked. In five minutes, she recovered enough to stand up. Zehra told them what Dr. Leonard had said. She watched the other two go through the same shock.

"It can't be," Detroit said. "Known that dude for years. Hollywood? No way."

Zehra picked up the office phone and called Bud Grant.

"You're wrong," he said.

"But Dr. Leonard's got the evidence."

"I personally recruited Hollywood. He's got an outstanding record with the police department, and even the governor put him on some commissions. Your expert must be wrong."

Zehra hung up and wondered to herself. Maybe Leonard's research was wrong. After all, it had seemed confusing to Zehra. Brown had disappeared for now, but that didn't mean he was the mastermind of an international trafficking ring. How could he be?

She pictured him in her mind, trying to pick out any clues he might have given in the past. Other than his insistent attempts to convert her, he was handsome, classy, and smart. Zehra had always sensed an inner toughness and ambition in him, but was he a criminal? Liz was in love with him and had been for years. It couldn't be true.

"What are you gonna do?" Detroit asked.

Zehra ran her hands through her thick hair, now tangled and fly away. "Don't know." She looked up at Detroit. "I just can't believe . . ." Zehra called Paul.

He answered. When she told him, there was a long pause of silence on the phone.

"Leonard's the expert, but I can't imagine Hollywood as a criminal. Of course, I always thought he was kind of odd. Not mean or cruel, but hard. Like there was always a chill when he came into a room."

"What should I do?"

"I'll cancel the meeting as soon as I can. Go back to Leonard's. I'll meet you as soon as I can."

She hung up the phone and turned to Barry. "Come on. We've got to tell Judge Von Wald about Sparkle's death. Get her to recess the trial until Monday."

At the judge's courtroom, Mezerretti fought hard to get Zehra to dismiss the case right on the spot. He was clever, and Zehra knew exactly what the stakes were. The Constitution prevented double jeopardy which meant a person couldn't be tried twice for the same crime. Since the jury had been impanelled, if Zehra dismissed the case, she could never prosecute Menendez for the murder again.

Considering it was Friday afternoon and the jury would be excused until Monday anyway, Von Wald agreed to let Zehra have the weekend to decide what to do.

An hour and a half later, Zehra and Barry drove in her new used Audi to Prospect Park. The car was one of the few luxuries she had given herself on a prosecutor's salary. Her old one had blown up—literally—when she had been involved with the terrorists and the Somali boys.

At Leonard's house a sharp wind blew out of the north. Zehra saw gray clouds bunched up in the sky trundling toward them. She'd lived in Minnesota long enough to be able to smell snow coming. She smelled it now.

Barry pulled up his collar around his neck. "Doesn't look good." He glanced up at the sky.

The door opened and Dr. Leonard waved them in as he talked on the cell phone at his ear. The warmth felt good in spite of the stink of stale cigar smoke. Although she'd never asked, Zehra was certain Leonard was single.

"What a dump," Barry whispered. "How does he find anything?"

"I once had a roommate in college, engineering major. Brilliant. Her room was always a cluttered mess. I asked her about it, and she was upset but told me that what looked like a disorganizational method to me was perfectly organized to her. She knew where everything was down to her paper clips."

"So, this guy is wicked smart, huh?"

"Ms. Hassan. You'll be glad you came by. Come into the lab." Leonard motioned for them to follow him. He didn't seem to notice Barry. The doctor swung the rolling chair in front of his PC, scrolled through several screens, and talked to himself.

Zehra interrupted, "Dr. Leonard, about the identification of the other phone. The 'decision maker' you told me about? How certain are you of the identity? Uh, Jeremy Brown?"

He paused to glance at her. Frowning, he seemed offended. "Perfectly certain. Don't you remember the charts I showed you and Paul?"

"Yeah, but . . ."

"There is no mistake about the frequency of communications and interpretations I made from the data. From that point, I have software to check with the phone company to find out who the number was assigned to. Jeremy Brown."

Zehra swallowed and stepped back. She took several deep breaths. She came back to the group. "What about the location?"

"Right. That's what I'm going to show you. You're familiar with Google Earth?"

"Sure."

"I'm going to superimpose the phone locations over a Google Earth map."

Barry interrupted, "How can you tell where the phone's been?"

"Almost all smart phones have a GPS in them, and they transmit thousands of signals all the time. We can plot these fixes on a Google Earth map." He reached around the back side of the screen to retrieve a Coke. Cracking the seal, he slurped loudly.

"Even when the phone is turned off?"

"Yes. I took Menendez's phone and tracked the GPS coordinates, focusing on northern Minnesota, which is where you're interested." He opened a Google Earth picture that covered the states of Minnesota and Wisconsin. He closed the scale until he had the northern half of Minnesota. Moving the cursor up the screen, Leonard could focus an even tighter scale to look at the area around the Canadian border.

"Now, I layer on the GPS fixes." With a click, the screen showed a series of red dots that followed a pattern. "See." He pointed to the trail of red dots. "Those represent the GPS transmissions from Menendez's phone. Now if I zero in on this part down here . . ." He brought the Google Earth map in closer and Zehra could see the dots lined up on Highway 169. She could almost see the phone moving north along the freeway as Menendez had traveled there.

"Amazing," Barry said.

"Show you something interesting." Leonard came in even closer on Interstate 35, and the screen showed the freeway looping onto an exit ramp. They could see trees and the white tops of houses and strip malls. The dots circled the parking lot of the strip mall, came to a point, and then left again for the freeway. "Probably stopped for coffee or to take a leak."

"You can pinpoint where he went on the border?" Zehra asked.

"Sure. I can even create a video that shows where the phone moved." His fingers blurred across the keyboard.

"Can you get us up to the border and identify where Menendez was?"

Leonard scrolled up the map to the northern half of the state. The red dots followed Highway 53 up past the Kabetogama State Forest into International Falls. A small spur of a road turned east and ran into the

Voyageurs National Park. At that point in the wilderness, the distance between Canada and the U.S. was the shortest.

"Can you tell if the phone used by Jeremy Brown was there also?"

Leonard sighed. "Can't work magic. I don't have that phone, so I can't get the GPS coordinates off it."

Zehra shrugged. "But we can probably assume that since he and Menendez were working together, if Menendez went to that location, Brown probably did too."

"Reasonable assumption," Dr. Leonard added.

"Can you print this out for us?"

"Sure. Give me a minute. My printer's acting up." Leonard got up and walked over to his printer, tapped it on the side, and came back. The printer whirred and colored sheets spit out of the bottom.

Zehra hesitated to ask again, but she had to be certain. "You're sure the other phone is Jeremy Brown?"

Dr. Leonard scowled at her in answer.

"Okay, okay. It's just that no one can believe he'd be involved in this."

Leonard smiled. "That's the beauty of my work. I don't have to interact with the messy parts of human life. Of course, in some ways, it's even creepier because I get to see what's happened to people, where they've been, who they communicate with, who they're having an affair with, see the embarrassing videos they've filmed, thinking they were private, the gross sex acts, and what secrets they hide from everyone but me . . ." He glanced up at them. "Hey, anyone want a Coke?"

They both shook their heads and reached for their coats.

"Almost forgot," Dr. Leonard said. "There's one other thing that's really odd. Look at this." He clicked through to another screen. "Menendez made several phone calls to eighteen other cities across the country. From New York, through the Midwest, and even out to the state of Washington."

"What for?"

"Don't know. The calls started six months ago. The same eighteen cities."

"Can you print them out also?" Zehra asked.

When Leonard had finished printing, he handed the list to her. She started to read:

McCandless, PA
Joliet, IL
Pasco, WA
Benton Harbor, MI
Monticello, MN
Green Bay, WISC
Toledo, OH

She folded the paper before finishing all eighteen.

Back in Zehra's Audi, the automatic fan kicked on to bring warm air into the car. She sat for a minute before driving away. "What do we do now?" Fat drops of rain splattered against the windshield. They seemed heavier than usual and rolled off slowly.

"Uh . . . suppose we should tell someone."

"Who? Grant doesn't believe me. Liz would think I'm crazy. I can't just call the police department and tell them one of their most decorated officers has gone rogue and expect them to drop everything to investigate."

"Paul Schmitt? How about those two guys that took you to Texas?"

"Tried them. They insist the southern route into the United States is the one the traffickers would use. The 'Milky Way,' they called it."

"But we've got proof now."

"Right." Zehra pulled her cell out of her purse and sent a text to both Mansfield and Long with a request to get back to her immediately. She looked at her watch and pulled the car out onto University Avenue, heading west for downtown Minneapolis. "We can't just do nothing."

In twenty minutes, they slid under the Government Center to the parking ramp and rode two elevators back up to Zehra's office. She checked her office phone and listened to a voice mail.

"Ms. Hassan, this is Kathy Johnson from the NorthStar Group and I'm, um, sorry to bother you again but I thought it might help you in your trial against Roberto Menendez because you seemed to appreciate the information I gave you the other day."

Come on. Get to the point, Zehra thought.

"Well, I have learned that the trafficking ring will be bringing in something huge this weekend across the northern border. Maybe a nuclear weapon. We're not sure where it will happen." Her voice rose with excitement. "I didn't know who else to call, but I thought since you're a prosecutor, you'd know what to do or know who to call for . . ." The message timed out.

Zehra sighed before responding to the empty air in front of her. "That's right: I'll know what to do. I'll know just who to call." She told Barry about the call.

"I don't know, Z, but maybe we should go north ourselves. Johnson sounds crazy, but what if she's right? Maybe we could get something to convict Menendez. Could you call your friend in the FBI for help?"

"Yeah. I forgot to call him back after we left. We should go, but not alone."

"Hey, you didn't know it, but when I was in the fifth grade I was a black-belt in karate."

"I feel safer."

She called Paul, got his voice mail, then texted him. Slumping into her chair, she needed a break. Too much had happened too fast. Fatigue fingered its way around her neck and shoulders, caressing her into leaning back, closing her eyes, and letting her mind drift.

Until she thought of Shereen.

Zehra slammed forward in the chair. Jagged pieces of Shereen's situation from the past week that had been resting in the back of Zehra's mind suddenly came together. Shereen had been so rebellious toward her parents, hung around at the Mall of America, and then she'd disappeared from the mall.

She didn't run away from her parents; she had been kidnapped by someone at the mall.

A thought so horrible that it made Zehra sick to her stomach popped up: could there be any connection between Shereen and Zehra's trial? Didn't seem likely. Still, she left a frantic voice mail to her mother to pass on to the police.

Where was Shereen right now? Should Zehra stay in Minneapolis and try to find Shereen, or should she go north to see if she could figure out the plot? Who would help her? Zehra felt like she had to get home, to feel safe, to stop running and think.

Her cell phone rang. It was Paul.

"Thank goodness you called," she breathed fast. "I need your help. Meet me at my place in an hour."

He agreed.

CHAPTER 25

Friday, November 4, Afternoon

JEREMY BROWN WAITED IN A DIRTY WHITE VAN at the arrival level of the Minneapolis/St. Paul International Airport. Painted along the sides of the van a sign read: "AL'S FISHING CHARTERS." The engine idled, and curling clouds of exhaust puffed out from the back end of the vehicle. Underneath the upper deck, Brown was out of the rain that had started earlier, gotten heavier, and threatened to turn into slush, the half-frozen version of rain in Minnesota.

He waited for his team to arrive. To make things easier for him, all the flights had been coordinated to come in at the same time. Each of them knew to look for the van. Once he picked up the men, Brown would head to a warehouse in Northeast Minneapolis where he'd stashed all the equipment—weapons mostly. It'd been easy to assemble the firepower by attending several gun shows over the past few months. And particularly as a former cop and an investigator in the county attorney's office, it had been even easier to buy what he needed.

Not that he needed much firepower. Brown didn't expect any problems because they had the righteous power of God on their side, but it was always good to be prepared in case of trouble. Along with the usual pistols and shotguns, he had also bought several weapons through the Internet. His favorite was the Noreen .338 Lapua semi-automatic rifle. It came with a tripod and a ten-round magazine. Although expensive at about $5,000 each, Brown wanted them for their light weight and firepower.

Once he'd received three, he'd taken them to an old friend who'd converted each one from semi-automatic to fully automatic—machine guns that could chatter through the ten cartridges in a few seconds. The same person had been able to alter the magazine to hold seventeen rounds. With the new design and a handful of fully loaded magazines, Brown knew he could hold off almost anyone.

An airport traffic cop waved to Brown to move along. In five minutes, he was back and saw the three men waiting for him. They didn't change their expressions, like most people did when their rides arrived with family or spouses to pick them up. Brown's men didn't smile at all. With a nod, they hefted big travel bags over their shoulders and came toward the van.

"Welcome to Minneapolis," Brown joked as they climbed into the van, one after another.

"You got beer here?" The Russian, Kanatchikov, got in first. He was pale, with pale blue eyes and a thin hollow face that looked like he never ate. "You promise beer, I work." He laughed and showed three gold teeth.

"You'll get all the beer you want when this op is over. We got some good locally brewed stuff for you. Me, I don't drink."

Milton, the guy from South Africa spoke out of the back seat. "You said you've got the weapons?"

"Right. I don't think we're going to encounter any opposition, but just in case, we'll be loaded to the max."

"And the pay?"

"Into your accounts when we get the shipment back here and off-loaded. Click of a button on my cell phone."

The last one in was Mercury Ferguson named "Snoop Dogg" after the rapper. Ferguson's dreadlocks swayed across his face as moved into his seat.

Apparently satisfied, they all sat back quietly. Brown cruised out of the airport and headed to the warehouse in Northeast Minneapolis. He turned on the radio to get the latest weather forecast. The announcer warned of a blizzard moving out of the west to hit the northern part of the state. Several inches of snow could accumulate over the weekend. Travel advisories were out, and people were cautioned not to go into the storm zone unless necessary.

Brown clicked it off and chuckled to himself. His mission was ordained by God, therefore, necessary. Along with the van and the truck that would be used to carry the cargo, he'd probably need to bring a few snowmobiles. They might be forced to cross wilderness where only old logging roads existed. If the snow got too deep, the only way through was by snowmobile.

He sighed. It would be slow and cumbersome, but he didn't have any other choice. Brown keyed in Paco's number and told him to line up some snowmobile rentals with trailers and have them ready immediately. At the thought of the convoy of snowmobiles carrying a group of Bibles across the wilderness, he allowed himself a smile.

Forty-five minutes later, he pulled the van around the back side of an old warehouse. The front of it contained two art galleries and a coffee shop that had four brass lanterns hanging outside over the picture window by the door. In the basement, two young kids had set up a recording studio on a shoestring and borrowed equipment. The old limestone block in the walls had been cleaned until it glowed tan and orange. Polished wooden floors creaked all over, but that gave the place a comfortable, worn feel.

On the back side, the owners had set up several private storage rooms that could be secured and rented on a long-term basis. Brown had done so months earlier and used them often. Today they contained the weapons and cold weather gear, including boots, coats, gloves, goggles, heating stoves, and some extra freeze-dried food. All the items were hidden inside banker's boxes or long, tan bags like those used to carry golf clubs on airplanes. Those concealed the weapons and ammo.

When he reached the sliding door into the warehouse, Brown backed the van up to it. He got out and used his key to open the door as it screeched along the track in the floor. The team cleaned it out in ten minutes, putting everything into the back end of the van. Snoop Dogg bobbed his head in time to the music from the buds in his ears. "Best reggae in the world," he said.

"I want to see the art gallery in front," Kanatchikov said. "I learn there is a Russian art museum in your town. Russian art the best in the world."

"Shut up, you old commie," shouted the South African. "African art is the best."

"Shut up, both of you," Brown said. "No time now. Come back on your own. But don't call me." He smiled, but the others would never understand unless they were Christians, and he doubted that.

Brown drove out of the city to the northern suburb of Crystal. It was a lower-income city with plenty of one-story ramblers that rented cheaply. On the way up there along Central Avenue, they passed the Karpet King warehouse of fine carpeting and the lowest prices, guaranteed. They passed three pawn shops before they arrived at a residential area.

Brown turned down the street, normally leafy and shaded. Today, the cold wind had torn all the leaves off, and the street was filled with deep puddles from the rain and clogged storm drains at the end of the block. The wet lawns looked shiny as the temperature dropped, freezing the rain on the grass.

Brown pulled into the alley behind the largest house on the block. It was red with white trim. At one time there'd been a sidewalk from the street to the front door, but it was too broken up to be useful. At the front door, wrought iron poles held up the narrow porch roof. The white paint on them had peeled off in several spots.

"You can crash here until tomorrow morning. Get good sleep; we've got a long day," Brown warned his team.

Most of the men had brought liquor with them and, as they settled in, drank the bottles dry. Brown found the South African in the kitchen. Milton was his name. He had light skin but African features.

"I never drink before a job." His face clouded over. "I grew up on the edge of Apartheid. I say the edge because my father was an Afrikaner who raped an African woman. I was the result and have had to fight all my life because I don't belong in either world. I can't afford to let myself go with alcohol until my work is done." His eyes expanded in intensity.

Brown admired the discipline and thought Milton was cold and tough. Brown was glad to have him on the team. "I agree. You can bunk in the last bedroom on the right."

He walked to the fridge and pulled out a mineral water. He screwed the top off and drained a third of the bottle. It tasted like stones. Brown didn't drink alcohol or smoke. He felt fatigue creeping up on him. He'd go to bed soon.

Paco came in the back door, shook rain off his black leather coat, and wiped his hands across his face. "Got the sleds. Two of 'em. Tough to find this time of year." He beamed with pride. "Hooked up to my truck and ready to go."

Brown sighed from tiredness. Then he stiffened his body, knowing it would be necessary to be fully alert for the next couple days. Once it was done, he'd have time to relax.

As Paco started to walk away, Brown thought of the girl and the idea forming in his head. "You got that Muslim girl here, like I told you?"

"Yeah. Somewhere downstairs." He blinked and waited for Brown's reaction.

"Good. I got a different plan for her. She's related to the prosecutor in Roberto's trial. We should've destroyed their case already, but just to make sure, I may need that Muslim downstairs to finish the job."

"What do you want me to do?"

"Get her ready to go with us tomorrow."

Paco frowned.

"You stupid idiot. Don't question me. Now get her ready, and I don't want any trouble from her tomorrow. You make her understand that." Brown glared at him.

Paco opened and closed his fists a few times, grinned and headed down the steps to the basement. "I'll make her understand."

From the living room, Brown heard laughter interrupted occasionally by angry words and arguments. He shook his head. How could he possibly keep control of these thugs? Paco had warned the weather was deteriorating. Brown felt like exploding himself.

He closed his eyes and prayed. For a moment, it almost felt like he was actually praying to his long-ago relative, John Brown, asking both him and God for strength. "I don't want to do this. I can't," Jeremy Brown moaned. "Take this cup from me. But, if it is Your will, I will obey."

Suddenly, like the burn of pain he'd get through his finger in the vise that flashed into pleasure, a bright golden liquid poured through him. A sense of peace filled him with warmth.

Brown knew he wasn't worthy or capable of finishing the calling, but with God's grace, he would persevere to the final end, no matter how hard Satan fought him.

CHAPTER 26

Friday, November 4, Night

Paul arrived at Zehra's high rise condo as she was feeding Larceny. She buzzed Paul up and waited by the unlocked door. Larceny ignored her as he gobbled his food amid an occasional purr.

When Paul came to the door, he rushed in, threw off his wet raincoat, and gave her a long hug. He felt strong and warm. Zehra could smell the dampness on his clothing and in his hair. Wouldn't it be wonderful if the case disappeared, she had already found Shereen, and she and Paul could sit in front of the sliding glass door that looked out onto the deck and Minneapolis below and watch the rain?

"I can't believe the bad luck you're having," Paul said.

"It's not bad luck."

"Huh?"

"Jeremy Brown is behind all of this."

"Zehra . . . I know Dr. Leonard ID'd his phone as the one Menendez communicated with but the witness in Texas? Your witness here?"

"He supposedly had the Spreigl witness in Texas all ready to come up here and testify. At the last minute, she got scared and refused. And isn't it coincidental that Sparkle dies just before she's scheduled to testify? Even though Detroit talked to her a few days before."

"I'm sorry, Zehra, but she was a prostitute. Any number of people could have killed her. Maybe it was an accidental overdose. Can the medical examiner say for certain it's a homicide?" He nuzzled his face into her neck while he talked.

"Well, not yet."

"And the witness from Texas? You always knew she was a long shot." Paul sniffed the air. "Make some tea for me, too?"

Zehra nodded and reluctantly let go of him. They walked into the small kitchen. "Sorry it's such a mess. As you know, I've been pretty busy."

"Hey, almost forgot." Paul ducked out of the kitchen, retrieved his limp raincoat, dug in the pocket, and returned with a gift for Zehra. "Godiva chocolate. But not too much to cause us any trouble." He patted his stomach.

Zehra smiled at his thoughtfulness. What a perfect gift at this time. "Here." She handed him a cup of China black tea. "Let's go over by the balcony." Zehra pulled two chairs in front of the sliding door that opened onto her small balcony. Pots of flowers and vegetables crowded the space. She loved to garden, like her mother, but since she didn't have much space or time, the pots on the balcony had become her garden, although her plants were sheathed in frozen globes.

They sat close to each other, nibbling bites of chocolate between sips of tea, and watching the heavy clouds cross the sky from the north. With dark bulging undersides, they looked pregnant with snow.

Paul leaned back and looked at her. "What can I do to help?"

"Remember I told you about my cousin Shereen? Well, it's been several days since she disappeared, and I'm worried she's been kidnapped and maybe it has something to do with my case. I'm just sick with worry."

"Nothing from the police yet?"

"No, and you know my mother. She's probably called them ten times every day." She gripped her cup so hard she realized that it might break.

"Even though the Bureau can't officially get involved until we know for certain it's a kidnapping, I assigned an agent to track it down like I promised. Same thing. She was out at the mall but the security there can't tell her much."

"When I last saw Shereen, told me she'd met the coolest guy ever at the mall."

"The security's really tight out there. After 9/11, they even started a counter terrorism unit that trains in the basement of the mall. They're on patrol all the time, stopping suspicious people who might be targeting the mall." Paul frowned.

Putting her cup down on the table, Zehra took a deep breath. She had to be careful how she broke this to Paul if she wanted his help. "I'm worried there's a connection between Shereen and the trafficking ring and Brown. That's why I'm scared."

Paul looked at her. "I know it looks suspicious, but we're lawyers. Where's the evidence?"

"The evidence is my gut feeling."

"Okay . . ."

"Paul, I can't just sit here waiting for evidence to appear. I have to do something." Her voice sounded scratchy. "Dr. Leonard pinpointed the spot on the map where Menendez has been several times."

"So what?" Paul said in an irritated tone.

She stood and walked next to the window. Rain splattered the mums, beating them down into submission before the storm. "What about Dr. Leonard's evidence?"

"That doesn't prove Brown or anyone else will be there this weekend."

"Come on, Paul. Isn't it obvious to you? That's the transfer point." Her voice rose.

Paul sighed and stood up. "I had another conversation with Agent Mansfield today. They're still convinced the southern routes through Texas and Arizona are the ones the traffickers will use. The snakeheads and drug smugglers have built up these routes over the years. Why would they abandon them now?"

"To avoid detection. I've gotten to know Brown. He's smart. While everyone's on the southern border, he slips across the northern one."

"You're going to ignore the expertise of these guys? Both Mansfield and Long have years of experience. What do you have to base your idea on?"

Zehra shuffled to the middle of the room. She hesitated to tell him about Kathy Johnson. But Paul would need all the proof she could provide before he'd be persuaded to help. "Remember the NorthStar Group? They told me. Brown's bringing a nuclear weapon across the border into Minnesota."

Paul's breath came out in a sarcastic cough. "You believe those people?" He flopped his arms in the air. "And, Zehra, think about it: it's impossible to bring a nuclear weapon into this country. You know how big they are? You can't just hide one in the trunk of your car."

Zehra's head bobbed as she thought. "Hey, Dr. Leonard also gave me a list of eighteen cities Menendez has called repeatedly. They must be important for some reason." She stood to circle the room. In a moment, she stopped, lifted her head, and a vacant, scared look crossed her face. She dashed for her laptop, propped it open, and battered at the keys, trying to get it to run faster.

"What are you doing?"

Zehra didn't answer. She kept clicking. "Oh no . . ." She fell back from the screen. "Oh no . . ."

"What?" Paul shouted. He hurried to her side.

Zehra struggled to continue breathing normally. With her finger, she pointed at the screen. In the upper left-hand corner an image of an atom showed in dark blue, followed by the letters U.S. NRC. The United States Nuclear Regulatory Commission. In the center of the screen, it read: "Operating Nuclear Power Reactors by Location."

Zehra scrambled to her briefcase and returned to the laptop with the list Dr. Leonard had given her. She felt sweat break out across her forehead. In alphabetical order, the NRC website listed the following locations of nuclear power reactors:

Beaver Valley, McCandless, PA
Braidwood, Joliet, IL
Columbia Generating Station, Pasco, WA
Davis-Besse, Toledo, OH
D.C. Cook 1, Benton Harbor, MI
Kewaunee, Green Bay, WISC
Monticello, Monticello, MN

Zehra scrolled through the entire list, matching all eighteen cities exactly. A hollow, jittery feeling coursed through her. "It's true," she mumbled.

Paul looked at the list and his face clouded over. "No one can get a nuclear weapon into the country," he insisted.

She moved toward him. "If I could be there when that happens, maybe I could find Shereen. Or maybe I could at least learn something to use in the trial on Monday. Don't you see? I can't sit still while she's in danger. Every minute I stand here talking with you could be critical for my cousin."

A crack of lightning lit up the room in blue-white color and was followed by the rumble of thunder.

"And what makes you think they'll take Shereen with them even if they have her? Why wouldn't they leave her here?"

Zehra didn't have an answer for that, but she had to act.

"Okay, okay. I want to help, but going up north is crazy. You can't go alone."

She walked toward Paul and reached for his arm. She tilted her head to one side. "I wasn't thinking of going alone."

Paul laughed. "Me? No, no way. I can't involve the Bureau's assets on evidence this flimsy. I still have to answer to the director."

"I'm not talking about the FBI. Just you and me."

"Crazy."

Her voice rose as she let all the worry and stress of the past weeks come into it. "I am going up there. With or without you. My trial has gone to hell and my cousin is in danger."

Paul threw up his hands in the air. He circled the room mumbling to himself.

Zerha went back to her chair, drained the last of the cooling tea and waited. She meant what she had said.

"Okay," he shouted. "I'm not happy with this. You can't go alone."

"I know. Brown is dangerous."

"Dammit, Zehra," was all Paul could say. "We'll have to move fast and leave first thing tomorrow morning. Weather forecast is horrible up there." He turned to face her. "We don't have any support. We're not exactly sure where we're going . . ."

"Yes?"

He mumbled to himself some more. "I could at least alert the Border Patrol, Air National Guard, some of the other resources that might be available." He looked up in the air. "Doubt they'll believe me."

"We still have to go." She smiled at him. "I knew you'd help. That's why I love you, Paul." She grabbed him in her arms to pull him close in a hug. "Look at it this way: what if we do find them up there and if they're stopped? Think of what it could do for your career."

"There were a lot of 'ifs' in that sentence."

They started to get Zehra's things packed for the trip on Saturday morning. She assembled all her winter wear, including the clothing she wore for snowboarding and her boots.

She checked her phone, and saw that Cindy Wilson had left a message with her cell phone number. Zehra called her.

"Hey, Z. How are you?" Cindy said. The sound of clinking bottles made her voice hard to hear.

"I'm stressed to the max. I got your other message."

"Yeah, I've got some good dirt for you." She turned from the phone and yelled at someone. She came back and said, "Sorry. Couple of us are at the local happy hour."

"What did you find out?"

"Told you, your guy had a child protection case opened a couple years ago. That's how I found it 'cause I'm working in that department. Anyway, I was able to get into the data base, found the mother, and checked on the reason child protection opened on the family."

"Yeah?"

"Domestic violence. Bad. Looks like your boy beat the shit out of this woman, Diaz."

Zehra's chest quivered. She sounded like a possible Spreigl witness. "What else?"

"Well, the county took the kids and tried to make Menendez go through domestic abuse counseling."

"Did he?"

"No. He boogied. But I did make contact with the mother, Ms. Rose Diaz. She hates the son of a bitch and can't wait to help put him away."

Zehra's breath came quicker. "Did you ask her if she'd be willing to come up here and testify?"

Cindy slurped from a bottle. "She can't wait. If you can pay for a plane ticket and hotel, I think you won yourself the door prize."

"I'll have one of our victim/witness counselors make contact with her and arrange everything. Tell her a nice woman named Detroit, that's 'De-twa,' will call her." Zehra's mind buzzed with the possibilities. She'd have to tell both the judge and Mezerretti as soon as possible. Of course, he'd object, saying it was too late. But the judge might allow the testimony of the Diaz woman. Maybe the case was still on track—with a few wheels hanging over the rails. She felt the excitement rise in her body.

When Zehra got back to her bedroom to close the suitcase, she found her hands shaking so hard she couldn't latch the top down. Standing back, her mind finally woke to what she was about to do.

Drive off into the wilderness, a blizzard, and for what? Zehra had staked everything on this mission: the trial, her cousin, her future career, and maybe even her life. If she failed, would that drive her back into the PTSD? The agents from Washington, Paul had warned her not to go. She could change her mind right now and no one would ever blame her.

Zehra walked the few steps back to the bed. With steady hands, she closed the suitcase and hefted it onto the floor for tomorrow, when she'd leave to go into the storm.

Chapter 27

Saturday, November 5

J EREMY BROWN AWOKE AT FOUR O'CLOCK in the morning on Saturday. They wouldn't leave for another two hours, but he was too wound up to sleep. He listened for the rain on the roof. Inside, silence surrounded him.

All that he'd been led to and worked for would be accomplished by Monday. The shipment of explosives would be headed across the country and for the nuclear plant at Monticello. He rose and prayed for victory and deliverance from sin. Then he went to shower to cleanse himself for the ordeal. It'd be a long day.

He made sure the team was awake and moving. No time to waste. Kanatchikov stumbled into the deserted living room. A crooked smile crossed his face until he saw Brown.

"Fucking good booze here," the Russian said. "Not as good as Russian vodka, though."

"You should confess your sins and pray for forgiveness," Brown advised him.

Kanatchikov blinked and said he was almost ready to go.

When Brown didn't see anyone else from the team, a sense of urgency gripped him. He went down the hall, banging on doors. He bellowed, "Get out of there. We're leaving." He opened the basement door and yelled for Paco.

In five minutes, Paco bounded up the stairs and grinned. "This is the day the Lord has made. We will be successful." He wore his leather coat over a bare chest like he'd just tumbled out of bed.

"Shut up and get the team going."

When Brown had everyone assembled around the breakfast table, drinking coffee and filled with eggs and bacon, he explained, "Change of plans. Because of the weather, we're leaving in ten minutes." People around the table looked at each other but no one spoke.

"We'll drive two vehicles north. Paco will pull the sleds and Kanatchikov will drive the panel truck. We expect bad weather and snow up there, which is why I want the Russian to drive." He turned to the end of the table. "Snoop, you're in charge of the weapons." He didn't trust Milton.

Brown ran through the procedure for everything, the preparations for the shipment and how they would make the transfer. Extra warm clothing was to be loaded and thermoses for hot drinks and more food.

Milton spoke. "What's the intel on border security?"

"The storm should actually help us with cover to get across. We will avoid the Border Patrol at all costs. Do not, I repeat, do not engage them in any way."

"Other bogies?" asked Snoop.

"Shouldn't be anyone. Besides, who would try to stop us? But if we're confronted, we've got the firepower to eliminate any threats."

"Which will draw God damn attention," Milton insisted. His eyes bored into Brown.

"That's why we avoid everyone."

"'Nother thing," Kanatchikov said. "Do we get time for any women?"

"You should pray for deliverance from your sins." Brown scowled at him. Little did this unbeliever know he probably wouldn't even be alive by then. Instead, he'd be in hell. When he'd finished the briefing and sent the men out, he turned to Paco. "Get the Muslim."

When she came into the kitchen, Brown could tell that Paco had been right: she wasn't cooperative yet. He assessed her. A tall, dark girl with a defiant way of standing. If she were dressed up, she'd be pretty. She had a long nose and dark-brown eyes that glared at him with a shiny stare. "Your name Shereen?"

She remained silent. Paco came over to her and whispered in her ear. "Yeah," the girl said.

"You're Muslim? Well, today's your lucky day. You're coming with us."

"Where?"

Something snapped in Brown. All the pressure and stress. He didn't have time for this insolence. He pulled back his hand to hit her but paused. Shereen didn't cringe. Instead, she looked at him with sad, large eyes. He dropped his hand. He felt sorry for this lost lamb. It wasn't her fault she was doomed as a Muslim.

What if his daughters had been born without the benefit of the Christian witness? "Disrespectful infidel!" he yelled finally. "You do what I say when I say it."

She nodded. A trickle of tears coursed down her cheek.

"Any trouble and I'll have to kill you." Brown pushed his face within an inch of Shereen's. "You got one purpose in this world: keep your relative, Zehra Hassan, from screwing up the Lord's plan." He shoved her out of the kitchen.

He checked the time and decided to make the call he'd been planning. He had Zehra Hassan's cell phone number. When she answered, he said, "Hi, Zehra. Sorry I've been out of touch. You know my sister in Boston has been really sick. But I'll be back in the Cities on Monday."

She remained silent for a long time. Finally, Zehra said, "Uh . . . yeah, sure. Where are you now?" There was a sharp edge to her words.

"I told you. I'm in Boston."

"Jeremy, when we needed you the most, you disappeared. Did you know the Guzman woman refused to come up here to testify? I thought you told me she was anxious to get back at Menendez." Hassan's voice rose and she talked faster. Angry.

"Humph. Sure thought so. 'Course, if you've worked with domestic assault victims, they're never totally reliable. They go back to the guy all the time."

"Sure, sure. I've seen that." She stopped talking for a while.

"Anything else I can do when I get back to help?"

"Bring back Sparkle from the dead."

"What? I can't believe . . ."

"It's a surprise to you?"

"I can't believe anyone would kill her."

"Who said anyone killed her? It was a suicide."

Brown coughed to cover his mistake. "Yeah. Listen, Zehra, are you still going ahead with the trial now that we've had all these setbacks?"

"Hell, yes. I think of that innocent victim. I'm not giving up."

"Okay." He gritted his teeth. "Hey, gotta run. My sister. I'll be back to help on Monday." He hung up quickly. Hassan's stupid resolve to keep going with the trial had just sealed the fate of her relative. Once he got everyone out of town, Brown would use the girl to destroy Hassan, end the trial, and get Menendez out of there before he revealed everything.

CHAPTER 28

Saturday, November 5

ZEHRA SLAMMED HER CELL PHONE on the kitchen counter so hard, she thought it might break. She waited for Paul to pick her up and go north out of town. Red hot anger bubbled up inside of her. She couldn't stand still.

That lying jerk! How could Brown act so surprised?

She wore a fleece sweater of dark blue that set off her dark hair and a pair of designer jeans. She'd put on her hiking boots and a down ski jacket. Zehra stomped around the living room. Frightened by her behavior, Larceny had hidden under her bed. All she could hear was his occasional mewing. Her mother would rescue him later and pamper the cat at her home for the entire weekend. Zehra had prepared a detailed list for Martha about how to feed Larceny, who was very particular about his meals.

But for now, she spun around the room like a revolving ride at an amusement park. She remembered the only question he had asked was if she was still going ahead with the trial. That was what concerned him. Made sense. If he and Menendez were in this together, Brown would want Menendez's case dumped so he could go free.

Zehra worked backward along the line of recent events. Brown must have hoped that sabotaging the case from the inside at the beginning, his lack of help, and the two witnesses' removal would stop the trial. Liz was so nuts in love with him that she'd been blind to his true involvement to stop the prosecution. When she got sick and Zehra took over, he was forced to take more drastic actions.

But they didn't work.

That led to her next thought: what would he do now? Zehra paced faster. He scared her in many ways. Not only physically, but also because he was smart and ruthless. She stopped and sank into the chair she'd just bought at Ikea.

What could she possibly hope to do against him? He was organized, must have planned it all out for years, was tough and dangerous. Zehra stared at the carpeting on the floor and saw pieces of cat fur she'd missed with the vacuum. Paul was right. This mission up north was crazy.

At least she had Paul on her side. He believed her . . . to some extent. Maybe he could organize the FBI once the traffickers got to the Twin Cities. At that point, he might have proof of a federal crime—trafficking illegal goods over international boundaries. The power of the federal government could be used to break up the network and stop it. Brown and his gang would be caught and prosecuted.

But what if the FBI failed to catch them?

Zehra's thoughts circled back to the same immovable point. She must go north to do what she could. If she and Paul were there, maybe they could at least assemble enough evidence for Paul to get the FBI involved.

And then Zehra remembered Shereen. Where was she? Zehra stood and circled the room again. Her phone rang and she answered her mother's call.

"Have you found out anything about Shereen yet?"

Zehra sighed. "No. I'm working on it. You're picking up the cat?"

"This morning. Sorry to ask, but I couldn't sleep at all last night. My sister is having a nervous breakdown. Your father and Shereen's father are out at the mall again."

"Good idea."

"Are you and Paul still going out of town?"

"Yes. He's picking me up any minute now."

Her mother sighed. "I still don't see how this will help find your cousin."

"I told you: I think these are the same people who took her. If I find them, I hope to find Shereen."

There was a silence. Then Martha said, "Are you and Paul . . . uh, are you sharing a room?"

"Mother."

"Okay, okay. I'll be there soon. Be very careful."

Paul buzzed on the door downstairs, and Zehra walked over to the release to let him in the building. In five minutes he knocked on her door. He was dressed like someone in an outdoor ad for beer or snowboards. Handsome and rugged. He'd grown up in St. Cloud, a small town in the middle of the state, trapped behind acres of pine forests and lakes. Paul often joked that he'd been born not behind the Iron Curtain, but behind the Pine Curtain. He kissed her quickly.

"I'm all packed."

"Weather looks like a mess up north. I switched to my Jeep."

She told him about Brown's call. His eyes opened suddenly and he said, "Must be getting desperate. Guy like him, we have to be really careful now."

"What do you think he'll do?"

Paul stopped carrying her things toward the door. He stood still and looked at her. "My guess is that he's used up all the tricks he had. Since you told him you're not caving on the trial, he has only one thing left to stop. You."

Zehra's breath caught in her throat. "Another reason not to go up there, huh?"

"Yeah." Paul's face tightened.

She didn't say anything. She lifted her overnight bag and her laptop onto her shoulder and started out the door. Paul followed with a load, and they descended to the parking lot where Paul's Jeep Laredo sat. He opened the back end, and they hefted her things into it. Neither of them spoke. One more trip upstairs and they had everything.

As Zehra set the last of her gear into the back end, she saw a pile of plastic boxes with curved corners. They were flat and looked too thin to carry much of anything. She asked Paul about them.

"Guns. You know how much I love my gun collection. Just thought I'd bring along a few." Rain started to drizzle on them.

"Thanks." She paused at the end of the Jeep and didn't move.

Paul hesitated. "What?"

Zehra chuckled. "All right. I may as well confess." She leaned into the back end and tugged out her light blue travel bag. She balanced it on the back end and unzipped the side. Reaching in, she pulled out a small, flat plastic case with rounded edges. She opened it and lifted up her Glock 26. She pulled the slide back to make sure the chamber was empty.

"I don't believe it."

"Had it since Mustafa tried to kill me . . . us. I took a few courses and spent a lot of time out at the range. Never thought I'd say this, but I feel good with this beside me."

Paul's face cracked open into a huge smile. He shook his head. "Good for you."

"You and me. Batman and Robin, huh?"

"Now that I know you can handle a weapon, I should appoint you a special agent of the Federal Bureau of Investigation. Temporary, that is."

"Get in the car," she ordered.

Paul pulled out of the lot and turned onto Interstate 94, which led northwest out of the city. Increased rain pelted onto the windshield in heavy half-frozen globs. It settled on the sides of the freeway to layer over the shoulders beyond in a gray blanket of slush. Paul switched the wipers onto high speed, and they slapped back and forth with an insistent sound. They hadn't gotten the early start they'd intended. Low, dark clouds gave the air a pearl color.

The traffic slowed as everyone tried to squeeze onto the freeway. Dozens of red tail lights dotted the road before them, reflected off the wet surface of the freeway. They moved in and out of the gray fog. Exhaust breathed out of the back end of the cars into the chilly air as if they were a huge herd of animals crowding together on a migration. In a sense, they were migrating to their homes, breakfast, shopping, and kids' activities.

"Can't you go any faster?" Zehra asked.

"Look ahead. The rain is slowing everything down to a crawl. Should open up by the time we hit Highway 169."

Zehra turned on the radio and fiddled through several stations, most of which ranted against the Democrats in Washington. A few country western stations twanged from the speakers. She shut it off. "Any CDs?"

"Uh . . . Rolling Stones, U2, and I think I've got the greatest hits of Frank Sinatra."

"You're kidding. We're going to be stuck in this Jeep for hours and that's all you got?"

He laughed. "A few hours ago, I didn't know I'd be doing this."

She twirled the dial until she came to a news show. They returned to the interview with their science expert, Dr. Nehru.

"The Japanese were very lucky at the nuclear reactor at Fukushima," he said in sonorous tones. "If a leak had occurred, the contamination could have spread for thousands of miles, depending on the wind. Thousands of people could have been affected, and unlike other disasters, there's absolutely nothing anyone could have done to prevent the harm. We'd all be powerless."

"Do we have prior experience?"

"The best history we have was the catastrophe at Chernobyl in 1986 in the Soviet Union. Besides the immediate deaths, it's the long-term results that trouble me the most."

"What are those?"

"The Chernobyl disaster released the most particulate and gaseous radioisotopes into the environment in the history of humans. It contaminated food sources, food distribution channels, the soil, particularly with strontium-90, which has a half-life of about thirty years. The contamination entered all the insects, animals, trees, grasses, lakes and rivers and even seeped into the aquifers. All of those contaminated items will create generations of problems."

Zehra switched off the radio.

Paul eased the car off of Interstate 94 to drive through Elk River and connect with Highway 169 which went north up into the state toward Canada. He said to Zehra, "Don't tell anyone, but after the Fukushima scare, the FBI doubled the security efforts around all the U.S. nuclear facilities. Trouble is, we can't possibly secure every single place twenty-four hours a day."

She waved her hand in front of her. "I don't want to hear any more. We've got enough problems right here."

They passed row after row of new shopping malls, new furniture stores, and new housing. At the north end, as they were leaving town, they stopped at a Dunn Brothers coffee shop and both ordered large black coffees to go. Zehra held herself back from adding a chocolate pastry.

Back on the road, the rain turned to snow. It drove against them in bone-colored clouds that whispered around the Jeep. North of Elk River, the traffic thinned, Paul sped up, and the lights of civilization dropped off into a long dusky gray even at this time in the morning. She didn't know what they'd find, but it was important to be taking action rather than simply sitting in her condo. Waiting, waiting.

Zehra made herself comfortable and wrapped both hands around the warm cup of coffee. The glow from the dashboard lit up Paul's face as she sneaked glances at him. It felt good to be with him, safe, and warm from the cold dusk outside.

Her mind drifted back to a late afternoon in August. Zehra had been sitting in a café on Hennepin Avenue near Uptown, drinking tea. A late summer rain crashed around her. She could hear the drumming on the roof of the café, saw it jump as it hit the sidewalk outside, and noticed the fresh mineral smell in the air.

When Zehra paused to look up, she saw Paul coming down the sidewalk with a large blue umbrella. She hadn't been with him for several weeks, and the clutch in her chest that she felt at seeing him surprised her. She smiled involuntarily and stood to run out of the café into the humid air. Without an umbrella herself, Zehra felt the rain pouring down on her, wetting her shoulders and hair. She ran after Paul, caught up with him, and ducked under his umbrella.

He held up and smiled at her.

"Hey, can a girl share your umbrella?"

"Sure. How are you?"

To show him, she reached up with both arms around his neck and pulled his face down closer to her own. A few inches away, she studied his eyes and nose and face down to his lips and slight smile.

"You smell good . . . and wet." Paul laughed as he ran his hand through her damp and frizzy hair.

The stood holding each other as the rain tumbled heavily around them, sealing them off from the street and sounds and sights surrounding them like an impenetrable wall. Inside the bubble of dryness, Zehra felt happy to see Paul. They laughed at the random good luck of running into each other.

As Paul ran his hand down over her back to pull her closer, he lowered the umbrella until it touched the top of his head. Now they were totally private even though they stood in the middle of an open and busy sidewalk. He leaned forward to kiss Zehra full on the lips as she listened to the rumble of the rain falling outside.

Rumbling north over the freeway on Highway 169, Zehra had a similar feeling. She set her cup of coffee on the holder in between the seats, leaned over toward Paul, and kissed him lightly on the cheek. "Thanks for your help."

He blushed and said, "Haven't done anything yet."

"You're here. I don't know what I'd do without you sometimes." Zehra leaned back into her own seat and sighed. She couldn't think of anyone else that she'd rather be with right now than Paul. When this was all over and Shereen was back home safe, maybe Zehra should think about him in a different way.

Thanks to her efforts and the presence of Paul in her life, she no longer suffered panic attacks. His steadiness and support had made it easier. Similarly, when the pressure of the trial threatened to overwhelm her, Paul had always been willing to talk and help. The guilt still dogged her, but now she felt like it was controllable. She'd gotten her life back again.

Zehra suddenly realized how good she felt—for the first time in months. She dressed up like she used to, felt engaged in life, the depression was gone, and she felt like getting more involved with Paul. Zehra thought of old friends that she hadn't seen in forever. When this was all over, she vowed to call them again.

A gust of wind swerved the Jeep to the right side of the road. It brought Zehra's mind back to what they were doing right now. "Want me to drive for a while?" she asked.

"Good for now. Later." Paul's head poked forward as he peered out the windshield. "Dammit. This stuff's turning to snow, and it's accumulating."

In the ditches to the side of the freeway, small humps of wet snow covered the ground. The surface of the road still shined black and clear of any snow. As she followed the beams of the headlights poking into the mist in front of the Jeep, hundreds of white blobs raced at them to bounce off the windshield.

Paul turned up the fan on the heater. The Jeep rocked back and forth in the wind. Zehra's cell phone played the Grateful Dead, and she pulled it out of her purse and looked at the caller ID.

It was Jeremy Brown.

CHAPTER 29

Saturday, November 5, Afternoon

J EREMY BROWN COULD SEE THE STORM COMING. Paco drove the pickup, pulling the snowmobiles on the trailer behind. North of the Twin Cities, they hugged the west side of Lake Mille Lacs, a huge body of water renowned as a "walleye factory" for its good production of the golden fish.

He gazed out over the flat gray surface that disappeared into the east. Whitecaps danced across the lake as if they were looking forward to the storm. His brilliant idea to hollow out the Bibles and fill them with plastic explosives had worked. He'd checked, and the entire load rested in Winnipeg right now. It was addressed to the Church of the Rapture in Hamel, it wouldn't make any difference because by the time the plant was blown, Brown and the Elect would be gone.

The load came in at ten pallets fully loaded. They'd be moved from the airport onto a truck that Brown had hired to drive south to meet the dozens of lakes that formed the border between Canada and the United States. The tough part would be off-loading the explosives onto boats to be sneaked across the border. Brown worried about that, but consoled himself with the thought that he was doing God's work. It would be okay.

A fierce gust of wind hit the side of the truck, and Paco compensated by pulling the wheel to the left. The trailer actually stabilized them and helped hold the truck on the road. Brown worried about the crazy Russian driving the van. But it looked okay close behind.

The road curved around the edge of the lake, sometimes no more than twenty feet from the shoreline. It was obvious the temperature had dropped since ice had started to form at the shore, reaching out in gray fingers toward the open water. At one turn, the road straightened and they could see, far off to the north, a high bank of black clouds. Underneath it swirled a gray mass of snow. They drove directly toward it.

"It'll still hit us," Brown said about the clouds, "but by the time the worst comes, we'll be there already." He glanced into the back compartment. The pickup had four doors, with two small seats behind the main ones in front. Sprawled across the back seats, the Muslim girl slept. Good. He reminded himself to make the call soon.

"Checked to see if the load got out of Winnipeg?" Paco asked.

"Called just before we left. Everything was loaded and ready to go." Brown turned back around to face forward. "Customs was a joke. If the timing works like we planned, they should get to the north side of the lake just as we get to the south side. Remember, we picked the narrowest point of water to cross for our route."

"What are we gonna do if there's a blizzard up there? How can those little boats make it?"

Brown squirmed in his seat. Paco was right. If they missed the window in the power plant shut-down, they wouldn't be able to blow it and the other seventeen nuclear plants would not be blown either. They'd fail at everything.

Besides, they'd contracted with some reprobates and sinners, who might not be dependable, to use their fishing boats to shuttle the shipment across Rainy Lake. Canadian Highway 11 came down to Fort Frances, across the border from the Minnesota city of International Falls. It was the official border crossing for miles in either direction. But before the road reached Fort Frances, it skirted the edge of Rainy Lake. At that point the two boats would meet the truck with the shipment of Bibles for off-loading.

The wind blasted against the side of the truck, but the trailer, heavy with snowmobiles, kept them going straight.

Between the two countries lay a small expanse of the lake, interrupted by a long island. Brown figured it would be easier for the small boats to avoid detection and hide, if necessary, around the island. Now it looked even smarter since the island would act as a shelter from any storms that might blow down the lake from the north.

After they'd crossed the lake, they'd reach a tiny island on the Minnesota side, with a town called Island View. The boats would ferry the explosives to that landing point, from which Brown and his team would distribute them around the country, including to the nuclear plant at Monticello.

Until people had actually been in the wilderness area at the border, they couldn't understand the vast expanse of forests, lakes, bogs, streams, and utterly wild wilderness that existed up there. Perfect for sneaking a load across.

Because they could only use two boats, the transfer would take a while. If the storm hit them hard, it would take even longer, and there was the added risk of losing some of the shipment overboard.

Brown's mind swirled like the storm ahead of them. What if the temperatures dropped below zero? Would they have enough warm clothing to keep the crew from freezing to death?

Could he keep control of his team? He'd purposely limited the number, but when he'd actually met them, Brown had been worried. These were ruthless killers who would only stay in line until they got paid. Then there was Milton who seemed too tightly wound for even a mercenary. Brown would have to be careful with him.

He looked out of his window to the side mirror. He saw the wind hit the big van. It rocked the vehicle. The back end skidded to the side of the road. Brown hoped the Russian knew how to drive in bad weather.

The van kept moving to the right. Brown could see the tires on that side bump down over the shoulder. The front end jerked to the left—Kanatchikov compensating for the sideslip. But he turned too sharply. Instead of straightening out, the van kept sliding to the side, the back end threatening to come past the front, meaning the vehicle had slipped into a deadly spin. The rain and snow created a slick surface that, once the van lost traction, caused it to slide even worse. Now the driver fought for control.

Brown screamed, "Paco." Paco pumped the brakes to slow down without putting the truck into a slide.

The van continued to skid sideways. Brown could see the Russian twisting the wheel in one direction then in the other. The van whirled out of control. The steering wheel didn't make any difference anymore.

Brown held his breath. If the van hit the tiniest bump in the road at this vulnerable point, it could roll. It would be destroyed, and he didn't have time to replace it now. He prayed Kanatchikov could handle it.

Still the van skated sideways. Since the road sloped slightly toward the edges for water to run off, the vehicle followed that slope down toward the edge of the lake. The shore, crusted over with frozen rain and snow, looked like a quagmire. If the van slid into that, it would never get free.

Paco slowed the truck, trying to stop it. They watched while the van drove backwards toward the lake. It slid across the road, took a huge leap into the air, the back tires spinning uselessly, and dropped heavily over the edge of the road, down into a deep ditch filled with snow and mud. At least it stopped moving.

"Turn around," Brown ordered Paco.

Careful on the icy road, Paco inched the truck and trailer around to head back toward the wreck. Could they save the van?

When they reached it, Brown jumped out of the cab and ran to the van. He didn't care about the men in it. Instead, he bounded over the shoulder and down into the deep gulley the van had fallen into. It looked bad. The van's wheels had sunk up to the axle in sand and mud. Stuck. The team crawled out of the van and shook themselves, glad to be alive.

There was only one thing that might work to save the mission. Brown pushed two members of the team toward Paco and shouted to him. "Unhook the trailer. Let's see if we can pull it out."

In ten minutes, Paco had backed the truck up to the front of the van, hitched a chain under the front bumper, and was prepared to pull. He inched forward, knowing that with the slick surface, he didn't want to lose traction. The engine of the truck groaned with the effort. Paco leaned forward, almost touching the steering wheel with his body, as if that would help get the van out.

The chain sprung taut, singing with tension. The van didn't move an inch. Brown ordered the team to get to the back of the van and push. Everything would help. They shouldered their way along the back end and gave a heave as Paco revved the engine in front. The van shuddered and started to move. Slowly, slowly it plopped free of the mud, and as it gained momentum, it bumped up over the gulley and finally struggled out onto the road.

"Son of a bitch," Snoop yelled, "didn't think the sucker'd make it." Loose snow dusted his dreadlocks.

They got back into their vehicles and started forward on the road again.

Brown slumped into the seat and looked out over the lake again. The flat, monotonous scenery and the adrenaline let down lulled him into relaxing. He hoped there were no more accidents. It was as if Satan himself had interfered with the plan.

He dreamt of the river valley that ran alongside his farm in New Mexico. He remembered the brilliant sun and the colors of the mountains that ringed and sheltered his home. He could smell the horses and the sweet odor of their dung before it had been cleaned out of the barn.

After reaching the small and smelly town of International Falls, they turned into a motel that offered vacancy. They were within ten miles of Dove Island, the last dot of land on the shore of Rainy Lake and their rendezvous point for the shipment. There weren't any lodgings open this late in the year on the island, so they were forced to stop for the night in International Falls.

"What stinks?" Paco said.

"Paper mills. This isn't bad. You should smell this place on a hot summer day."

Paco bumped over the rutted gravel parking lot. Snow filled the holes until the truck crashed through to crunch on the gravel along the bottom of the holes.

Brown was glad he'd thought to get some snowmobiles. Although they'd beaten the worst of the storm, snow was piled up to the height of the truck's tires and was still falling. They parked the vehicles in a circle, and the men unloaded to find their rooms. Brown ordered them to stay inside, avoid the numerous bars all around, and get some sleep. Tomorrow would be busy.

Suddenly, he remembered to make the call. Brown worried whether he'd still be able to get a signal. Luckily, there was a tower in International Falls.

He pulled out his iPhone and dialed Zehra Hassan. The heathen. If she was too stupid to understand why she should dump the murder trial, he'd have to hit her hard.

He listened to the buzzing of the ring, the heard her voice, slow and sleepy. "Jeremy?"

"Yeah. Listen, Zehra, we got a new plan now."

"What?" Her voice was coming alert, sharp at the edges.

"I don't have time to go into the details. You don't seem to get it that the murder trial has to stop. God has ordained this. You've got to let Menendez walk, or he's gonna bring everything down. I cannot have that happen."

"I'm not surprised, Brown. I know what you're up to."

Brown paused for a moment. Was there any way she could've figured it out? She was bright, but he'd covered himself every step of the way. "Here's what's important for you to know. I've got your relative, Shereen."

She gasped over the phone. Silence for a long time.

"Yeah. Thought you'd listen to that. It's real simple. On Monday morning, first thing, you file your dismissal of the case of *State v. Roberto Menendez*. I want him out of jail before noon."

"So double jeopardy will apply and I can't prosecute him again, right?"

"I always knew you were smart. You don't do that you won't see Shereen ever again. Cooperate and I'll return her unharmed."

"Where?"

"I'll tell you then . . . if she gets returned." Brown twisted in his seat, reached back to the sleeping girl, and flicked open a small knife. He jabbed her in the leg until she woke up. The act of coming out of sleep and seeing the knife and feeling the pain spurred the reaction he'd hoped for. He held up the phone for Zehra to hear.

Shereen screamed loudly and then broke off into a long cry.

CHAPTER 30

Saturday, November 5, Evening

"WHERE THE HELL ARE WE, KEVIN?"

Kevin leaned forward over the steering wheel, staring into the gray swirl before them. Snow curled around the Prius and obliterated any landmarks. He could hardly see the white lines in the road.

"Slow down," Kathy screamed.

Kevin jammed on the brakes. The Prius, light as it was, slipped to the side.

Kathy yelled at him, "Just tap the brakes, you idiot! We don't want to lose the grip on the road."

"Yeah, yeah." A sheen of sweat glowed across his forehead in the light from the dashboard. The colorful graphics warned them they were only getting six miles to the gallon in spite of being a Prius. He righted the car and took her advice, tenderly touching the brakes to slow them down. "Can't see a God damn thing."

"I saw a sign back a ways that said Grand Rapids. It must be coming close. Maybe we should stop, Kevin."

"Fuck no. We're losing time in this storm, we haven't met our guys, and we got a long ways to go to the border."

"Don't be crazy. If we're slowed down, the rest of them are also. You can't even see where you're going." Kathy balled her fists in her lap and felt the tightness of the seat belt across her shoulder. It gave her a little sense of safety with Kevin driving. From now on, she'd insist on driving. "Where are we supposed to meet the guys you're talking about?"

He didn't answer as he moved his head back and forth, trying to see through the blizzard ahead. "Huh? I don't know. They're supposed to call when they get up here, but this storm has made the cell phones worthless."

Kathy let out a big breath. "So what the hell are we doing? Let's stop and wait out the storm. At the rate we're going, we won't get there tonight anyway."

Kevin's hands gripped the wheel so hard, his fingers turned as white as the snow. "Maybe."

Kevin had never had a good car, so they'd taken Kathy's. The back end was loaded with winter clothing, some camping equipment, sleeping bags, a Coleman gas stove, boots, and their laptops. They'd packed food in case they got stranded, and Kevin had insisted on packing enough marijuana to last for several days' emergency. At the last minute, he'd shown Kathy a pistol that he'd packed in his duffel bag. "Just in case those guys want to play rough."

Kathy had almost laughed at the idea of Kevin with a gun until she noticed the serious look on his face. His eyes glowed and he held his mouth tight. If that made him happy, okay. For herself, she'd been more interested in packing personal items. Kathy had put in her nicest jewelry for the evening. Extra make up, perfume, the see-through nightgown, the low-cut bra—black, of course—and the bikini panties were the first to go in her suitcase. She'd brought extra protection in case they were stranded in some nice place and the only thing they had to do was make love for a few days.

She didn't have many expensive bottles of wine at home, but what had been in the cupboard above the sink now rested in the back of her Prius. As Kevin fought the storm, she heard the bottles clink against each other, and she worried they might break.

Despite the tension created by the dangerous weather, Kathy was having a great time. She really didn't think they'd find anything or stop anyone. How could they, when they didn't even know where the bad guys were?

In the isolation of the little car amidst the storm, Kathy dreamed about what it'd be like. They'd probably stop in a cozy place with cabins that had knotty pine walls that reflected the golden glow of a lamp in the corner. A huge bed with a down comforter would warm them until body heat took over. She could see the scene: an empty wine bottle knocked over on its side from when they'd first rushed for the bed with mounting passion. Her bra would be carelessly tossed onto the overstuffed chair next to the bed. Kevin's thin body would feel hot and slippery from their exertions. Her own would be firm and willing. Not too willing, but in the end . . .

The car slipped to the side, and her stomach lurched with the sickening feeling of loss of control. When she looked over, Kevin jammed the brakes too hard once again. She shouted at him, he let up, and the car straightened out. "Dammit, Kevin. We've got to stop."

"I drive." He hunched over the wheel.

When a window opened in the blur of snow, Kathy saw the sign that said: "Welcome to Grand Rapids. The Home of Judy Garland!" They crawled along the main street. It was early evening and the storm blotted out the sun, making it seem like early evening. Yellow globs of light poked out of the dusky blur of snow.

"Okay, if you're so smart, where are we gonna stop?" Kevin relaxed and leaned back, his face covered with sweat. "Nothing open."

They drove slowly, trying to spot anything in the twilight. Block after block, everything was closed and looked abandoned. Out of the gloom, one bar shone with a neon sign that said: "The Last Fishing Hole. Beer and Set-ups." At the door a hand-lettered sign read: "We Got Shiners." Kathy hoped they wouldn't have to stay there for the night. How horrible. She could imagine them unrolling their sleeping bags on top of a pool table, smelling the spilled beer from underneath it.

Then she saw another sign. "MERLE & MAMA LOU'S MOTEL. HOME COOKING." "Kevin. Over there," she pointed. "That's open, and looks like they've got food."

He turned the Prius into the parking lot, and they felt it wallow through the deep drifts of snow as it plowed toward the door. Trying to stop, Kevin slid about ten feet before the car halted.

Kathy peered out her window. Cozy cabins? All she saw was a solid motel wall that ran away from them into the darkness dotted by several doors. Two trucks were backed into parking spots directly in front of two of the doors. Above each door was a short metal awning held up by wrought iron posts. A pyramid of snow settled on the top of each awning.

Kevin gunned the engine, trying to get closer to the office door. The front wheels spun in a high-pitched whine. They were stuck in the middle of the lot twenty feet from the door. "Fucking worthless car," Kevin swore. He glanced at Kathy and said, "Here's the end of the line, babe."

It sounded like something out of a movie, and Kathy laughed. "You make me feel like we're Bonnie and Clyde, hiding out."

"We are outlaws."

"Knock it off, Kevin. I'm tired and anxious to get out of the storm." She opened her door against the wind and stepped into deep snow. Trudging up to the door, Kevin followed and they burst through into the lobby.

It was quiet, warm, and had red wallpaper. A lamp in the corner shone brightly and two more stood over a narrow counter covered with some magazines. They walked across the linoleum-covered floor to the counter, tapped on an upside-down silver cup bell, and waited.

In a few minutes, an older woman came out from the door to the left. She was overweight and wore a gold sweatshirt with a maroon letter M in the front. Below that, it read "Gopher Hockey" in maroon lettering. Thin gray hair stretched from her face to the back of her head to end in a limp ponytail. A cigarette dangled from her mouth, and when the smoke curled up into her face, she squinted and turned her head to the side to avoid it. Must be Mama Lou.

"Shitty night, huh?" she said.

"The worst. How's the road north of here?" Kevin asked.

Her laughter gurgled into a wet cough. "Closed. All the way to the border. Nothin's gettin' through. Want a room?"

"Sure. What's it look like for tomorrow?"

"Clear. Storm's movin' east."

"How long will it take to open the roads?"

"Geez, let's see. If Ronnie's on duty at the county highway department, I'd say you're good to go by nine. But if Len is on, forget it. He'll still be hung over at noon." She laughed again. "We got breakfast at seven. I only cook once, so don't miss it." The ash fell off her cigarette onto the sign-in paper she filled out for them. She swept it away onto the floor.

"What's for breakfast?" Kevin said. "I'm looking forward to those famous north woods blueberry pancakes."

"I got eggs and bacon."

"Pancakes?"

"I got eggs and bacon."

Kevin turned to Kathy. "Damn. I was so busy preparing for the mission I forgot my plastic . . ." He patted the pockets in the front of his jeans.

Mama Lou took Kathy's card and laid it in a slot on top of a triplicate piece of paper on a flat metal machine. With her other hand, she pushed the handle across the card and the machine. She returned it and peeled the paper off for Kathy to sign. "Extra towels cost extra." She thought that was funny, although she'd probably said it a thousand times, and laughed anyway.

They both left and tramped back to the car to try and carry into the room what they needed for the night. After the last load, they were locking the car when they heard a sharp barking sound that leveled out to a long howl. It echoed around the trees at the edges of the parking lot. The howl started again, lonely and fierce. This time, other howls joined in.

"What the hell is that?" Kevin ducked his head as if avoiding a blow and looked around.

"Wolves. Gray wolves are all over northern Minnesota." She laughed at him.

"They sound too fuckin' close for me. Come on, let's get inside."

The howls started again, hollow and almost human sounding. Kathy strained to see around the sides of the parking lot. In the dim light cast by the neon motel sign, she spied two gray shapes ghosting along under the pine trees, bobbing in a loose walk.

In spite of being afraid, Kathy felt a tingling low in her stomach as they sought shelter in the room. She smiled at the thought that the white wine from the trunk was probably chilled already from the weather.

A warm bath first, finish the wine, roll back the down comforter, and it would be just she and Kevin. He probably wanted to get high. That was okay, since he usually performed better that way. Safe and warm inside, while outside the blizzard battled to reach them but couldn't.

Then she opened the door to the room.

CHAPTER 31

Saturday, November 5, Evening

After Brown's call, Zehra sat silently while Paul drove. The numbing hum of the tires over the snow-crusted road, the monotonous scenery, and the closeness of Paul all helped her stay calm and not let panic overwhelm her. Should Zehra call her mother to at least tell her Shereen had been found? No, Martha would ask too many questions and the full truth would come out, upsetting her mother to no end.

Zehra told Paul what Brown had threatened.

"That son of a bitch," Paul growled.

"At least we know who Shereen is with now."

He nodded. "If nothing else, we can rescue her."

"And it confirms all that I thought about Brown. I'm amazed at how he fooled so many people for so long."

"The good ones can do that. I've interviewed dozens of con men, guys who run Ponzi schemes. They have two qualities: guts and the ability to fool people. It's a personality type that lots of criminals share. They're so self-centered that whatever they think must be the truth. Consequently, they can lie without blinking an eye because they believe it so strongly themselves."

"That's Hollywood." He reminded her of Mustafa, who had charmed Zehra into thinking she might be in love with him—until he tried to kill her. How could these guys do it? To be so ruthless and unfeeling. Of course, there were always clues one saw in retrospect, but the guys were so disarming it was hard to notice the warning signs along the way.

Zehra glanced at Paul, his face contorted in concentration on the driving. What about him? She smiled to herself. He was different. He had saved her life from Mustafa. Steady and predictable. Maybe that was worth a lot more than she had ever given him credit for.

The Jeep shuddered as Paul hit a drift of snow spread across the road. "It's getting worse. I don't think we can go much farther," he said.

Zehra's stomach tightened. "What about Shereen?"

Paul looked over at her quickly, then studied the road again. "We can't work a miracle here." He fought the wheel to the left and then to the right. "You said Brown would wait until Monday before he did anything. That means he has something else planned that he needs to keep her for. Must be whatever they're bringing across the border."

"Yeah. But I don't want to wait 'til the last minute." She faced him. "You didn't hear her scream. I did."

They came around the north end of Lake Mille Lacs, past Grand Casino, the Native American museum, and hundreds of small ice fishing shacks. They stood along the shore of the lake, painted in bright colors with stovepipes sticking out of their roofs. As soon as the ice was thick enough, all the shacks would be dragged onto the lake to create a weekend community of hundreds of fishermen. To call them all "shacks" was misleading. Many were furnished and decorated as nicely as anyone's home, with cooking and sleeping facilities. Once the ice on the lake was frozen thick enough, trucks would pull the houses into place.

When he saw Zehra looking at the village of shacks, Paul laughed. "Hey, what a fun time I am. I took you north to go ice fishing. Impressive, huh?"

"Can you see me? You ever go?"

"Naw. Too boring for me. But I've got some friends who were up here last year. Coldest damn night of the year. They told me there were hundreds of people partying 'til late. While they were in their shack, a woman came to the door dressed in a full snowmobile suit. When she got inside, she unzipped it. She was completely naked and offering her services."

Zehra shook her head. "Can't wait to try fishing."

Paul's cell phone rang. He fumbled with it until he held it next to his ear. He answered Agent Mansfield's call. "I'm heading north with Zehra Hassan."

Paul listened for a long time, then said, "I disagree. You do what you want, but we've got good evidence they're coming across the northern border. I'm alone for now, but I'll call for assets just as soon as I can."

He listened again. His voice rose. "You're making a big mistake. These guys are different. I know it'd be hard to get anything in through Canada. But they're coming across today or tomorrow."

After the agent talked some more, Paul shouted, "Don't tell me what I can and cannot do. I don't work for you." He snapped the phone off and turned to Zehra. "We're on our own."

"Isn't there something you can do?"

"I don't know. I can't really call in the FBI assets with the weak evidence we have now. Let me think." He tapped his hand on the wheel. "There's an old friend in the Coast Guard in Duluth. Maybe."

"Why not call him?"

"Yeah. Renko Sarinen."

"Who?"

"Commander of the Duluth station. I'll give him a call." Paul scrolled through his phone numbers until he found the commander's number. He waited through several rings. It was an office number and on Saturday, no one answered. Paul left a message to call back right away. "He owes me a favor."

"Doesn't the Coast Guard work on water?"

"Right. But they also have helicopters that can carry troops and armament. If we need back-up . . ." He took a deep breath. "We'll need enough evidence to convince him to act. That'll be hard. A commander doesn't scramble his air power on a hunch or as a favor to me, even though I'm FBI."

"But they're in Duluth. We're out here in the middle of nowhere."

"Well, I've got one more asset. Another friend from a law enforcement training school. I think he's still the sheriff somewhere up here. When I get a chance, I'll contact him for help on the ground."

Zehra let out her breath. At least there was the possibility of help.

Paul turned the wipers on full speed. "Can't see a damn thing. We gotta stop, Zehra."

"Where? I didn't bring my arctic sleeping bag and tent."

"I think Grand Rapids is the next town."

By now, the snow had obliterated the road ahead, covering the lines and hiding the shoulders which made driving extremely dangerous. Paul couldn't judge how far to either side he could go without dropping off into the steep gullies that ran along the shoulders. Snow piled even deeper in those crevices and covered mud, sand, and broken tree trunks that would destroy the Jeep, trapping them in the clutches of the blizzard.

He slowed to a crawl, trying to feel his way along the road. He got a sense of the edge because the road was banked in the middle, sloping down to both sides. When he felt the angle of the Jeep change, Paul drifted it back to the middle. Still, it was just guessing and hoping he wouldn't slide off entirely.

In the growing darkness, the headlights illuminated a sign: "WELCOME TO GRAND RAPIDS. HOME OF JUDY GARLAND!"

Paul let out a big sigh. "Almost there. I can't keep this up much longer."

"Why don't I drive tomorrow?" She turned quickly to the window and looked out into the gloom.

"What's wrong?"

"I can't stop thinking of how Shereen sounded when she screamed. What did he do to her? Do you think she's still okay? He's going to kill her no matter what." She twisted her hands together. "I don't want to stop."

"We don't have a choice. Forecast is for the storm to blow through us and move to the east. Maybe we can get going first thing tomorrow."

They inched their way down the main street. Streetlights poked out of the dusk to illuminate various stores and buildings. They were all closed. Paul tried to steer in the middle of the street, but the snow was so deep, it dictated where the tires of the Jeep went. Paul hung on, trying to maintain some control of the vehicle.

Near the end of town, they spotted Merle & Mama Lou's Motel. It was open.

Paul steered toward it, but with the snow drifts it was more like a controlled slide into the parking lot. They saw a stranded Prius parked in the middle. It looked abandoned. As they cruised up to the front door, Paul pulled in close and shut off the engine.

"I wish I could've taken you to Paris, but Grand Rapids will have to do."

Zehra laughed. "Come on. We've got a lot to do."

They tramped around snow drifts to reach the lobby and entered. Two lamps in the corner glowed golden against the red fuzzy wallpaper.

"Nice place," Zehra joked with him.

They tapped a small bell and waited. In a few minutes, a heavy-set woman came out from the door on the left. She was dressed in a gold sweatshirt that proudly supported the University of Minnesota Golden Gopher hockey team. A cigarette dangled from her mouth. "Help ya?" she said.

"You got a room?"

The woman laughed, as if that were funny. "We got a few." She walked behind the chest high counter covered with linoleum and pushed a paper toward them. "Sign here."

Paul signed in and asked about the weather.

"No problem. You guys from the Cities, right?"

"How'd you know?"

"Snow's movin' to the east over Lake Superior. Going north?"

"Yeah."

"Son of a bitch. Everyone's going north. I just checked in a couple who are going north too. Doesn't look like they know what they're doing." She coughed in a wet gurgle. "We got breakfast at seven. I cook, so don't miss it."

"Got it," Paul said. He noticed the sign behind the counter: "PRAY FOR SNOW."

They took the single bronze key, struggled back to the Jeep and unloaded just enough for the night. They opened the door to the room, and Zehra laughed. "Thanks, Paul. This is just what I expected."

A clean room opened to them. Gold drapes hung around the large picture window that looked out on the parking lot and the storm. Two double beds with one pillow each were flanked by small side tables. A Bible sat on one table and a rotary phone on the other. The bathroom had a thin white towel on the floor and a plastic curtain with yellow flowers embossed on it separating the toilet area from the shower. The linoleum floor felt slick with dampness.

A chill surrounded Zehra. "Turn on the heat," she asked Paul.

He studied a tan box that hung from the wall. "It's on all the way."

"Great." She sighed. "I'm tired." For a moment, they looked up at each other. One bed or two was the question that wordlessly bounced between them. "I'll take this one," Zehra said to avoid the issue. Actually, she was too upset for anything else tonight anyway.

After she'd brushed her teeth and changed into a flannel nightgown, she climbed into her bed. Propped up with the thin pillow the motel offered, she checked her email on her cell phone. Zehra saw a text from Detroit. After she opened it, a smile creased her face. "Hey, good news," she called to Paul, who was in the bathroom.

"Wha . . . ?" His mouth sounded full of toothpaste.

"Detroit has already made contact with the woman in Texas. The new one." She shouted around the corner of the bathroom.

"Yeah?"

"Well, it looks like the snow cleared enough so that Detroit's got her already booked on a flight to Minneapolis today."

Paul came out of the bathroom with only a towel wrapped around his waist. Black hair curled off his chiseled chest, and his body tapered down to a narrow waist. He was in great shape, and Zehra couldn't help but study his bod. Nice. If she wasn't so tired, who knew what could happen? Besides, they were on a mission to rescue her cousin. Things were too complicated at this time to even think about his body right now.

"That's if you still have a case Monday morning," he reminded her.

"Don't know what I'm going to do. But I will fight."

CHAPTER 32

Sunday, November 6

At daybreak, Jeremy Brown traded driving duties with Paco. They drove straight east from International Falls on State Highway 11 to poke their way through dense forests and finally reach the tiny town of Island View, if you could call it a town since it was unincorporated. It stood in the middle of Dove Island, the last landfall until Canada to the north. A perfect place to make the transfer without anyone knowing about it.

In the brief summer, the population doubled due to the fishing and boating resorts. Now, with the exception of snowmobilers, the town shrank to a handful of year-round residents. And with a blizzard of this force, they'd all be huddled in front of TVs or in bars waiting for the Vikings to play football.

The blizzard had moved off to the east, toward Duluth and Lake Superior. Bright blue skies canopied over the team. Brittle, dry and cold air froze their nostrils as they loaded into the van and truck. Cold wind had come with the tail end of the storm and still buffeted them.

Dove Island looked on a map like a puffy "T" that jutted out into Rainy Lake. Over a small channel of water, less than a thousand feet across, stretched the immense Voyageurs National Park, a wilderness area that the government prohibited anyone from building on. The wilderness protected the right flank of Brown's operation from prying eyes and people who might call someone when they spotted boats ferrying back and forth.

Less than a mile to the northeast, a group of deserted islands spattered across the half way point between Canada and Dove Island. The smuggling boats would weave their way through those islands to avoid detection and also for protection from the bitter winds blowing out of the northwest from across Canada's plains.

Brown steered the truck with the trailer onto a long bridge that crossed over Krause Lake to get on to Dove Island. Low guardrails, no more than two feet high, offered little protection from sliding over and into the cold lake below. Bullying everything before it, the wind whipped up the lake into ferocious whitecaps. The truck swayed to one side as Brown crossed the exposed bridge until he bumped onto solid land again.

Huge granite outcroppings bulged out of the ground to plunge into the water at the shore of the lake. Growing in the tightest crevices, pine trees clung to the very edges of the rock. Thick lines of the trees formed impenetrable fortresses against the open water and wind beyond.

Brown knew that the truck from Winnipeg carrying the shipment would travel on Canadian Highway 11 until it hit the edge of Rainy Lake. The boats waited there to pick up the load. Once filled, the boats would head southwest toward the big deserted island of Sandpoint Island Provincial Park. Using the island to screen their movements, the boats would poke their way along its bays until they crossed another open section of the lake to reach Harrison Island, and finally come through Tango Bay for the last run to Dove Island. The entire distance was about eight miles. At least each one of the open sections of the route was limited to no more than about a mile each.

Brown worried about everything. Would the boats be able to handle the rough water, or would they capsize? Could they make the long crossing quickly enough to avoid detection? Would he lose any of the heavy cargo overboard in the choppy water?

He would have preferred to make the transfer under the secrecy of darkness, but that was impossible in this weather. That was why he'd hired the team.

Brown passed the park and continued to drive toward the farthest end of the island. It formed the right arm of the "T" of the island. Sheltered on the underside of the right arm were several boat docks that protruded into the cold, deep water as if they didn't really want to be out there at all.

He pulled up to the first dock on the right, the public landing. The Sha Sha Resort, with its cabins wrapped around the eastern tip of the island, was closed this time of the year. The dock Brown chose was the longest one, constructed of metal to withstand the brutal winters and freezing water. The van parked next to him.

Their cover story, if they were questioned, was simple. The sign on the van read, " Al's Fishing Charters." They were scouting spots for next year's season, when they'd bring up rich guys from the Twin Cities and make them believe the charters were dangerous adventures in order to charge a lot of money. The locals would understand the scheme and probably even laugh in recognition of the scam also practiced by a lot of the expensive lodges on the lake.

While waiting for the boats, Brown would keep the men close to the van. He'd use them to help with the actual transfer, but their main purpose was defensive in case any strangers caused trouble. Armed, they kept a lookout. He posted one man at the close end of the bridge that crossed Krause Lake to spot for incoming trouble.

He ordered the snowmobiles offloaded and set up on the perimeter. Paco fired up each one of the engines to make sure they would start. These were also defensive and could be used to escape, if necessary, into terrain where a vehicle couldn't follow. Only he and Paco had the keys, however. Brown had no hesitation about leaving the rest of the team to fight for themselves. They were heathens anyway and doomed.

Ferguson set up two of the machine guns to cover anyone coming over the bridge and one to defend against an attack from the water.

The van was parked at an angle to give them shelter from the wind at the point where the dock met the land. After they got the explosives off the boats, they'd be shuttled into the back end of the van. After giving Shereen heavier clothing and a blanket, Brown left her in the locked truck. In a short time she seemed to doze off.

Some of the men set up the Coleman heating units and they huddled around each one. They drank hot coffee from a thermos and bitched about the rough conditions. Kanatchikov was the loudest, as usual. "Fuck. This ain't nothin' compared to Siberia," he boasted.

"I'm sick of hearin' your shit, Russkie," said Snoop.

"You shut the fuck up."

"Don't make me come over there and shut you up," warned Snoop.

Kanatchikov stretched up to his full height and started to move around the heater.

Brown noticed and hurried over. "Stop this crap," he yelled. "I know you're tired of being cooped up in there." He nodded toward the van. "But we're almost done. Focus. Stay alert and watch for local trouble instead of fighting."

The team backed down and resumed their places. Brown ordered Milton to stand guard to the west. Then Brown wandered over to the front end of the van and leaned against it, squinting into the bright colorless sun that glistened on the snow all around. It hurt his eyes until he put on the sunglasses Brown had insisted they bring with them.

Brown went back to the dock, shaking his head at Paco.

"I'll be surprised if these idiots keep it together long enough to finish the mission," Paco said.

"Occupational hazard," Brown sighed. "When they actually see the cargo, it'll get real for them and they'll perform well." From a pocket inside the down parka he wore, Brown pulled out a small radio. He clicked it on, dialed the pre-selected frequency, and keyed it to "Send."

Static cut through the noise of the wind. Brown repeated the code words over and over until he heard the reply. "Shipment has reached the transfer point in Canada. Loading as we speak."

"Give me updates about your progress over the route."

"Roger that, Horseman."

"How's the weather there?"

"Clear but very windy."

"Can the boats handle it?"

"Roger that. We are using the ones with the larger bows to deal with the waves. Don't expect a problem."

"Any problems so far?"

"Negative."

"Be careful. That shipment's worth a lot."

"Yes, sir. Out."

The radio went dead in Brown's hand. He placed it back in the pocket and pulled up his sleeve to check the time. In practice runs before, it had taken about an hour and a half. With the weather conditions today, it would probably take longer. He noted the time and planned for the arrival.

Now, the only thing left to do was wait and depend on God.

CHAPTER 33

Sunday, November 6, Morning

KEVIN SHOOK HER AWAKE. "Come on. We gotta saddle up and get on the trail," he insisted. He jerked around the room in several kung-fu stances to loosen up.

"Knock it off, Kevin. You'll hurt yourself."

"Gotta be ready for those bastards." He whirled his arms around his chest. In a few minutes, he panted and stopped the antics.

Kathy slumbered with her head under the thin pillow. Merle and Mama Lou certainly didn't spend any money on décor or supplies. The room was barren and cold. The garish gold drapes couldn't keep out the bright sunlight. Kathy swung her legs over the edge and felt the shag carpeting touch her feet. She wished for a pair of slippers, because who knew what lived in those fibers?

Kevin told her, "Shower's free. 'Course, there isn't much soap. They only gave us one of those little bars and uh . . . I used a lot of it."

She frowned at him. She ran her hands up underneath her hair and lifted it out several times as if to clear her brain. Her hopes for a romantic evening had stopped at the doorway to this dump. Even Kevin had said the beds were so thin they reminded him of his dorm at prep school. They had opened a bottle of wine and started to drink it. Kevin smoked some grass. As Kathy came out of the bathroom dressed in her see-through negligee, Kevin was so exhausted from driving and fighting the storm, he just fell asleep. She had rolled him over on his back and tried kissing to wake him up. When that didn't work, she wedged her breasts against his face and wiggled. He was out cold.

Now he was wide awake, trying to get her to move faster. "Remember, Mama Lou said if we aren't at breakfast on time, we miss it. I'm starving. I got the munchies."

"Kevin, you get the munchies *while* you're high, not the next day. You passed out too early to even think about food."

"I did, huh? Hey, I'll make it up you later, babe."

She sighed and headed for the shower.

In twenty minutes they had packed the few items carried in from the Prius and walked out into blinding sunshine. At least it gave Kathy a lift to see the sun. It sparkled over all the new snow piled like down pillows on top of everything. Even the sign for the motel had a rounded cap of pure white snow. The cold air stung her nose and mouth.

As she looked up, dark evergreens groaned under a load of fresh snow on each branch. Above them arched a sky blue and high. A wisp of faint cloud stretched off to the north.

Kathy blinked several times, trying to adjust her eyes to the brightness. She stumbled through the snow drifts to the Prius. Someone had plowed carefully around it, freeing the car from its trap of snow. They heaved their bags into the back and locked up the doors.

Back in the motel, they walked around the counter in the lobby, through a door to the left, and into a small dining room. The same gold drapes hung over a small window high on the far wall. Three tables sat in the middle. Metal legs held up the red linoleum tops streaked with capillaries of color to resemble marble.

Two silent men sat at the first table, faces propped in their palms as their arms steepled over the table for support. Cigarette smoke curled up from one face. He wore a camouflage military field jacket, the other a blaze orange hunting coat.

"Thought there was no smoking in this state?"

"Doesn't apply up here. These are real men, Kathy. They drink and smoke and work hard."

"How would you know anything about the hard work part?"

When they sat, Mama Lou came out quickly with a tan plastic coffee pot. The smell wafted around them, and Kathy looked forward to a full cup. When the lady set the pot on the table, part of her cigarette ash dropped to the surface. Mama Lou brushed it aside onto the floor and said, "Betch're hungry." Before waiting for a reply, she walked back into the kitchen.

"Wonder where Merle is?" Kevin asked.

"Probably back there cooking our bacon and eggs. 'Course, that's all he knows how to cook. Do you recall if Mama Lou asked us how we would like our eggs?"

Kevin laughed with her. "I'm sure you'll find out soon enough. Merle can only do them one way." He slurped from his cup. "Ahh . . . that's what I needed. We got a lot of ground to cover today."

"Uh, Kevin?" He turned his face to her. "Where are we going?"

"North . . . north to Alaska." He grinned, then shrugged. "I don't fuckin' know. I still haven't gotten any communication from our troops. I hope they're not stranded somewhere."

"You sure they're coming?"

"Hell, yes. These guys are tough as nails."

Kathy gave him a skeptical look. "Kevin, do you know what the hell you're doing?"

Before he could respond, Mama Lou came back to refill their coffee pot. She brought the smell of bacon with her. "Be out in a minute."

The door to the dining room opened and Kathy gasped. Zehra Hassan and a tall, good looking man walked in.

CHAPTER 34

Sunday, November 6

ZEHRA WOKE EARLY WHEN A SHAFT of bright sunlight sneaked through the gold curtain, reflected off the knotty pine walls and crossed her face. She peeled back the covers and, hugging herself, moved to the window to peek out. The sharp light reflected off mounds of snow hurt her eyes.

She came fully awake and remembered what they were doing there. Waking Paul, Zehra urged him to get going. She didn't want to wait for breakfast. Paul insisted that he was hungry and had to eat. They assembled the few items they had carried from the Jeep and brought them out of the room. The lot was fully plowed, leaving a periwinkle Prius marooned in huge sea of white color.

When they entered the small dining room, Mama Lou told them to sit and wait for their breakfast. Zehra's body stiffened. Across the room Kathy Johnson looked up and saw them standing there. What were the chances they'd meet up here? Johnson walked over to Zehra and Paul. Kevin Stout remained at the table, head hung low.

Johnson stuck out her hand to Zehra, withdrew it, and pushed it out again. "Hi, Ms. Hassan. So, you're after them too, huh?"

"Who?" she said and introduced Paul.

"So are we." Kathy waved over at Stout.

Zehra didn't respond. It felt awkward. Johnson shifted from one leg to the other. Low in her stomach, Zehra felt heat grow inside her, like turning on the burner of a stove. "What are you really doing here?"

"We're going to intercept the crazy militia."

"I don't believe that. You're following me." Zehra's voice rose.

"Following you?" Kathy shook her head. "I tried to warn you, to help you," she insisted.

"That's crazy." The two guys in the far corner tilted their heads toward the noise. Their cigarettes continued to smolder.

Kathy shouted, "How dare you say that? I can't believe you're so inconsiderate."

Kevin unrolled his long body, stood up, and came over to the argument. "What's the problem, babe?" A coffee cup smoked steam into the cool air as he sipped on it occasionally.

Zehra felt the heat inside her rise to a boiling point. "We don't need your interference, so butt out and leave us alone."

"Hey, let's chill here." He smiled weakly.

Zehra stepped into him and pushed her face up to his. His eyes popped open and he stumbled backward. "Let's chill? Chill? Mr. Stout. Do you think Elizabeth Alvarez is 'chilling' right now? Thanks to you, she almost died," Zehra yelled at him from a few inches away.

Stout backed up further and held his cup before him as if for protection. "Wait a minute . . ."

"I'm sick of phonies like you."

Paul moved closer to Zehra's side and placed his hand on her shoulder. "Zehra . . ."

She twisted her shoulder. "Back off, Paul," she warned him. She turned to face Stout. "It's so easy to criticize us. You have no idea how hard this has been on all of us, how hard we've worked." The words didn't seem to come from her, but from some stranger. Zehra opened the wells of frustration and let it all out, directed at Kevin Stout.

Kathy interrupted, "I'm sorry about your colleague, but we do have a right to do our work also. You're way out of line."

Even Mama Lou came out from the kitchen. Her cigarette went out as it hung from her mouth.

Paul stepped forward. "I'm with the FBI. I'm warning you that you shouldn't be involved in anything that could be this dangerous."

Stout snorted and laughed. "Not involved? Man, you feds are so busy chasing foreign terrorists you can't see the home-grown ones we got right next door living among us. Even worse, they're united across the Internet, all feeding off each other to commit violent acts of terror. Even the politicians pander to 'em, trying to get support and money. I tried to warn you guys about these extreme groups, how dangerous they are, and no one would believe me." He grunted. "Well, we're gonna take care of 'em."

"You're not going anywhere," Paul ordered.

Stout snorted and turned away. From over his shoulder he mumbled, "Stupid prick."

Paul slammed his hand into the middle of Stout's back. He arched forward while his stomach smashed into the closest table. He rolled onto the floor in a crumpled heap. Shaking his head, Stout yelled, "I got a shitload of lawyers who'll sue your ass off for that."

Kathy Johnson moved between the two men. "Stop it," she yelled. "You're both acting like children. Go to your corners."

Suddenly, the room went silent, but the yelling echoed as if the argument were still going on. Both women paused and took a breath. The silence rang with anger. Zehra wanted to strangle Stout. This wasn't like her, but after weeks of stress it felt good to let someone have it. And Stout certainly deserved his share.

"Just back off," Zehra said in a low voice she hoped would sound menacing. "Stay away from us."

Kathy glared back and circled around the table to help Kevin stand up. "Don't worry. I'm never doing a damn thing to try and help you. Ungrateful bitch!"

Zehra and Paul sat at the far table and hurried through dry scrambled eggs and thin coffee. "Son of a bitch. Amateurs," Paul grunted. "I don't want that guy anywhere near us. He's dangerous because he's so stupid."

After a few bites, Zehra shoved her plate away. She could hardly sit still, from the blowup and from knowing what they had to do later. Eating quickly, Paul finished everything on the plate and stood to leave.

Outside, they climbed into the Jeep. While the engine warmed, Paul called his friend from the sheriff's office. After several rings, Henry Yellowfeather answered. "Sorry to bother you on your day off, Henry."

"No prob. Anything for a friend. What do you need?"

"Not sure. We're just leaving Grand Rapids."

After Paul told him about their situation, Henry said, "I'll wait for you at the sheriff's department in International Falls. I'll get things ready on this end." He gave them directions.

Zehra looked out the window and sighed. "Sorry to make a scene in there. I don't know what happened. I'm just so sick of these people harassing us."

"Let it go. You think it's easy being an FBI agent? Not only do we get it from the public, but our administration is equally difficult sometimes."

Paul wheeled the Jeep out of the lot. A blue, clear sky curved over everything. The air felt sharp as Zehra took a deep breath. What a difference a few hours made. They took Highway 38 north out of Grand Rapids. The entire road was plowed clean.

"Not like Minneapolis or St. Paul," Paul laughed. He pushed the Jeep up to eighty miles per hour. With the stiff suspension, everything rattled inside, but they made good time. Twenty minutes later, Paul glanced in the rear-view mirror. "Oh, no," he groaned.

"What?"

"There's been a blue Prius following us all the way from Grand Rapids."

Zehra twisted around in the seat. As the Prius crept closer, she saw the shaggy head of Kevin Stout. Turning back, she said, "It's Stout, dammit."

A half hour later, the rocking of the Jeep lulled Zehra into a dreamy state. As far as she could see, mounds of fresh snow were piled among dense, dark forests. Trees and bushes grew outward endlessly in different shades of green, each color indicating a different type of plant, crowding and shouldering each other in a greedy effort to live.

Living in an urban environment, Zehra forgot how plants could predominate over human habitation. Boasting thousands of species compared to people, plants thrived and adapted everywhere on the planet. They had existed long before humans and had more practice in growing, reproducing, and defending themselves—against human invasion—and they still survived. Maybe they would prevail over humans in the end.

Zehra turned on the radio. Only the AM stations came through, most of them live church services. On one station, two men talked about the upcoming ice fishing season.

"She's gonna be a cold one, Elmer."

"You betcha. It's so cold in winter, my email will freeze." They both laughed for a long time.

In a few hours, they approached the small town of International Falls on the Canadian border. Stout and Johnson had fallen far behind. Paul slowed as he drove into the city. Except for dozens of trucks parked outside each of the one-story bars, the streets were vacant. Even though the wind had dropped its load of snow, it still felt cold and fierce coming out of the northwest.

The Rainy River looped to the north around the town and created the international boundary before it flowed east into Rainy Lake. They passed the Falls International Airport and entered the city.

Paul turned east on Fourth Street. To the left, they saw Smokey Bear Park with a white band shell that looked like someone had cut a basketball in half. Zehra chuckled and pointed out to Paul, "There's a beach here. Can you imagine?"

"Must only get used one month a year."

On Fourth Street they came to a two-story old stone building with a gold dome on the top. The sign told them it was the Koochiching County Courthouse. When Paul turned around the corner, they saw a tan Yukon in the parking lot. A sign in the shape of a badge with a yellow and tan star on the side read "KOOCHICHING COUNTY SHERIFF." On a trailer behind the vehicle, two snowmobiles rested, strapped down with bungee cords. Paul stopped beside the Yukon.

From the left, two men hurried out of the sheriff's office with their heads lowered against the wind. They both wore tan ski jackets with yellow edging and brown trim. Official clothing.

The first man looked up, waved, and smiled at Paul with recognition. "Great to see you again, Paul. This here's my undersheriff, John Hansen." Yellowfeather had glistening black hair worn long. He was short but muscular. He and Paul discussed the situation. "There's a road goes straight east of here to Dove Island. About ten miles. You sure that's where they are?"

Paul looked at Zehra and back again to Henry. "We have GPS evidence that a co-conspirator spent a lot of time at that location."

Henry nodded. "If I were smuggling anything over, that's where I'd go."

"Okay. Let's roll."

"We'll pull the sleds in case we need 'em out there. Snow's pretty deep, and there's only one road onto the island." He paused. "Why don't we lead? We know the terrain, and our vehicle is bullet–resistant."

They left and caravaned along Highway 11. Stands of fir trees hugged both sides of the narrow road, growing right up to the edges. Even out here, the road had been cleared of snow. The Yukon slowed just before it disappeared around a curve. Paul slowed to a stop.

Henry came back around the curve, jogging toward them. At Paul's open window, he said, "Stop here. The island's right around the corner, connected by a low bridge. Let's go on foot into the woods and reconnoiter first."

"Right."

Paul got out and walked to the back end of the Jeep. He removed an automatic pistol and a snubby gun that looked like a machine gun. He held it up to show Yellowfeather. "Here's one of my favorites. The American Tactical 522 Lightweight rifle. I've got the nine-barrel attached and the extra-long clip." Paul tilted it to the side to show the curved banana clip that stuck out from the bottom. "Extra clips right here," he patted an outside coat pocket, "and I can slam 'em in in less than two seconds."

Henry lifted his eyebrows and admired the weapon. "Light?"

"Feather weight, but it carries one hell of a punch. And," he looked around them as if someone might hear, "I got a friend of mine to alter it to fully auto." Paul grinned with pride.

"We can't afford those on our budget up here. 'Course, the worst problems I usually have are drunken brawls between ice fishermen."

Zehra pulled out her own small Glock 26 and, lifting the cuff of her jeans, she strapped it on her left ankle. As Mavis had taught her, she practiced drawing it out to make sure it didn't snag on any clothing. Zehra rolled down her pants leg.

After everyone had armed themselves, Paul told her, "Whatever happens, don't leave the vehicle." The men started forward toward the curve in the road. Paul slipped among the trees on the right and the sheriffs disappeared to the left.

The Jeep's engine idled and warm air curled around Zehra's feet after she crawled back inside. She rolled down the window next to her. High in the trees she heard the whistle of the wind as it bent the tops over. On the ground it was silent.

Then Zehra heard a chirping beside her, chattering and insistent. She saw two squirrels chasing each other. They played in the snow, running over bare branches to dive into snow banks like they were jumping into a swimming pool.

She waited. The engine of the Jeep rumbled monotonously.

Zehra strained to hear anything from in front of her. Time ticked by while she waited. After she crossed her legs again, they felt cramped and needed a stretch. Zehra looked around outside the Jeep. The squirrels had left. Nothing moved. She opened the door, remembering Paul's warning, but decided it would be okay if she remained next to the Jeep. She stepped out and shut the door quietly.

She looked down the road where it curved to the right. What was happening? Was Paul okay? Had he found Shereen yet? Zehra glanced to her left and right, listened, heard nothing, and inched forward along the road where the men had gone.

She heard the crunch of her boots over the snow. The air smelled dry and cold and crisp as if it could shatter like frozen glass.

Then a stretched-out rifle shot cracked through the silence, followed by two more.

CHAPTER 35

Sunday, November 6

"GOD GRANT US PATIENCE. WHERE ARE THEY?" Jeremy Brown studied his watch as if that would make the transfer go faster. "It's been two hours since they left." He couldn't raise the boats on the radio.

Paco tried to calm him down. "It's rough out there. Maybe they're going slow so they don't tip over."

"Capsize is the word, you idiot. Get out of my way."

Paco jumped back as Brown stomped off the end of the dock onto dry land. He yelled at the men squatting around the heaters. "What are you doing? Taking a shit? Keep a lookout."

Paco came up behind him. "Why don't I go to the other side of the island and glass the water? See if I can spot 'em." More than anything, he wanted to get away from the fury of Brown. Paco worried about that. The guy was unpredictable.

"No. I'll go." Brown shuffled off past some deserted log cabins with green roofs and reached the north shore of the island. He pulled out his Steiner binoculars and scanned the open water ahead of him. Nothing. His eyes hovered over the horizon. The easiest way to spot a boat was to look for specks on the horizon that interrupted the flat expanse. There. Far off to the right he spotted the bow of a boat heaving up and down in the waves. It would ride up one side, crest it, and plunge down to disappear through a spray of white mist into the trough below. Brown let out a whoop. It looked like the boat carried a full load. "All praise be to God," he shouted to the trees huddled around him.

He ran back to the dock. "Here they come," he yelled at Paco. "I want them offloaded in less than five minutes to pick up another load."

Just as he got to the end of the dock, they heard the high whine of a four-stroke outboard motor. The boat rounded the tip of the island, plowing a white wake on either side of the bow as it entered the calm shelter of the island and turned in toward the dock.

Brown could hardly control himself. The plan was going to work. He jumped off the dock into the bow of the boat before it snugged tight against the rubber tire fenders hanging from the dockside. He wallowed back and forth to keep his balance. Once stabilized, Brown grabbed at the first of the wooden boxes. Heaving it up, he shoved it off the boat to Paco above. Then he lifted the next one. He kept pulling them out of the boat as fast as he could.

Some boxes teetered on the edge of the dock and almost fell into the lake. Brown pushed at them and at Paco and at the driver of the boat. Like a madman, he lifted and shoved until the boat was empty.

"Get them in the van," Brown screamed. Paco started a line of men in a bucket brigade and managed to get all the boxes off the dock.

Kanatchikov came over, his mouth open as he stared at all the explosives sitting in the back end of the van. "One hell of a bang," he wheezed as he pushed his hat back on his forehead. He helped the others move the shipment forward deeper into the van.

On the dock, Brown helped cast off the lines to the boat. "Other one coming?" he asked.

The man driving the boat was covered from head to toe in heavy clothing and had frozen spray crusted white on his beard. "Right behind me. But the water's rough and colder than a witch's tit." The driver looked up at him. "Got any hot coffee?"

"Get going." Brown used his foot to push off the boat from the dock. Then he hustled off the dock. When he got to the large van the Russian had driven, he looked in to see the load stacked at the front end. Not yet enough to complete the job at all the nuclear plants.

Soon, Brown heard the whine of the second boat coming around the point of the island. He felt great. The transfer was going better than he'd expected. A few more hours and they'd be done and out of there.

He waved the boat in toward the dock. "Hurry up," he yelled over the biting wind. When they got closer, he saw the load, spread out along the bottom of the boat in order to avoid the worst of the water splashing into the bottom over the gunwales.

Brown went wild. He almost jumped off the dock into the boat. "Stupid clods," he yelled at the driver. "Why weren't these covered? Paco, get these boxes out of here and up to the van."

As they marched off the dock for the seventh time, carrying the heavy boxes, Brown heard shouting from the left. He looked up to see Milton running hard down toward the camp with his rifle slapping against his thigh. "Bogies. Bogies over the bridge," he shouted. "Get the weapons."

Brown met him at the edge of the van. "What'd you see?"

"Law. Lots of 'em across the bridge. I tried to take one out. Think I did."

Brown felt the heat rising in him again. Uncontrollable. His arms and shoulders shook with blind holy anger. In one step, he crossed to Milton and ran his hardest uppercut punch into Milton's gut. Brown turned his shoulders and hips into the blow for maximum power. Milton's face opened in surprise and pain. He dropped the rifle and staggered back a couple steps before collapsing on his back into the muddy snow, writhing in pain and coughing while his legs jerked spasmodically.

Snoop laughed at that.

"I told you not to engage. Not to let anyone know we're here. Now you've screwed it up for us all. I should kill you right now," Brown screamed until spit came out of his mouth, stretched wide open.

Milton rolled to his side and threw up. Finally recovered, he shook his head and dragged himself up in round house steps until he could lean against the van. He pulled the rifle with him, lifting it in shaking hands. He pointed it at Brown. Milton tried to steady himself to fire. Brown beat him to it. He pulled out his Ruger. His arm stuck out straight, the pink bracelet hanging from his wrist, and he shot Milton in the face.

The back of his head exploded from the impact of the bullet. A spray of red and gray mist and pieces of skull blew out over a section of clean snow. Milton followed it down by rolling back onto his butt and lying out like a pancake on a breakfast plate. Spread eagle with arms thrown wide, he didn't move.

Shocked silence spread through the camp.

"I hate to waste an asset, but that sinner may have just cost us everything," Brown growled. "Get into your defensive positions. You've got to hold 'em off 'til Paco and I get the last crates unloaded. Put all the Noreens on their tripods toward the bridge."

The remainder of the team grabbed pistols and rifles from the van. They switched the rifles to automatic fire to turn them into machine guns. Carrying extra ammo, they sprawled into the deep snow, hidden behind logs and rocks in a perimeter around the camp, all facing west toward the bridge. They had enough firepower, Brown figured, to hold off an army—at least for a few hours until the last of the boats arrived.

Back at the dock, Paco looked whiter than the snow. "Uh . . . what do you want me to do?" he chattered.

"Get the sleds ready. While our guys hold off the law, you and me'll sneak around the edges with the snowmobiles and flank them. Won't know what hit 'em." He grinned briefly. "Then we get out of here. With or without those idiots." He nodded at the team on the ground.

Paco nodded but was too afraid to say anything more.

CHAPTER 36

Sunday, November 6

PAUL RAN UP TO ZEHRA, FURIOUS. "I told you to stay in the Jeep. Someone fired on us over there." He pointed up the road to the bend. They met with the sheriff and his partner next to the Yukon. "See how many?" Paul asked them.

Henry had been in front and had drawn the fire. "One guy. At the other end of the bridge. Probably a lookout."

"Damn. Wish we had some air cover."

"What're we gonna do?"

Paul thought for a moment. "I don't know. Is there any other way onto the island besides the bridge?"

"No. If we had a boat . . ." Hansen said. "Can't we just wait for reinforcements? Trap 'em on the island?"

Paul shook his head. "I'm sure they're trafficking the stuff over with boats from Canada. They could get off the island using the same boats and escape."

Henry said, "They could go anywhere. There are over 200,000 acres of water out there with thousands of bays and places they could put into. Depending on how fast they moved, they could come into one of these little towns and disappear before we could mobilize a containment plan."

Zerha inched back into the group. "Is the lake frozen enough to drive a snowmobile on it?"

Hansen shrugged. "Not unless you got a floating snowmobile. And I ain't never heard of such a thing." He spit into the snow.

"But are they frozen along the shores yet?"

Hansen started to protest until Henry waved him back. "Wait a minute. We've had enough below zero weather at night that the water close to the shore may be frozen in the shallow spots. If you know where those spots are located. What're you thinking?"

"You said the bridge is the only way to get on the island, but what if you could sneak across some ice at a different part and surprise them? After all, won't they expect you to come over the bridge?"

Paul smiled and turned to Henry. "Think it could work?"

He sighed. "Don't know. It's pretty dangerous. If the sled goes through the ice, it's all over, baby. That water will freeze your ass solid in about five minutes. You can't even swim that fast. And think about all the clothing you're wearing, weighing you down, and even if you made it to shore, you'd freeze standing there before you could get the clothing off, get dry, and get into . . ."

"But *could* it work, Sheriff?" Paul interrupted.

Henry blinked. "Maybe."

"Maybe might be all we have now."

Yellowfeather and Hansen unloaded the two snowmobiles quickly. Firing them up, they revved the engines and checked the gauges. Satisfied, they climbed off and came back to Paul and Zehra. "So, now what?" Henry asked them.

Paul's face twisted. "We've got to maximize our force. Or at least, make them think we've got a huge force. They don't know how many of us there are."

"How do we do that?" Hansen said.

"Confusion and surprise."

Henry frowned. "Me and John could cross the channel under the Krause Lake Bridge. I know a spot that might be frozen enough."

"Once you're over, split up. Makes more noise and they might think there are more of you."

"Yeah. Okay. So we go around the bridge and hit the beach with the sleds, driving into the interior. I think we should be firing our weapons as we come across. Try to confuse them."

"Right. You said your Yukon is bullet proof?"

"Well, not like an armored vehicle. The windows are bullet resistant, they tell us. The sides are made of thicker steel, but I don't know if it would hold off a high-powered rifle."

Zerha said, "Sheriff, do you have a map of the island?"

He laughed. "It's too small and unimportant to be mapped, but I can draw you a picture." He pulled out an official notebook with the sheriff's logo on the cover. "Here we got the only road down the middle to the public docks. The entire eastern end is the Sha Sha Resort. Closed for the season, but it has a big lodge and a ring of cabins along the north and south shores. If we could at least stop these guys for a little while, I could scramble the deputies from the surrounding counties. Maybe even our National Guard unit in International Falls. Take a while, but we could get help."

"Key is we can't let them escape off the island."

"Shit, I don't know." Henry sighed and stepped back into the road. "I don't know. I was in Iraq and had bullets flyin' all around me. It ain't no fun. And it's dangerous." He frowned. "We can't wait?"

"No. Those assholes can escape and carry out their plot. We'll never stop them."

Zehra thought of Shereen. "I'll go with you," she said to Paul.

"No you won't," Paul said. "I know you're worried, but no."

She stood in front of him, face within inches of his. "She's my family. I'm going with you. At least in the sheriff's Yukon."

Paul sighed, knew he couldn't fight her, and thought of the time sliding away. "Okay. You ride in the back seat and duck down. Do not, and I repeat, do not leave the vehicle until I personally come to get you."

"Aye aye, sir."

Paul and the sheriffs prepared their weapons. Their plan was simple. Paul would drive the Yukon and nose it onto the bridge, hoping to draw all the attention of the enemy. While they focused on that, Henry and John would charge across the channel and attack from the north side of the island, hoping to confuse them. If lucky, they could surround and capture the criminals quickly. The fallback plan was to work their way toward the main lodge building for protection, pin down the enemy, and wait for reinforcements.

"And if they try to get off the island with a boat?" Hansen asked.

"Intercept them with your snowmobile. Try to slow 'em down. Remember, we'll be sheltered in the trees and they'll be exposed, naked on the beaches with the lake behind them. I don't think you'll get much of a fight in that situation."

Hansen nodded in agreement. He turned to the side, a spat into the snow, and wiped his mouth off.

Zehra climbed into the Yukon with Paul. She sat in the back seat while Paul laid out an arsenal of weapons across the front seat. "Scared?" she asked.

He nodded but didn't answer. He adjusted the mirrors in spite of the fact it wouldn't make any difference, started the engine, checked his watch for the coordinated time with the sheriffs, and said, "You can't think about what might go wrong." He turned back to face her. "Zehra . . . I uh . . ." His face clouded over. "You're wonderful, and I promise to look for Shereen as soon as I can. Even though they know we're here, they don't know how many we've got, and if we move fast enough, we should overwhelm them."

She searched his eyes and wanted to say something meaningful to him. Something about the way she'd come to feel about him and her thankfulness and how handsome he was, but the time ran out. Maybe the look that passed between them was enough anyway.

"Don't get out of this vehicle," he warned her again. He turned forward and put the Yukon in gear.

He crept along the two-lane road that curved to the right. As they rounded that, the narrow steel bridge came into view. It spanned a short stretch between the big lake to the left and Krause Lake to the right. Paul slowed as they came closer. No one appeared on the other side of the bridge.

Ducking down behind the steering wheel, Paul came across the bridge. No one stopped him. He inched forward until they came down a slight incline. Still, no one appeared. Moisture sprang over Paul's forehead. He breathed faster.

They drove along the two-lane road, surrounded by evergreens on both sides. Zehra felt like a sitting duck. Hidden from view along the entire road, anyone could pop out and blast the Yukon from the undefended sides.

The trees closed in around them even tighter and blocked the wind. Inside the cocoon of trees, silence enveloped them. The crunch of the tires seemed very loud. Paul crept forward.

On his cell phone, he called to Henry. "Across the bridge. No engagement yet. Hold off 'til you hear action."

A few yards further, the road dipped to the right again. Off through the trees, they could see the gray and tan of the beginnings of a beach. Must be getting close now.

Nothing moved except the Yukon crawling forward. The next turn took them into an open area to the right that sloped down to the long beach. To the left, trees hugged the side of the road, thick and dark. At the far end of the beach, they saw a large white van, a truck, and two snowmobiles. No humans were visible.

Then, like the sudden onset of a tropical monsoon, that even when it's expected shocks onlookers with the fury and encircling noise as it hits, the attack against the Yukon came just as suddenly, with uncontrollable fierceness.

CHAPTER 37

Sunday, November 6

BULLETS SPLATTERED INTO THE YUKON until Zehra felt like she was stuck inside a metal garbage can while someone pounded hammers against the sides. The windshield splintered into dozens of crooked cracks, but held without shattering. The passenger side rear-view mirror fell off after disintegrating under the punishment of rifle fire.

In order to flank the attackers, Paul bailed out of his door and rolled into the protection of the heavy woods that hugged the left side of the car. Zehra flattened onto the floor of the back seat, wishing she could somehow get even lower. The shooting continued without let up.

The two right side windows crumpled under the bullets and blew inside with a rush of shattered glass. Zehra, face down on the floor, felt the deadly debris scatter across her back. Her ski jacket protected her. Down there, the shooting sounded like firecrackers exploding in long strings of noise. She heard thuds, twanging sounds, crashes, and metal parts breaking in screeching pain.

Was Paul okay?

At a brief pause in the attack, she heard the distant whine of a snowmobile to her left. Then another one came from the right of her, around the back end of the Yukon. She couldn't see anything but the shooting stopped suddenly. The sheriffs? The noise died. Zehra heard more gunfire, but it was coming from far in front of her. She raised her head to peer over the door.

To the right of the Yukon, the trees, bushes, and branches were stripped bare from the gunfire. The door on the right side was crushed in from the firepower directed against it. Zehra surveyed the area around the truck. Nothing moved.

Sliding across the seat, she tried the opposite door. It opened, and Zehra was about to climb down when Paul's warning came back to her. "Don't leave the Yukon until I come to get you." She hesitated and retreated to the back seat.

She heard more snowmobiles whine. It sounded like an army of them, crisscrossing somewhere in front of her. More gunfire. Tree branches cracking.

Zehra couldn't sit still. Worrying about Paul, Shereen, and not knowing what was going on scared her. Should she leave the truck? And do what? She looked out to the sides, and forward, trying to see what had happened.

Nothing appeared. What could she do?

When she calmed down, Zehra noticed that she was damp inside her ski jacket and jeans. Sweat from fear and adrenaline soaked all over her. She unzipped the jacket and peeled it back to let cool air refresh her. Zehra breathed deeply and forced herself to calm down. In spite of what she'd just been through, she could control her panic.

She tried to think rationally.

It had sounded like the sheriffs had moved forward of the Yukon. Paul had probably crawled up there too. Were they okay? Her mind ticked back and forth like the pendulum on a clock. What should she do? Paul had told her to stay with the vehicle. And in her gut, Zehra felt relatively safe inside now that the shooting had stopped. She sat back in the seat.

A girl's scream gashed through the still air. Shereen!

Zehra jumped out of the truck to land in a deep pile of new snow. A few feet in front of her stood a thick stand of trees, the same ones Paul had hidden between. She started to climb over the drifts to reach the safety of the tree line.

Behind her, she heard the whine of a snowmobile. It gained in volume, obviously coming down the road in front of the Yukon. Zehra clambered into the trees and sank behind a mound of snow. She kept her head low but looked down the road toward the direction of the beach.

The sound echoed off the trees on either side of the road as if she were in a Gothic cathedral where the trees formed the narrow walls. A snowmobile burst out of a mound of snow on the road as it climbed up over it. Zehra could see the treads on the front end chewing ahead as it rose into the air. When it crested the mound and dropped down on her side, she gasped.

Jeremy Brown stood in a crouch behind the handlebars, driving the sled as fast as he could. When he came down onto the road, the snowmobile slewed to one side, and he leaned in the opposite direction to maintain control. A jet of snow erupted from the back end. The machine dug into the muddy road and straightened out.

She was going to hide behind the trees when something behind Brown caused her to pause. Someone hung on the back end of the snowmobile.

Then Brown noticed the Yukon in the middle of the road. He slowed to check it out. Brown angled off the road to the side and ducked behind the protection of some trees. He inched forward toward the abandoned truck.

That's when Zehra saw the other rider—Shereen.

* * *

JEREMY BROWN HAD KNOWN THERE WAS trouble when he killed Milton. The law enforcement wouldn't go away. His only hope was that the team could hold off whoever came at them for a short time.

He radioed the final boat load, and found out it was about ten minutes out from the island. He yelled at them to hit it at full throttle. Brown ordered Paco to get the snowmobiles started and ready. "And get that Muslim infidel out here. I may need her yet."

Paco's face went slack with fear. "Yeah," he mumbled. This was nothing like hustling kids at the Mall of America. He wished he were back there, eating at McDonald's and acting like a big shot around the stupid babes. Paco was determined to survive. He raced to the sleds and fired up each one, leaving them to idle as he climbed off.

The next boat curved into the dock, and Brown went berserk in his efforts to get the boxes unloaded quickly. Brown heard the first of the gunfire as he got the last of the crates into the van. The two remaining team members had moved to a forward position and were firing on full automatic. It sounded like a shooting gallery at the state fair.

Brown stayed to unload the last boat. He called Paco over and told him to support the fire team. Paco trembled at the thought, and Brown realized he was worthless as a fighter. Undisciplined and faithless. He couldn't face a real opponent. Time for Plan B.

Brown raced to the truck. Inside, he searched quickly for the Muslim. There she was, near the back, hiding underneath the blanket, sitting with a vacant look on her stiff face.

Brown leaned past the front seat to reach Shereen. When he got there, he pulled her up by her wrist. He told her to come with him and not to try anything brave.

She stumbled after him as he led her from the truck. She was dressed for the weather but didn't have a hat. No time for that now. He signaled to Paco to forget about the last boat and to mount the snowmobile.

Brown straddled his sled and made sure he was armed with two semi-automatic pistols, and he laid a sawed-off shotgun across the seat in front of him. A "street sweeper," the "gangstas" called the weapon because the shortened barrel assured that the hundreds of pellets exploding from the barrel would disperse in the widest pattern, assuring an easy kill at close range.

When Paco was equally armed, Brown leaned over to give him orders. "You angle to the north and try to flank them from that direction. I'll go along the beach and come up at 'em. When you see them, shoot to kill."

"What about Snoop and the Russian? We're just gonna leave 'em?"

Brown barked a short laugh. "They are sinners and lost forever anyway." He twisted the throttle on the snowmobile, made sure the girl was on tight, and he rocketed forward to follow the shoreline to the left. He hoped that if he could knock out the enemy, he could still get back, pack up the rest of the shipment, and get out all right. It could work.

As he skimmed along the edge of the lake, he still heard heavy fire to his right. Probably the team engaged with the enemy. Good. That meant it would be easy for him to sneak up and attack their undefended side while Paco came in from the opposite direction.

He felt Shereen start to sag off at an angle. He stopped and propped her up again. "Hang on," he screamed at her. "You're gonna get me out of here."

He pounded ahead until he figured he was behind the enemy. He circled up the slight incline toward the road. He wanted to come in behind them and kill them easily. As he rose over a mound of packed snow on the edge of the woods, he leaped over it and thudded down on the far side.

Ahead of him stood a shot-up Yukon. He slowed as he came closer to be careful. It looked abandoned. Brown decided to check and, if necessary, kill any survivors inside. He idled up to the side of the Yukon, holding the sawed-off shotgun in front of him pointed toward the vehicle. Any movement would cause him to shoot. He swung his leg over the saddle of the snowmobile and stood.

Brown sensed movement behind him. He spun and saw Shereen rising up to dismount. "Don't even try it," he growled. "I can shoot you faster than you can run." She sat down in the saddle.

He turned back to the Yukon and when he rose on his feet to look inside, he saw it was empty. That caused him to worry, and he looked around quickly in case the occupants were lying in the trees, ready to ambush him. He surveyed the trees from a low crouch. He saw nothing except squirrels that played over the tops of the snow piles.

From behind him, he heard a familiar female voice. "Put the gun down, Hollywood."

CHAPTER 38

Sunday, November 6

B ROWN PIVOTED SLOWLY WITH A WIDE GRIN on his face. He pulled Shereen close to him with an inescapable grip. "Hey, Z. Looks like we need to make a deal."

Zehra felt fear rising from her stomach, causing her extended arm with the Glock to quiver. She tried to maintain control. She thought of Mavis Bloomberg and her training with the gun. Deep, slow breaths. Don't jerk the weapon or squeeze it too tightly. Aim for the largest body mass. "I'll trade you Shereen for not shooting you. Let her go." Zehra was proud of the false authority in her voice. It sounded good.

Brown didn't fall for it. He edged closer to Zehra, pulling Shereen along with him. "Not a real trade. How 'bout you give me the gun, I leave with Shereen, and I don't kill you."

Zehra forced herself to focus, to keep calm. Fear coursed through her as she faced Brown. She couldn't swallow, couldn't talk.

He inched closer. When he got within a few feet of her, he dropped his arm and stuck his hand into a jacket pocket. He smiled at Zehra and looked her dead in the eyes.

She felt her legs shaking and hoped it didn't show. An image of Mustafa from a year ago crossed from her memory into her consciousness. The rain had soaked all their clothing including his long hair as it hung on either side of his face that contorted into the horrible shape of a gargoyle as he tried to kill her. She had shot him instead, killing him. The guilt from that washed over her in an instant, and Zehra realized that she couldn't kill Brown.

Then her eyes found Shereen again and Zehra fired the Glock twice, quickly.

Brown roared in pain, which distracted Zehra long enough for him to leap at her, raising his arm from the jacket pocket to swing and knock the gun from Zehra's hand, sending it up into the air, where it came down to sink into a snow drift. He grabbed her still outstretched hand and twisted it fiercely.

Zehra screamed and dropped to her knees, turning involuntarily to avoid the pain. She ended up on her back. When he let go, she realized her arm and shoulder were numb. Brown threw Shereen down into the snow next to Zehra. They met each other's eyes and rolled enough to hug each other. Shereen cried and said, "I'm sorry. I'm so sorry." Brown kicked them apart.

When Zehra looked up, she saw a bright red streak on the sleeve of his jacket. She must have wounded him. He had a gun pointed at them about twice the size of her little Glock. "Get up," he growled. His face twisted from the pain. "How many are with you?"

Zehra didn't say anything.

The explosion of the gun in his hand was so loud that it hurt her ears. A clod of earth and snow jumped up from beside Shereen. "How many are with you?" he asked.

"Uh, Paul and two sheriffs from International Falls."

"What's their plan?"

Zehra felt her eyes brimming with tears. She'd failed in so many ways. And to now be facing death at the hands of this man, unable to even protect her cousin, was crushing. "They . . . they are going to circle around the beach and surprise you. They're armed and know what they're doing."

Brown laughed. "I've got the army of the Lord to stop them."

"And the Coast Guard is on the way with helicopters," she lied quickly.

That made Brown think for a moment. He stepped to the side and looked around him, back toward the beach. "Okay. Here's what we're gonna do, girls. I'm not giving up and you two are my way out." He flicked the gun up to indicate they should stand. Both of them scrambled up from the snow. "Zehra, you get in the front on the snowmobile. Your cousin goes next, and I get on the back with the gun pointed at your heads."

"But . . . I can't drive . . ."

"You'll learn. If a ten-year-old kid can do it, so can you."

Zehra threw her leg over the saddle and scrunched forward. She felt Shereen climb on behind her and squeeze close. She felt the weight of Brown as he mounted the back end.

"So often, I offered to tell you the Good News of the new kingdom, but you refused to listen. Now you will be lost like all the others, except for the people of the truth," he called to Zehra. "Muslims aren't promised the kingdom of heaven."

Brown pointed to the handlebars. "Put your hands on the grips," he ordered. "Now see that red button by your thumb? Press it." When she did, the engine roared to life. "In your right hand is the throttle. When you turn it toward yourself, it goes faster. Now, all you gotta do is steer us out of here."

Zehra tentatively pulled on the throttle. She gave it a lot of gas, and the sled leaped forward with a jolt. She hung on and eased the throttle back a little until she felt comfortable. As she became more familiar with the snowmobile, she increased the speed. She heard Brown yell over the noise of the engine. "Head for the bridge."

Zehra followed the trail along the road, still increasing the speed. She thought maybe if she could get going fast enough, she could swerve the sled and throw Brown off the back end. Then she remembered he had the gun. A trained man like him could easily kill them both, even on a speeding snowmobile. She saw the narrow bridge with the low guardrails on either side as they curved around a turn in the woods.

She was about to start across the bridge when the blue Prius appeared suddenly from around the bend in the road beyond the bridge. Stout and Johnson. Now what?

Zehra heard Brown yelling behind her to get across the bridge. She twisted the throttle and felt the track underneath the snowmobile churn with power. They raced up onto the bridge.

At the far end, the Prius skidded to a stop and blocked the exit off the bridge. Stupid Stout, Zehra thought. Brown will simply kill them. She throttled back until the sled stopped along the guardrail at the edge of the bridge. What would Brown do?

When Zehra looked back at the Prius, she saw something that stopped her breathing. Stout and Johnson had scurried around the side of the Prius. From behind its protection, Stout's hand poked out with a pistol in it. "Stop it right there," he yelled. "Freeze!"

Didn't he know who was sitting behind her? Zehra wondered. Stout couldn't possibly win this battle. Brown dismounted and fired three shots at the Prius. The first took out the windshield and driver's side window in a disintegrating shower of glass. The second flattened the front tire, and the third hit metal somewhere and twanged off into the woods. Stout ducked but came up with his own shot, which went off into the woods.

Zehra yelled to Shereen to get down. They dove behind the side of the machine and burrowed into the snow on the bridge. She heard more shooting back and forth. Where was Paul? Would he hear the noise and come to see what it was?

Next to her feet, Brown crouched and, propping the barrel of his big gun on the saddle of the snowmobile, he took careful, timed shots. He looked relaxed and smiled as if this was simply a shooting range. He knew that eventually, he would win.

Zehra pushed Shereen in tighter to the edge of the sled. She tried to keep down as far as possible. The gunfire stopped for a moment. Brown peeked over the top edge of the machine. He started to straighten up and in a crouch, moved forward toward the front of the snowmobile. He crabbed along the side until he was next to Zehra. He was close enough that Zehra could smell the coppery odor of fresh blood on his sleeve.

He slowly unfolded himself to stand up and study the Prius for any life. He growled at the women, "Get up on the sled. We're getting out of here, or I may just kill you now."

Zehra rolled to her hands and knees. Brown stood about two feet away with the guardrail against his lower left leg, studying the Prius. She knew what had to be done.

Putting her right foot underneath her body, Zehra pushed with all her strength and launched herself at Brown. She hit him just as she extended fully, knocking against his upper body from his blind side.

He tried to get his wounded arm up but was too late. Off balance and unprotected, he teetered at the guardrail, his arms windmilling until he tipped over and fell down into the choppy water of Krause Lake below the bridge.

Zehra panted from the exertion and from the fear that shook her all over. She knew enough to flop down behind the snowmobile again. All they had to do was wait for Paul to rescue them.

On the road behind her, she heard the whine of another snowmobile. Then she heard a second one. As she and Shereen lifted themselves up enough to see, the first snowmobile roared up the road. The driver was bent down and frowning.

"Paco," screamed Shereen. "He'll kill us."

The driver must have seen the congestion on the bridge because at the last minute, he veered off the road and slid down toward the edge of the lake. He chose a point next to the bridge where a sheet of ice stretched across the channel to the far bank. He lifted himself up for a moment to study the escape route, glanced behind him to see the second snowmobile chasing him, and launched his snowmobile out over the ice covering the lake. He skidded across the surface. That's when the cracking sound boomed like a cannon going off. A hole in the ice opened up before him, he hit it, and with the nose of the snowmobile digging down into the open water, the track of the sled still churned furiously to send a geyser of foam high into the air. Paco and the snowmobile sank below the surface.

Paul roared up, stopping when he saw Zehra and Shereen. She warned him to stay down because of Stout. Then Sheriff Yellowfeather skidded down the embankment where Brown had fallen in. The sheriff saw the situation, stopped to retrieve a long rope from his snowmobile, and threw it toward Brown. Paul called over to Stout and ordered him to stop shooting.

In ten minutes, Brown was on dry land, shaking so hard he couldn't even stand. Henry was trying to get his body temperature warm enough to avoid hypothermia. Paul found Stout, wounded in the stomach, and Kathy Johnson crouched behind the shot-up Prius.

Paul's phone rang. It was Commander Sarinen from Duluth. "Hey, Paul. Weather cleared unexpectedly and those choppers should be with you any time now."

That's when they heard the high-pitched whine of an outboard motor as one of the enemies escaped off the island.

CHAPTER 39

Monday, November 7, Morning

THIS IS LITIGATION BY AMBUSH," thundered Mezerretti.

"I agree," said Judge Von Wald. She glared at Zehra from up on the bench just before the jury was to come into the courtroom. "Counsel, you're aware of the Criminal Rules of Procedure, Rule 9.01, Subdivision 1-1, that mandates you give notice of who your witnesses are going to be and any statements to defense counsel? Suddenly, you claim to have another Spreigl witness, a Ms. Diaz from Texas, who will be called?"

"I know," Zehra said. "As an officer of the court, I can tell you as soon as we learned of her existence I notified both defense counsel and the court. Rule 9.03 indicates that both sides have a continuing duty to disclose evidence *as we learn about it.*"

"The prosecutor should be sanctioned to exclude this witness from the trial so the jury will never even know she exists," demanded Mezerretti.

"You have the witness here in town?" the judge asked.

"Since Saturday night. I notified Mr. Mezerretti by email right away. I was in Northern Minnesota until Sunday night, conducting an investigation into this case. I just returned."

Conducting an investigation. Zehra thought that sounded quaint for almost getting killed. After the Coast Guard had arrived, it was easy for them to round up the traffickers still on the island and take them into custody. With the exception of Jeremy Brown, most of them talked. Zehra knew they'd be convicted easily.

And she had rescued Shereen.

Zehra purposely turned toward Mezerretti and Menendez sitting next to him. She said, "Yes, we finished our investigation and successfully stopped the trafficking of explosives into the country that was the cause of this murder. Law enforcement captured the network and they revealed the entire plot."

"Alleged murder," Mezerretti grunted.

Zehra watched Menendez closely. Although he didn't change his expression, his eyes twitched back and forth. His head bowed slightly. Maybe her plan would work after all. It was all she had left in order to get the conviction.

"Calm down, everyone." The judge patted the air in front of her with her palms. "Question is, what do we do now?" The judge nodded at Zehra, apparently agreeing. "Child protection case, huh?"

Zehra waited a moment hoping the judge would let Zehra take the next step. Then she said, "I can give the court an offer of proof."

Thankfully, the judge agreed. "Read it into the record."

Zehra glanced at Barry sitting beside her. He smiled tightly as he handed her the file folder containing Ms. Diaz's statement. Zehra opened it, paused again to make sure Menendez was listening, and started to read.

"When called as a witness, Ms. Diaz will testify that two years ago, she was the wife of the defendant, Roberto Menendez, and the mother of two of his children. They lived in El Paso. When the children appeared at school with bruises on their bodies, the school reported this to the police, who brought in the El Paso County Child Protection department."

She repeated word for word what Cindy Wilson had told her about the Texas case. Zehra took a breath and looked over at Menendez. Black eyes glared back at her.

"He would use electric cords, belts, and his fist against each of them for a variety of reasons. Ms. Diaz was also concerned about his chemical use, since the violence escalated when he was drinking or using drugs."

Mezerretti jumped up so fast, he tipped over the stack of papers on the desk before him. They flittered down to the floor like dead leaves in the fall. "I object! There's no proof of my client's drug or alcohol use other than this biased witness. She's got an axe to grind."

"Objection noted, but this is merely an offer of proof." The judge looked at Zehra as a cue to continue.

"Further, Ms. Diaz will testify that on several occasions, Mr. Menendez sexually assaulted his daughter."

"I object," Mezerretti yelled again. Next to him, Menendez half-stood in his chair. His face clouded in a deep red.

"Sit down, Mr. Mezerretti," the judge ordered him.

The judge rolled backward in her tall leather chair. After a few minutes, she turned and looked down at the parties before her. "I'm concerned about the surprise nature of this witness and the defense's inability to fully prepare for it. I'm ruling that the witness may not be called in the government's case in chief right now, but can be recalled in rebuttal after the defense has presented their case to the jury."

It wasn't much of a win, but Zehra hoped the psychological time bombs she'd tried to plant in Menendez would explode soon enough. It was a risky move, considering she hadn't been able to present enough evidence to the jury during the trial. Zehra would "rest" and conclude her part of the case, prevented from ever giving any more evidence to the jury except for a rebuttal.

Thoughts jumped through Zehra's mind. The first meeting with Grant and Liz, the work they'd all done on the case, Hollywood, the dead witnesses, the innocent victim of the murder, and Shereen. Zehra took a deep breath and took the gamble. "Thank you, Your Honor. The government rests."

The jurors filed into the two rows of chairs in the jury box. Some looked tired, others carried notebooks, and several shut off cell phones as they took their seats.

The judge turned to Mezerretti. "You may call your witness."

Mezerretti stood tall, his huge stomach bumping up against the counsel table. He glanced down at Menendez, looked up, and announced in a loud voice, "The defense calls Mr. Roberto Menendez."

The defendant stood, tugged at the front of his suit coat, and walked up to the witness chair next to the court reporter. He stood, a little bow-legged, as he raised his right hand and swore to tell the truth. He climbed into the swivel chair and looked out at the courtroom. It had filled with the usual media, spectators, homeless people looking for warmth from the snow outdoors, and many people from the NorthStar Group.

Mezerretti began slowly. "Tell us where you were born and raised."

Menendez took a moment. He blinked his eyes several times and said, "I born in Ciudad Juarez on the border with El Paso. I grew there until I sneaked into America."

"How many kids were in your family?"

"Twelve. Wait . . . two died, so ten."

Mezerretti smiled. "What work did your father do?"

"Don't know. Never met him 'cause he left us early."

"Did you finish school?

"Yo. Graduated high school."

"Work?"

"Right. Worked in factory that ship computers to America. Fourteen-hour day."

"Why did you work so hard?"

Zehra peered at the jury. Four of them had their eyes fastened on Menendez while he spoke. The others looked up at the ceiling or down at their laps.

"I work to support my new family."

"Who was in that family?"

"Wife, Rose, and two kids."

"Why did you all come to the United States?"

"Hey, man. I want to make better life for me and my family. I want to work hard and become American." He grinned proudly.

Mezerretti took him skillfully through more of his background to "humanize" Menendez before the jury. For days, they'd heard all the gruesome facts of the murder. Mezerretti wanted to remind them they would soon pass judgment on a real human being—something that was often difficult for a jury to do. "Where did you live . . ."

"Never on welfare neither." Menendez smiled briefly.

"When you got to the U.S., where did you live?"

"El Paso 'til I got the job in Minneapolis."

"Did you abandon your family in El Paso?"

"No way. I send money back every week. *Re-embolsos.*"

"Yeah. What kind of work did you do here?"

"I work as janitor in a church."

Zehra almost started to laugh because it seemed so unbelievable. She couldn't help but smirk a little.

"You're telling us you came all the way from El Paso for a job as a janitor?"

"Paid well."

Zehra knew it was a lie, which seemed obvious to her, but when she looked back at the jury, she found seven of them hanging on Menendez's words. She sat up and had a hollow feeling in her stomach. Zehra began to pay closer attention. Mezerretti had worked wonders on this creep. Menendez actually looked sympathetic, honest, and just as gentle and quiet as could be. Mezerretti took him through more details about his life and background. She took a deep breath and hoped everything would work as she had planned.

"Were you working at the Church of the Rapture the night of the shooting?"

"Uh . . . yeah." He looked up from under his dark eyebrows at the jury. His eyes sagged with pain.

Zehra felt uneasy and had a hard time sitting still. To occupy herself, she scribbled all over her legal pad. Meaningless gibberish.

"I was tol' I would be janitor and clean up at night."

"Were you there the night of the shooting?"

"Yeah. For little while. I work the early shift and leave before anything happened."

"Did you know the deceased?"

Menendez frowned. "Kinda. Not too well."

"Do you know anything about a shooting down the street from the church?"

"Never saw nothing." He tightened his lips.

"Did you shoot and kill Marko Sundberg?"

Menendez paused. He'd been coached well. He glanced at the jury and said, "No."

Ten of the jurors studied Menendez when Mezerretti stopped questioning and turned him over to the prosecutor.

Zehra was scared to death. Menendez had killed the victim, but he'd also just killed Zehra and her case. He had been totally believable. Even Zehra had almost believed him. She started to question him slowly, remembering what her psychologist, after reading Menendez's psychological evaluation, had coached Zehra to do.

"How many nights did you work in the church?"

"Five to six, depending on the meetings."

"Meetings?" Zehra asked.

"See, they think the world come to an end real soon."

"What did they do at the meetings?"

"Pray, sing songs. Pastor St. Peter, he talked a lot about the mark of the beast and the Rapture."

"What did he say?"

"First, people have to believe in Jesus. Then, they have to be re-born and then, third step, they have to go through Pentecost. Then he always ask for more money."

"Did you ever have any trouble with anyone there?"

"Naw, man, I mean ma'am."

"Ever get violent with any of the women?"

His eyes flashed obsidian at her. "Hey, I'm not like that."

Zehra let the exposed emotion hang in the air before her next question. "You ever take money from them, beat them up?"

"Objection."

"Sustained."

"Who else worked with you?"

"Just me for little time. Usually had a boss."

"Who?"

Menendez's head jerked up, his expression startled. "Uh . . . Pastor, sometimes others."

"How about 'Horseman'?"

Menendez looked down and refused to answer. Mezerretti jumped up. "Objection! This is irrelevant to the murder case."

"Sustained," the judge said.

Zehra continued, "Horseman set you up to be the security at the church?"

"Naw."

"You were hired to keep everyone in line, and when Marko escaped, your job was to stop him any way you could, even if you had to kill him."

Mezerretti yelled, "Objection. Scope of direct."

"It's starting it get beyond the scope of direct, but I'll allow it for now," the judge said.

Zehra lowered her voice and took a breath. She felt frustration bubbling up inside her. Menendez was a killer, and here he was, denying any responsibility for it. Zehra thought of all the deaths and suffering tied to this case. Her anger threatened to get out of control. She knew to direct it toward Menendez and the questions. If she could provoke him enough . . . maybe. "Mr. Menendez, besides being a janitor, you were hired for security at the church, right?"

Menendez hesitated. "Sometimes."

"And how about your family?"

"Huh?"

"Your family in El Paso. Why didn't they move up here with you?"

"Uh . . . we got problems . . ."

"Problems?"

"She don't respect me and I have to set her straight once in a while."

"You were violent with them?"

"Naw." He looked up to the judge. "Hey? I gotta answer this shit . . . er, questions? She's dissing me bad."

The judge sighed and leaned over to address him. "Turn around, calm down, and yes, you must answer all her questions."

While the judge talked to the defendant, Zehra opened another file and skimmed the psych done on Menendez.

> Diagnosis of Antisocial Personality Disorder . . . they have little tolerance for frustration and exhibit moodiness and irritability. These individuals often show intense feelings of anger and hostility, which are sometimes expressed in negative emotional outbursts when triggered . . .

The judge nodded at Zehra. She asked, "Do you support your family in El Paso?"

Without answering, he pumped his head up and down. "Yeah."

"So, if Rose came in here next and testified that you haven't given them a penny since you abandoned them in El Paso, she'd be lying?"

Before Mezerretti could heave his bulk up for an objection, Menendez yelled, "She's a liar. Yeah, stinkin' liar."

Zehra felt that she'd hit a sensitive spot with him. "If she testified that you beat her with an electric cord, she'd also be lying?"

Menendez gripped the edge of the granite top before him. His eyes jiggled. "Liar!"

"Your Honor." Mezerretti was up again, moving to head off the questioning. "May we take a brief recess? My client is obviously upset by these terrible lies. It's also way beyond the scope of direct . . ."

"The defendant 'opened the door' to this by his own testimony. Sit down, Mr. Mezerretti," the judge said. "Continue."

"If she said you used belts on her and on the kids, she'd be lying again?"

"She used to steal my money. See other men. I can't stand only so much." He waved off Mezerretti, who tried to object again. "What can I do? When I complain about her to others, she just laugh at me. Disrespect me to everyone. No man take that from a woman."

"Oh? Did you also hit your wife and your children when they dissed you?"

"Not hard. Just 'nuff to get 'em obey me. Like they supposed to do."

"So, you did hit them?"

"No . . . yeah," he screamed. Red color rimmed his blazing eyes, and his hands squeezed the wooden rail before him. "Sometimes," he yelled again. "I want to explain . . ."

"I'm asking the questions, not you." She looked into his eyes and she saw a cauldron of hate.

Menendez sat back for a moment. Then he was up again, agitated, angry, and flushed in the face. He shook his head back and forth. "No . . ." he mumbled.

Zehra waited to let his frustration build again. Then she asked, "What if your wife came in here and said you sexually abused your daughter? That you sexually assaulted her?"

He rose from the chair is if he were on a diving board about to jump off. He stood and pointed at Zehra and yelled, "No." Alarmed, two of the four deputies in the room converged on him. When Menendez saw them come closer, he sat down and calmed himself.

"How about the murder of Marko?" Zehra bored in again. "Did he disrespect you like your wife and kids did?"

"No."

"Why did Marko run from the church?"

"Don't know."

"But you were hired to stop things like that, right?"

Menendez wouldn't answer.

"Who hired you?"

"Uh . . . Horseman is all I know his name."

"He warned you to never let anyone leave the church with information about what was going on there? About the plot to blow up eighteen nuclear power plants? When Marko tried to leave with that information, you knew he must be stopped. Isn't that why you killed Marko?"

Menendez shook his head and for a moment, it looked like his eyes had lost their focus. He shook it again and said, "Wasn't my fault. Paco and the Horseman, they scared me. Tol' me to just keep the people in line. "

"Objection, Your Honor. Defense asks for a recess," Mezerretti said.

"No."

"I keep the people in line. That's my job. That night . . ." His eyes moistened and his voice rose. "That night . . . Marko just laugh at me. Disrespect me. When he run out with the flash drive, I have to stop it. He disrespect me just like the wife and the kids. I can't stand it. I probably snapped, or something and just . . . I don't know what happened. Marko ran out of the church, I know if I don't stop him Horseman will kill me. I know he won't fuck around. Just kill me," he admitted. "Not my fault. Don't remember much after that . . ."

Behind his eyes Roberto felt a red hot poker that hurt so badly he worried it would burst his eyeballs and jelly would dribble down his cheeks. No one ever listened to him. He twitched with anger and with trying to hold himself back from all the days in court when he wasn't allowed to tell his story and how he had held himself back when people told lies about him and right now holding himself back from jumping over the top of the witness stand and scrambling up to the prosecutor's table to strangle that whore with the curly black hair that look like a woman's crotch and her big fucking nose so that he could smash it in and kill her right there to stop the disrespect like so many people did to him all the time. He'd rape her to teach her to respect him, hurt her, knock her fucking ass around, and smack her down, and then kill her to stop it all. Dead.

He was panting and suddenly stopped talking. He blinked his eyes as if he'd been dreaming for a while. Silence echoed around the courtroom and everyone stared at him. Whatever he'd just done, damn it was cool, 'cause they all looking at him right now. He was the boss and they all finally listened to him.

CHAPTER 40

THIRTEEN MINUTES. THAT'S ALL IT TOOK for the jury to convict Roberto Menendez of first-degree murder," Zehra bragged to Paul. She glanced at her watch and remembered that she had an appointment with her psychologist in a half hour.

They were finishing a two-hour lunch at Broder's Pasta Bar on Penn Avenue in south Minneapolis, a small, cozy restaurant that specialized in locally-grown, wonderful food. She and Paul had worked on a bottle of Pinot Noir earlier, with Zehra apologizing that, as a Muslim, she normally didn't drink anything. But after all that they'd been through, she justified a glass.

Besides, they were celebrating her victory in the trial.

Paul laughed. "I gotta admit that first day we met at Dunn Brothers for coffee, I didn't tell you the truth. Didn't want to discourage you. I thought your case was a dead-bang loser."

Zehra crossed her eyes and nodded. "Think I didn't know? Probably good you didn't say anything, although I still don't think we'd have dumped it. Both Liz and I really wanted to get that guy off the streets. We were convinced he was the shooter."

"How's Liz?"

"Better. The win really helped."

"And Grant?"

Zehra huffed with a laugh. "Suddenly wants to promote me and get me out in the community to speak to groups. Guess I'm the 'token' Muslim." She frowned. "Told him I'd think about it. This time, I'll put *my* career ahead of what *he* wants."

Paul studied her. "You look great. New clothes?"

"Yeah. Figured I deserved them."

"And I haven't seen you this happy for months. You smile like . . . uh, before."

The waiter brought two coffees and cream out to the table.

"What happened at the nuclear plant?" Zehra asked.

"Brown wouldn't talk at all. He's in custody. Didn't surprise me with a guy like him but after fishing Paco out of the water our agents interrogated him about the federal crimes. He's the one who led us to the plant and a guy named Bernie. Scary stuff. He planned to get the explosives into the plant past the security and set the charges."

"And the militia?"

"Paco also coughed-up a lot about them. You were right about the other seventeen power plants. The plan was to blow each of them at the same time. The resulting panic and fear would ripple across the country."

"Crashing all the first responders, rescuers, medical, and law enforcement?"

"Right. There's no way we could keep up with a disaster like that. Their theory was that people would be so scared they'd turn on each other in a desperate fight for survival, leading to Armageddon." Paul leaned back and took a deep breath. "If they'd succeeded, the result would've certainly been some kind of Armageddon."

"There was something Stout told me. He said the FBI spends all its time investigating foreign terrorist threats and misses all the scary people living and plotting right here in our neighborhoods."

Paul swept his hand across the table as if to dismiss the idea. "Not true. Homeland Security tracks many of the extremist groups in this country. We're not naïve to the existence of home-grown terrorists. But it's hard to investigate them all."

"He told me about some blogs and chat rooms that NorthStar found."

"Yeah. The Internet really gives these nuts a chance to connect with each other. Now isolated crazies begin to feel like they're not alone, that their ideas are really mainstream because they find lots of support on the 'Net."

"Can it happen again?" She looked up at Paul.

"Sure. Have you heard from Kathy Johnson?"

Zehra laughed. "She called and apologized. Said to thank you also for saving them. In order to help Stout recover from his wounds, she was going out of town with him to a continuing legal education seminar . . . that she paid for. But Stout promised to get divorced." Zehra changed the subject. "How about the church?"

Paul said, "We're investigating the whole church. Seems they're tied into lots of other 'end of time' churches across the country. We'll prosecute those members involved in the plot. Without Brown, we suspect the church is extreme but not necessarily violent."

Zehra wagged her head back and forth. "Hollywood sure fooled me."

"Fooled lots of people. Classic definition of a sociopath. They believe so firmly in their bizarre world they convince themselves it's really true. From there, it's easy to convince everyone else. Besides, Brown drew a parallel with his ancestor, John Brown. Almost like Jeremy was channeling him. Saw himself on a mission from God to be a savior for the 'true believers.'"

They sipped coffee and privately contemplated how close Brown had come to winning.

"How's Shereen?" Paul asked.

"Fine. I think she grew up about twenty years during the time Brown had her. She's back in school and doesn't go anywhere near the Mall of America."

"What about you?" Paul set his cup down and looked into her eyes.

Zehra shrugged. "I'm fine. The PTSD seems to have disappeared. I don't know if I'll ever be 'cured,' but I can control it now. I feel engaged with life again. The depression's gone. My career's back on track, and Grant thinks I can walk on water. Wait a minute, wasn't that a Christian miracle?" She laughed a white smile across her dark face. "Even wants to use me in his upcoming election as a speaker. So, I guess I'm okay."

"Uh, what about me and you? A Christian and a Muslim."

Her eyes rose slowly to meet his, held them for a moment, and then circled his face. "I think we should escape for a long weekend. Just me and you. Let's look for a deal to a beach somewhere. I've been thinking of beaches a lot lately, and I'd love to share one with you."

Zehra leaned back in her chair, still watching Paul's face. She heard gulls cawing in her mind, felt the sun warming her back, around her shoulders, and down her chest. The hot air smelled salty, a little like fish. She closed her eyes.

Her watch beeped. Time for prayer, Zehra remembered when she glanced at it. Then she realized that she'd missed her appointment with the psychologist.

It didn't matter.

CHAPTER 41

A T THE SAME TIME PAUL AND ZEHRA were sipping Pinot Noir, Jim Moriarity waved an unmarked truck into the cavernous bay at the Monticello Nuclear Power Plant.

Jimmy worked at the final security check-point for any material entering the facility. The large truck had already passed through three security stops outside. Jimmy's jurisdiction consisted of a large room with two steel doors on either end that could be raised and lowered into the walls. The inside door formed the last barrier to entrance into the nuclear facility. Lately, they'd been having problems with the doors. Sometimes, they refused to go up or they fell unexpectedly on the way down. Something was screwed up with the computers that ran them.

Since his wife had told him she was pregnant with their third child, Jimmy had been angling for a promotion and more pay. That was dependent, almost entirely, upon his immediate supervisor, Rueben Holton, the Chief Security Officer, Grade 4.

Today, Jimmy signaled the driver of the truck to stop when the front tires touched a yellow line on the oil-stained floor. Hundreds of trucks came through the bay every month and all needed to clear this last security point before entering the plant. Around them, steel and concrete block walls rose up two stories in height. Everything was painted tan including a small office along the side of the room. It had large glass windows, a steel door that could be secured from the inside, and four computer monitors that were wired to several cameras both inside the bay and immediately outside. For security purposes, there were two land lines to phones inside the facility. One connected directly to Chief Holton who had called five minutes ago demanding to know where the last truck of rod blade replacements was.

Jimmy heard the driver shut off the engine and saw him climb down from the cab. He held an iPad in his hand and came around the truck to meet Jimmy. The driver stuck out his hand and shook with Jimmy.

Jimmy took the iPad and scanned the credentials of the driver, whom he didn't recognize. "You new?" Jimmy asked.

"Yeah. Other guy got sick at the last minute. That's why I'm late. Sorry."

Jimmy glanced at the digital clock on the wall. Nodded in agreement. "We've got to get these control rod blades changed like, yesterday." Two other employees of the power plant stood by the office door. No one could tell by looking at them, but they were heavily armed with automatic rifles.

The driver's documents looked okay. Jimmy handed the iPad back to the man and noticed his hands. They were thin, delicate, and the finger nails were so long they almost curled over the tips of his fingers. Not the hands of a truck driver. "Can you open the back and let me look?" Jimmy asked him.

"Sure." The driver had a Russian accent and moved to the back end. He used a key to open a padlock and threw the doors open.

Jimmy climbed into the truck's large interior. Something nagged at him about this driver. Something wasn't right about him. The hands? Jimmy saw several long, rough wooden boxes piled in rows. He carried a bolt cutter with him and started to snip off the metal bands that wrapped around the boxes. Burned into the wood like a brand on a cow's hide was the name of the manufacturer: Marathon. Once Jimmy cut the metal bands, he used a short crow bar to open the top of the box. He went down the long side, heard the screech as nails in the wood gave-up their grip reluctantly, until he finally reached the end. When he lifted the wooden top off, he saw clear plastic packing material. Pulling that aside, Jimmy assured himself that the first box contained only control rod blades, as ordered for the switch-over.

He was about to open the second box when he heard the phone ring. To make sure it could be heard, the phone in the office had an amplified ringer. Jimmy crawled down from the truck and ran up the metal stairs to the office. It was the chief.

"What the hell's taking so long down there?" he yelled at Jimmy.

"Just checking the cargo now."

"Well, get your ass moving. The Vice-president called for the third time this morning to chew my ass. They got the inspectors from the NRC in tomorrow morning at six o'clock and we gotta have those blades changed over and tested."

"Yes, Chief."

"'Cause if we don't, it's my ass and if my ass is out of here, so is yours. Got it?"

Jimmy swallowed hard. "Yes, Chief." He hung up and went back into the truck. The driver waited beside the back wheels. Something else bothered Jimmy about the driver, but he couldn't put his finger on it. Besides, Jimmy had to hustle through the inventory. After he had opened two more boxes, the phone rang again.

Back to the office, he listened as the chief yelled again, "Get that truck out of security and into the plant. Right now," he demanded.

"But I'm not done checking . . ."

"I don't give a shit. This is our last load of blades and we gotta get 'em mounted."

Jimmy thought to say something to the chief about the driver. But what could he say—that he had long fingernails? What was the reason Jimmy felt uneasy about him? He couldn't identify anything more. "Yes, sir." Jimmy hung up, ran down the stairs, and waved the driver back into the cab. He watched the man put his foot on the steps and climb into the truck. The driver started the engine. It groaned with a low roar and he shifted into gear. Jimmy went back to the office and punched the button that ran the door. The computers kicked-in and the heavy steel door began to rise in front of the truck.

Then, it struck Jimmy. This driver wore brand new, expensive running shoes. Something like a marathon runner might wear. In all his years at the company, Jimmy had never seen a driver wear anything but some kind of a boot. He thought to call the chief. But again, what would he say? The guy wore running shoes? Was that enough to stop him and the truck? When the chief called once again, Jimmy was relieved to tell him the truck was on its way inside.

He waited until it cleared the door and then Jimmy hit the button to lower it. Halfway down, the steel door broke loose and crashed to the cement floor. In the confines of the steel and concrete room, it sounded like an explosion, so loud it could even be heard outside as the noise rolled out across the fields.

AFTERWORD

Some of the scenes portrayed in this story involve violence toward women. For instance, the Mexican *paseo* of prostitutes and the "rape tree." Unfortunately, the scenes are all based on true facts. If anything, I minimized the violence and brutality that I discovered in my research. Although I added these scenes for dramatic effect, I was upset by instances like the "rape tree" and decided to educate readers about the criminal networks that traffick in many illegal items, including humans.

If you are troubled by these activities, there are things we can all do to make a difference. I've included a short list of web sites for you to investigate—there are many more—but these will give you a start.

As for me, I pledge to donate five percent of the sales of this book to the organizations that fight to expose and stop the trafficking of humans around the world.

www.polarisproject.org   www.humantrafficking.org   www.safehorizon.org